THE BIG HAPPY

DAVID CHADWICK

The manufacturer's authorised representative in the EU
for product safety is Authorised Rep Compliance Ltd,
71 Lower Baggot Street, Dublin D02 P593 Ireland (www.arccompliance.com)

Troubador Publishing Ltd
Unit E2 Airfield Business Park,
Harrison Road, Market Harborough,
Leicestershire. LE16 7UL
Tel: 0116 2792299
Email: books@troubador.co.uk
Web: www.troubador.co.uk

ISBN 978 1836284 680

British Library Cataloguing in Publication Data.
A catalogue record for this book is available from the British Library.

Typeset in 11pt Minion Pro by Troubador Publishing Ltd, Leicester, UK

For my fellow authors and wonderful friends
Ros Davis, Iris Feindt, Nicky Harlow and Alison Ward

ALSO BY DAVID CHADWICK

Novels
Liberty Bazaar

The Nixon's America Trilogy:
Tin Soldiers
Headload of Napalm
Hot Metal Hobo

The Big Happy

Non-fiction
High Seas to Home – Daily Despatches from a Frigate at War (with Shirley Morgan and Allan Seabridge)

Short stories
Panopticon (edited with Nicky Harlow)
Weird Love (edited with Nicky Harlow)

ABOUT THE AUTHOR

David Chadwick is an author, historian and award-winning journalist whose novels include his Nixon's America crime trilogy and debut novel, Liberty Bazaar. David uses his experiences reporting crime, politics and business to inform his fiction.

He divides his time between homes in Bolton, Greater Manchester and Almeria in southern Spain.

1

LAS VEGAS, ENGLAND
Right now – Friday April 13, 4050

'We could have builded Jerusalem here,' tattled
Isambard Kingdom Confucius in his rumbly Royal
Shakespo vox. 'On England's green and pleasant
land.'[*]

He swivelled from the window, specking me bolshy-
boohoo. 'But all they wanted was another Las Vegas. And
the overspend on casinos left no money for climate control.'

We was in a luxury suite at Caesar's Palace in Vegas,
England – zact rip of the rijnal Sin City and the party cap
of Europe. Place were monsta snapped, no truer words. But
Confucius were right about the weather. Rain come bullety
cold from led-zep clouds, fat bellied and stormbroody.
Wuddabin six day straight, this being Old England.

---

[*]   Appendix – A Scientian Visitor's Guide to IngoLingo®© can be
found on page 438

1

I zeroed Confucius. 'Do I really gotta gab like this?'

He maked an outta-my-graspers spresh. 'While you're in the Popular Republic®©, Miranda, I'm afraid you must. They insisted on regional language modification. Besides, your knowledge of IngoLingo®© will help your investigation. And credit to you – you're talking like a native.'

I weren't monkeyed by this butter-up. 'You sure I can gab proper again the nanosec we leaves?'

His Mount Rushmore viz maked a bitty smile. 'I am.'

This come as a bigmost relief. See, IngoLingo®© were gobspew street-English, spawned by the fads and whims of smin knowed as the Vox Popeye®©. But, as Confucius splained, I never got no choice. Every word I speaked come out like this. And me schooled at Boiloil Coll, Oxfy and all.

He were right, too, about tattling with the local lawdogs and I went back to the reason I were here.

'I better get to it,' I gabbed.

'One of my people will go with you.' He waved to one his dark-earled scurity detail but I nay-shaked my fusebox.

'Gotta do this solo,' I tattled. 'Ebbathin gotta be zamined ultra careful. Less ins and outs the betterest.'

He taked my point and gimme a yo-nod.

A Lincoln Conty with black tinteds were waiting outside and I were drived eight clicks north to Vegas Boul and Fremont.

As I stepped outta the limo, I specked this Army jack legging by, brassy bold in his camo garb and sarge stripes and thanked him humble for His Service to The Flag. Confucius told me the nabbers here was often casting for any what dissed The Flag. And though a ranking lawdog myself, I never wanted no bother right then.

I set off along Fremont, neon glowing blurry in the wet. Puddles sheened the sidewalks – dark mirrors flecting jiggly glares. High up, a giant horseback cowboy rippled smeary. Street scran sellers touted badger burritos, eelgut broth, flamingo chop suey and udda grub. This were a jungle for sure, and in more ways than one. I specked showgirls in ostrich feathers; prosts in leopard-print skimps; yeggmen in croc skin boots; and rookie punters in way over their fuseboxes. Then I zeroed the unglueds – jacked up and junked out. And blade boys lurking mean. Nuff to freddykrueger the stoutest spud.

The gaff where I were headed weren't hard to find – lights of lawdog cruisers and amblances maked gaudy images in the squishy street, mingling in ripply pools of red. Cuddabin the gore from them poor cut-up popeyes in the flat above, I thinked.

The nabber at the door scanned my ID and let me in. Confucius gimme the rank of Det Top Boss and I hoped he were right about this helping with local law forcement.

I climbed the stairs frisky to the third floor flat where Det Boss Tom Roscoe was waiting in the lobby. He were a gnarly old lawdog with wet rubbery puckers that give him a gog of Edward G Robinson in a 1930s gangsta flick. He were with the crime scene uber and both was decked in full barrier whites. They waited as I got togged up, then taked me to the crime scene.

'The parents is a hitched pair,' the crime scene uber gabbed over her shoulder. 'Kanye and Kiera Sinatra. Kids is Jay-Z, seven, and Beyoncé, five.'

Roscoe paused at the door, scanning me cocky. 'Not pretty in there. Got a tough gut, Det Top Boss?'

'Don't fret about me,' I telled Roscoe. 'I specked all and more.'

He pushed back his hat, Edward G-like. 'You ain't not specked nada like this.'

I keeped my gobbler shut, moved by him.

The man and woman was in the living room, both naked. Kanye – early fifties, strong build – were tied to a chair, his viz bruised and clarety, one slot swelled shut. Strangled with a ligature I guessed. Lot more gore round his groin. Genitals gone but not hard to find. Kiera were much younger – mid-thirties I guessed, slim and limber. Fusebox tilted back, gobbler wide, hubby cock and balls jammed right in there. Legs wide, vagina and inner thighs bruised bigbad. Left nipple slit off. I zeroed udda cuts and stabs and stopped counting at twenty. Choked to death too. Lotta gore spattered and pooled but no defence wounds, no sign of struggle. Kanye were a big jack, fit too. Wuddabin hard to put down. So how did the killer take control? Were he smoddy the family knowed? Smoddy they trusted?

Perhaps they was subjugged smuddaway.

The crime scene uber come up to me.

'You CSIs done?' I asked.

'They is,' they gabbed. 'Want me to leg you through?'

'I'll go solo for the first pass.' I gogged the four doors what come from the living room – two bedrooms, bathroom and kitchen. 'We can gab when I'm done.'

The kids' bedroom were nearest and I went in.

The scene were off-planet, gottasay, even for a hard bit lawdog like me. But not off-planet how you mighta

4

thinked. The lad and his sis was togged full-smart – Sunday best, as we tattled in the wayback. They was laid on neat-maked beds, feet together, gipsies folded across their chests. White candles was lit at the corners of each bed, spectful like. They give off a fruity scent – apple blossom praps. Over this, I niffed a spiky smell – smin I knowed but couldn't pin. Nail varnish mover, mebbe, or pear-drop candy.

The childs zeroed like they died peaceful – no obvio sign of injury; slots and gobblers shut; hair neat. And shapes cut from yellow cloth was laid on either side of each. Meant to rep angel wings were my best guess. Curtains from the kitchen windows and scissors on the floor showed where the killer got the cloth. More of a shrine than a kill scene.

But why so tender with the kids and zact oppo the growns?

End of the day, though, the bastard still went and killed them childs. And they wasn't just co-lat. He knowed they'd be here; *needed* em to be here. They was as much a part of this show, this display, as ma and pa.

Then it come to me that the peeky niff were knock-out gas. Seemed Jay-Z and Beyoncé got a lethal dose. The tox rep would tattle all.

I toured the udda rooms. All was normal but in the way of a nightscreamer that were still to come. I were gogging snaps of what family routine were like a nanofrag fore it weren't.

Roscoe and the crime scene uber taked off their barrier whites and was waiting in the lobby.

They asked what I thinked and I telled em.

'Same signoff, same guy,' Roscoe tattled when I were done. 'We all agree?'

I maked a dubio spresh. 'I ain't not zeroed any udda crime scene reps yet.'

'Say what?' Roscoe lighted a smoke and peeked at me through the fumes. 'So how does you know this is part of the series?'

'I don't. Not yet.' I specked him straight. 'I come to zero the crime scene here, nada more.'

He grunted like he weren't hearing proper. 'What sort of a lawdog is you, coming to my kill scene not proper briefed?'

I shrugged. 'The kind that come with no precons and no assumps. And this ain't not *your* crime scene. Not no more.'

He were obvio musked off but I were in no mind to play nice. So I tattled even morester blasé. 'I'll read them previo reps later. If I specks smin what you needs to know, I'll give you a skrike.'

'That why they calls you Serial Killer Miller?' The cigarette wagged in his damp puckers. 'Coz you can do stuffs beyond us reglar nabbers?'

'I never picked that moniker.' I zeroed him stern. 'The media did.'

This were true. It zucked me off bigmostest. They also called me Red Randy and that zucked me off even moster bigmostest.

I turned to the crime scene uber who I liked better. 'How you thinks he got in?'

She glanced at the door. 'No signs of break-in or forced entry. We is working the theory that they let him in. Either they knowed him, or he were a stranger what they trusted.

He probs got here round dinnertime so not a late caller that might raise spicion.'

I gogged Roscoe. 'Sveylance cams?'

He nay-shaked his fusebox. 'Killer knocked em out. Some sorta sonic pulse gun we thinks.'

'Witnos?'

'Nada.'

'*Nada*?'

He gimme a you-heard-me gog.

'Curio,' I tattled frowny. 'This a busy neybrud. Lotta night-biz down on the street so tough to get in and out unspecked. Udda tenants come and go frequent, famlies and buddies calling round, not to mention kids playing out, pizza delivry spuds and whatnot.'

Roscoe gimme a blank speck. 'Popeyes here is proper three monkeys.'

'Even with spuds getting tortured to death and small childs snuffed?'

I zeroed Roscoe spiky but his offhand spresh stayed.

I turned back to the crime scene uber and asked her to tell me the nano any of the lab reps come in.

Then I left.

2

Outside, rain still come bludgeony, slants flickring garish in the neon. Neybas wuddabin hunkered, punters staying inside casinos. Even the prosts was off the street, standing shivry in doorways. Unlike the weather, their biz was drying up.

This were when I zeroed the radiant angel.

He come along the street, haloed in light. It flected bright off his silver coat. And when he crossed the street, the halo followed. The popeyes what flocked round him was the oppo – dim critters lurking on the edge of angel-shine. They was calling out to him, cries of worship, shouts of joy. Was he a movie star, or a big plitiko or some kinda gospler?

Specking squinty, I gogged he was coming right at me. *Holy Cowell*, I thinked, *what the zuck is this?*

As they got close I specked this were no angel but a celeb shined up by a boom-lamp gripped by a lighting tech. Nearby were anudda boom, this with a fuzzy kebab mike at one end and a sound lad at the udda. Ahead of em were a popeye with a TV camera – doing a capboggly job of legging backwise.

They come nearer still and I got a better speck of this shiny jack. He were high – six-three or four – with a honed body-shape and square viz. His rug were slick, pomaded up top, shaved at the sides. I guessed this were the fash. Glinty blue slots zeroed me and his puckers parted, flashing schlocks what shimmered dazzly.

'Well. Here I am.' He lifted his gypsies and maked a small bow, ziff I shuddabin specting him.

I made a monkeyed spresh. 'Who is you?'

'Who is *I*?' He chuckled chummy, like I maked a monsta bojo and he were happy to forgive.

The crowd behind him was giggly too.

He twirled to face em. 'Tell the pretty lady who I am!'

They chanted the rejoinder monstamostest loud, 'He's Bogart Wham!®©'

This Bogart Wham!®© turned to me, looking somewhat musked off. 'Nubdy tattled you I were on your team?'

I nay-shaked my fusebox. 'I never knowed I were getting no team. Only they'd be helpers here in PopRep®©, plus the nabbers.'

He come closer. When he tattled, his vox were low so nubdy could earwig. 'They called me a *helper*?'

I shrugged. What were I meant to do?

He snorted. 'Trump in Stormy, I ain't not having this. "Helper" makes me sound like smoddy outta Santa zucking grotto.'

'Scuze me, Mr Wham!®© but – '

'Call me Bogart.' His floodlight smile made me wish I'd bringed sungogs.

'Apols, Bogart, but does you know who *I* is and why *I* is here?'

'Why you is Det Top Boss Randy Miller – Miller of the Yard. And you is here to catch Family Guy, the franksteiny serial killer.'

'So what kinda lawdog savvy you got?'

The smile stayed. He mightabin hunky and ripped and stacked. I mighta zucked him if I weren't into women back then. But I come to wonder what were upstairs. 'None,' he gabbed, 'as such.'

'So how, *as such*, you thinks you can help?'

He gimme a gog that showed he didn't get me not getting him. 'I'm the Numero Uno Celeb Influsser in PopRep®©. I opens doors, makes stuffs happen. I'm the fluent in influence.'

I scanned him puzzly. 'But there ain't not no fluent in influence.' Why were I even having this eastbound convo?

He tipped me a wink. 'They will be soon. I spinning up a Vox Popeye®© what gonna make it so.'

'Apols,' I gabbed, 'but I don't not need no celeb… influsser.'

'Well I apols too, but whether you needs me or not, you got me.'

'How so?'

'All part of the deal what bringed you here. You get a… *helper* from each fedration.'

Bogart Wham!®© were obvio big boohoo at the lowly job title he got gived. I never knowed why, but I cut the lad some slack. 'I cudda not heared em proper,' I tattled. 'Thinking back, the words they used cuddabin *spesh counsler.*'

Acourse this were bullshit but if I gotta to work with this Wham!®© I wanted him sharp not sulky.

My ploy come off. A childy-happy spresh crossed his viz.

Then I quizzed, 'So who these udda spesh counslers?'

'Apols, dunno. Never knowed *I* were on you team till this morning.'

He zeroed up at the window of the Sinatra gaff. 'I'll take my popeyes in now. We can grab some intro shots.'

He come forward but I shoved him hard in the chest. 'The zuck you can. This a kill scene till I gabs uddaways. Nubdy goes in less they abso gotta.'

'Don't I abso gotta, Randy?'

'No you don't abso gotta.' I keep the flat of my grasper on his chest and shoved him back. 'And don't call me Randy. Ma'am, boss, guvnor, take your pick.'

This jack were one of the vainest I ever meeted – and I meeted many. And yet he were brassy and sassy and maybe this might come in handy.

'When the frensics spuds is done, you can take a look.'

Again his mood lifted. 'Thanks, boss. I'm sure there'll be lotsa stuffs I can use on ClapTrap®© and YakityYak®© – '

'You can't use nada nowhere. We ain't not gonna go public. Not yet.'

'But when we can – '

'When we can, Bogart Wham!®©,' I tattled, 'you is the man.'

It were a daft thing to gab but the part-rhyme bringed anudda laddish beamer from my sparkly helper.

How many more "spesh counslers" like Bogart Wham!®© could I take before my fusebox caved? More crucial, I were a stranger in a strange land, so how were I gonna catch this Family Guy who were monkeying the bestest lawdogs on earth?

You gotta stick with it, Randy, I telled myself. *When you got morer better used to it, this gaff won't seem so bojoed.*

I never been more wronger though. The more I cogged about this zucked-up world, the more baddest allstuffs got.

Wanna know how much morest baddest?

Stick close, I'll gab all.

3

PARIS-SUR-EUPHRÈTE

Seventy-two hours earlier ...

D id I exist?

This was the first of three questions.

I shouldn't exist. I'd never had a consciousness. Not as such. I did now though. A past, a memory too. Yet also an awareness that these things had been applied, inserted. Some sort of intervention had happened to bring me to this dark city street. Its cobbled surface was wedged between tall brick-and-mortar buildings – warehouses or factories. The only light came from an iron street lamp. Its lemony glow reflected off the pavement. Bags of garbage hunched against an overfilled dumpster. An aluminium ventilation duct poked through a wall, whisps of steam drifting into the sombre sky. The air smelled of boiled cabbage, fried food, damp clothes. I had no idea where this was.

Which brought me to question two: Who was I?

My name was Miranda Miller and I was a criminal investigator. This didn't answer the question though because I had never been a real person. I was a work of fiction, an alloy of various detective tropes. Or a shameless rip-off, depending on who you listened to. What I was above all else, though, was a spoof, a send-up. I was never meant to be taken seriously.

The third question was, what should I do about the man coming at me with a knife?

He'd appeared from the shadows of a side street, eyes fixed on mine, walking at first, then charging.

In that instant I wondered what would happen if I did nothing. Could I be killed if I was never alive?

My body's response was a massive catecholamine hit.

Which put me in the fight.

My attacker started circling, looking for an opening.

I slowed everything right down, visualizing, anticipating, shifting. His blade gleamed and danced in the murky light. His expression was deadpan, eyes unblinking.

The attack came in a flurry of lunges. I felt the knife whisk the air millimetres from my face, my throat, my chest.

I ducked and weaved and kept moving.

When he lunged again I was ready. Shifting under the arc of his arm, I drove my elbow hard into his face. There was a crackle of crunching teeth, a spatter of blood. The knife tinkled on the ground and I kicked it away. He staggered back.

Pressing my advantage I spun around and moved towards him.

That sort of impact, he should have been down and out. But somehow he stayed on his feet.

Wiping blood from his mouth, he looked at me through cold eyes, but I couldn't detect any hint of anger or fear. Or anything.

I went again, fiercer this time. His guard went up, parrying my salvo of head punches.

I moved back, sweating, breathing hard.

Yet he seemed unaffected. He shimmied right, went left. I read his move, adjusted mine.

Then he feinted again, switching back to my unguarded right. My slo-mo moves went to shit. Before I could react he landed a hefty blow on the side of my head.

I fell backward, hitting the ground, hanging onto consciousness.

He loomed above me in the swaying corona of a street lamp. I felt myself slipping away, enveloped in a welcoming numbness.

He raised one foot and aimed it at my head.

Somewhere deep inside it, I found a slither of something.

His boot swung forward. I raised both hands, caught it by the toe and heel, twisted outward. A muted snap told me the fibula and talus had parted. He should have been yowling. But his expression was one of bafflement. Still gripping his boot, I pushed him back. He stumbled, one knee buckling, then keeled over onto his back. His head struck the cobblestones hard. He should have been out cold, but he'd already shown astonishing resilience. I had to be sure. Casting around for a weapon, I grabbed a half house brick from a pile of building rubble and raised it high above my shoulder.

My attacker just stared at me, no hint of fear or desperation, not even blinking.

I tensed. I was going to kill a man. But if one of us was going to die, it wouldn't be me.

Before I could smash his skull the street was illuminated by powerful lights.

I hesitated, looked around, realized this wasn't a street, not a city, but a movie set.

4

Twenty-four hours earlier ...

f I believed what I'd been told – and I wasn't at all sure I did – I had arrived at the Élysée Palace in Paris-sur-Euphrète.

A kilometre to the south, the great river of ancient Babylon drifted by the gold dome of les Invalides, towards the Louvre then on past the cathedral of Notre-Dame. Of course, none of this "neo-paleo" architecture was original but it looked every inch the real deal as I was driven by. So too did the channel of the Euphrates that had been reshaped to the precise dimensions of the Seine as it passed through Paris in France.

The man I was here to see was Isambard Kingdom Confucius, Citizen Ascendant of Scientia. Whatever that meant. He awaited me in the baroque splendour of the Salon Doré, the traditional office of French presidents. As I was ushered through the ornate double door, he crossed the room to grip my hand and invited me to sit opposite him on a matching pair of dark wood sofas upholstered in cerulean silk.

My host was a physically imposing individual in his middle years with a fiasco of dense grey hair and a heavy Beethoven brow. His eyes were dark, intense, the moustachioed mouth downturned, the jaw chevroned by a pointy beard. His attire was equally impressive. I saw a crafted elegance in the cut of his suit, perfect symmetry in the knot of his tie and the fit of his collar. This man was a statue waiting to be carved.

Two days had passed since I was attacked, although the medics who treated me explained that the venue wasn't a movie set but a simulation facility for special forces operators. Which also explained my assailant's indifferent reaction to injuries that should have been crippling. He – or rather *it* – was a "combot", an android designed for close-quarter fight training. The blood, the breaking teeth and snapping bones were, I was told, functions designed to mimic "kinetic authenticity".

My own head injury had largely healed – the concussion cleared up in less than twenty-four hours and the abrasion on my right cheekbone had almost vanished. However, the question of whether I actually existed made me wonder if I'd simply benefited from the impossibly fast recovery time you see in action movies. Something else: I looked suspiciously better than when I last glanced in a mirror – middle-age didn't seem hang so weary on me. The lines were still there and I could see a few strands of grey. Also, my eyelids remained slightly hooded, my skin a little slack when I put makeup on. I might have been halfway glamorous if I'd made an effort, but this rarely happened because I never found the time. My nails often needed doing. My roots showed. My work suits got crumpled from sitting at a desk too late, or in a car too long. This said, I was still trim and slim and in relatively good shape. I'd run my last 10k in a respectable time and was weirdly confident I could improve on this if I started right now.

Isambard Kingdom Confucius examined some data on a translucent screen on his lap, then switched off the device and set it to one side. 'You have exceeded our expectations, Miranda. Your synaptic reactions in the combot test were remarkable and your cognitive analysis results no less impressive.'

'That's good to hear,' I said. It wasn't really but I couldn't think of anything else to say.

After the "kinetic simulation" I'd been taken to a room with white walls and no windows where more medical types examined me. Then there'd been a meal break and I ate a passable vegetable lasagne before drinking a pot of coffee that I had to say was excellent. Next came a series of interviews with another set of white coated people. And finally some seemingly random tests and exercises on a computer screen.

The citizen ascendant sat back and gave me an avuncular smile. 'I trust you have been treated well? Has your accommodation been satisfactory? Food and drink to your liking?'

'Thank you, yes.' I'd been given a suite at the Paris Ritz on the Place Vendôme and my every request had been granted without delay. Thin-crust pizza, pint of Guinness, even a pack of Gauloises cigarettes. Nothing was too much trouble. The view across the city was special although the manager was clearly under instructions to provide only limited information. Nor could I do any exploring because

I wasn't allowed to leave my suite. At first I'd thought about escaping. But where to? And what for? So I stayed put, went into sofa-spud mode and watched TV re-runs until my summons arrived an hour ago.

'You must be wondering why you're here.' His kindly smile stayed put.

'More like *if* I'm here.' I glanced around the room. 'You do know, don't you, that I'm not real?'

'You *weren't* real in the sense that you were created by your author as a fictional character.' His smile broadened. 'But you're real now. We have made you real. It's a procedure we call actualization.'

I took a few seconds to absorb the implications. 'So what are you saying? You can "actualize" any individual, real or imagined?'

He nodded.

'Then why me? Why not – I don't know – Abraham Lincoln or Winston Churchill? Albert Einstein or Marie Curie?'

'They weren't investigators.'

I laughed at that and reeled off a list of real and literary cops, gumshoes, legal eagles and hotshot reporters.

'Your background is simply more suitable.' He steepled his fingers and leaned forward, elbows on knees. 'You specialize in apprehending exactly the type of criminal we are pursuing. You rose to the rank of detective chief superintendent at Scotland Yard, having done your most notable work at sergeant and inspector levels. You worked for some time with the FBI's Behavioral Analysis Unit and received a citation for your odontometric work on the Rumpelstiltskin case. Yet your origins were humble –

raised by working class parents in a poor neighbourhood of Manchester, England. None of which prevented you from obtaining a first class degree in politics, philosophy and economics at Balliol College, Oxford.'

He paused to pour two glasses of water from a jug on the low table between us.

'You don't get it, do you?' I accepted the glass he extended and took a sip. 'The reason my author gave me that improbable backstory, those unlikely qualities, was that I was intended as a spoof, a sendup. I wasn't meant to be taken seriously.'

'*We* take you seriously, Miranda. Seriously enough to give you all those skills and experiences *for real.*'

'But what is "for real"? What does it mean?' I struggled to keep my cool. 'Why should I believe anything you say?'

'Why shouldn't you?' His tone stayed stubbornly reasonable. 'Where is the sense in not?'

'So explain how I came to be here.'

'It's not straightforward.'

'In a nutshell.'

The citizen ascendant made a yielding expression. 'You were actualized by our transmutative technicians and physiological initiators. They used bio-chemically accelerated milling, psycho-generative sculpting and sub-atomic mapping processes.'

'That sounds like random words tossed together.'

'Perhaps so. But does it matter?' He tilted his head to one side. 'If you tried to explain the workings of a car engine or a smart phone to someone from the Middle Ages how do you suppose they would they have responded?'

He had a point.

'Look,' he said, 'I can show you some of the technology. I can set up demonstrations. But ultimately you still have to believe or disbelieve what you see.'

He had another point.

'Or,' he went on, 'we can have a philosophical conversation. We can discuss Plato and Aristotle. Explore Cartesian logic. Talk about existentialist theory – Sartre, Kierkegaard, Heidegger, whoever. But you'd still be left to make up your own mind.'

This was yet another point.

He sipped his own water and put the glass back on the table. 'Also, you have your memories – family, childhood, relationships, career.'

My recall was sharp enough. Part of me wondered if it was a little too sharp. I thought of my mum and dad, parents at eighteen; my dad a factory worker, my mum a house cleaner. We never had much but I was never short of love and always had strong roots. Growing up in Strangeways in the 1970s and 80s was tough, though I didn't think so at the time. My playground was the back streets around the Victorian prison, Boddington's brewery and the banks of the dirty brown Irwell, where trash was treasure and magic always close. Despite all this, I did well at school. I won a scholarship to Balliol College, Oxford and then, against all advice, became a street cop. The brass wanted to fast-track me for senior management but I liked the down-and-dirty business of proper police work. I rose through the ranks, sure, but I was never interested in going further than chief superintendent and refused promotions from sergeant and inspector roles because I wanted to stay close to the action. I remembered my lovers too. Not many and rarely for long. Patrick and Emma were my two longish term relationships, one bitter-sweet, the other just bitter.

'So,' I said, 'is that what I am – the sum of my experiences?'

'Isn't that what any of us are? That and assorted anatomy parcelled in skin – complicated burritos if you will. And don't we ask same questions? *Who* are we? *Why* are we?'

He racked up a further point. By now I'd stopped counting how many points he had racked up.

Besides, where would denying my existence take me except on an endless expedition up my own arse? So I decided to roll with Confucius, at least for now.

'Okay.' I gave him a straight stare. 'Tell me *where* I am. What is this crazy world? And what happened to *my* crazy world?'

'I don't want to burden you with too much information at once.'

'A two-minute summary will do.'

'Two thousand years in two minutes?'

'Just the headlines.'

5

He pursed his lips and took a few moments to think.

'Very well,' he said at last, 'you know already that this year is 4050.

'What you don't know is that the world you knew ended in the middle of the 21st Century. Civilization was destroyed in a period of mutually-compounding catastrophes. Extreme temperatures, flooding, pandemics, drought and famine, lawlessness and nuclear wars brought about the collapse of civil society. It was the nightmare envisaged by Thomas Hobbes, the Enlightenment thinker whose work you read at Oxford.'

I drank more water. He seemed to like dropping the names of full-fat philosophers and I started to wonder why. But I saw no reason not to cooperate and gave him the quote he wanted. "'No arts; no letters; no society; and which is worst of all, continual fear and danger of violent death; and the life of man, solitary, poor, nasty, brutish, and short.'"

I put my glass back on the table. 'Is that what happened?'

'It is.' He straightened his legs and his gaze seemed to fall on, yet pass through me. 'After what we call the Second Dark Age, new civilizations began to emerge. We had to learn a great deal from scratch, but we made real and lasting progress. Then, five hundred years ago we made an epoch-changing discovery. Deep under the Urals we found a bunker complex containing every form of artistic and technological knowledge that had gone before the Great Calamity. Standing on the shoulders of giants, as Newton put it, many generations devoted their lives to developing new arts and sciences. We had in our hands every fruit of the human mind from the ages of Knossos and Mycenae to Athens and Rome; from the Renaissance and the Industrial Revolution to the time of nuclear, digital and nano technologies.'

'That's a lot of know-how.' I refused to be impressed. 'But it didn't do my people much good. Not in the end. At least not from what you just told me.'

'Unlike your people, we *learn* from our errors.' His condescension was irritating. 'Ultimately our knowledge enabled us not only to build our own world, but also to *re*build yours. We have before us – if you will forgive the cliché – the best of both.'

He made a sweeping motion with one arm. 'Our artbeiterbots for example, built Paris-sur-Euphrète, complete with a northern European climate, in the land you would have known as Iraq.'

'But what's wrong with the original Paris?' I frowned. 'The one in France?'

He made an uncomfortable cough. 'The site doesn't belong to us.'

My frown deepened. 'Who *does* it belong to?'

He crossed one leg over the other and laid an arm across the back of the sofa. 'Our world is divided into three large federations. Ours, Scientia, comprises the whole of Asia and Australia, along with Siberian Russia and Russia-in-Europe. Our constitution is founded on principles of freedom of expression, knowledge, learning, egalitarianism and social welfare.'

'And let me guess, the power that owns France doesn't possess these civic virtues, and nor does the third one.'

'I'll let you be the judge of that because at some point soon you'll see for yourself. But France, as you would have known it, belongs to the Popular Republic, or PopRep®© as they prefer to call themselves. Their territory includes Europe and North America and, as their name suggests, they are a society based on populist capitalism. They are shallow, materialistic, fickle and avaricious.' He made a whimsical smile. 'But then I would say that, wouldn't I?'

'And what would you say about the third federation?'

His smile vanished. 'The Holy Trumpian Empire, also called Trumpia, is a theocratic dictatorship occupying South and Central America and Africa. Their only religion, the Church of the Holy Quadity, is practised with intolerance, bigotry and brutality. Heretics are slow-roasted at the stake in huge microwave ovens, lesser offenders have limbs and other body parts surgically removed. Like the PopReppers®© they eat the flesh of other creatures – known in Scientia as anibalism – but with even greater barbarity. Women are oppressed, abused and powerless – they are not allowed outdoors unless on a lead and under the control of a responsible male.'

'A responsible male?' I made an ironic expression. 'Is there such a thing?'

He indulged my weak joke with a polite chuckle. 'Allegedly.'

'What about international relations? Have there been wars?'

'Many. Almost all between PopRep®© and Trumpia. Our advantage in technology keeps us out of most conflicts.'

'What causes these wars?'

He made a scoffing laugh. 'What does not? Twenty million perished in the War of Trump's Ear, waged between those who believed God blew on the bullet fired by Thomas Matthew Crooks, causing it to miss Trump's head; and those who believed Crooks was just a bad shot. Millions more died in the first and second Wars of Trump's Golf Handicap, the Wars of the Donald's Deity and the Holy War for Righteousness as it was known in Trumpia, or The Even Holier War for Even Morer Right-tity-ness, as it was called in PopRep®©.'

'At least that one wasn't about Donald Trump.'

'I'm sorry my, dear, but it *was*.'

I frowned. My opinion of Trump had been much the same as that of any one else with centrist views in early 21st Century western society. 'So why was Trump the source of those conflicts?'

'The two federations interpret him differently.' He rubbed the tip of his V-shaped beard between his thumb and index finger, as if teasing out an apt response. 'The Holy Trumpian Empire orthodoxy is that Donald Trump was "raised up" by God and deified as the "Second Cousin of God". What was once the Holy Trinity, according to Trumpian doctrine, is now the Holy Quadity.'

He seemed to read my thoughts and held up one hand. 'Beyond absurd, I know. But these people are fanatical believers and one must deal with them on their own terms.'

'And, what? The PopReppers®© don't go along with this Trump-in-Heaven business?'

He made a whimsical expression. 'Sometimes they do, sometimes they don't. The issue of Trump's deity in PopRep®© depends on when you ask the question. Those people have had so many populist referenda on the topic that one loses track. They have abolished and reinstated God three times in the last twenty years. Hell has been and gone and come back again. Trump has always been revered in PopRep®© but largely as the father of populist government. Each time they vote to make him one of God's relatives, relations with Trumpia improve. Each time they reduce him to a mortal, there is tension, often war.'

'What about opposition to these wars?'

Confucius made a rueful smile 'In PopRep®© every referendum is regarded as an expression of democratic will. But then their "Vox Popeyes" are won and lost on the basis of which side can create the most persuasive disinformation. So, no, there is no effective pro-peace lobby – unless the oligarchy decides it's time for a period of peace. As for the Holy Trumpian Empire, disagreeing with the theocratic state is heresy, punishable in all sorts of horrible ways.'

'What about here? In Scientia?'

'The right to protest is constitutionally enshrined. There is always a rigorous debate before we ever go to war.

When this becomes inevitable we use our combots. So there's no loss of life on our part and we win almost every battle.'

'Do the other federations have these combots?'

'We sell some to PopRep®© with software that guarantees they can't be used against us. But they never have enough funding to purchase an entire army so a portion of their people are conscripted.'

'And Trumpia?'

'They can't afford *any* combots. They have a massive agrarian population and it's their people who go into the meat grinder. Having said that, volunteers are plentiful. They believe that to die in a Holy War is the fastest way to meet Jesus and his most trusted friend, Donald J Trump.'

There was a brief gap and I welcomed it because I had a little time to process the landslide of information that had fallen on me.

At last I decided to go back to the reason he'd brought me here. 'Who is this criminal you want catching?'

He appeared happy with this subject change. 'He is a particularly sadistic serial killer who is terrorizing communities in all three federations. The best law enforcement minds on the planet have been unable to make any significant progress. We are turning to you because, as I mentioned earlier, your track record says you're the best.'

'You're talking about a track record from a satirical novel.'

'Nonetheless, the attributes we have given you are authentic – as you demonstrated with your engagement with the combot and in the subsequent interviews and tests.'

I decided to go along with this. What option did I have? 'Very well, tell me what you know about this serial killer.'

'The media have named him Family Guy – and yes, we *are* familiar with the American TV show from your era.'

'Presumably his victims are families?'

'Quite. Specifically heterosexual families in which the man is much older than the woman – on average the age difference is eighteen years.'

'And how many children?'

'Typically two, although there have been cases involving one child and four. Age and gender of the children don't seem important. Moreover, where there is sexually fixated torture of the adults, he kills the children quickly and with minimal suffering.'

'But he kills them anyway?'

'He does.'

'How many in his series?'

'Twenty-three in two time-frames. There were twenty-one events in a five-year period that ended fourteen years ago. Eighty-nine men, women and children were murdered in that period. Then, for whatever reason, we believed he had stopped.'

He made a sour expression. 'We couldn't have been more wrong. Thirteen months ago the killing started again. Since then we have had three events and twelve homicides – from children as young as six to adults over seventy.'

I did the arithmetic. 'About three months between each event in the first period as well as the current one?'

'Essentially, yes.'

'So he will be nineteen years older than when he started out. What sort of age do your profilers think?'

'Probably mid-twenties when he began, which would put him in his late thirties now.'

'What about the type of work he does?'

'Our profilers say he's well educated and from a professional background, probably an engineer in the technology sector.'

'You said he kills in each of the three federations – that must say something about his MO.'

'Indeed. We believe there is a strong probability that his MO is connected to his apparent freedom of movement. He kills here in Paris-sur-Euphrète; in Rio de Jerusalem in Trumpia; and in Las Vegas, England in PopRep®©. So clearly he has a job, or the resources that mean he can travel internationally.'

I sensed there was a catch. 'But?'

'Each of these locations is easily accessible and has large visitor numbers. Paris-sur-Euphrète is the capital of Scientia; Rio de Jerusalem is the main destination of Trumpian pilgrims; and Vegas, England is the entertainment capital of Europe. In each city, the non-resident population is greater than the permanent population throughout the year.'

My next question was pre-empted by a tap on the door. A sharp-faced woman in a dark pantsuit half-entered the room. A telepathic message seemed to pass between her and Confucius. He explained that this was his principal private secretary and asked to be excused.

There was a whispered conversation at the door. He glanced grim-faced in my direction and returned to the sofa.

'Family Guy has killed again,' he said. 'You can take a look at his work for yourself.'

6

LAS VEGAS, ENGLAND
Back to now – Saturday April 14

Morgue air were chocker with pongs I knowed too well – formalin, ammonia, inosine. Then there was the vingry niff of formic acid. Plus a conkful of bone-dust, chalky-sour and scorchy-rank from the lectric brain saw.

Kanye Sinatra and the two kids been autopsied aready and was lying on gurneys, bare skin marble pale and statue smooth. Y-shaped suture lines with franksteiny stitches showed where their torsos was fixed back together. Kiera were next up.

Baudelaire Dodgson, the path-doc, had maked the Y cut and were ready to go inside the torso. With the outside exam, X-rays and cap work done, this were the last part of the last autopsy. Dodgson would not gab to me till all were done so I were keen for him to crack on.

Picking up a pair of rib cutters, he specked em smiley.

'Brand new and top of the range.' He shoved his new cutters near my viz. 'Splendid, are they not?'

I shrugged. 'They could be garden shears for all I knows.'

'That's exactly what they are – ninety frogs from Home & Garden SupaSave. I acquired them when I arrived in Old England yesterday.' He grinned. 'Say what you like about the PopReppers®© but they make quality products at a fraction of Scientia prices. Look at this craftsmanship – chrome-vanadium blades, edged to perfection. You'd be looking at two hundred frogs for surgical rib-cutters in Paris-sur-Euphrète. And these do a better job.'

If the lad were tryna impress me, it never happened. Most path-docs I knowed bought their own gear from all kinds of gaffs. I knowed a couple what used butcher blades and uddas what got spine chisels from hardware stores. So pruning shears wasn't so hard to gulp. And since path-docs wasn't doing no micro-work, subtlety weren't not so crucial.

Dodgson were a funny one, though, even for his centric profesh. Late mid-age, long and narrow and bendy like he'd got squeezed from a toothpaste tube. Scrawny neck and beaky conk give him a vultry look. Slots was icy blue, cold as his clients. Up top, the rug were a spikey tangle, ziff a hundred volt cattle prod got sticked up his vance. Voice was reedy smooth, though, and manner friendy. Morer importanter, he was one of the best path-docs in all the feds. And even mostest importantest of all, he'd worked on all one hundred and seven previo homicides in this series. If any spud knowed Family Guy, Baudelaire Dodgson did.

'All right,' he said. 'Let's see what these beauties can do.'

Gripping the new cutters, he parted Kiera's sternum and ribcage with a satisfied grunt, then opened her chest and abdo with a scalpel. The big organs was fragged savage. You never needed to be a path-doc to cog that much. He taked em out – colon, liver, tiktok, breathbags and so on. Each went on the scales butcherwise with an autopsy tech recording Dodgson's path gab, all big-word lickertangle to me.

With all the organs done, the path-doc mopped his brow with the back of his hand and sighed heavy. 'This is hungry work and one must sustain oneself.' He glanced at his helper. 'Would you oblige?'

The tech lad bringed a pizza box and took out a slice for his boss to gobble. I'd knowed path docs who noshed in the lab office, but never at the slab. Then again, Dodgson been working bonus giddy-up with few breaks and needed the scran.

Biting off a gobful, he began packing Kiera's innards in a thick plastic bag.

'I love pizza,' he tattled as he ate. 'My guilty pleasure – banned as gutter-food in Scientia. Another reason I never refuse a visit to PopRep®©.'

He bit more pizza, munching hearty.

Into the bag went the colon, clipped sausagey at the duodenum and anus. Then the tiktok, breathbags, liver and so on.

When he were done noshing the pizza he put the organ bag in the cavity, picked up a heavy Hagedorn needle and started stitching.

'*Now*,' I tattled, 'can we tattle about you thinkings?'

He gabbed nada till he snipped and knotted the thread, then zeroed me grim. 'I understand your impatience,

Detective Superintendent, but I thought it important to evaluate the entire… *ensemble* before venturing an opinion.'

Curio slection of words I thinked.

'These are, of course, my preliminary views. My full report will follow.' He pulled off his latex gloves with a double snap. 'But in anticipation of your first question, yes, the pathology is wholly consistent with the work of Family Guy. His signature is everywhere – bondage, torture, humiliation and the exercise of total domination over his victims. Then there is the picquerism – the excessive stabbing and cutting of the female victim, the object-rape of the vagina and rectum, along with the insertion into her oral cavity of the male's severed genitalia. The absence of ejaculatc tells us, once more, that although the killer is frenzied, he is also in control of every aspect of his actions, every square inch of the crime scene.'

I knowed this kinda killer. They was the toughest to nab coz nada were left behind – no body fluid, no dedo prints, no trace mats. And their self-control was capzucking. They delayed the big payoff till much later, typico with smin taked from the kill zone to max-up the jerk-off sperience for weeks. Sooner or later, though, the high died and they'd hunt new vics.

'Kiera Sinatra's cause of death was asphyxiation,' Dodgson gabbed, 'the mechanism, a thin ligature, although she would have been close to death at that point as a result of massive exsanguination from the stab wounds.'

I pointed to a mush of pulpy flesh on her right upper arm. In size it were smare tween the wideness of a lemon and an orange. 'What you make of this?'

He give it a quick zero. 'A focused cluster of stabs.

I didn't see anything quite like it on other victims but overkill of this nature is in keeping with his signature.'

I glanced at the nearest of the three gurneys. 'And Kanye Sinatra?'

'Castrated ante-mortem then made to watch what Family Guy did to his wife. He put up a valiant struggle though – which may go some way to explaining why he took so many blows to the head. Family Guy does not like to have his authority challenged. Also, Mr Sinatra almost severed his radial arteries trying to free his wrists and there were extensive contusions around his ankles. When Family Guy was finished with the wife, he strangled the husband, probably using the same ligature. As you know, this wasn't left at the crime scene. However, from the indentations around their necks, it looks some sort of synthetic cord.'

'What of the childs?'

'Killed as they slept and posed in the manner you saw for yourself.'

'Knockout gassed?'

He nodded. 'The full toxicology report is yet to come but early indications suggest you were right about the odour. Sevoflurane, I suspect. My guess is that Family Guy got into their bedroom and used the anaesthetic to render them unconscious.'

'Then maked shrines for em,' I gabbed sarcy. 'How considrate.'

He give me a bleary look. 'This would be another aspect of his signature. He's used anaesthetic previously.'

'You used the word "ensemble" previo,' I tattled. 'Am I right to think Family Guy specks his killings as creations, works of art?'

'You'd need to talk to a psychologist about that. But from a pathological perspective, I'd say the significant amount of research, planning and labour he puts into each element of his signature speaks for itself.'

'So we can say for sure the Sinatras is victims of Family Guy?'

He started taking off his surgical apron. 'As far as the pathological examination goes, absolutely.'

Smin in his vox give me an odd gutfeel. 'Does the path exam go far enough?'

He hung up the apron and led me to his office at the back of the morgue.

Sinking his long bendy body into the desk chair, he lighted a smoke, jetting fumes through his hairy conk holes. 'The pathology is unambiguous. But this latest series follows a fourteen-year hiatus. That's a long time for a serial killer to stay silent.'

He were right. Smimes they did quit. Smimes they stayed quit. But udda times they went back to it. Like a dried-out boozer what falled off the wagon.

He zeroed me quizzy. 'You saw the reports on the previous three?'

I give him a yo-nod. I spent the night previo specking reps, spections, pics, vids and whatnots of Family Guy's latest outings. These was the ones what marked the "rebirth" – and give Confucius the capwave of "actualizing" me. Far as I could speck, they aligned perfect with the first wave – one in each fedration. No pattern or theme in vic slection. One family were wealthy, one mid-class, the udda low-income. And the killing crossed ethnic lines, which were rare though not unknowed. Also, they was a sameness to the sign-offs what did not bode good. This work were ultra-precise, just like fourteen year previo. I readed them case files also, all twenty-one. And though the stabbing and slashing in each were frighty frenzied, I picked up a curio calm in the fury. Mighta seemed outta control, but he were never. This lad knowed just what he were about and this freddykruegered me bigmost.

'So,' I gabbed, 'you thinks smin cudda gone down during this dormant period – smin not path-related?'

'It's possible.' He pinned me broody. 'We don't know why he stopped or why he started again. It's fair to say, though, that information held back from the public may have been leaked – by accident or for a price – over such a long period of inactivity.'

'Who might leak them stuffs?'

He shrugged. 'Someone in the justice system of any of the three federations. Folk in various law enforcement organizations. And politicians are rarely beyond reproach.'

I got what he meant. Fourteen year, that a monstamostest bigwhile for a monstamostest lotta folks to get skint or shaked down or plain monkeyed. 'Is they any udda way to tell deffo this ain't not no ripcat?'

'Potentially.' He sucked his smoke pensive. 'He sometimes left handwritten notes. I examined most of them for bloodstain and trace evidence but found nothing. Even so, the writing was haunting.'

'How so?'

'Well, the style was fussy and over-wrought. The tone came over as both over-familiar and condescending. Once read, never forgotten.'

He stabbed out his smoke in a tin ashtray. 'But this is outside my field. You should talk to the forensic linguistics people for more on those handwritten notes.'

I zeroed what he were getting at. 'You think them old notes got lingo detils what no ripcat could mimic?'

He specked me knowy. 'Don't you?'

7

Me and Wham!®© left the Big Copshop on Martin Luther King Boul and drived south to the Strip, leaving the motor at Spring Mountain and Sands. We was in a plain car but even so I thinked it best to leg a few blocks so as not to get specked by them as we was specking.

Not a good night for legging though. Wind come razory, clouds stormbroody. They maked the Strip speck dreary, spite the shimry razdaz. Or, more like, dreary *coz* of it. Weird, I knows, but what you zeroed mostest were not the parade of rainbowy neon but the grey nada between the dazzles. I been to Vegas, Nevada – the real Vegas, the hot sunny Vegas – in the wayback and it never grabbed me like it done udda spuds. The never-stop changes, the sparkly fresh-builds, the big-budget rips, they striked me as kinda frantic. Ziff the city always gotta look like smuddaplace. Ziff it could never stand still. And for every Sammy-D songster, every billyaire roller, there was a godzillion slot-slaves and blackjack bums, wretchy and boohoo and zucked. They sitted in them casinos with last night's whisky dregs and piled-up ashtrays and coin-roll wrappers dropped at their feet. Take all that and stick it in the climes of Old England and, well, you gets my drift.

'Where we going, boss?'

Bogart were at my elbow like a too-keen mutt. 'You'll know soon enough.'

We went from Venetian Vegas and its rips of St Mark's and the Rialto Bridge to Paris Vegas with mimics of the Eiffel Tower and Arc d'Triomphe and whatnot. And it come to me ironic that we just legged from one fake of a fake to anudda fake of a fake. But then you might tattle that about the whole of Vegas, England.

'Hungry, boss?' Bogart specked the street food rigs we was passing.

Their lights was fuzzy in cook steam and rain dripping from canopies and punter brollies. I got a conkful of niffs: sizzle fat, peeky spice, unwash pitstink, and the gore of critters killed fresh as punters chosed. There was nought I fancied shoving in my gobbler: grilled gibbon fajitas; chop suey toucan wings; armadillo steak with mouse-tail noodles. Maybe washed down with a paper cup of crushed wasp tea – *"The brew what come with a sting!"*.

'Mind if I grab a bite?'

I give him an if-you-wants shrug.

He maked a sheepy spresh. 'Lend me ten frogs?'

I frowned puzzly. 'Ain't you not got you own gelt?'

He specked me barrassed 'Temp gelt-flow prob, boss.'

In my sperience when popeyes tattled temp gelt-flow probs they meaned permo gelt-flow probs. But I give him the ten frogs and he went to get some scran.

He come back sinking his schlocks into a parakeet burger and off we setted.

We heared the demo a bigwhile before we specked it. Chants of 'Two sylls good, four sylls bad!' come rolling down the street.

'What this about?' I asked.

He finished the burger and tossed the wrap. 'Vox Popeye®© demo, boss.'

I make a curio frown. 'What might them be?'

'They's part of our constution. Ebboddy gets a Popeye®© a week on smin what we picks. Could be any stuffs from import tax on frozen badger to nuking a Trumpian city. *A Vox Popeye®© a week give ebdy a treat*, that the motto.'

'So what this one about?'

'Them as backs it wants morer shortester words. Right now sixty per cent of IngoLingo®© words got two sylls and ten per cent four sylls with the rest at three. This Vox Popeye®© aims to raise two syll words to seventy per cent and cut four sylls to five per cent.'

'But this gobspew lingo is kiddy enough aready,' I tattled. 'This would make it babby-gab.'

My slots was drawed to a bonfire near the south end of the Bellagio Fountain. Young popeyes was tossing red-cover books onto it. Loud cheers went up each time a book landed in the flames.

'What's with the book burning?' I quested. 'Whiffs Nazi.'

'We don't got no Nazis here, boss – them's in Scientia.' He gimme a dulgy grin like I tattled smin brickthick. 'They blazing old dictionies as a ClapTrap®© stunt what's backing the word-shrink Vox Popeye®©.'

I wanted to ask why Nazis wuddabin in Meso-Liberal Scientia but, right then, this dictiony biz were the morest big quesh. 'So what's going down? Them dictionies getting torched got too many big words?'

He specked me muddly.

Smoddy pushed by me with an armful of dictionies, dropping one in their rush. It landed open but all I gogged was blank pages. I picked it up and skimmed it giddyup, cover to cover. Nada on any of the pages, save for the words *PopRep®© Dictiony – 345,567*th *edition* on the front.

'This a tickler?' I quizzed.

Anudda muddly gog.

'A dictiony with no words,' I splained. 'Gotta be a tickler for the bonfire stunt, ain't it not?'

He nay-shaked his fusebox. 'Ain't not laughy, boss. In PopRep®© we got an unwroted dictiony, unwroted lottsa litry stuffs.'

'What, like an unwroted *Complete Works of Shakespo*?'

He yo-nodded like this were smin to be proud of.

'But that ain't not poss.'

'Tis poss, boss. We also got unwroted laws and an unwroted constution.'

I rolled my slots. 'How the zuck does that work?'

'Just does. It's all in the 43,813th Mendment.'

I were capblown, no truer words. 'But how can you make mendments to a constution if it ain't never wroted?'

'Ebba spud in PopRep®© knows our constution by tiktok.'

'Ebba word? That gotta be tough to member.'

He gogged me ziff I were eastbound. 'Ain't not so tough, Boss. Fifteen words is all.'

I asked what these was.

He shoved out his chest and gabbed lofty, '"We The Popeye is titled to The Big Happy and all as come with it."'

'That it?'

'What more could any spud want?'

I tried anudda proach. 'These mendments, they unwroted too?'

He nodded. 'We got monstasmart popeyes what members em and tattles us when ness.'

I shaked my fusebox, gobblerwhacked. 'So nubdy in PopRep®© knows their rights?'

'Some does. As an influsser I knows them as is importanterest.'

'Aright,' I gabbed, 'does you know what the 43,812th Mendent were about?'

He nodded vigrous 'Ebdy above avrage, nubdy below. It were put in our constution only last week: "All popeyes is sprogged above avrage".'

This were getting morer and morer eastbound by the nanofrag. 'But that ain't mathly poss.'

'We let the smart spuds worry about rithtik.'

'So you bosses just tattle shit and make stuffs up as they goes? That it?'

'Works though, boss.'

'You think?'

'Only Alisters gets to think.'

I specked him puzzly but before we could gab more we was into the demo. Popeyes ebbaplace, bawling vilent, spit spraying from snarly gobblers, shoulders barging, boots stamping. Some toted placards, uddas honkers, one waved The Flag.

Bogart gripped my gipsy, his vox panicky. 'We gotta go, boss.'

8

As he were yanking me way from the scrapping I specked a bunch of hippy spuds with a banner that read *SOUL – Save Our Language*. A nanofrag later they was swamped by a bunch of Two Syll goons. One SOUL lass went down and were kicked savage. An old lad with thick-lens gogs gawped as a Short Word stormtrooper come at him, clenched buckets swinging. One blow landed flush and this old lad crumpled sacky, gogs smashed, one slot a bojo of clarety glass.

Bogart went on pulling me outta the trouble spot. The Short Word yeggs was intrested only in bashing the SOUL popeyes. And the SOUL popeyes was intrested only in getting the zuck out.

When we was safe distanced I turned and were stonished to speck a line of nabbers what was standed still, like nada were happening.

'Why don't they break it up?' I skriked. 'Smoddy's gonna get killed.'

Bogart frowned grim. 'Ain't not what them nabs is here for, boss.'

He pointed to three janes and two jacks on a raised platform behind the nabbers. They was togged in high-end earls and silk frocks. All coiffed fashny, all wearing gold lapel studs and lofty spreshes.

'Why is the nabs shielding em?' I quizzed.

'Coz they is Alisters.' Wham!$^{®©}$ spit the words bitter. 'Billyaire bastards what thinks their shit don't stink.'

I give him anudda quizzy gog.

'In the wayback they wuddabin called A-Listers,' he splained. 'Below em come B-Listers, C-Listers and so on. Down to G-Listers.'

'And them Alister popeyes are, what? The ruling class?'

'You got it. Alisters is the top of the pile – star-spangly influssers, bigshot media billies, glammy playjacks and pop divas. It them what rules the roost in PopRep$^{®©}$.'

'And you ain't not one of em?'

He zeroed me like I shudda knowed betterer. 'I is a rookie Blister, recent as last year a struggling Clister. But I always been an outsider with too much ambit for the liking of them sticked up Alisters.'

'So why you wanna be one of em?'

'I never.' His spresh were fierce. 'I wannabe an Alister, sure. But not like them. What I done, I done by my own ennaprize. Not like them privleged pricks with silver spoons up their vances. Ebbathin I does I gotta fund with my own cheddar. That why I ain't not never got nuff. Smimes not even for a flamingo burger. It why I wanna be a billy – so as I can buy all the flamingo burgers I wants.'

From smare close by come a crickly crack and yowly screech as smon's arm were snapped. Anudda lad's fusebox were splitted with a steel knuckler. And from inside the tangle of scrappers come a flow of gore.

Seemed the vilence were spreading to where we was. Spuds all round us was getting real freddykruegered as the Short Word stormies cast about for smoddy else to bojo. Bogart taked my arm again and tugged me outta the danger zone.

We legged tward the Eiffel but gone less than fifty metres when some juiced-up spud skriked, 'Holy Cowell! Ain't you not that influsser lad? Him off GibGab®© and ClapTrap®© and Howler®©?'

'No I ain't not.' Bogart quicked his strides.

'I know who *you am*,' this gobby spud yelled, 'you Bogart Wham!®© – the best there am!'

When we rounded a street corner Bogart gimme a sidewise gog. 'Apols, boss. I get that a lotta times, even when I ain't not glitz garbed.'

He weren't wrong. Same thing happened again as we ducked under the Paris Vegas balloon. Then for a third time at the Arc d'T. There were no more unwanted attention though after we turned into Paris Drive, then went right at Audrie.

'Where the zuck we going, boss?' he quizzed as we reached East Harmon. 'Shudda bringed my hike boots.'

'Right there.' I pointed to a night club named Fifi's with a neon display of a high-kicking can-can dancer and the *tricolore* flag of Old France. 'This is where your lesson in victolgy starts.'

He gogged me quizzy. 'There smin you ain't tattling me, ain't there not?'

I stopped at the entrance. 'Kiera Sinatra worked part-time gigs at Fifi's. And hubbie never knowed.'

'How you find that out?'

'Det Boss Roscoe is spozed to be co-opping but he ain't never.' I give Bogart a cheeky wink. 'So I hacked his hard-drive and that were real helpy.'

9

Coming to the nightclub were a bad idea. But even a bad idea were better than no idea. Which were all we got when we left the cop shop.

'This gaff is mighty frighty, boss.' Wham!®© gabbed nervy as we went inside.

He weren't wrong. The scene were a jux of flickry dazzle and dungeony gloom where popeyes was getting blowed and licked and zucked upright. Light-sabery strobes cut the air, smoke-chocker and reeky of sweat and sex and cheap scent. In the centre of the space, real snapped jacks in roxy earls and trouser-arouser janes in next to nothing was sucking shots and sniffing lines of hokey-cokey at candle-lighted tables. These was ranged round a stage got up for turns by songsters, magic trickers and tickler-tellers. There were also a dancefloor where spuds was jiggling punky. Smov em specked eastbound I thinked – lads in high waist drainpipes and checkety shirts and lasses in spray-on minis and stiletto thigh-boots. But then I membered how I gogged when I were that age, clubbing at the Hacienda in Manchester, thinking I were jawdrop cool with my spikey garb and jivy moves.

Round the bog doors, blade boys was dealing horse, meth, and crack; uppers, downers and sidewaysers. Yeggmen was pimping scams, whispring orders to sex-jacked lads and ready-for-it lasses. They zeroed punters like wolf packs zero sheep flocks. Vilence were "when" not "if".

Wham!®© drained his whiskey glass. 'Do we gotta be here, boss? Can't you not teach me this victolgy smuddaplace?'

'We got no alts, Bogart,' I tattled, 'part from this, we got nada.'

I splained that we come here coz it were the gaff Kiera Sinatra worked as a songster and I were keen to find out more. Hubbie Kanye were prinspal of a community coll and the two hooked up when he were an IngoLingo®© teacher and she his pupil. This splained their sixteen-year age-gap – but not why Kiera been keeping this part-time gig from Kanye. Praps she were just staying in touch with a previo life. Praps that previo life were staying in touch with her. Fifi's were a Mecca for crim gangs. If some street boss still had hooks in her and she stepped outta line, that wuddabin plenty to get her killed. And a Family Guy ripcat play wudda maked a cute smoke screen. A thin lead for sure, but who knowed what crawled out when you turned a stone?

A drunk spud tripped and lurched against our table. He tattled smin lickertangle, belly-belched and went on his way, joining a party of rowdies.

'They is slaughtyhouse workers from Trumpia,' Bogart splained, dabbing specks of spilled beer from his shirt.

'They gets paid eastbound wages and spends it ziff there ain't not never gonna be no tomoz.'

He paused to sip his drink. 'And smimes there ain't not.'

'What you mean?'

'Holy Cowell!' He cut over me, squozing my gipsy. 'That's Plato Tomsky! The lad hisself!'

'Who?'

'Plato Tomsky. Bigestdickest media olly in Scientia. Bigestdickest here too. Bigestdickest ebba place. He's knowed as the Maharaja of Media – and with good cause. Ziff that ain't not enough, he also the sixth richest popeye on the planet.'

By now, Bogart's freddykruegers was banished. All the lad could do was gog this Tomsky.

I zeroed him at a table a few yards from ours. Thick yellow rug swept back tarzany from a deep-tanned viz. Slots was bright-lit and schlocks as gleamy as them of Bogart. Togged in a crumply linen suit and canvas loafers, he were lopey-limbed, long and lithe. Three glam janes was sitting close, hanging on each word what come outta his gobbler and chuckling when propriate.

I turned to Bogart but he were gone – half way to his hero.

Gottasay I were specting my compadre to get the old heave-ho but he never. Instead, this Plato Tomsky greeted Bogart hearty, shaked his grasper and bid the janes make room at the table. Sitting close to Tomsky, Bogart tattled rapid. The olly chuckled lots; so too did the janes. And for the first time I zeroed how my lad Wham!®© could wow spuds – even this so-called Maharaja of Media and sixth richest popeye on the planet.

Also no needed to hold Bogart's grasper gimme an oppo to quiz round the club for any what knowed Kiera. The bar spuds and off-stage artists was smiley-chummy but not so helpful. I sensed more was knowed, but nubdy were keen to tattle. All I learned were that Kiera were a poplar lass, well-liked and much missed. Just as well Bogart weren't not paying attention coz he wudda learned nada from this lesson in victimol.

He specked me return to our table and come to join me – his new bro and the glam-janes headed for the exit. When they was gone Bogart would not shut up about how mad-daddy snapped Plato Tomsky were, his cowelly chrisma, and how the lad abso bezossed The World of Media.

Soon enough though, his frighteners come back. Again he were casting round the dark edges of the dancefloor, body-lingo rabbity, slots twitchy.

With good cause.

This meaty honcho in a white tux come outta no place and standed at our table.

'You been asking about Kiera.' His vox were gravely – maybe Old New York City or Old New Jersey. He specked me mean – murky slots in mudslide viz. Batter-ram brow and anvil jaw. I guessed mid-forties. 'Why you quizzing?'

I flashed my shield. 'And who is you?'

Rumbly laugh come up from his belly. This were echoed by two yeggmen close behind. They called to mind sliverbacks in earls and ties.

'I'm Gonzales Smedge. This is my gaff.'

Wham!®© come to his feet, schlocks on high beam, vox chummy. 'Hey, my bro, we don't want no trouble – '

'Sit the zuck down, pretty lad.' This Gonzales Smedge zeroed Bogart fierce. 'Or my yeggs here will put you down.'

Obvo the charms Bogart used on Plato Trotsky was not gonna work on the gang boss. Wham!®© stayed upright though. Had moxie, gottasay.

I standed beside him, gogging Smedge. At five-eight I weren't not a short lass but the gangsta boss mustabbin a solid six inches higher. His two yeggs was higher still. I keeped my tone smooth. 'You really wanna rumble with nabbers?'

'You ain't not nabbers in this city. Not on my turf. See, I got this greement with the chief. He wudda telled me you was coming.'

'I ain't got no chief,' I gabbed. 'Not in Old England or any uddaplace in PopRep®©.'

'Well, I spoze we gonna find out.' He grinned big then swivelled and moved away. To the yeggmen, he skriked, 'Sling em, boys.'

Silverback One come at me, bucket cocked. But the swing never got no further. A jane I never specked moved in sudden and taked his wrist, levering him backwise sharpfast. Radial tendon ripped at the elbow. He slammed to the floor bawling shrieky. Silverback Two were still gogging his bro when this newcomer palm-striked him sturdy on the jaw, again, again, again. Silverback Two shaked cartoony, over and over, like Tom getting done good by Jerry. Then the lass looped one foot round the back of the lad's right heel and sended him down crashwise with a punch to his conk. He joined his amigo on the deck, gore squirting from his bojoed nose. All this time the lass were moving frisky slick, delivring ultra vilence and never breaking sweat nor stride.

'Whoever you is,' I tattled, 'thanks.'

'You could have dealt with those dicks easily enough.' The firstest thing what striked me were her casual tone – ziff she just done some small favour. And the secondest thing were that she were gabbing Trad Ing. Not from PopRep®©, then.

'But I'm here,' she went on, 'so you don't need to get distracted by stuff like this.'

'Gotta name?' I queshed.

'Liz Comanche.' She holded out her grasper.

I shaked it and zeroed her closer. High and lean like me but ten year junior – late thirties, early forties. Features slopey and smetric, skin creasy round tawny slots and a broad gobbler. No make-up and raggedy rug, cut short of the shoulders. Sorta viz that come from high mileage on hard roads. Still tractive, though, in a rugged sorta way. And togged in biker gear – beat-up leather jacket, threadbare jeans, tatty T.

Well and good, I thought, but we weren't not outta this.

Gonzales Smedge were coming through a side-door, slots widening as he specked Silverbacks One and Two on the deck. Over one shoulder he skriked, 'Trump in Stormy! Look what they done to my lads!'

A squad of yeggmen flooded the room and come right at us.

Only they was never yeggs.

They was nabbers.

10

Det Boss Tom Roscoe were Edward G to a T as he gogged Wham!®©, Comanche and me getting frogged cross the bull pen and throwed in the tank. The grin on them moist rubbery puckers tattled all. He were never gonna lift a dedo to help.

When was behind bars, our cuffs was taked off and we was free to mix with the drunks, prosts and unglueds. Some was gogging us leery. One stare from this Comanche lass, though and they turned away ultra ferrari.

We been arrested at Fifi's right in front of Gonzales Smedge and his yeggs. This were spite my surances that I were a ranking nabber. A knuckle-viz sarge done the formal arrest and we was shoved in the back of a van what been pissed and puked in real recent. Then we was drived to a local cop shop where they done justice like Mackie D's done food. Under the gloaty gaze of this knuckler sarge we was processed and banged up frisky. It were obvio to me now that Gonzales Smedge were not lying when he tattled about a greement with the local nabber boss. This, cording to Bogart, were the chief nabber of the whole city.

Lawdog cruption, Bogart splained, were bonus bad in Vegas, England.

'Can't you do nothing?' I turned to Wham!®© as we rubbed our cuff-chafed wrists. 'What with all this celeb influsser stuff you got?'

He nay-shaked his fusebox. 'To be honest, boss, I just gotta be happy this ain't not on the PubComPlats. Normal circs, celeb like me gets nabbed, it wuddabin all over ClapTrap®© and YakityYak®© and all the others.'

This were puzzly. 'So why ain't it not?'

He zeroed me grim. 'This shit we in come from high up. Mebbe even higher than the chief of nabbers.'

This were a worry, no truer words.

For now, though, I wanted to learn more of this Liz Comanche, parently the second of my three spesh counslers.

I sitted next to her. 'You done good work back there, Liz.'

'Call me Comanche.' She gimme a small smile. 'Everyone else does.'

'You my spesh counsler from Scientia?'

She yo-nodded.

'So what's your background??'

This fetched a sarky titter. 'Only in a universe of opposites. I'm a career criminal.'

Wham!®© earwigged this and gabbed, 'She means *celeb* crim, boss. She been one of Scientia's Top Ten Most Wanteds longer than she ain't not.'

'Fuck off,' Comanche telled him. Then to me, 'I hate that media shit. I'm not a new age Robin Hood. I steal from the rich, true, but I give nothing to the poor. If they had any shit worth stealing, I'd rob them too.'

I studied her a short while. 'Why you here?'

'They gave me two options: work for you or do a twenty stretch.'

Zucking-A, I thought: a biker gang jailbird added to my celeb influsser.

That tattled, she obvio come with uses. 'Where you learn to rumble like you done at Fifi's?'

She gimme a lazy shrug. 'Started out on the backstreets of San Fran del Mediterraneo in Old Turkey. That's where I grew up. If you couldn't scrap you didn't matter. I learned even more from my biker friends and more still at the University of Alcatraz.'

Figured, I spozed. If you gonna build a rip of San Fran you gotta do Alcatraz too. 'How long you do inside?'

'Ten years.' She grinned whimscal. 'That place educated me better than any real university. Fighting, sure. But school stuff too – I got a bachelor's degree in accountancy and a master's in business administration.'

'Lemme guess, you did your thesis on the import/export trade. Which were real handy in the narco biz.'

Her grin stayed. She weren't tickling. Me neither.

'I went in a busted bank robber and came out a criminal entrepreneur. Alcatraz gave me an eye for opportunity and the contacts to exploit it.'

'Confucius and his honchos must love you.'

She maked a brief chuckle. For a nanofrag she gogged much younger, all care lifted. If this lass were ebba happy, pissing off the bosses were how she done it. 'They hate me,' she tattled, 'because they think I'm a rebel without a cause. And they fear me because they think I might find one.'

'So what you crime sociates think of you working for a nabber like me?'

'I'm the boss, I do what I want. But in this case they understand that unless I help you they'll be looking for a new boss. Also, they know people like me don't grow on trees – although we sometimes hang from them. And besides… ' There were a catch in her vox. Her words petered and she specked away. 'My people aren't serial killers. We aren't murderers of children. Going after this bastard isn't the same as turning state's evidence.'

I understanded this much. Even so, it were gonna be off-planet weird me oprating with her and she with me.

'What do you have on this born-again Family Guy?' she asked.

I tattled all. I done this aready with Wham!®©, so why not Comanche? She listened careful and showed keen intrest in the idea of scluding a ripcat. And she thinked Dodgson were right that a hand-wrote note from Family Guy hisself would set us straight one way or the udda.

We both glanced up at the scrape of a key turning in the cell door. The knuckly sarge come through to the cells and skriked my name, Wham's!®© and Comanche's. Gogging quizzy at one anudda we was taked – *un*cuffed – by this sarge into a lift, then up ten floors to a marble hallway carpeted plush. We stopped at a double door where the sarge knocked, waited and went in. The room we entered were the abso oppo of the tank. Gleamy cut and chrome décor with a jawdrop speck of the city. At one end were a monstadick desk with a high-back visitor chair.

'The lad at the desk,' Bogart hissed, 'is Chief Nabber Derangère.'

I thinked the sarge were gonna bojo Bogart for tattling outta turn. But he never.

Instead we was ushered nearer the desk. This Derangère standed as we got close. He were high and lithe, smooth skinned and handsome, with the bearing of some noble spud wroted by the lad Shakespo. Tough to picture this popeye taking bribes and kickbacks, but I stopped getting sprized by this work many a year back.

'Det Top Boss Miller,' he tattled, 'I apols humble and spectful for the palling worstermost way you and your team was treated.'

Them words come as the biggester shock I got in a bigwhile. And there were more. 'Sarge Connery here weren't never following no orders when he nabbed you. He also got smin to gab.'

The sarge also apolled humble and spectful. He were full shamed of his trocious acts and sweared by All What Were Orange never to repeat em. Then he left the room, pursued by Derangère's surances of badmost punishings.

This was when I zeroed smoddy in the high-back visitor chair.

He come to his feet as the sarge shut the door and I specked a low fella, slight build and old – mid-sixties praps. Polywoved suit, shiny with wear, knitted cardy and crepe fabric tie. Deep lines was scribed ebbaplace on a viz what minded me of a dried walnut. Up top, the combover specked like broked guitar strings laid sidewise on his shiny scalp.

'I'm Bob Puritan.' He smiled toothy. 'Attorney-at-law.'

Smin odd about his schlocks – a front incisor were missing and the dark gap give him a trampy speck.

Then he gogged me straight and I seed one slot were gone and, in its place, a pale glass ball what never budged.

Longer I zeroed, the more downy-outy this old lad zeroed. That Oldy Testy line, *A slot for a slot and a schlock for a schlock* come to mind and I couldn't believe I were the first to note this.

'The three of you are free to go.' He gabbed in a vox samesec raspy and suave. 'I took the liberty of commencing wrongful arrest proceedings and withdrew them in return for your immediate release.'

'Smart lawjaw work, Mr Puritan,' I tattled. 'And proper giddyup.'

'Wrongful arrest?' Comanche's viz were a mix of mazement and curio.

Puritan give a small shrug. 'You were arrested for one offence – causing affray – but charged with another – inflicting grievous bodily harm, for which you had not been read your rights. Under any test of PopRep®© law this adds up to wrongful arrest. Chief Nabber Derangère has already had the paperwork drawn up.'

Derangère viz were ultra boohoo as he nudged three sets of legal docs cross his desk and asked us big nice to sign.

11

We drived back to the Big Cop Shop in a gleamy Roller what Puritan had waiting on the street. Tacky ads was blazoned on the side of the car and this were a big puzzler. *Wanna Ride Like this?* skriked the ad, *Call ARM AND A LEG LAW For The Compo What You Deserves.*

'Apologies for the tasteless advertisement,' Puritan tattled as we settled in the back seat. 'But my PopRep®© practice has to compete in the PopRep®© market.'

Clever bit of biz, though, I thought. What better motor to use for a persnal injri compo ad? Didn't do much for the Roller brand though.

Old fella mightabin reading my mind. He gimme one of his gappy grins. 'Rolls Royce is offering me a significant cash settlement to stop using their vehicles for this purpose,' he splained. 'We're currently in advanced negotiations.'

Cleverer still, I reckoned.

'Apols for my bluntness, Mr Puritan,' I gabbed, 'but why is you here?'

He gimme a wink with his only working slot. 'Why do you think?'

I zeroed him piercy. 'You ain't not just no random lawjaw is you?'

He fiddled with a big hearing aid jammed behind his cabbagey lug. It were maked of beige plastic and minded me of them National Health Service ones in Old Britain from the 20th Cent what made R2D2 noises when you justed em. But what were a lawjaw in a Roller doing with this ancient tech? Then it come to me that it were a marketing tool – like all else about this old lad. He wanted to come over messy and muddled when, in truth, he were the exact oppo. Praps to monkey his foes; praps to draw to clients; praps both.

Then he tattled, 'I've been sent by the Holy Trumpian Empire to assist your Family Guy investigation.'

And then lottsa stuffs maked sense.

And, I flected rueful, my team of "spesh counslers" was maked up of a crusty lawjaw, a crime boss and celeb influsser what cudda made Narcissus blush.

As we drived back up Vegas Strip we gogged these monstadick vid screens on the sides of buildings. There was slo-mo shots of Army jacks and Navy janes strutting patrio with The Flag rippling pompy behind em. These clips melted into uddas of this mid-age mumsy lass I knowed to be Dreezy Simz, Uber-Top-Boss+++®© and ruler of PopRep®©.

'They's gearing up for the next big show,' Bogart tattled. 'Hiking the punishment for dissing The Flag gonna get Vox Popeyed®©. Them as backs the move wants to hike the max from two year in stir to ten year with backbreak labour. As you can zero, the Uber-Top-Boss+++®© herself is behind it. So it's gonna happen for sure.'

Confucius warned me against doing anything what cuddabin specked as dissing The Flag so I asked Puritan what this meant in law lingo.

'Anything,' he splained, 'and nothing. I've defended clients myself. A sight-impaired woman failed to give a civilian salute to the PopRep®© Flag, even though she couldn't see it and in any case there was no legal requirement to do so. In another case a teenaged boy was sitting on a park bench wearing full-immersion head gear – Pink Floyd at Radio City as I recall – when a soldier walked by. Understandably the lad didn't notice the soldier and therefore failed to "thank him humble for His Service". I could go on… '

'You winned all them cases?'

He gimme anudda franksteiny grin. I wished he'd stop doing it. But acourse he winned. This lad never did nada but.

When we got to the Big Cop Shop, Puritan gabbed smin about a bit of biz he gotta finish at his office cross the street. I specked him moving limpy long the sidewalk, old wood stick to keep him from falling – and probs yet anudda part of the walking ad what this canny old fella maked hisself into.

The three of us went to the incdent room. The crazy board showed nada helpful– a blank sea of white round vizshots of the Sinatras and udda famlies what maked up Family Guy's "new wave" victims. Multi-coloured twine, marker pens and jars of thumbtacks sitted useless on a table, minding me what little progress we maked. True, I were gonna pin up a piece of red string linking Kiera Sinatra to a pic of Gonzales Smedge, though I doubted this were to do with the main event. But keep an open cap, Randy, I told myself.

Besides, I got udda stuffs to deal with. Turning to Wham!®© and Comanche I nodded for em to come into my office.

'I wanna know what you two thinks about this Puritan,' I gabbed. 'We all gonna be working with him so I gotta know.'

Bogart never dithered. 'Best lawjaw in the three feds, boss,' he tattled. 'That lad is bigbad news for them as wrongs his clients. They sees Old Bob coming, they better run.'

I zeroed Comanche. 'You ever come cross him?'

'Not directly,' she said. 'But, like Bogart, I know him by reputation. As you've no doubt figured, the disfigured old bum look is part of his schtick.'

'So how come he got to be like that in the first place?'

Comanche taked out a pack of smokes but never lighted one. 'Story goes that he was a gifted criminal psychiatrist who was framed by one of his clients for blasphemy – speaking ill of Blessed Steve Bannon.'

I frowned capboggly. 'Sloppy Steve, as Trump called him?'

'The Holy Quadity re-wrote a lot of history.' Comanche splained. 'Including Trump's spat with Bannon. He came to be regarded as one of the major prophets of the Holy Trumpian Empire.'

'So what happened to Puritan?'

'He was sentenced by a religious court to lose an eye and a tooth.'

'Holy Cowell,' I tattled. 'Where them Trumpian spuds at? They sounds like smin outta the Dark Ages.'

'They uses mod surgry, boss,' Wham!®© tattled. 'Crims gets anesticked before the blade docs starts chopping. So not quite sames as Dark Ages.'

I shaked my fusebox in disbelief. 'What kinda society uses mod medico techniques to maim its own popeyes?'

Comanche maked a sympo spresh. 'After Old Bob's punitive surgery, an audio recording of the alleged blasphemy was shown to have been faked by his client. The culprit was microwaved at the stake in the Arena of the Redeemer. But that was no comfort to Bob. From what I heard, he gave up his psychiatry practice and retrained as a lawyer. At first he focused solely on clinical and forensic negligence claims. His dad was a religious scholar and taught the boy every Trumpian scripture back to front and upside down – the scriptures, you see, are the basis of Trumpian law. And there are a fucking lot of them.'

'Since then,' Bogart rejoined, 'Old Bob repped monstaloads of spuds what had body bits lopped unfair. Lotta knife-docs was over-zealy and taked off more than they shudda. Also, lotsa nabbers broked rules and judges was slapdash with scripture law. Old Bob done off-planet class actions against em all. Winned every case and got godzillions of shekels for them as he repped.'

'Them Trumpian bosses mustabbin real happy with Old Bob,' I gabbed sarcy.

Comanche lighted her smoke. 'The bosses in Scientia and PopRep®© weren't too pleased either when he set up practices in their federations.'

'He cogs Scientia and PopRep®© stuffs as well as Trumpian legals?'

'He's a great litigator with exceptional recall,' Comanche tattled. 'Everything he experiences goes into that mainframe brain of his. Most cases, just the prospect of facing Bob Puritan in a law court brings opponents to the settlement table.'

Intresty I thinked.

The convo ended when the old lawjaw come into the room, grinning that gap-toothy grin. 'Good news, my friends,' he gabbed. 'I just got off the phone with the lawyers representing Gonzales Smedge. I assumed you'd be happy for me to file for defamation and they agreed a settlement of two hundred million PopRep®© dollars.'

'*Each*?' This were Bogart.

The lawjaw done a yo-nod.

The three of us specked him capboggly.

'You sued a gangster for *libel*?' Comanche sounded stonished as I feeled.

He give a so-what? shrug. 'Mr Smedge unwisely posted security camera footage of the two of you being arrested. The post appeared on Claptrap®© and Howler®©. It had been, I suspect, intended to showcase Mr Smedge's power and influence. However, it backfired. The formal admission by the chief nabber that the arrest was unlawful made the post defamatory.'

My phone ringed – it were Confucius.

'There are some people you need to meet,' he tattled. 'In Paris-sur-Euphrète.'

12

PARIS-SUR-EUPHRÈTE

Confucius was as good as his word: the compulsion to speak IngoLingo®© vanished the moment the solar-atomic arrow plane left PopRep®© airspace. Glancing around the executive cabin, I struggled to conceal my instant and overwhelming joy.

Then I started talking. Not gabbing. Not tattling. *Talking.* I talked just because I could. I talked because it sounded so good in my throat, my mouth, my ears. I was talking shit, I knew this. Still I talked.

Only when my three companions started glancing at me askance did I realize I was making a fool of myself.

What puzzled me though was why Wham!®© continued talking in IngoLingo®©. I asked him about this.

He made a rueful expression. 'Would you prefer if I spoke IngoLingo®©? Like everyone in PopRep®© I'm quite capable of speaking in Traditional English when I'm abroad – if I choose.'

I gave him a second look. Was this the same person I'd met decked out in a silver tux on Fremont Street? His words came in a silky baritone, smoothly modulated and enunciated with perfect clarity.

'However,' he went on, 'unlike most of my compatriots, I prefer to stay true to my roots. I've never been pretentious in that way and don't intend to be, irrespective of any political success that may come my way.'

I had to admire his commitment, his refusal to be cowed by the snobbism that appeared to be directed at PopReppers travelling outside their federation. Besides, he sounded downright weird in Traditional English. I never thought I'd find myself admitting this, but in Bogart's voice IngoLingo®© sounded natural, sometimes bizarrely eloquent. I just wished *I* didn't have to use it.

The plane droned on and I turned my thoughts to graver considerations.

Like Family Guy.

So I called a team meeting and went through the elements we needed to keep in mind. I discussed the MO and signature, victimology and the importance of what was *not* at the crime scene – the lack of forensic evidence meant we were hunting a man driven by fury yet constrained by immense self-possession. I also mentioned the possible, if unlikely involvement of the gangster boss Gonzales Smedge in the murder of Kiera Sinatra, his former employee. And I pointed out the need to rule out the admittedly small chance of there being a copycat killer. I explained how a handwritten note could do this, or another aspect of the latest killings unique to the Family Guy of fourteen years ago.

Later we sat back in the luxurious seats and relaxed over food, drink and idle chatter. My team was a mixed bunch for sure. Would I have chosen any one of them for this work? Absolutely not. Did I think they could do the job? Well, maybe. Bob Puritan's multi-jurisdictional legal knowledge would clearly be helpful, but I also wondered about his previous career as a criminal psychiatrist. Looking across the aisle to Comanche, it was obvious that she wasn't just an enforcer. A criminal history like hers would give me a perspective of the other side of the law enforcement fence, not to mention her contacts. And Wham!®© was a curious mix of vanity and loyalty. He wasn't as daft as he often sounded and could form fast and easy relationships with important people. Like Plato Tomsky. Just as crucially, he'd stood by me when the chips were down with Smedge's yeggmen at Fifi's.

One important thing the three of them had in common was an anti-establishment attitude – albeit for different reasons. Puritan had made a career out of suing the system; Comanche out of robbing it; and even Wham!®© was bent on disrupting PopRep's®© A-lister dominated regime. These oppositional views would, I hoped, give me a valuable counter-narrative to the sanitized puff I suspected I'd been hearing from Confucius.

When we were done eating, Wham!®© turned on a television screen and pictures of Dreezy Simz filled it. The Uber-Top-Boss+++®© of PopRep®© was addressing a mass rally in Trafalgar Square, London in support of the *Two Sylls Good, Four Sylls Bad* campaign. Her yellow hair was tied in a practical bun and she was wearing a sensible tweed suit that spoke of family values, straight-talking and elbow-grease politics.

'You recall,' she said, sounding like Huxley's Mustafa Mond with a Liverpool accent, 'that monstamostest inspo gab of the Great Gove's: "The people of this country have had enough of experts."'

'"The people of this country,"' she repeated slowly, '"have had enough of experts."'

Whoops and cheers rang out, finding echoes in the stately masonry of Admiralty Arch. Horatio Nelson himself, gazed down approvingly from his column.

The crowd chanted, "Michael Gove! Michael Gove! Michael Gove!"

I thought of the jingoistic British politician who uttered these words during Brexit – the chaotic referendum campaign in 2016 that resulted in Britain exiting the European Union. Gove hadn't liked the anti-Brexit warnings of authoritative economists so he chose to reject them, lending legitimacy to an anti-intellectual free-for-all. In this sense, I guessed, Gove had earned a place in populist iconography.

The crowd roared louder still as Simz hit full throttle and it was as if everyone who ever knew anything actually knew nothing. She pointed a Gove-Knows-Best finger at the TV camera and Plutarch and Livy were on the run. She waved a back-to-basics wave and Augustine of Hippo and Nicolo Machiavelli, Charles Darwin and Karl Marx, got trolled. She shook her head with an anti-liberal-elite shake and Taxila and Al Quaraouiyine and Bologna turned to ash. She laughed a Will of the People laugh and instead of the Sorbonne and Heidelberg, Oxford and Cambridge and the Ivy League, there were theme parks. She talked Common Sense and Common Sense vanquished Byzantium and the Renaissance and the Age of Reason. More Common Sense – Ibn Khaldun, Jean-Jacques Rousseau and Emile Durkheim got out of Dodge. Common Sense – the work of Montesquieu, Malthus and Hegel returned to factory settings. Common Sense – John Stuart Mill, John Maynard Keyes, Robert Dahl, who the fuck? Common Sense – art. Common Sense – science. Common Sense – knowledge. Common Sense –

I needed a drink.

The flight from Vegas, England to Paris-sur-Euphrète was nearly three thousand miles but the arrow plane, flying at supersonic velocity, began its descent a little after three hours. As we came in to land I peered through my seat window and saw dawn light on the copper-ochre ramparts of the Zigurrat at Ur of the Chaldees.

Dating from 3,800 BC, the archaeological city was the birthplace of Abraham and first recorded in the 26th Century BC. If you wanted a marvel of ancient history on your doorstep, this would be tough to beat. And given its location near the Euphrates, it was probably the real deal. The kind of place, I thought, that would be anathema to Dreezy Simz – and, indeed, Mustafa Mond – but enrapture Isambard Kingdom Confucius and his Meso-Liberal Party friends.

We landed smoothly at Charles de Gaulle where a slender woman in a black business suit was waiting on the apron of the private arrivals terminal. This, according to my briefing notes, was Wu Mei Leclerc, director-in-chief of the FIB – Federal Intelligence Bureau – an organization combining the espionage and counter-espionage roles of the CIA and FBI in Old America.

She moved forward to take my hand as we stepped off the plane, introduced herself and guided me to a black SUV. Wham!®©, Comanche and Puritan were taken to a second vehicle and we set off in a small convoy with FIB escorts at the front and rear.

As we left the airport I said, 'Who are these people I'm here to meet?'

'You'll find out soon enough.'

I gave her a closer look. She was one of those women whose age was hard to judge but I guessed around fifty. Her features were almost genderless, slopey and thin with lively eyes and stylishly dishevelled hair. She was a fraction taller than my five-eight with a sinuous frame and no discernible figure – the build of a long-distance runner or maybe a high-jumper.

'Must be important, though, otherwise I wouldn't be here.'

She made a tight smile. 'So must you, detective superintendent. Otherwise *they* wouldn't be here.'

Clearly I wasn't going to get much from her so I sat back as the convoy cruised along the A1 past the Parc Georges Valbon then turned south with the Stade de France on our left.

'I'll be frank with you, Miller, I didn't want you for this role.'

'Sherlock Homes not available?' I continued to gaze out of the window. 'Philip Marlowe out of town?'

'I mean no disrespect.' She sounded a little miffed by my sarcasm. 'I just don't think you're the right fit.'

'To be equally frank, director, I don't think I'm the right fit either. I don't think I'm even here, even real.'

'This isn't easy for you. I understand that.'

I kept quiet as we drove past the tall town houses of the Boulevard Malesherbes.

At last she said, 'May I offer some advice?'

'Sure.'

'Don't trust anyone.'

'Thanks, but that's kind of a given in my line of work.'

'I mean *anyone*.'

'Not you? Not Confucius?'

She shook her head.

'What about my team?'

'Not even them.'

'Not even myself?'

'Especially not yourself.'

I gave her a hard stare. 'That's the most paranoid advice I ever heard.'

She took a few moments to consider a response. I suspected she never did anything without having examined every angle.

'This business you're involved in,' she said as we arrived at the Élysée Palace, 'it's deep and dangerous. And you're obviously a stranger to everyone and everything. So feel your way in. Don't take anything at face value. Keep your options open.'

I wanted to ask her to be more specific, but the SUV came to a halt in the gravel surfaced courtyard. Two men and a woman were standing at the entrance. One of the men was Isambard Kingdom Confucius; the other, I presumed, Judgment Jesusly, First Father of the Holy Trumpian Empire. I recognized the woman as Dreezy Simz, whose "Two Sylls Good, Four Sylls Bad" speech I'd watched on the plane.

I gave Wu Mei a curious look. 'Simz was addressing a rally in London an hour *after* our plane took off. So how come she arrived here so far ahead of us?'

'She travelled in her low-orbit space clipper,' Wu Mei said. 'So did Jesusly. Very, very fast, but very, very expensive. Top echelon world leaders only.'

I looked through the side window at the global rulers and the pliant media folk – not so much a hack pack as a schlock flock. And sensed I was enmeshed in a power play for which everyone knew the rules except me.

'Remember,' Wu Mei whispered as I followed her from the SUV, 'nothing at face value; options open. Also, don't promise anything you can't deliver.'

As guidance went, I couldn't imagine anything more vague.

13

followed Wu Mei from the SUV past a strangely deferential group of reporters, photographers and television camera crews. They went about their work with unobtrusive murmuring in a marked-out area in front of the three leaders – not exactly the hack pack I was used to.

First, I was filmed being presented by Confucius to Dreezy Simz who looked better in person than on the TV screen. Since then, her hair had been arranged in a stylish bob and she'd changed into a chic business suit. That low-orbit clipper from London must have travelled even faster than I thought – she'd clearly had time for a make-over in Paris before our arrow plane arrived. She took my hand and we turned to face the cameras with smiles as false as the city we were standing in.

Next I was introduced to Judgment Jesusly. I'd been expecting some pharisaic holy man in religious regalia but this fellow looked more like a country boy from the American south-west. His olive skin was contoured by handsome face bones and he was wearing an Italian silk suit that flattered his lean build. I guessed he'd be mid-fifties. He and I did the obligatory handshake pose for the cameras before I was invited indoors with the three leaders and Wu Mei.

I followed them into the baroque shock of the Salon Pompadour, all fluted columns and gilt frame mirrors, intricate tapestries and sculpted flourishes. The leaders sat in gold-frame chairs with pale blue upholstery arranged around a low table. There was a brief pause, then Confucius invited Wu Mei and I to sit.

Confucius started the meeting by apologizing to me for the short notice and explaining that this was necessary because of the complex security arrangements for bringing the world leaders together.

'Isambard already met ya'll,' said Jesusly. His accent was heavy-duty west Texas and he pronounced Isambard as Eye-zam-bard. 'But me and Dreezy here, we wanted to see you in the flesh, so to speak.'

'Me and Judgment know all about your track record, Randy. It's nice to get up close and personal though, isn't it?' Simz's Liverpool accent was much less broad than in her Trafalgar Square speech. Equally surprising, she was talking in Traditional English, not IngoLingo®©. The former, it seemed, was the language of diplomacy.

Jesusly leaned forward, elbows on knees grinning, his teeth a similar kilowattage to Bogart's. 'We want to go back home and tell our folks we met with the *Top Detective Of All Time* and she's right across this gosh dang awful Family Guy business.'

I was struck by Jesusly's and Simz's informality, their regional accents, their use of pet names – including mine. This made a sharp contrast with Confucius's aloof erudition, his pedantry and fondness for referencing big names in philosophy and literature. Then I imagined the demographic profiles of Jesusly's and Simz's constituents and the folksiness made sense. Jesusly's tone would play well in the religious communities of rural Trumpia, just as Simz's would strike a chord among the junk culture consumers of PopRep®©.

'Can you give us an update?' Simz asked. 'How close are you to catching this monster?'

I glanced enquiringly at Confucius and Wu Mei, then gave Simz and Jesusly a summary of the investigation.

When I was done Jesusly set down his glass of water and gave me a stern look. 'Gotta say, Randy, you're not filling us with a whole lot of confidence.'

I shrugged. 'I'm sorry, but there's no use pretending this is going to be quick or easy.'

'You can't have got nowhere?' Simz's Liverpudlian cadence went up half an octave. 'You must have *some* leads?' She swivelled to face Confucius. 'She must have *some* leads?'

Wu Mei made a polite cough and a small smile. 'I'm sure that is so. But with serial killer investigations, all intelligence has to be carefully guarded.' She gave me a slightly irritated glance. 'Isn't that right, Superintendent?'

I took the hint and nodded. 'I am pursuing a number of lines of enquiry. And Director-in-Chief Leclerc is correct, I have to keep them confidential for operational reasons. If we show our hand, Family Guy will become evasive and even harder to catch.'

'But surely you can tell *us*.' Simz's head traversed like a tank turret from me to Confucius. 'Surely she can tell *us*?'

Mount Rushmore man seemed to take Wu Mei's steer. 'I'm afraid not, Dreezy. I'm not party to this information either, but if the superintendent is to succeed we have to accept that she knows best what can be shared and what cannot.'

Coming from Confucius, she seemed to accept this although clearly wasn't happy.

'But she is going to catch this bastard, isn't she?' This time her eyes darted from Confucius to me. 'You are going to catch this bastard, aren't you?'

'I'm confident, yes.'

'Very confident?' Jesusly asked.

'Confident,' I said.

Jesusly looked at Confucius. 'Okay we'll leave it at that. But this is on you, Isambard. She's your pick. I hope she can deliver like you say she can.'

I didn't like the way he talked about me in the third person, as if I wasn't there. And I liked even less the casual menace in his folksy accent.

Confucius ended the meeting with some vapid comments about how well things had gone and how another meeting should be arranged, perhaps in Trumpia or PopRep®©.

I was glad to be out of the room.

Wu Mei appeared at my shoulder as I walked across the courtyard towards our SUV.

'You really should have known to play along with Simz and Jesusly. They needed reassuring words to take home, not the blunt facts you gave them.'

There was a terseness in her tone that annoyed me. 'And you,' I said, 'really should have known that I needed a proper briefing before plunging me into a situation like that.'

'I didn't have time. Everything was hushed up and locked down for security reasons. You weren't supposed to know Jesusly and Simz were here until you went into the meeting. I thought you could handle it.'

We both backed off, sitting in silence as the SUV nudged through the city centre traffic.

After a time I said, 'You know I'm not a proper detective, don't you? That I don't really exist?'

She gave me a bleak look. 'Do you want to exist?'

I thought about it. 'Since I don't know what the alternative is, I suppose so.'

'Then I wouldn't talk like that when Trumpian folk are around. Jesusly's zealots already think you're a demon conjured by diabolical technology. If you repeat that sort of thing when you're in the Holy Trumpian Empire, they may make sure you don't exist.'

'Is that where I'm going next?'

'Where you go next is largely down to Family Guy.'

14

left my car in the underground car park and headed for the elevator. We'd been given office space at FIB headquarters at 36 Quai des Orfèvres on the Île de la Cité – the address of the Old French Sûreté. Its central location gave us efficient access to most areas of the inner city and it seemed as good a place as any to continue the investigation in Scientia.

The snarl of a powerful engine reverberated off the concrete walls and I turned to see Comanche arriving on a sleek motorcycle. She stopped near the elevator and I walked toward her.

'Nice bike,' I said. It was too – a sleek black and chrome machine with graceful lines and a lot of raw power. As I got closer I saw that it was a Vincent Black Lightning.

She made a clumsy shrug and I got the impression she was uncomfortable with compliments.

'I used to have an old Triumph Bonneville,' I said. 'Not a patch on one of these though.'

She gave me a curious look. 'I'd never have put you down as a biker.'

'There's a lot you probably wouldn't have put me down as.'

'Is that so?'

She examined me as if we'd never met. Her dark purple eyes met mine and there was an uncertain moment. Then she smiled. 'You can look,' she said, 'but not touch.'

I made a mock frown. 'I'm disappointed.'

She gave me a playful look. 'Maybe later.'

'Could I take a ride?'

'Maybe.'

I leaned forward, checking out in the big speedometer and rev counter. The tachometer read 89,507 miles. Which was puzzling. 'That's a lot of miles for such a great looking machine.'

'I've rebuilt the engine three times.' She turned off the ignition and dismounted. 'But this is the original bike with the original engine casing.'

We went into the elevator and up to the incident room on the fourth floor.

Through the open door of my office I watched Comanche standing by her desk. She looked awkward, as if not knowing what to do, and I guessed she didn't. Spend the whole of your adult life as a member of a motorbike gang, why would you know about white collar practices? She said something to Bob Puritan whose work station was opposite hers and finally sat down. Even then she seemed at a loss. So was I. So, probably, were we all. We'd been given the resources normally available to detectives on a murder investigation team. But we weren't detectives. I could hardly ask Wham!®© to do some door-to-door work; or Comanche to check in with her informants; or Puritan to come up with a profile of Family Guy.

Or maybe I could.

I called the old timer into my office. He shuffled across the incident room using his wooden walking stick and sat opposite me in the visitor chair. He looked more tramp-like than ever in his two-sizes-too-big polyester suit, food-stained cardigan and open-toe sandals.

'You used to be a criminal psychiatrist, right?'

He looked at me suspiciously through his one eye. 'I did.'

'Have you heard of George Metesky, the New York "Mad Bomber"?'

'I have not.'

'He planted more than thirty bombs in public places over a sixteen year period in the 1940s and 50s. Twenty-two of these devices exploded, injuring fifteen people.'

'So?'

'His arrest was in large part due to the work of James Brussel, a criminal psychiatrist who created an uncannily accurate 'portrait' of the perpetrator.'

'So?' Now his question was freighted with suspicion.

'So I was wondering if you could work up a similar portrait of Family Guy.'

He ran his fingers through the raggedy strands of his combover. 'Not my field I'm afraid, boss.'

I sucked in a breath and waited a few seconds. I was hoping to do this without losing my temper. 'Look, Bob, what we're being asked to do isn't anyone's field.' I tried to sound reasonable. 'We must all adapt or face the consequences of failure, whatever they are.'

'But you already have profiles drawn up by profilers in all three federations over many years. There's nothing I could add.'

'Actually, there a great deal you could add,' I said. 'You could bring a different perspective, a fresh approach – and the fact that you're not a law enforcement profiler is a benefit, not a problem. Yes, we know that Family Guy is classified as a "power-control, anger-excitation killer with a torture signature". That's fine as far as it goes. But I want more. I want a medical opinion, not another application of investigative technique.'

'You realize I haven't practised psychiatry for thirty years? I'm a lawyer these days, not a doctor.'

'Then you can also use your legal insights. You've defended a lot of people on murder charges. How would you defend Family Guy? What pleas of mitigation might you enter?'

'I wouldn't. He's a monster.'

'Indulge me.'

There was a pause. I sensed his discomfort. The audio output in his ancient beige hearing aid crackled and chirped. 'This is all very unorthodox,' he said.

Again I struggled to keep my temper at bay. 'Have you got anything else to do right now? Or tomorrow? Or next week?'

'Well, no.'

'Then do this for me. Think of it as a creative exercise. I want to know what you think is inside this man's head. Give me his story. Tell me why he thinks he's the hero of it. Write a portrait of this killer like Brussel did of Metesky. Use your experience, use your imagination, use anything. Because right now, we have nothing except three very anxious world leaders, including the man who put you here.'

This last point scored a hit and he made a gruff noise. 'Very well, I'll see what I can do. But I'm not confident so don't raise your hopes.'

As Puritan left I saw Wham!$^{®©}$ glance across from his desk and come rushing into my office.

'It Plato Tomsky, boss – he just called. He wanna meet!' The words stampeded from his mouth, each trying to get ahead of the one in front. I'd never seen a child at their own birthday party this excited.

'That's great work, Bogart,' I said, without really meaning it. There were times when it was best to treat my celeb influsser as a child, and this was one.

'Plato. Tomsky.' He pronounced the name slowly, each syllable pleasuring his tongue.

'I don't know what to say,' I said. This, at least, was true.

'This gotta be monsta for my career, boss. Monsta!' He was already planning his speech for the Oscars, or whatever they had in PopRep$^{®©}$.

'This is exciting news, Bogart,' I said, 'but in order to get back to your career, we first have to sort out this Family Guy business. How do you think Tomsky might help us?'

'C'mon, boss.' He fashioned a sheepish grin. 'You gotta know he the bigmosterest speshlist on the planet on allstuffs Family Guy. Ain't nada worth knowing what Plato don't not know. He made a capblowy docmentry fourteen year back. He gonna wanna make anudda now Family Guy come back. We gotta help him.'

'I'm more interested in how he might help us,' I said. 'Anyway, go to this meeting and find out what sort of information he has.'

He dashed off and I returned my attention to my computer screen. Less than thirty seconds later, he was back.

'What is it now, Bogart?' I tried to rein in my irritation.

'It's lunch.' I looked up and saw Wu Mei standing at my office door. 'And a bottle of something nice. One o'clock sharp.'

Eating out with a high-up was not something I fancied. But although she was smiling there was a flinty edge in her voice. I wasn't being asked, I was being told.

15

On the Quai des Orfèvres a sharp April wind veered off the river. Tree branches were hazy green with spring buds and the sun was shining. Even so, a stack of sombre rainclouds was approaching from the east. I reminded myself that the river wasn't the Seine but the Euphrates; that, despite the weather, this wasn't north west Europe but southern Iraq.

And I could not exist, yet did.

'I thought you needed a break from the office,' she said.

This wasn't true – Wu Mei's type didn't take lunch or drink wine in the middle of the day without a reason. I was going to be briefed, examined, probed or tested. Nonetheless, a decent meal and a glass of wine would be a refreshing change from a sandwich and bottle of water.

We headed towards the Pont Neuf. 'Any news on your investigation? Your man Wham!®© seemed excited about something.'

I told her about Bogart's meeting with Plato Tomsky and she gave me a look of astonishment. '*Tomsky* contacted Wham!®©?'

In that moment I realized what a big player Tomsky was – and what an achievement this was for Bogart. 'He won't shut up about his new best friend's deep knowledge of Family Guy. Apparently Tomsky's documentary got rave reviews. Maybe he can be useful.'

'Maybe he can.' She gave me a wary look. 'But you should be very careful with what you share with Tomsky. He's an oligarch and a Great Elector. Yes, he has some talent. But he's also an ego-driven narcissist.'

This was interesting, I thought. Not because I disagreed with Wu Mei – on the basis of what I'd seen of Tomsky at Fifi's, he was exactly as she described – but because she had clearly gone out of her way to bad-mouth him.

As we approach the bridge I was distracted by a group of municipal workers cleaning graffiti from the side of a building. "One person, one vote", it said.

'What's that about?' I asked.

'Populist nonsense.'

'I thought populism was what PopRep®© was about?'

'That's not to say we don't get a version of it here.'

'But what's so nonsensical about one person, one vote?' I gave her a baffled looked. 'Surely you have universal suffrage?'

'We do.'

'Then why the graffiti?'

'Some people have more than one vote.' She paused until we were passed a busker with a guitar and harmonica. 'Those Leveller types want to abolish capacity-configured electoral input.'

She read my confounded expression. 'Our electoral system recognizes that some people are better equipped to decide socio-economic and geo-political questions. So, for example, the head of a large corporation or a university president has more votes than, say, a manual worker or a factory operative. Somewhere in between there could be a school teacher or the owner-manager of a mid-sized business.'

'How many more votes separate the top from the bottom?'

She seemed a little uncomfortable. 'It's a complex algorithm that depends on a broad range of factors.'

'It's a lot, isn't it?'

We walked a little further. 'Give me an example.'

She shrugged. 'I suppose, hypothetically, a highly qualified, talented and experienced individual may be awarded a weighting factor of more than one million.'

'Compared to, say – ' I glanced across the street at the municipal workers cleaning up the graffiti ' – one of those people?'

'Well, one.'

I was curious about something else she'd mentioned about Tomsky. 'What's a Great Elector?'

Once more, she looked flustered.

I gave her a prompt. 'I can look it up easily enough.'

'Very well,' she said after a few more strides, 'it's a term used to describe people with more than fifty million votes.'

'So you'd need enough factory operatives to populate California and New York City combined to scrape together enough ballot slips to equal, say, Plato Tomsky's?'

'In theory, yes. But it's not that simple.'

Nothing ever was, I thought.

'Scientia isn't an oligarchy,' she said. 'We're a sophocracy, from *sophos*, the Ancient Greek for wisdom.

And there's nothing undemocratic about giving a greater political voice to those who know how best to use it.'

'Including Tomsky?'

She didn't answer that.

We turned right and headed across the Pont Neuf towards the right bank.

'I mean,' she said, 'you wouldn't want a bunch of graffiti cleaners running this city, whereas a group of top people with proven management and administration skills would be a different matter.'

I'd heard this argument for elitism before. But I kept quiet.

'In Scientia everyone is *morally* equal but we are wise enough to recognize that people have different gifts, abilities and intellect. You've seen for yourself what happens in the Great Populist Experiment of PopRep®©. Las Vegas, England, for example, with extra hotel casinos but no weather control. Also, we have superb social mobility. People can rise to the top exclusively on merit.'

I'd heard that before too, but she wasn't done. 'The best education system in human history is state-funded from pre-school to doctor's degrees – and with each qualification beyond high school diploma come additional votes. So a corporate middle-manager with a bachelor's degree or vocational equivalent would get a thousand votes. If that person took a master's degree and became a senior manager, this number would rise to one hundred thousand. We have the best educated, highest skilled and most insightful electorate on the planet.'

I was getting tired of this, so I said, 'Let me guess. Everyone is above average, just like in PopRep®©?'

She gave me a dismissive glance but didn't reply and I was happy to leave it at that.

The first building I saw on the right bank was the Paris office of Arm and a Leg Law. Clearly, Puritan hadn't been exaggerating when he said his firm had a strong presence in all three federations.

Wu Mei was taking me to a little place called La Papille Gustative, which I knew translated as The Taste Bud, located on Rue Rivoli opposite the Tuileries Gardens. There, she assured me as we walked along the east side of the Louvre, I could choose from the best menu on the right bank.

As we headed into the Louvre I noticed a statue of a woman holding a basket of bread in one hand and, in the other, a rifle raised above her head. Her expression was fierce, uncompromising, her gaze one of far-sighted determination. It reminded me of Soviet-era statues of idealized heroism.

'Jemima Gage Pankhurst,' Wu Mei explained, 'The founding mother of Anti-ism.'

'Anti what?'

She made an indulgent sigh. 'Every citizen ascendant in Scientia for nearly three hundred years has been an Anti-ist. The ideal society is The Ismless State and we all strive towards it. Simply put, Anti-ism opposes every form of Ism, from zooism, visionism and weightism to fascism, evilism and hatredism.'

That was a lot of isms, I thought.

We continued into the Napoleon Courtyard, Pei's glass pyramid at its centre. I had visited the real Louvre in my previous "life" and knew that queues for the museum were often long. This one, though, was like nothing I'd experienced. Starting at the pyramid entrance, it zig-zagged many times around and across the courtyard before vanishing into the distance towards the Tuileries Gardens.

'It's the global premiere of a new exhibition,' Wu Mei said. 'Animal Revisionism, I believe.'

An electronic information board stood at the pyramid entrance and I went across to see what the fuss was all about.

It seemed that fifty Old World masterpieces that misrepresented or disrespected animals had been "enhanced". Notable examples were the removal of the horses from Edouard Manet's *Horse Race in Longchamp* and replacing them with "running jockeys"; taking away the frilly collar and bells from the pug in Francisco Goya's *The Marquesa de Pontejos*; slimming down the pig in James Ward's *Gloucestershire Old Spot*; and giving Salvador Dali's *The Elephants* legs in proportion to their bodies instead of the stalk-like limbs the artist had originally given them.

Wu Mei asked me what I thought and I said, fine, if people wanted to replicate these pieces and re-interpret them, why not?

'These aren't replicas,' Wu Mei said. 'The originals have been reworked to reflect what the artists would have painted if they had the correct sensibilities.'

Deep inside I found myself hoping that this consciousness of mine wasn't real, that two-thousand year-old masterpieces had not been vandalized by animal-obsessed anti-ists.

'Look,' she said, 'they're even setting up a funfair.'

I followed her gaze to the Place du Carrousel where three articulated trucks were moving off the road and stopped at the edge of the Louvre courtyard. The sides of their trailers were emblazoned with images of dodgem cars, a waltzer, helter-skelter and other attractions.

The arrival had also come as a pleasant diversion to the people queueing for the Louvre. Some of the parents with kids were probably thinking a carousel ride and candy-floss would be something to look forward to after the exhibition. I could even see kids tugging on their parents' coat sleeves and pointing to the funfair vehicles.

'I didn't know about this.' Wu Mei's voice sounded tense. 'My office wasn't told about traffic congestion. There was nothing on the news.'

Rumbling noises came from inside the trailers. It sounded as if heavy objects were being shifted or arranged. Then the sides of each trailer fell away, revealing three guillotines on each of the three flatbeds.

A gasp went up from the throngs of tourists.

On each guillotine a victim lay prostrate, their arms tied behind their backs and their necks secured in wooden stocks. The victims were wearing white boilersuits with blue plastic aprons and hair coverings. I had just enough time to notice a banner on the crossbeam of each device that read DEATH TO ANIBALS.

'Slaughterhouse workers,' Wu Mei said.

The slanted steel blades flashed in the sunlight.

I recalled Wham!'s®© unexplained comment at Fifi's nightclub – the one about abattoir operatives getting huge wages and spending it "ziff they weren't gonna be no tomoz". Now I knew why – he was talking about danger money.

And there wouldn't be any tomorrow for these poor bastards.

Nine guillotine blades fell with a shuddering rumble that ended with a brief crackle of steel cutting through vertebrae. Almost simultaneously eighteen blue-capped heads rolled forward into wicker baskets under the stocks.

The crowd groaned.

I'd always believed my world would be judged by future generations for our treatment of animals. We deserved to be. But not like this.

The masked figures who had operated the guillotines scattered, some on foot, others on bicycles, others still on motorcycles and scooters.

'That shouldn't have damn well happened,' Wu Mei said.

As understatements went, I'd never heard one bigger.

16

Wu Mei took out her phone and spoke to one of her senior people. She said something about Zooist extremists. Her voice stayed calm, even measured. But I sensed fury, fear, frustration. She was Scientia's security chief and eighteen people had just been executed by terrorists in front of an audience of thousands, right under her nose. The event would have been live-streamed and that would put the number of global views into the billions. The Scientian government had just been humiliated for the world to see. I recalled Confucius's smug assurances just a few days ago. *We have had nothing remotely approaching what happened before the disintegration of the Old World.*

You have now, I thought. The spectacle at the Louvre would have put any Islamic State outrage in the shade.

Heads would roll, maybe Wu Mei's.

Fuck, heads *had* rolled.

She ended the call and turned to me. 'Go back to the office. Go straight there. Do not talk to anyone. Do not say anything about what you just saw.'

I made it back to the Quai des Orfèvres in ten minutes.

The first thing I noticed was Comanche's Vincent motorcycle. The second was Comanche leaving the office and heading for the bike.

She seemed surprised to see me.

'Going somewhere?' I asked. 'There's been a major incident and I'm calling a team meeting.'

She made an apologetic expression. 'Sorry, boss, but I'm leaving town for a while.'

'This is important.'

'I know about the beheadings at the Louvre. The Zooist ultras streamed it live. But it's not really our business, is it?'

'It might be. If you come to the meeting you'll find out why.'

She held my stare.

'Listen,' I said, trying to sound reasonable, 'I know you're not used to being on this side of the fence, but if we're going to work together you can't just take off whenever you like, without telling me. Not with a federation-wide emergency about to be announced.'

Still she kept quiet. She was digging her heels in, this much was clear.

'Where do you need to get to in such a hurry?'

She mounted her machine. 'That's my business.'

'Right now, it's *our* business. I have an investigation to manage and you're a senior member of my team. If you're going to be somewhere, I need to know where. I need – '

She started the engine, twisted the throttle. The engine roared, drowning out my voice. As the engine noise settled down, she said, 'If you really must know, I'm going to see an old friend. In Qatar Prison.'

'That's a very long way.'

'I'll be back in a couple of days.' She tipped me a wink. 'Then I'll give you that ride you asked for.'

She revved the engine again and was off.

I stood there awhile, not quite sure what I felt. Angry, snubbed and unsure what to do. I couldn't fire Comanche and I was reluctant to take this to Wu Mei. And I felt something else – a fugitive admiration for her ballsyness, an uneasy excitement at that cheeky wink and outrageous innuendo.

17

Wham!®© was waiting for me in the lobby as I stepped out of the elevator. He must have seen me walking back from the Louvre.

His mouth worked like a machine-gun, words hitting me in frantic salvo. Plato Tomsky – now known simply as Plato – was going to help us catch Family Guy. There was nothing Plato couldn't do, no introduction Plato couldn't make happen, no audience Plato couldn't reach. Yes, of course Bogart had heard about the guillotining and it was horrible, horrible news. But the good news – "the off-zucking-planet news" – was that now Plato was working with us everything was going to work out fine. Finer still, Bogart added, because Plato had promised to swing some lucrative influencer contracts Bogart's way. His "temp gelt-flow probs" would be over.

I didn't have the heart to tell him about Wu Mei's reservations. And in any case, the security chief hadn't told me *not* to work with Tomsky, just to be careful what I shared with him. So I muttered words of praise and gratitude as Bogart followed me puppy-like from the lobby and into the incident room.

I could tell from Puritan's expression that he, too, had seen the live-streaming but I called a meeting anyway. I didn't agree with Comanche that it didn't concern us and wanted to discuss this with my two remaining advisers.

'I presume this sort of thing has happened before,' I said as we gathered around the conference room table, 'and that the authorities will come down hard on anyone suspected of involvement.'

Puritan sipped vending machine coffee from a paper cup and grimaced. 'You're right, boss,' he said, 'about this having happened before. It's the work of Zooist ultras but this is a new tactic, obviously designed to generate maximum impact. They've brought their horror show to the capital of Scientia and introduced guillotines as a *coup de théâtre* – clearly to draw parallels with the Reign of Terror during the French Revolution. The spot they picked is a very short distance from the Place de la Concorde, where the mass guillotining took place in 1793 and 94.'

'So how do they *normally* kill their victims?'

'Smimes they uses a bolt-gun,' Bogart said, 'and uddatimes they slits they throats, same as what happens to hogs and cattles and sheeps and chickens in them slaughtyhouses.'

'You're right too about a security crackdown,' Puritan added, 'although there are plausible rumours that senior people in the Scientian government are Zooist fundamentalist sympathisers.'

Bogart looked at me thoughtfully. 'You thinks any whipcracky clampdown gonna make Family Guy go low?'

'Figures,' I said. 'If so, it might buy us some time. God knows, we need it.'

'Smin else niggling you, ain't they not, boss?' Bogart was fast on the uptake. The better I knew him, the more I realized he wasn't just a six-foot three infant.

I ran my fingers through my hair. 'The pressure from Simz and Jesusly is one thing. This terrorism stuff is something else – another layer of political complexity. Who the fuck are these Zooists? How do they stand with the Anti-ists?'

'The Anti-ism movement is bitterly divided,' Puritan said. 'On one side you have the Zooists and on the other, Anthrocrats.'

'Anthro what?' I placed one hand over my eyes, massaging my temples with my thumb and forefinger.

Puritan looked into his coffee cup but decided against another sip. 'Anthrocracy is the old political order, a humanist philosophy rooted in the spiritual and physical needs of common people. Although all Anti-ists are vegan, Anthrocrats prioritise human needs above those of animals and this was the cause of the Zooist schism. It began eighty years ago in central and eastern Asia. Now, Zooist governors control the whole of Old China and Old India. They've exerted enough pressure to gain devolved powers. And the more power they get, the more they want. There's an increasingly well supported campaign for independence from the Anthrocrats and the rest of Scientia.'

'So where do theses Zooist ideas come from? What makes these people tick?'

Puritan made a longsuffering expression. 'Their fundamental belief is that all creatures have equal ethical value and homo sapiens is a pestilential species. So much so that we have a duty to eradicate ourselves, or at least to radically reduce our numbers. Some Zooist states are running Neanderthal recreation programmes with the ultimate aim of replacing us with our ancestral cousins.'

'They blieves them Neandies was kinder and more co-oppy than us Homo spuds,' Bogart said. 'They thinks Neandies got extincted coz we gobbled em.'

The lawyer acknowledged that Bogart was correct and pressed on with his own narrative. 'The Zooist states in the east have punitive animal welfare legislation. This ranges from the death penalty for killing an animal to an on-the-spot fine for forcing a dog to go on a walk against its will.'

I looked at him aghast. 'There's dog police?'

'That and montamostester,' Bogart said. 'You don't zuck with the four-leggers over in eastern Scientia. Well, one spud did – sexed a donkey, that is – and got his dick limped permo.'

Puritan nodded. 'There's even talk in Old India and Old China of direct political representation for animals.'

'How would that work?' I went to the vending machine and got a coffee despite Puritan's misgivings.

'They are proposing a system of Zoological Representation by Proxy,' he said. 'Animal interests would be served in state parliaments by species-attuned legislators.'

I made a puzzled expression. 'Like animal whisperers?'

Puritan nodded. 'In a manner of speaking.'

I returned to the conference table with my coffee. 'And what do Confucius and his people think about this?'

Bogart shrugged. 'They ain't not happy, boss.'

'Animal representation is the least of their concerns,'

Puritan went on. 'The Zooist ultras have pushed technology further than anyone could have imagined. For example, there are "animorphic" individuals who "autospect" as mammals. Latest developments mean the genomes of species can be transferred to "animorphs". As a result they become more and more like the animals they believe themselves to be. Eventually they transmogrify entirely into this creature and retain none of their human physiology.'

I took a drink of my coffee. Puritan was right, it was dreadful. 'Sounds complicated.'

'It absolutely is,' Puritan became more animated. 'Last year I represented a client autospecting as a Bengal tiger.'

I thought, *Of course you did*. But I kept quiet.

'My client had pounced on a woman in a supermarket and bit her arm. She wasn't seriously injured but pressed charges. It was a precedent-setting trial. The whole world was watching.'

'Must have been fascinating.'

My voice had a hint of sarcasm but Puritan was so caught up in his story that he didn't notice.

'I used a previously un-tested defence,' he said. 'I argued that my client was simply behaving as a Bengal tiger would at that point in his transmogrification programme. And the jury agreed. My client was acquitted. Made the headlines around the world.'

It would have made more than just the headlines – Puritan would have been even more filthy rich with a result like that.

Good for him, I supposed, but I was more interested in the terrorist movement. 'How does this relate to the militant element?'

He finished his coffee, grimaced and tossed the paper cup into a waste bin. 'At least in public, the Zooist state governors accept that the other federations have a right to decide for themselves on their animal welfare policy. But the hard-liners want to decide *for* them – hence the capture and execution of meat industry workers like the poor bastards guillotined today.'

'What we gonna do next, then, boss,' Bogart said, 'if this whipcracky stuff happens and Family Guy hunkers?'

I made a you-tell-me shrug.

'Maybe Comanche has some ideas,' Puritan said.

Bogart frowned. 'Anyways, why she gotta be smudda place right now?'

'Said she had someone important to visit,' I said.

'She a bad un that lass.,' Bogart said. 'You should never trust her.'

Puritan agreed with Wham!®©. 'She's a dangerous type,' he said. 'You should be careful with her. We all should.'

'I know she's dangerous,' I said, 'and I certainly don't trust her.'

I did like her though. I liked her audacity, her wildness, her refusal to compromise. In more ways than I liked to admit, she reminded me of me.

18

The weekend arrived and I spent it looking for myself. I'd decided to leave questions of my existence until after the investigation. But still they niggled me – more so on an empty weekend like this. If I did exist, I wanted to know more about the I fictional character whose identity was supposed to be the basis of mine. I wasn't sure how seeing myself in print would dispel any doubts or corroborate a sense of reality. Even so I was determined to find out.

An online search gave me nothing. Nor did calling at the big book retailers. After a hurried lunch I turned to small independent book stores. They proved equally fruitless. Until I came across a little second-hand shop called Abbey Books on Rue de la Parcheminerie in the Latin Quarter. My head was aching, my throat parched. This place specialised in Canadian English literature, making it an even longer shot than the other long shots. But the slender aisles immured by book spines exerted a strange attraction. And the almond-coffee-vanilla whiff of old books completed the allure.

I went to the sales counter and asked the woman behind it if the store stocked any books about a spoof detective called Miranda Miller. Of course this woman had no idea I was Miranda Miller, but I still felt absurdly self-conscious.

She asked if I knew the author and I said no. The title? ISBN number? Publisher? No, I was sorry, but all I had to go on was the protagonist's name. I'd inquired at the big book stores but they had no record of such a character. She peered at me a while over the frames of half-moon glasses. She didn't use the phrase "needle in a haystack", but didn't need to. She told me she'd never come across this character and without more specific information, couldn't help. However, the store had a large selection of out-of-print independent titles in the basement. I was welcome to take a look. I made a what-the-hell? expression and followed her directions to a flight of metal stairs.

The basement had an arched roof, its odours of stone and mortar adding a layer of sourness to the sweeter book tangs. I stood there a few moments, gazing through the dusty light at thousands of books, some on shelves, others in stacks, others still in unpacked crates.

After an hour of rummaging among the obscure, the forgotten, the unwanted, my resolve began to fizzle.

A further thirty minutes made my head hurt with fresh intensity.

This was more than a headache, though.

I felt as if my head as swelling; that my brain was going into labour; that it was delivering something. What sort of a brain did this?

Not mine, I thought, not mine.

Holy fuck –

I stumbled, clutching my temples. I became aware of a fundamental wrongness in the fabric of my surroundings – not just the bookstore, or the city, or even the entire planet. I was overwhelmed by a sense of suspension. Of not really being here and, at the same time, of being everywhere. My vision blurred. The room tilted. I thought I was going to slip sideways. But the direction of gravity shifted. It held me still.

My sight cleared.

The room levelled.

I felt perfectly fine. No headache, no dizziness. Like nothing had happened.

Right in front of me was a small pile of old paperbacks.

I picked up the one on top and scanned the cover:

Not Happy
Miranda Miller # 1
Nico Nyro

The design showed a snub-nose revolver silhouetted against a white background with a line of blood running from the top and pooling at the bottom.

With trembling fingers I open the book. On the leaf opposite the title page, I read:

Also in the Miranda Miller series

Slap Happy
Get Happy
Happy Never After

And below this:

Out soon: *The Big Happy*

Snatching up the other three titles in the stack, I wasn't surprised to discover they were numbers two to four of a quintet that excluded the upcoming *The Big Happy*. Nor could it have been a coincidence that these same three words of the forthcoming title accounted for twenty per cent of the PopRep®© constitution – *We The Popeye is titled to The Big Happy and all as come with it.* There was no information about the author, this Nico Nyro. There was no year of copyright and the publisher – Red Rag – gave no address or contact information.

Nonetheless, this was a massive discovery. I hurried to the counter and paid for the books.

*

I spent the rest of the weekend reading all four titles.

They were decently written crime novel send-ups with me as the protagonist. And as mind-blowing as this was, the books didn't tell me anything about myself that I didn't already know or couldn't have figured out. The physical description matched mine, as did the backstory. The sardonic humour produced wry smiles rather than belly laughs. The writing style and attention to certain types of detail told me the author was a woman. But that was as much about her as I could discover. And unless these paperbacks were two thousand years old – which they obviously weren't – they would have been written as historical novels. Well researched, I had to admit.

I finished the last one – *Happy Never After* – with a sense of unrealized expectation, especially after the effort I'd put into finding them.

Then there had been the strange experience in the bookstore. The feeling of otherness, the sense of universal artifice, the slanting room, the blurry vision, the appearance of the books and – weirdest of all – the inexplicable pain of their "delivery". This was disturbing on all sorts of levels.

*

Comanche arrived back after a seventy-two hours absence. She was wearing her leather biking jacket, falling-apart jeans and yellow bandana that I guessed had some sort of biker gang significance. Without a word to anyone, she went to her desk and stared at her blank computer screen.

I went over. 'You okay?'

'Fine.'

'Did you do what you needed to?'

'Yes.' She looked up, expressionless, but at least I got a few seconds of eye contact. 'I did.'

'I've just sent you a full FIB intelligence report on the guillotining. It sets out the new high-alert security environment Family Guy will have to operate in. Not just here in Scientia but also in PopRep®© and the Holy Trumpian Empire. Their whole meat processing sectors are in a state of crisis. Strikes are expected, supply chains disrupted and there's widespread panic buying. We all need to keep it in mind because it *will* affect our work.'

'Then I'll look at it.' She turned back to her computer, switched it on and started to read the lengthy report.

When I was sure she was focused, I left the office and went down to the underground car park.

I'd asked her to read the FIB report because what I told her was true – Family Guy may go to ground; or he may spot fresh opportunities. But I also wanted her distracted while I checked out her story.

Her Vincent Black Lightning was easy to find. It looked remarkably clean for a machine that had just completed the 1,200 mile round-trip to Qatar. Of course, she may have washed it after returning to Paris, but I thought not.

What I was more interested in though was the tachometer. I recalled our conversation three days ago, about the high mileage – 89,507 miles. Leaning over the speedometer I read the new number. If she had been to Qatar and back, the tachometer reading would have been well over 90,000. But it wasn't. She'd added less than thirty miles.

The Vincent hadn't been any further than the outskirts of Paris. Maybe she'd flown to Qatar. But then why didn't she correct me when I commented on the long ride?

Whatever she'd been up to in the last three days I was convinced she hadn't been to Qatar, or anywhere else outside Paris.

Maybe after all this was something I'd have to take to Wu Mei.

Then again, the security chief was in the midst of a global terrorism crisis and –

'Boss! Come quick!' Bogart was calling from the opposite side of the car park. 'Family Guy! He striked again!'

19

BERLIN UNTER DEM HIMALAYA

The arrow plane came in from the west, losing height much faster than the commercial airliners I was used to. Below, the green pastures of Uttar Pradesh surrendered to the Himalayan foothills, which were in turn defeated by the shimmering white sawblade of the Everest range.

As we circled to land I saw the Tiergarten, the Reichstag and Brandenburg Gate at the eastern end of the tree-lined boulevard of Unter den Linden.

The flight had been dull. Even at supersonic speed we'd been in the air three hours. I told my team I didn't want them to speculate about these latest homicides. When we got to the crime scene, I wanted them to see what they saw, not what they expected to see. Besides, there was very little information. The area had been sealed off by the local cops and FIB field office. When the first responders had done their work, no one had been allowed through the inner cordon – not even senior law enforcement and CSIs.

The first sign of how Berlin unter dem Himalaya was being run was that we landed at Tempelhof rather than the more modern Berlin Brandenburg airport. I'd last visited Berlin in the 2010s when Tempelhof had been redeveloped as a park with picnic areas and sections of runway used for cyclists and runners. Now, it had had been restored to its pomp of the 1930s – sweeping art deco architecture with clean lines and graceful curves. The place had been a venue for Nazi rallies in the 1930s as well as the Berlin Airlift in 1948-49. But it was the former activities that snagged my attention.

After leaving the plane we were greeted by Adolfa Hegelfrume, the state chancellor, a squat built woman in a light brown trench coat with scarlet lapel facings. I could have been looking at Herman Goering's twin. She stepped forward to shake my hand and I found myself looking into eyes of Aryan blue in face of Aryan symmetry, framed by short centre-parted hair of Aryan blonde. The face may have been the real deal but I suspected the eyes were coloured by contact lenses and the flaxen hair by peroxide-based product.

'Thank heavens you are here, *Hauptkommissar* Miller,' she said in German. 'I have a car waiting to take you and your team to the scene of this heinous crime.'

She glanced at Puritan. 'You're the fellow who got an acquittal for the Tony the Tiger.'

The lawyer nodded. 'I am indeed, *Frau Kanzler*.'

'You're very welcome here in Zoosylvania, Herr Puritan.'

The kindly expression vanished as she turned to Wham!$^{®©}$ and Comanche. 'I know you two also – and you're *not* welcome here.'

To Comanche she said, 'You better watch your step.'

And to Wham!$^{®©}$, 'And you, your mouth.'

Her thick neck swivelled like a panzer turret and she trained her eyes on me. 'My people are waiting. Anything you need, tell them. Anything they can't get you, tell me. I want this bastard caught and caught fast. Is that understood?'

I said yes it was.

She about-turned, trundled to her black Mercedes Hum-Vee and was driven away amid flashing red and blue lights and a phalanx of motorcycle outriders.

When we were in our own vehicle, I said, 'Are these people Nazis?'

'Depends.' Puritan paused as his mesozoic hearing aid started fizzing and whistling. He adjusted the setting then refocused his attention. 'On your definition.'

'All right, to what extent are they National Socialists defined as the party that governed Germany from 1933 to 1945?'

'To every fucking extent.' Comanche didn't look away from the tinted window as we crossed the Landwehr Canal and headed north towards the city centre. 'Pompous, arrogant, despotic bastards.'

'I done this docmentry on em five year back,' Bogart chipped in. 'Went down led zeppy herebouts. But that what you gets when you tattles truth to power like what I does.'

'You can't even speak English,' Comanche said, 'never mind truth.'

Bogart looked at me with an outraged expression. 'You here what she just gabbed, boss?'

'Let's cool down,' I said. 'We've got to work together or we'll find out how people like Hegelfrume reward failure.'

'They aren't Nazis as you'd define them, boss,' Puritan said. 'They call themselves Hitlerians.'

I raised an eyebrow. 'Which means what exactly?'

'They believe Hitler was the first political leader to give animal welfare the policy priority it deserved. According to official Zooist doctrine, Hitler and Göring were proto-Zooists who were betrayed by senior lieutenants including Himmler, Heydrich and Eicke, who were the true architects of the Holocaust. *Mein Kampf* was a forgery and it was the treacherous lieutenants who developed the bogus science of racial superiority, along with *Lebensraum* – the need for Germany to possess "living space" in Slavic countries.'

He broke off to peer through the windscreen as we moved along Unter Den Linden and the premises of Arm and a Leg Law came into view. This was an elegant stone building with a façade of Corinthian columns overlooking the equestrian statue of Frederick the Great. There, the defence strategy for Tony the Tiger would have been planned.

'Zooist orthodoxy accepts that this happened,' the lawyer resumed, 'though not on the scale claimed by the Allies. After the Second World War, Hitler was grotesquely misrepresented by 20th and 21st century historians.'

'I knew Hitler was a teetotal vegetarian,' I said, 'but he was still a genocidal monster. This sort of revisionism is unbelievable.'

Puritan made the smile I wished he wouldn't make, the one that didn't so much show the teeth that were there as the one that wasn't. 'Are you familiar with the Nazi animal welfare legislation?'

I shook my head.

'You will be soon. It's the bedrock of their political beliefs.'

He reeled off a list of animal welfare reforms from the 1930s including Germany becoming the first country in the world to ban vivisection; abolishing kosher butchery; curbs on hunting and trapping; the prohibition of boiling lobsters and crabs; and plans to outlaw all slaughterhouses after the war. Offenders could be – and were – sent to concentration camps. Göring, for example, sent a fisherman to a camp for cutting up a live frog as bait.

'But it was Hitler's treatment of humans that made him evil,' I said. 'He was responsible for the deaths of six million Jews and twenty-five million Russians – not to mention the eleven million Germans who died in the war he started. If he'd valued human rights as well as those of animals, there wouldn't have been a war or a holocaust.'

'But that's the whole point of Hitlerism,' Puritan said. 'Like him, these Zooists are more concerned with animal life than human. That's why they idolize the *Führer.*'

'They's proper eastbound,' Bogart said. 'Up to them, we all be gobbling nought but leaves and berries and no flamingo chop-suey for yours truly.'

I recalled him telling me at the dictionary burning "event" in Vegas, England that there were no Nazis in PopRep®© but plenty in Scientia. Now I understood why.

As we glided past the Brandenburg Gate I noticed a twenty foot high statue of Hitler with a German shepherd dog at his side. The words carved on the plinth read *der Führer mit seinem treuen Begleiter Blondi.*

'Tell me more about your client Tony the Tiger,' I said to Puritan. 'Presumably there was more to the case than a random guy who fancied himself as a big cat and attacked a hapless shopper?'

'You're right, boss.' Puritan's palaeolithic hearing aid started making noises again and he started fidgeting with it. 'Tony was undergoing animorphic transmogrification. In a nutshell, this is a genome replacement programme that involves a sliding scale of human/animal characteristics. When the proportion of animal physiology reaches a certain level, the patient is accommodated in a special compound, rather like the big cat houses they have in PopRep®© zoos. My client had reached this threshold and should have gone into his compound the week before the attack. However, an administrative oversight meant this was postponed by two weeks. So when he attacked that poor woman in the supermarket, it wasn't his fault, but that of the Animorphic Transmogrification Unit management team. Also, the case took six months to reach court and by that time Tony was seventy per cent tiger, so there was also a question of fitness to plead.'

'Is he out there now?' I asked. 'In the jungles of Bengal?'

Puritan nodded. 'Transmogrified animorphs are electronically tagged and released into the wild when they reach one hundred per cent animal. Observations show they generally thrive in their new environments, though there have been tragedies. Peter Rabbit, for example, was killed by a fox just days into his rabithood. It transpired that the fox was not only a former human but also an old business rival of Peter's. Nothing was ever proved, of course, but it could hardly have been a coincidence that

Reynard the Fox happened to be in the vicinity when Peter was set loose in that meadow.'

'I guess that's one way to out-fox the law.'

He gave me a reproachful glance and continued his explanation. 'Also, mammals are one thing; birds, insects and fish, are something else. Experiments in this field are ongoing, though test results are encouraging.'

I was wondering what sort of a person would volunteer to be turned into a pigeon or a bluebottle or a haddock when we turned into Ebertstrasse, then left onto Hannah-Ardent-Strasse where the Memorial to the Murdered Jews of Europe was located.

It seemed much the same as when I last visited, though its acreage had been vastly reduced and its name changed. A large sign informed visitors they were about to enter the *Memorial to the Gingers, Gays, Gipsies, Socialists, Communists, A-socials, Work-shy vagrants, Useless Eaters, Criminals, Sundry Others, and Jews, whose lives were unjustly terminated ALBEIT WITHOUT THE KNOWLEDGE OR CONSENT OF THE FÜHRER OR REICHSMARSCHAL GÖRING.*

'Holocaust exaggeration is a felony crime in Zoosylvania,' Puritan said. 'This redesigned memorial is meant to be proportionately sized and appropriately named.'

'It's obscene.' I watched the small field of flat and upright concrete slabs until they vanished behind us. 'A fucking disgrace.'

'Wait till you see what's standing right next to the crime scene,' Comanche said, still without turning from the window. 'For once I agree with Bogart – these people *are* off-planet crazies.'

20

We arrived a few minutes later outside the home of Family Guy's latest victims, Sigismund and Brunhilda Mozart, aged fifty and thirty-two, and their six-year-old twins Ludwig Van and Elise. Their apartment was on the fourth floor of a building overlooking the parking lot where the *Führerbunker* had been located until 1945.

Only the parking lot was gone and the *Führerbunker* was back.

I'd visited Berlin many times and even parked here once. After the war, the Soviets demolished the Reich Chancellery buildings below which the underground complex had been built. Later, the East German government filled in and sealed off the subterranean chambers to stop them becoming a shrine for Neo-Nazi pilgrims.

Which was exactly what had happened.

The line of Hitlerian devotees snaked twice around the rebuilt chancellery buildings before vanishing around the corner of In den Ministergärten. A burger and kebab trailer had been set up near the entrance, and next to it a hot and

116

cold drinks vendor was doing brisk business. There were even public conveniences with baby-changing facilities.

Floodlight towers at the four corners of the area suggested these crowds also came at night, which would have made it hard for Family Guy to move around unseen.

So why had he chosen such a high-risk place?

I thought back to the home of the Sinatra family on Fremont Street. That too was a well-lit area, busier at night than during the day. It, too, would have been much more difficult for Family Guy to access than somewhere dark and quiet.

So why had he targeted the Sinatras and the Mozarts? There must have been similar families living in less visited districts.

I called Puritan over.

Wham!®© was signing digital autographs for people in the line and Comanche had just lit a cigarette, despite – or more likely because of – a no smoking sign.

'Buzz-buzz-buzz,' went the tall man in a yellow and black onesie with plastic wings on his back. 'Buzz-buzz-buzz.'

He skipped and gambolled back and forth along the line then came right up close and buzzed in my ear.

'Buzz off,' I said with a smile.

'He's autospecting as a bee,' Puritan explained, 'but the transmogrification process for insects is very much at the experimental stage. So he may have a long wait. One could say, I suppose, he is a wanna-bee.'

I acknowledged the weak joke with a short chuckle.

The bee buzzed in Puritan's ear and moved off to irritate others.

He recognized Bogart, took out his phone and asked for a selfie. Bogart grinned and obliged.

The bee's next target was Comanche. He came frolicking over to her.

'Buzz-buzz-buzz,' he said.

'Fuck off.'

'Gimme a drag!'

He made a grab for the cigarette and Comanche whisked it away.

'I said fuck off.'

'Bees can smoke. Who says they can't? Gimme a drag! Buzz-buzz-buzz!'

He pranced around a bit, then leaned towards her again. 'To bee or not to bee,' he said, 'that is the question.'

Her head butt sent him reeling, blood and teeth exploding from his mouth.

'Not to bee,' she said. 'That's the answer.'

I moved in fast, pulling her away. 'You didn't need to do that.'

She took a drag in her cigarette. 'He didn't need to piss me off.'

'A tap would have been enough. Why did you hit him so hard?'

'Why not?'

Poor impulse control, I thought. It was common in violent criminals but I thought an organized crime boss like Comanche would have her shit together.

The bee was sprawled on the ground clutching his face, gore oozing between his fingers.

Fortunately, ambulance crews were already at the crime scene and a couple of paramedics came over to examine him.

While this was happening I didn't notice Wham!®© come striding towards Comanche.

'You,' he said, 'is a zucking cut-hole.'

He shoved her hard in the chest. 'Wanna rumble smoddy what gonna rumble back?'

Comanche tossed her cigarette aside and squared up. 'Bring it on, Tweetie Pie.'

'Stop this right now!' I shoved myself between them, extending my arms to push them away from one another.

'He started it,' Comanche said.

'No, *you* did. *You* capblasted that wispy spud just for going buzz-buzz-buzz and tryna scam a toke of you smoke!'

'Listen up, both of you.' I gave each of them a hard stare. 'We have enough problems without you adding to them. There's a murdered family up in that apartment – a couple mutilated to fuck and two young children gassed to death. Can we please focus on catching the bastard responsible?'

They nodded like sullen teens.

To Comanche, I said, 'You need to cool the fuck down. Go to the hotel – Hegelfrume's people will tell you which one. Get a drink, watch some TV, take a shower, whatever it takes to get your head straight. We can talk later.'

She opened her mouth to protest, saw my expression and thought better of it.

'You're the boss,' she said, turned, and walked away.

I went to ask if the zoanthropic bee was going to be okay. The lead medic said probably. His lip needed stitches and four teeth would have to be replaced. There'd also be some concussion, but a thorough hospital exam would hopefully rule out any long term problems.

Puritan was standing at my side. 'You'd better hope the bee doesn't want to make a complaint – especially as a bee rather than a human.'

I gave him a questioning look.

'Causing actual bodily harm to a human carries a maximum penalty of six months in prison; for the same offence against a non-human you could get up to five years.'

'Can you smooth it over?'

'I can, but surely Wu Mei could get any charges quashed.'

'I'd rather Wu Mei didn't find out about this. Chancellor Hegelfrume too.'

'Very well,' Puritan said, 'I'll deal with it.'

Why was I protecting Comanche? The bee had been a pest, but didn't deserve to be in hospital with broken teeth and concussion. Comanche, on the other hand, deserved everything that would have been coming to her. Did I really need her on my team? To the extent that I was putting it at risk?

'By the way,' Puritan added, 'did you want something from me, earlier? Before this bee incident?'

My thoughts returned to the high-risk environment for a serial killer getting into and out of the crime scene, here and in Vegas, England. I mentioned this and asked if any of the other families murdered by Family Guy lived in similar locales. His astonishing memory went into action and he shook his head no. Before the Sinatras and Mozarts, all three families killed since Family Guy made his comeback lived in much quieter areas. So too did the twenty-one families targeted in the five year period that ended fourteen years ago.

'Good stuff, Bob,' I said. 'I knew that brain of yours would come in handy.'

'I'm here to serve,' he said with an edge of sarcasm.

As we moved towards the crime scene outer cordon, I said, 'By the way, how are you progressing with that Family Guy portrait I asked you to paint?'

I ducked under the black and yellow tape and he followed. 'I've made a start.' His functioning eye went up to the fourth floor flat. 'But I suspect there's going to be a lot more material up there.'

21

The scene in the Mozart family's living room was very similar to what had been left behind in the living room of the Sinatras. Or the three other families before them. Or the twenty-one families butchered before Family Guy rebooted his career.

The man and woman were both naked and had been strangled with a ligature. The man was tied to a chair and the woman supine on the floor, legs wide. Of course there were differences. Sigismund Mozart, for example, was older, smaller and less honed than Kanye Sinatra. His face was unbruised and unbloodied, suggesting he'd put up less of a struggle. His muscle tone was flabby, skin pale and loose. A small belly sagged over the bloody mess where his genitalia had been. And the age gap between the older husband and younger wife was greater. At fifty-five, Sigismund was four years older than Kanye, while Brunhilda was thirty-three, a year younger than Kiera. The forcible insertion of the man's penis and testicles into the woman's mouth remained central to the signature, as did the severing of the woman's left nipple and extensive knife-wounds – picquerism as it was known – to her torso. Again, no defence wounds indicated that Family Guy had been invited inside and took immediate control of his victims.

It was all numbingly familiar.

I squatted near Brunhilda. I wasn't surprised to see bruising in and around her vagina and thighs where she had been object-raped.

Something I *was* surprised to see, though, was a small group of stabs and cuts on the right upper arm. I recalled a similar cluster in the same place on Kiera Sinatra. The pathologist said he hadn't see anything like it on previous victims, though he had emphasized that overkill was consistent with Family Guy's signature. Even so, it would be worth asking the bendy man to look into this apparent development a little more closely.

He had arrived shortly before we did and, according to the senior FIB agent, was examining the two children in their shared bedroom.

I was halfway there when he called out, an edge of alarm in his normally measured tone.

'The boy is alive!'

Dodgson was on one knee beside seven-year-old Ludwig Van. He looked up as I rushed in.

Over my shoulder, he shouted, 'Get the paramedics up here right now!'

'Will he survive?'

'Too soon to tell.'

He moved to the other twin, Elise, feeling for a pulse and a heartbeat. At last he looked round and nodded yes to my unasked question.

'How the fuck did this happen?' I asked. 'When did the first responders get here?'

'Five hours ago.' Dodgson stood as paramedics came into the room with their gear and a pair of stretchers.

I went to the side of the room with the pathologist. 'This must be the most monumental incompetence I've ever come across.'

Dodgson made an unsure expression. 'I wouldn't be so quick to judge. The vital signs are almost undetectable. They looked dead when I got here and it took me a while to realize what had happened. And remember, the paramedics were under strict instructions to work fast, then get out until we arrived.'

Of course he was right. Even the CSIs had been forbidden to enter before we did – something unheard of in the place I came from.

Puritan came into the room with a bleak expression that told me he'd found nothing useful.

I watched the paramedics at work, hoping and praying the twins would pull through.

Dodgson had a point though. Instead of seeing this as a huge blunder we should be viewing it as the biggest break in the long, long hunt for Family Guy.

I turned back to the pathologist. 'Is this his first mistake? Or did he spare them for some reason?'

'I don't know. We may never know. Even if we catch him, he may or may not tell us the truth.'

'That's right, boss,' Puritan said. 'Given that he's a sociopathic narcissist it's unlikely he'd admit to a cock-up – unless he could see a way of playing it to his advantage. Even then, we could never be sure, not with a mind like his.'

'Can sociopaths develop consciences?'

'They can certainly change,' Puritan said. 'Family Guy himself stopped killing for fourteen years. And although it could have been down to any number of reasons, some approximation of conscience could be one of them.'

We watched the paramedics carrying the twins from the room, strapped to stretchers and linked to intravenous drips.

'Hey, boss!' Bogart was easily excitable so he didn't get my immediate attention. 'Lookee here!'

He did though when he added, 'Family Guy – he wroted a note! To you!'

22

I n his full barrier whites, Bogart resembled a well-stacked yeti. He was standing by a small writing bureau in a corner of the living room looking down at a sheet of A5 paper on a green leather writing surface. An old fashioned fountain pen had been placed diagonally on the paper, its silver nib pointing to the bottom left corner. There was also a scatter of paper clips half on and half off the note, and a six-inch plastic ruler across the top right corner. Family Guy had clearly arranged this desktop tableau with intricate care. Whether it meant anything was a question for later.

I recognized the handwriting from Family Guy's original notes and, at first glance, it seemed genuine.

The note was easy enough to read, even with the stationery items on and around it.

Dear Det Supt Miller, Miller of the Yard, Serial Killer Miller — Miranda, if I may?

I do hope you are a worthy opponent. I really, really do. Because quite frankly, I am quite

*bored with the amateurish toiling of the law
enforcement clowns in the three federations.
They didn't come close to catching me all those
years ago and are failing again now. Failing
miserably. How dull is that?*

*I hope, too, that you are impressed by my
latest creation. This one I crafted specially for
you. I thought about you throughout my labours.
My adult subjects were agreeably compliant – at
least until my serious endeavours began. As for
the innocents, it was an immense pleasure to
work with twins for the first time. So much so
that I left the subjects unembellished. This aspect
of the piece speaks for itself, wouldn't you say?*

That is all for now.

Seth

The name, I knew, corresponded with that of Seth
MacFarlane, creator of the *Family Guy* TV show. The
killer had used it many times before so this wasn't of any
significance – except perhaps to re-emphasise his belief
that his atrocities were creative masterpieces on a par with
MacFarlane's multi-award winning TV series.

Nor was there anything obviously different about the
taunting and self-aggrandizing language of the note with
its customary artistic pretentions. It would be analysed by
the forensic linguists team. If there was anything useful to
be found, they would find it.

There were, however, two significant departures from
the other murders since Family Guy's comeback. First,

he had left a note. If it was authenticated, we would have solid proof that we were dealing with the original Family Guy and not a copycat. Second, he had written the note specifically to me as the senior investigating officer. This, he had never done before in his entire career. What might it mean? Almost anything, I thought, but nothing good.

23

The Mozart twins were going to live. The chief paediatrician called me with her prognosis early the next afternoon. The children would be kept in hospital under observation, but so far the signs were encouraging and no complications were expected. However, if a fraction more Sevoflurane had been administered, Ludwig Van and Elise would be dead. Could Family Guy have controlled such a small amount of anaesthetic? I didn't expect a useful answer and I didn't get one. Maybe he did, maybe not, which did nothing to advance my understanding of Family Guy's current psychology.

The initial victimology reports hadn't revealed much. Sigismund Mozart had been a neurology assistant working on the Neanderthal Programme. I wondered for a moment if he could have been attacked by one of his subjects. But Wu Mei assured me the entire Neanderthal community of two hundred could be accounted for. And besides, Neanderthal people were being reintroduced precisely because they were inherently less aggressive and more cooperative than homo sapiens. Brunhilda worked as a paralegal at a small downtown law firm. She was too junior to have made enemies through her work, and in any case worked in a tax law team.

An hour later, the forensic linguistics lab phoned to confirm the note was indeed from Family Guy. The florid idiolect, said the specialist, the fussy syntactical structure, specific turns of phrase, everything pointed to the same author before and after the fourteen year hiatus. Just as crucially, the handwriting specialists had carried out their own examination and came to the same conclusion. The note was one hundred per cent Family Guy.

I finished reading the two detailed reports in my office and looked up to see Wham!®©, Puritan and Comanche at their desks – the latter using hers only as a foot rest. We'd been given offices at the State Police headquarters in the old SS-Gestapo building on Prinz-Albrecht-Strasse. When I last visited the real Berlin, the building had been razed and a museum built on the site. Also, the street had been renamed and the last ghosts of the Nazi terror exorcized. Not in this Berlin though. First Tempelhof airport, then the *Führerbunker*, now this. It seemed the Zoosylvanian regime was recreating these temples to Nazism across the city and I felt more than a little uncomfortable working in this environment.

Puritan saw me looking and came unsteadily to his feet. He should have been using his walking stick I thought as he approached my office.

'I've finished my portrait of Family Guy,' he said. 'Would now be a good time to discuss it?'

I said sure and ushered him to the visitor chair.

'You saw the forensic linguistics and handwriting reports?'

He nodded. 'The authenticity of the note is certainly interesting, though we should keep in mind that Family Guy would have known this when he wrote it. He'd have crafted his message accordingly.'

I was curious about his use of the word "crafted".

'It chimes with his grandiose self-perception,' Puritan said. 'What I can tell you from my own observations is that we're dealing with a genuinely creative, genuinely intelligent and genuinely talented individual. He sees his "work" as art and sees himself as the Michelangelo of serial killers. He is no doubt charismatic, socially connected and a charming dinner party companion.'

This was helpful. It ruled out ninety-nine per cent of the global population. But it also left a good few million.

'What might he be like as a work colleague?'

Puritan shook his head. 'It would be nightmarish to work *with* him; even worse to work *for* him; and worse still to manage him. He's an obsessive perfectionist and won't tolerate any criticism of his work, whatever it is.'

Too many people I'd worked with fitted this category. And they'd likely have said the same about me.

'So what type of work does he do? Your best guess?'

'I can't argue with the FIB profilers about him having a professional background, though I think more likely in the creative sector than technology, which was the initial hypothesis. And I believe he's been highly successful in his work whereas earlier profiles suggest a talented but stifled and under-promoted individual. Maybe he works in fine arts, the music industry, photography or fashion design. He may even be a writer.'

I made a dubious expression. 'With prose like that?'

'If he's as clever as I think, he could have written in that style as misdirection. Or as the voice of an alter-ego. Also, he may be patronizing us.'

Puritan was making a lot of disturbing sense. I asked for his views on Family Guy's decision to address his note to me.

'You're the senior investigator,' he said, 'but also a celebrity cop whose arrival was much trumpeted by the authorities in all three federations. Since he also sees himself as a celebrity, it would make sense to him to pit himself directly against you. It's all grist to the enormous mill of his narcissism. He'll be loving this.'

'And therefore even more incentivised. Which means my appointment has backfired.'

Puritan made a kindly expression that only drew my gaze to the eye that wasn't working and the tooth that wasn't there. 'Possibly, but if that's so, it isn't your fault.'

'Thanks, Bob,' I said and meant it. 'What's your take on the surviving twins? A show of mercy or a mistake?'

He gave me a who-can-say? look, just like the paediatrician did.

Then he surprised me.

'If I had to go one way or the other, though, I'd say he wanted to spare them, or was ambivalent about taking their lives. He has always gone to great lengths to make sure his child victims never suffered. This suggests he sees them as innocents caught up the perceived wickedness of their parents or adult carers. As the FIB analysts and others have noted, the big age difference between the older men and younger women may indicate incestuous sex between a father and daughter – possibly Family Guy's father and his sister or step sister. He may have witnessed this as a boy. He may even have been forced to witness it.'

'He's still killed a lot of kids.'

'But reluctantly, caringly if you can see the byzantine logic.' He ran his fingers through his stalky strands. 'Then there's this business with angel wings and scented candles, brushing the children's hair, dressing them in their best clothes, placing treasured toys on or near them. I think he identifies with the children because he suffered as a consequence of *his* parents' actions. So he takes revenge on the adults and creates these respectful, even worshipful tableaux with the children. He may well be preparing them for their arrival in heaven. One could go further and speculate that he thinks he is helping them escape from abusive parents and reach a better place.'

This was a helpful analysis, though one aspect still left me unconvinced. 'The paediatrician says the anaesthetic levels in the twins' blood is right on the cusp of lethality. If he did mean to let them live, it would have been very difficult to control the precise amount he administered.'

Puritan lifted a knowing eyebrow. 'Which would play directly to his narcissism, his unerring belief in his own genius. By pulling off something as challenging as this, he'd be saying to the world leaders "Look on my Works, ye Mighty, and despair!"'

'And even if it went wrong and the children died, who would know he failed?'

'In any event, this is a huge departure. Whether he's blundered or shown mercy, there's been a notable shift in his psychosis. We've seen nothing like this from him before. It's almost as if we're looking at two different people.'

I considered this. 'Or the same person fourteen years on. He may have thought he could start again where he left off, and that may have worked for his first outings, but then something happened. It seems he's lost his mojo.' I gave him a searching look. 'Could we be seeing some kind of late career burn-out?'

He made a philosophical expression. 'Not so much burn-out as ennui. It could be that things ain't what they used to be for him. Perhaps he isn't hitting the heights he once did. He may even be thinking about stopping again.'

This was a good point. 'He used the word "bored" and "dull" in his note,' I said. 'And there was a virtual appeal to me to do make a better job at catching him than my predecessors.'

'It's possible that he addressed the note to you to shake things up, make his game more stimulating.' Puritan seemed to be warming to this theory too. 'He's a man who gets a thrill from overcoming challenges. Harder tasks deliver greater rewards.'

'Which may tie in with another possible change,' I said, 'the high-risk locations of the last two crime scenes.'

The more I thought about this, the more it added up. 'Of course, he could have been forced into these busy locations because there were no suitable families elsewhere. But I think not. I think he's been taking higher risks to get greater satisfaction. Hence the note and the last two venues.'

'Agreed,' he said. 'There's something else you should consider – I believe he's much older than originally thought. Not early-twenties when he started, then early forties when he resumed. More like early-thirties first time out and early-fifties now. A late developer in the serial killer world, you might say.'

'Why would you say that?'

'No more than gut instinct.' His walnut face looked especially mournful. 'There's a world-weariness about this latest note that I experienced as I got older – as I suspect you did. A sense that this is how the world is and it isn't going to change for the better. So you reluctantly accept it.'

I nodded yes and said he wasn't wrong.

'And even with his earlier notes,' Puritan went on, 'he displayed insights and observations that I'd have associated with a man of greater maturity than a twenty-something. Which ties in with his background – successful and creative rather than frustrated and technical. As a rule, success comes mid-career, not when you start out.'

This was good work. I told him so.

He seemed a little embarrassed at the praise, as if he wasn't used to it despite his household name status. He fidgeted with the ancient hearing aid in his right ear. The device moved slightly and I saw that a small part of his ear was missing. A perfectly L-shaped section had been removed.

I asked what had happened.

'Contempt of court. The judge sent a seventy-eight-year-old woman to the Big Oven. She – like me – was aurally-impaired and failed to obey her husband because she hadn't heard him calling. Unfortunately this happened in public. The husband, also elderly, pleaded for his wife to be spared. But the judge wasn't interested. When the sentence was handed down, I spoke my mind. The judge didn't like what he heard and ordered me to have two thirty-ninths of my ear cut away. However, the surgeon took *three* thirty-ninths. I sued for clinical negligence and won record damages. I wasn't too worried about my ear – I had already lost my eye and tooth and was never oil painting to start with.'

I could tell he hadn't finished and waited. After a few moments, he said,

'I forced myself to watch as they put that frail old lady in the microwave chamber. I saw her shrieking when her skin started to roast. You couldn't hear anything – the Big Oven is sound-proofed. But somehow the sight of sound was more harrowing than the sound itself. Then her eyeballs exploded and her muscles spasmed. I thought the agony would never end. Finally, her internal organs boiled and ruptured and she died.'

'That must have been unimaginably horrific,' I said.

He shook his head and rolled his eye. 'Even the monster who is Family Guy could learn and thing or two about cruelty and suffering from those judicially sanctioned monsters in Trumpia.'

I reached forward and squeezed his arm. 'What happened to that poor woman wasn't your fault, Bob.'

'But she *was* my responsibility.' He gave me a desolate look. 'Afterwards, I swore I'd never lose another case, and I never have.'

Now, I though, *now* I understand what drives Bob Puritan.

My videophone rang and I saw the caller was Baudelaire Dodgson.

The bodies of Mr and Mrs Mozart were ready for autopsy.

24

Dodgson's post-mortem was much faster than his last. The twins had survived and whether this had been an act of mercy or a mistake, it meant a lot less work for the pathologist. It was still an unpleasant affair though. Unlike Dodgson's profession, I had bever been able to dissociate the body on the slab from the horror that put it there.

Puritan was also there, a billionaire with a 1970s hearing aid and threadbare cardigan. As was Wham!®© with his money problems, hundred dollar haircut and Milanese suit. They made an odd pair, I thought, though not as odd as Comanche who had refused to attend. Of the three, I'd have put my mortgage on her being the most comfortable in the aftermath of violent death – she was, after all, responsible for a lot of it. She hadn't said why, but then she rarely said much. Also, I was still angry with her over her unexplained disappearance for those three days and the alleged 1,200 mile round-trip to Qatar that had added less than thirty miles to her bike's tachometer.

Puritan had used his own funds to negotiate a

generous settlement with the bee identifier who had been head-butted by Comanche. Bogart had also helped out by visiting the bee in hospital and posing for selfies at the bee's bedside. Comanche, meanwhile, showed neither remorse nor gratitude and this made me even angrier. As much as I sometimes liked her don't-give-a-fuck attitude, there was only so much slack I was prepared to cut her and she was running out fast.

Dodgson worked with routine efficiency, his narrow frame craning over Sigismund's body, head bobbing and tilting this way and that. He had seen nothing new or unusual in his external examination and now set about opening up his subject with the pruning shears he'd bought in PopRep®©. He handed the organs to his assistant who took them for weighing and measuring. They might have been working at the counter of a delicatessen.

With Sigismund's autopsy complete and nothing new to report, Dodgson turned his attention to Brunhilda.

'This contusion in the centre of the forehead is interesting.' He indicated a livid bruise about the size of a two pound coin from early 21st Century Britain. 'Blunt force trauma but no impression of a tool or other implement.'

'What might it mean?' I asked.

'I'm not entirely sure.' He raised Brunhilda's right hand, then her left. Both had deep wounds where the synthetic cord had bitten into her skin. The lesions were similar to those on Kiera Sinatra but deeper and more extensive. He then looked at her forearms, also bruised.

'She must have put up some resistance,' Dodgson said. 'These forearm contusions are defensive wounds from a blunt force attack. But again, no tool marks. She was likely fending off punches or kicks. And the deep wrist lesions indicate a sustained struggle after she was tied up.'

Wham!®© leaned nearer to Brunhilda's face. 'This bruise on the brow, Doc, is it poss Brunhilda cap-butted Family Guy when he come too close to her?' He gave me a sly look. 'Like what Comanche did to that poor bee?'

'Quite possibly.' Dodgson looked at Bogart as if he too had realized the celeb influsser wasn't as daft as he sometimes sounded.

'She musta gotted some balls,' Bogart said.

'She certainly did.' Puritan made a grim expression. 'Unfortunately they were her husband's and they ended up in her mouth.'

'I like Bogart's idea of a head-butt.' I turned to Dodgson. 'Would this have left any traces of DNA?'

The pathologist frowned. 'I'd say not. The skin on Brunhilda's forehead hasn't been broken so she hasn't lost blood externally in or around the contusion. She may, though, have hit Family Guy hard enough to make *him* bleed. I'll put some skin tissue under a microscope. Please don't get your hopes up though.'

I asked about DNA from Family Guy's sweat or some other body substance.

The pathologist looked again at the bruise. 'Unlikely. But, again, worth checking out.'

'This is interesting.'

His tone told me he'd found something significant. He pointed to a fuzzy-edged rectangular bruise around a particularly nasty stab wound to Brunhilda's outer left thigh.

'What you speck doc?' Bogart asked. 'What is that thing?'

'I can't be certain.' Dodgson pushed his face near the bruising, squinting as his eyes moved slowly around the edges of the injury. 'But I think a contusion like this could have been caused by the cross-guard of a bladed instrument – most likely a knife – being thrust into the flesh with extraordinary ferocity. This would also be consistent with Brunhilda having put up a fight, even injuring Family Guy, and then struggling even after he had her bound.'

He took a step back from the slab, bulldozing bony fingers through his hedgerow hair.

After some time I said, 'What are your thoughts?'

'This sort of ferocity is normally associated with intense, spontaneous anger. Which is unlike Family Guy. It could mean he lost his self-control due Brunhilda's resistance – perhaps including a head-butt. As well as the forehead contusion, we also noted the defensive wounds on her arms.'

Puritan gave Dodgson a curious look. 'Aren't all this man's attacks frenzied and furious?'

'They are.' Once more Dodgson shoved his nose close to the bruised rectangle of flesh. 'But Family Guy's hallmark is controlled frenzy, constrained fury. And far from spontaneous. Amid all his stabbing and slashing, he is always following a predetermined pattern, a unchanging template. For sure he uses force, but not wild force. He is always in control of himself and of the crime scene. That's what makes him so tough to catch.'

'So this potential head-butt could be his second mistake?' Puritan went on. 'If leaving the twins alive *was* a mistake.'

I could follow Puritan's reasoning. It tied in with his theory about changes inside Family Guy's head.

Dodgson nodded. 'Regardless of his intent with the twins, we are looking at two significant departures from what has been, until now, a flawlessly consistent series.'

This wasn't a breakthrough, a punch the-air moment. But it *was* something. And the survival of the children combined with this apparent tussle would widen the scope of our enquiries.

'He losing it?' Bogart asked.

'That's worth considering,' I said. 'Fourteen years have passed since he ended his first series. So he'll be an older and possibly less able man. He may have suffered a debilitating illness or had some kind of life-changing accident. If we work from Bob's new hypothesis that he was in his mid-thirties when he started his career, that would put him well into his fifties now. Not quite ancient but he'll inevitably have taken some wear and tear over such an extended period.'

'So we gotta speck for morer cock-ups?' Bogart said.

I nodded. 'And hopefully something that'll give us a better handle on him.'

I turned back to Dodgson. 'What about the cluster of stabs and cuts around the upper right arm? They look very similar to those on Kiera Sinatra.'

'Indeed,' the pathologist said. 'They are almost identical in both the area they cover and their anatomical location. But both are entirely consistent with previous episodes of picquerism. They don't in themselves represent a change in his signature.'

'An evolution perhaps?'

'You're the serial killer specialist, Superintendent.' Dodgson bent down to look again at the wounds to Brunhilda's upper arm. 'What do you think?'

'Once is happenstance,' I said, 'and twice is coincidence. And you know what cops say about coincidence.'

'I'm afraid I don't.' He didn't look up. 'Enlighten me.'

'There's no such thing.'

He stayed bent over, extending his right arm behind his body and wiggling his fingers.

As if by telepathy, the assistant seemed to understand exactly what his boss wanted and went to fetch a powerful magnifying glass.

With the lens between his eye and the ravaged skin, he adjusted his stance, moving his head from side to side, then up and down.

Wham!®© was the first to run out of patience. 'What you speck, Doc?'

'I'm not sure.' More finger wagging and this time the assistant brought a hand-held spectrophotometer. 'Might be something, might be nothing. But I need some time without distraction.'

Still without looking up, he said, 'I'll let you know if I find anything.'

25

Comanche was waiting outside the mortuary smoking a cigarette, flicking ash at passers-by and looking for a reaction. She joined us on the four-block walk back to our office in the recreated SS-Gestapo building.

I caught a waft of tobacco fumes as she came alongside and had to admit I enjoyed the experience. I'd quit fifteen years ago but often felt the urge to smoke just one. Or maybe two, or five, or the whole pack. And that not-even-one rule was how I stayed stopped.

She asked about the autopsy and I told her.

'Good for Brunhilda,' she said. 'At least she stuck one on the bastard.'

'Didn't help her any in the end.' I spoke in a curt tone but she didn't seem to notice. I sucked in another lungful of secondary smoke.

She quizzed me about the cross-guard indentation and the cluster of wounds similar to the one found on Kiera Sinatra. I said I didn't know any more than I'd already told her. Dodgson was carrying out further examinations of both.

After a few more paces, she said, 'I've picked something up that could be important.'

'Yeah?'

'We have a tail. A woman – quite old from what I could see – followed us from the office to the mortuary.'

'How do you know she wasn't just going the same way?'

'She waited across the street until you came out. And when you did, she took pictures. When I tried to get closer, she vanished. A bus went by. When it had gone, so had she.'

'Clever fieldcraft,' I said. 'If that's what it was.'

'I'm sure of it. She was watching me watching her. And I'm good at watching people without them knowing.'

'What did she look like?'

'As I said, old-ish but sprightly – maybe in her sixties. Average build, wearing a grey raincoat and dark green headscarf. Glasses, flat shoes.'

'That's not much to go on.'

'That's what I'm telling you. She couldn't have been more of a grey woman without being invisible.'

I kept quiet as we walked another half-block. There was no reason to doubt what Comanche had told me. It should have come as no surprise that we were being observed. We were all well-known people – on my part thanks to an unhelpful publicity campaign before I was actualized. And we were involved in a high-profile investigation. This grey woman could have been one of Wu Mei's people; an agent of Adolfa Hegelfrume's state police; a Zooist agitator; even a journalist – especially given the photos she was taking.

As we crossed a side-street, Comanche said, 'What do you think?'

I didn't look at her and kept my voice brusque. 'Let me know if you see her again.'

*

Baudelaire Dodgson was excited. This was obvious because he arrived unannounced late the next morning still wearing his white lab coat and powder blue Crocs. He saw me in my office and came loping towards me on his giraffe legs.

I invited him to take a seat.

'We have a breakthrough,' he said. 'In fact, two breakthroughs.'

Now *I* was excited. My team followed him into the room. They too had caught the buzz – even Comanche.

There was a stiff hiatus as we waited for Dodgson to give us the good news. But this abrupt focus seemed to bring out the physician's code of caution and caveat.

'Neither are *breakthrough* breakthroughs,' he said, 'but they are definitely breakthrough-ish – '

'For fuck's sake,' I said, 'tell us what you found.'

He gave me a slightly offended glance, then began his explanation. 'I was right about the contusion around the deep stab wound. I had some X-rays taken after you left and this is what it revealed.' He opened his leather satchel and pulled out an X-ray image that he laid on my desk. It showed Brunhilda's pelvis and femur glowing pale against the engulfing darkness.

But there was something else, something that didn't belong. I looked closer and saw the tip of a broken knife blade deep inside the quadricep muscles.

'The knife-tip must have snapped off when it struck the femur,' Dodgson said. 'The blow would have been dealt in a fit of boundless rage that I've never before seen in any of the one hundred and seven autopsies I've carried out on Family Guy's victims.'

'How does this help us?' Comanche sounded dubious. 'Unless we can match the tip to the knife, it's useless. And a killer as smart as Family Guy will have made damn sure it will never be found.'

'What about DNA on the tip?' Puritan asked.

'Unlikely,' Dodgson said. 'I sent it for tests but I'm not optimistic. Comanche is right. Without the rest of the knife, this in itself won't bring us any closer to Family Guy.'

Wham!®© made a puzzled frown. 'So why was you so excited bout a breakthrough, Doc?'

'Because of what this signifies.' Dodgson gave us all a don't-you-get-it? look. 'The survival of the twins – intended or not – along with the loss of control that snapped a steel blade represents a radical shift in his behaviour.'

'From a psychiatric point of view, I agree,' Puritan said. 'When I compiled my portrait of this man I suspected something fundamental had altered in his psychopathy. Now it seems certain – and this could work to our advantage.'

'We should keep this in mind,' I said to the group. 'On the one hand Family Guy may be discovering some sort of conscience about child-murder. That would be a first. On the other hand, he lost it bigtime with Brunhilda. And that would be another first. He also seems to be selecting families in town centre locations that present greater challenges than any of his previous outings. So clearly there's been an important event or development in his life.'

I turned to Dodgson. 'What about your other discovery?'

After the lukewarm reaction to his first announcement, Dodgson sounded somewhat prickly. 'The cluster of wounds to Mrs Mozart's inner thigh may have been intended to destroy a tattoo.'

He scanned the room like a teacher making sure his pupils were paying attention.

Which irritated the shit out of me. '*And*?'

Again, the vaguely affronted expression. 'I thought I'd seen an ink trace with the small spectrophotometer but didn't raise it at the autopsy because I couldn't be sure. Anyway, I sent a tissue sample to the lab and they ran some tests with a neutron activation analyser. The results came back just now.'

Once more he dipped into his satchel, this time bringing out a dense laboratory report. I skimmed through the sheaf of highly technical data and went to the conclusion. But even this was unintelligible. I placed the report on my desk and looked at Dodgson. 'What's the upshot?'

He made a tight smile. 'The ink is, indeed, a tattoo fragment. The sample was far too small even to guess what the tattoo depicted but the ink specialists carried out further research. They discovered that it's an unusual and very expensive tattoo ink.'

I frowned. 'Expensive why?'

He picked up the report and riffled through its of pages. Without looking up, he said, 'It's a compound of exceptionally rare synthetic chemicals. The manufacturing process is complex and costly and specialist equipment is required. This means high barriers to market. So the few manufacturers that do have the wherewithal can set their prices as high as they like.'

'So why are people willing to pay the extra money?' This was Puritan.

Dodgson glanced at the report and turned to an annex at the end. 'They spend huge sums on marketing.' He gave Wham!®© a harsh look. 'Especially celeb influssers like Mr Wham!®© here who have endorsed the product.'

'Hey, I ain't never not dorsed no inky stuffs.' Now it was Bogart who sounded miffed.

The pathologist ignored him. 'These high-end manufacturers have also gone big in other media sectors such as television ads, articles in glossy magazines and displays on the sides of prestige buildings. Dreezy Simz herself said in an interview she would "never get a tat with any other ink".'

Dodgson's gaze returned to the appendix. 'The colours are "from the palette of pigment prodigy Pierre-Yves Cousteau" and are described as "lustrous hues that radiate vibrant yet subtle allure" and "marvels of the spectrum to die a thousand deaths for".'

'Did the analysis show what pigment was used?' I asked. 'Or any other way of narrowing down the ink type found on Brunhilda Mozart?'

He flipped back through several pages. 'The fragment showed a traces of three different colours – red, yellow and green. Database cross-referencing revealed that these very specific pigments have been produced and marketed as Billion Buck Vermilion, Canarybreath and Vert De Cyclops.'

'So where does this take us?'

Dodgson opened his mouth to speak but Puritan got there first. 'Tattoos are outlawed as ungodly in the Holy Trumpian Empire and regarded as socially unacceptable here in Scientia. But there's a thriving industry in PopRep®©. And there can't be all that many high-end ink manufacturers.'

'We gotta go to PopRep®©,' Bogart said. 'Right, boss?'

My mood plunged at the prospect but I said nothing.

Puritan came to my rescue. 'Hold on a moment,' he said to Bogart. 'This tattoo ink business may be important, but it may also be a dead-end. Am I wrong, Doctor?'

'No, you're not,' Dodgson said. 'Kiera Sinatra had a similar cluster of wounds but I found no evidence of a tattoo. This could be because it was totally obliterated; or it could be because there *was* no tattoo.'

'Let me make sure I have this right,' Comanche said. 'The clustered wounds have been inflicted only on Kiera Sinatra and Brunhilda Mozart, but evidence of a tattoo has only been found on Brunhilda. So the discovery of tattoo ink may not mean anything?'

'It may not,' I said, 'but I think it does. These tightly grouped wounds would be an ideal way for Family Guy to destroy a link between the two latest female victims without us knowing. If they had the same a tattoo in a similar area, we'd have established a direct connection.' I glanced around the faces around my desk. 'We need to look more closely into victim selection in these two latest cases. I'd bet my boots Kiera and Brunhilda have something in common. And until we know for sure that Kiera *didn't* have a tattoo, I want to work on the theory that she did.'

'You cogs Family Guy maked anudda bojo?' Wham!®© asked.

'We shouldn't take anything for granted,' I said. 'But there's a good possibility that we're much closer to catching him now than we were yesterday.'

'So is we gonna go back to PopRep®©, boss, or ain't we not not not not?' This was Comanche mimicking Wham!®©.

There was an exchange of hostile glances but I let it pass.

'At some point soon,' I said, 'we'll have to.'

26

The venue of Plato Tomsky's fiftieth birthday party said more about his bohemian airs than his status as the world's sixth richest individual. He was throwing the event not at some big glitzy venue like the *Berghain* nightclub but at the *Eschschloraque*, a small counterculture bar at the end of a cobbled alley off Rosenthaler Strasse.

I didn't want to be here but had finally buckled under Bogart's pestering. When we arrived, though, I had to admit I was impressed. The alley walls were covered in a sense-shock of street art – representations of David Bowie and Siouxsie Sioux, Batman, Cat Woman and a weeping bunny girl, Anne Frank and Frankenstein's monster as a clown. Then a Soviet cosmonaut shaking hands with a caveman. Next, a groovy skeleton carrying a ghetto-blaster. On it went.

The bar was located in a four storey building at the end of the alley. Crumbling concrete walls were veined with dead branches and besieged by huge steel sculptures of insects. These, apparently, belonged to the *Monsterkabinett*, an old warehouse opposite that was crammed with even more mechanized horror. The overall effect of somewhere between Hammer horror and David Cronenberg.

The alley led us to a cobblestone courtyard where canapes were being served. We were greeted by a hefty man in a black T-shirt and jeans who looked like Tomsky's minder. The birthday boy was expecting us, he said, as he escorted us into the main bar space. Vinyl jazz from the 1970s was playing – Chick Corea's *Return to Forever* then Herbie Hancock's *Watermelon Man*. The air was crowded with chatter. People were dressed as hippies, glam-rockers, punks, goths and a whole lot else. They sipped bottles of Pabst beer and fritz-kola. The vibe was louche-lite, conservatively outrageous. But I was cool with this.

The man with fifty million votes came across to greet us, hand extended, ski-piste teeth competing with Bogart's. With his blond rug side-parted and a long quiff spilling across his brow, he had the look of a middle-aged Andy Warhol. Plastic-frame glasses and a badly knotted tie added to the East Village arthouse deal.

He greeted Bogart like a brother, then turned to me. He took my hand and kissed it. It was so very good of me to come, so very, *very* good. I wished him a happy fiftieth birthday but he made a rueful expression and said what was happy about being fifty? He called me superintendent and I said Miranda was fine. Miranda it was and what could he get Miranda to drink?

I asked for a fritz-kola and Bogart wanted a Pabst.

Tomsky signalled a bartender and the drinks arrived quickly.

We were guided to a small side-room with two black sofas on a dinted concrete floor. Two walls were bare brick, the third was painted pale blue with big yellow flowers and there was no fourth, creating a feel of inclusive privacy.

Tomsky gestured for us to sit and sat opposite, placing his fritz-kola bottle on the glass topped table between us.

'So, how goes the investigation, Miranda?'

'Well enough.' I said, 'though not as well as I'd like.'

He leaned forward, elbows on knees and looked at me through his luminous eyes. In that moment I wondered which were brighter, the eyes or the teeth. 'You know from my good friend Bogart that I want to help,' he said. 'I want to help and I *can* help. There's little about Family Guy that I don't know. And, of course, you'd have all my resources at your disposal.'

'Sright, boss,' Bogart said. 'They ain't not nada what Plato can't not do, get gotted or get finded out.'

The proposal was reasonable enough, but I didn't like the way I was being hustled – by Bogart as much as Tomsky. And if Tomsky was such a valuable advisor, why had Scientia given me Comanche and not him? Maybe it had something to do with Wu Mei's oblique warning. She hadn't told me *not* to work with Tomsky but she had warned me to be wary of him.

'Your offer is very generous, Plato,' I said. 'Let me think about it.'

In the corner of my eye I saw Bogart make a crafty nod, as if to say, *go-on-tell-her*. When we arrived I thought Wham!®© had been primed for this meeting by Tomsky. Now I wondered if it was the other way around.

'Something else I can bring to the table, as it were, is unrivalled knowledge of and access to the family and friends of Family Guy's victims.' He spoke a little sheepishly at first, as if embarrassed by Bogart's unsubtle hint. But as he continued, I sensed rising authority. 'I interviewed more than fifty people in Family Guy's first and his latest sub-series. Some were used in my documentary fourteen years ago; others in my film last year. But many were never used. Miranda, I really think some of this archive footage may be useful to your inquiry.'

Now I was interested. This sort of access would be especially useful in focusing our efforts on victim selection because no one knew the victims like their surviving family and closest associates. What these people had to say about their murdered loved ones could inform our understanding of these and other. Maybe there were links such as Brunhilda Mozart's almost obliterated tattoo – links that had been missed in earlier cases.

Nonetheless, I didn't want to give Tomsky – or for that matter, Wham!®© – the impression that I could be played. Although I had become fond of Bogart I didn't kid myself that his interest in Tomsky was also related to the success of his own career.

So I ended the discussion by thanking Tomsky and saying he'd given me a lot to think about. He could leave it with me and I'd get back to him soon.

I took a cab back to my accommodation soon afterwards, leaving Tomsky to debrief Wham!®©, or maybe it was Wham!®© debriefing Tomsky. In either event, they were thick and thieves and needed watching. For all their bromantic chumminess I had no doubt they were using one another and I was determined not get manipulated by either or both.

27

I f I'd had time to be scared, I would have been.

The slim figure silhouetted by moonlight at my living room window turned towards me.

An arm came up. A pistol.

I expected a bullet.

But I got a woman's voice. 'You should take better precautions when you go out.'

Wu Mei turned on a table light and I realized the object in her hand wasn't a gun but a ceramic figurine from the windowsill.

'After this,' I said, 'I won't go out ever again.'

She moved to the drinks cabinet and helped herself to a glass of brandy. 'Can I get you something?'

I asked for a stiff anything.

'How are you finding your accommodation?' She crossed the room and handed me a glass of brandy.

I gulped a mouthful. I needed to get a grip, alleviate the adrenalin still stinging my veins.

The apartment I'd been allocated was a lavish affair in a stately Belle Epoque building on Unter den Linden. I'd have preferred something more spartan but it would have been churlish to complain so I told her it was perfect.

She sat in one of the armchairs. I assumed I was meant to do likewise and took a seat facing her.

'You're not here for a housewarming drink,' I said. 'What can I do for you?'

'It's more what *I* can do for *you*.' She took out a pack of cigarettes and made a *May I?* expression.

I said yes of course and brought an ashtray. The secondary smoke, I told myself, would help my nerves.

'I'm aware of certain tensions within your team,' she said, lighting up. 'And I'm here to ensure they are resolved. It's in all our interests to make sure you and your people are functioning as efficiently as possible, without distractions.'

I frowned. 'Certain tensions?'

'You know what I mean: you and Comanche, Comanche and Wham!®©, Comanche and the whole fucking world.'

I drank some brandy and waited for her to continue.

'It's my business to keep you on track,' she said after some thought. 'I know you checked the tachometer on Comanche's motorcycle. I know you suspect she never left Paris when she went AWOL. And this means I know you know she lied when she said she was going to see a friend in a Qatari jail.'

This shouldn't have come as a surprise – maybe the grey woman Comanche spotted outside the mortuary *was* one of Wu Mei's agents. The fieldcraft Comanche spoke of would point in this direction. All the same I was pissed off that the security chief knew so much about my business and my team's business.

I swallowed more brandy. 'So how do you propose to ease these tensions?'

'I have information to share. Relating to Comanche. It's highly confidential and nobody outside this room can know.'

'Even Comanche?'

'Especially Comanche.'

'Very well. Nothing goes beyond these walls.'

Wu Mei leaned back and tilted her face to the ceiling, as if seeking inspiration, as if this was going to be difficult.

I finished my brandy. I wanted another but I also wanted a clear head so I stayed put.

At last she looked at me direct. 'Comanche has a daughter.'

I hadn't seen that coming and I was sure my expression said so.

'The girl has just turned sixteen. She was born in prison and, not surprisingly, has spent her whole life in care. However, Comanche has been allowed contact and even though she's a psychotic violent offender, she's never failed to attend. She might hate humanity but she loves her daughter.'

This explained Comanche's extended absence and the deceit surrounding it.

'So what's the deal?' I said. 'Not many people know about Comanche's daughter and this is how she wants to keep it?'

'You got it.' Wu Mei picked up her cigarette from the ashtray. 'The more people know about the girl, the greater the danger she's in. I'm sure you don't need telling that Comanche is a prolific enemy-maker. There's nowhere in the world of organized crime or law enforcement – or any other world – where no one has a score to settle.'

I understood the situation perfectly. The best way to get to Comanche would be through her daughter. And if she loved the girl as much as Wu Mei said, Comanche would go to any lengths to keep her safe.

'So.' Wu Mei took a last drag on her cigarette and stubbed it out. 'Now you know the reason for her deception, I expect your working relationship to be more productive.'

I gave her a studied look. 'What about Wham!®©?'

'His loyalties are to himself, you and his career. Probably in that order. Which is some achievement on your part. If your relations with Comanche come back from the edge, so will his.'

'You underestimate him.' I said. 'He's his own man and he's not stupid. I made the mistake of thinking otherwise when I first met him.'

'Nonetheless, you're their leader.' She looked at me with a sternness that told me this was a command not a request. 'It's for you to set the tone. If you set the correct one, I'm sure things between Wham!®© and Comanche will become less antagonistic. Are we clear?'

There was only one acceptable reply so I said, yes, absolutely we were clear.

She was headed for the door when the second-hand bookstore where I'd found the Miranda Miller books came to mind. 'By the way,' I said, 'do you know an author named Nico Nyro?'

'No,' she said, rather too quickly. She turned, smiling, and added in a more relaxed tone, 'That's not a name I'm familiar with. Why do you ask?'

'I overheard it,' I lied. 'Somebody in a restaurant was talking about a novel written by this Nico Nyro. It was called *The Big Happy*. Have you heard of that?'

She said no she hadn't. Why was I so intrested?

'No reason,' I said. 'Sometimes I hear a title that piques my curiosity. Same with music albums and movies. Doesn't that happen to you?'

'It doesn't,' she said with a blasé shrug. 'Now, if there's nothing else, I'll leave you to the rest of your evening.'

When the door was closed I poured myself another drink and wondered why I'd lied about where I came across the name of my author. Reading her books hadn't enlightened me one bit. But the act of possessing them, of linking them to the author's name, to a concrete reality, made me want to protect my source.

Moreover, Wu Mei told me not to trust anyone, including herself. Including *my*self. And there'd been something about that too-fast denial that told me she *had* heard of Nico Nyro. That whoever she was, she was real.

28

I went to bed with too many questions and got up the next morning with little sleep and no answers.

The Nico Nyro matter was intriguing and concerning. But what had really kept me awake was Comanche having a daughter. And the question that kept coming back to me was this: What wouldn't a mother do the protect her child? I'd never had kids. But if I *had*, the answer would be simple: Nothing.

Comanche was hardly a paradigm of motherly virtue, but the toughest shell sometimes contained the most sensitive organism. And this made me realize how little I really knew about her. Clearly I'd made some wrong assumptions. But, given what I knew at the time, who wouldn't have?

When I arrived at the office, Puritan was working on his updated portrait of Family Guy and Wham!®© was at a meeting with Tomsky. I had no doubt he could justify it but I didn't need to hear it and had nothing for him to do anyway. Comanche had put away her tobacco tin and cigarette papers and was at least pretending to be looking at her computer screen.

I said good morning to both, and both reciprocated – a first for Comanche.

Later that morning Puritan went on an errand, leaving me and Comanche alone.

I hadn't heard her come into my office and was startled when she coughed to catch my attention. I made an obliging smile and asked what I could do.

She stopped in front of my desk looking awkward, even embarrassed – another first. It seemed she had something difficult to say so I gave her the time she needed.

'About what I did to the bee… ' she said at length.

I waited some more.

'Listen, I don't have a problem with people who autospect as critters – even insects… ' Another few seconds of hesitation. 'But that guy – that bee – was right in my face. I can't say he deserved to wind up in the hospital but I'm not a good person to piss off.'

'Thanks for clearing that up.' I was aware that this was as close to an apology as she was going to come and decided to take the win – particularly after my fresh orders from Wu Mei.

The cynical side of me wondered if Comanche had been given a similar dictate to mine. But did it really matter? As much as I distrusted Wu Mei, she was right about the smooth functioning of my team. If we didn't pull together we'd never pull at all.

'I also know how you've cut me a little slack. Not just over the bee, but in general.' Once more, a difficult moment. 'So I guess I should say thanks.'

I thought, Wow! Her first "good morning", her first approximation of an apology and her first show of gratitude, all in one morning.

In that instant my suspicion that Comanche had also been given a talking to became a certainty. But my main instinct remained correct: this outcome was no bad thing.

I glanced at my watch. 'Lunchtime,' I said. 'Do you fancy something? Perhaps with a glass of wine?'

She nodded. 'Come on, I'll give you a ride on my bike that we talked about.'

*

The Vincent Black Lightning was one cool machine and Comanche one mean rider. I didn't know what else I should have expected but I was awash with epinephrine before we reached the end of Quai Voltaire.

I gripped her waist tighter, tighter still as the 998cc twin-V engine powered us through the western outskirts of Paris and towards Ville d'Avray. She had to slow down in the town centre traffic which gave me time to shake the pins and needles from my arms as we rolled along the picturesque streets. When I took hold of her again I felt her lean waist and hard muscles. And picked up a lemony vanilla scent in the slipstream of her hair – when I'd asked about wearing helmets she gave me two options: I didn't wear one or we didn't go.

Then she turned onto the Route de l'Impératrice, an open road that cut through the densely wooded Forêt Domaniale de Fausses Reposes. She opened the throttle and the crotch-rocket really took off. We went from 0-60 in under three seconds. Moments later we were clocking 100 mph, then 120, and finally 140. She would probably have gone faster yet but we were running out of road. I felt a strange mix of relief and disappointment as she began to brake.

We stopped at a roadside café-bar called the *Cabane de Christophe* on the edge of the forest. It wasn't what I'd had in in mind when I suggested lunch – a biker's hang-out with sun bleached beer ads on the timber frame walls. But there was parking at the back and a small grassed area with tables.

Christophe, a big beardy man with more tattoos on show than skin, wiped his hands on his apron and embraced Comanche like a sister. She nodded to a few leathered up comrades at the bar and we went outside with a menu. It was, of course, strictly vegan and I ordered a dish called *ragoût de la forêt* while Comanche opted for chilli beans and rice. To drink, she ordered a bottle of *La Goudale* and I followed suit. So much for the wine I'd been looking forward to, though the beer was good and strong. The food was served in enamelled metal bowls that had a prison kitchen vibe. But my reservations vanished when I started eating. Christophe could serve this dish at a Michelin-star restaurant in Saint-Germain-des-Présn and the patrons would be in raptures.

I couldn't ask about her daughter so I did the next best thing and asked about her parents.

'They died when I was a teenager,' she said between mouthfuls of food. 'They were both arseholes and I never shed a tear. Oh, wait. Yes I did – of joy.'

'I'm sorry.'

'Don't be – I'm not.' She swigged some beer. 'What about your folks?'

I told her about my mum and dad and my working class childhood in north Manchester. And, without really knowing why, about my actualization from an improbable character in a satirical novel. As a result, I didn't know if that past and those parents were real.

She chewed some food and thought about this.

'I don't know much about that actualization stuff,' she said at length, 'but you look real enough to me. And all this shit around us – ' she whisked the air with her fork, as if to indicate the whole of creation – 'is all too real. I wish it wasn't. If there was any chance of it not being, believe me, I'd take it.'

'Really?'

'If you aren't real, boss, you're the luckiest person I ever met.'

She looked down at her food, shifting it around her plate as if she was trying to re-order the universe. I guessed this bleakness had a lot to do with her teenaged daughter. I sensed deep regret, even an edge of despair.

To fill the silence, I said, 'When it's just the two of us, call me Randy.'

She let her cutlery fall into the dish and looked up with a weary smile. 'Okay then, Randy, it is – when no one's listening of course.' She finished her beer and smiled again, this time with a little humour. 'You can carry on calling me Comanche.'

I grinned back. 'Why did you choose that name?'

'It means enemies forever,' she said. 'With everyone.'

She ordered another beer for each of us, despite my protests about drink driving.

'Where did you learn that about Comanches?'

She downed most of the fresh bottle of *La Goudale* and wiped her mouth with her sleeve. 'In a movie,' she said. '*Hell or High Water*, 2016 neo-western. Great film.'

'It is for sure.' I took a few swallows of my beer. 'But stuff in movies isn't necessarily true.'

She shrugged. 'I don't care. Sounds right. That's all that matters.'

'Anyway,' I said, '*I'm* not your enemy.'

'Not now. But you will be. Sooner or later.'

I took her hand and squeezed it hard. 'It doesn't have to be like that.'

She looked at me with a forlornness I couldn't fathom. 'I wish it didn't. You can't imagine how much I wish that.'

'Things are rarely as bad as they seem.' I wanted to tell her that I knew about her daughter, that I was sure she would keep the girl safe. But I couldn't admit to this knowledge, still less give any such assurances. Instead I made a pragmatic expression like the one my mum made when my dad lost his job or when we'd received an eviction order or she'd been diagnosed with cancer.

'Another beer,' she said.

'We shouldn't drink and ride.'

But she was already signalling Christophe and two more *La Goudales* were on their way.

We left the *Cabane de Christophe* much later and having drunk more alcohol than we should have. She promised to take it easy but the open road was too tempting and the Black Lightning was soon clocking 120. My adrenalin spiked fast and stayed spiked all the way back to the underground car park. But at least the journey was short.

As she dismounted Comanche said, 'About earlier. All that heavy shit I laid on you ...'

'Don't be silly.' I put my hand on her shoulder.

'Everyone gets down. And any time you want to talk, I'm here. For you.'

I leaned a little closer and her lemon-vanilla scent filled my nostrils.

She mirrored my movement. Our bodies were almost touching. This shouldn't be happening. But in another way, it should. It felt right. Fuck, it felt inevitable.

I titled my face to hers, our lips touched. Hers were damp and smooth and –

She stepped back fast, the growl of a car engine filling the garage.

At the same moment Bogart's rented Porsche Stuka rattled down the entry ramp and he drove towards us grinning.

'I'll catch you later.' Comanche headed for the door. 'I really don't want to hear whatever shite Tomsky has filled Tweetie Pie's head with.'

29

One of the first things I learned as a senior detective was that investigations are like sharks. They must keep moving even if they aren't sure exactly where they're going. The more you move, the more you start to see things. The more you sniff the sharper your scent.

The sniffing I was doing involved Brunhilda Mozart and Kiera Sinatra. Apart from the remnants of Brunhilda's tattoo and my assumption that Kiera's had been obliterated by the stab cluster, there was nothing concrete to suggest a link. All the same, my instincts told me these two women had been singled out in a way other victims hadn't. If I could confirm this it would be a big step forward. It would go to motive and a whole lot of other places. So I re-read the reports on both women – personal, employment, education, lifestyle and others. I looked again at their social activities and political affiliations. I re-examined statements from friends, family and employers. I requested comparative DNA checks. And I ran facial recognition pictures.

Also, there remained a possibility that Kiera had been targeted due to her secretive employment at Fifi's nightclub by Gonzales Smedge. I wondered, too, if Brunhilda had also worked for the PopRep®© crime boss. It seemed she had never visited Vegas, England. But things were seldom as they seemed.

I saw Comanche talking to Puritan at his desk and my thoughts catapulted back to our motorbike ride and lunch at Christophe's place. And of course to the kiss that never got off the launch-pad. By the time I'd listened to Bogart's account of his meeting with Plato Tomsky and got back to the office, there was no opportunity to talk to her in private. Apart from the occasional meeting of glances, we didn't communicate for the rest of that afternoon. We did, though, speak briefly in the elevator on our way out of the office. I said we should talk some time, maybe over a drink and, rather too quickly, she agreed. That would be nice, she said. We should definitely do it. Then the elevator doors opened and Wu Mei was standing in the lobby, waiting for me. Comanche touched my arm and was gone.

Wu Mei watched her leave gave me a cautionary look. Comanche was on our side now, she told me, but that could change. She was a sociopathic criminal and there was only so much control one could exert. Wu Mei walked with me to my car. I got the impression she didn't like to have conversations anywhere that might be surveilled. As we walked across the car park she explained that Judgment Jesusly wanted me in Rio de Jerusalem. The folksy First Father of the Holy Trumpian Empire was keen for his people to see me at work in their federation. He wanted this even though it was clear that the high profile foisted on me had already backfired. So I told Wu Mei my time would be better spent catching Family Guy than playing politics. It was my decision, she said, but Jesusly was not a good guy to piss off. I asked her if she thought I gave a shit and she said no, she didn't think I did. We left it at that.

My videophone beeped.

It was the facial recognition specialist. She had a hit. Kiera Sinatra and Brunhilda Mozart had flown into the seaside resort town of Blackpool in Old Britain on the same plane fourteen years ago. At the time, Kiera would have been aged twenty and Brunhilda a year younger. The names on their passports were different – aliases, no doubt, to cover their activity. The facial recognition expert said they'd left Blackpool three months later, travelling together on the same arrow plane to DJT airport in Old New York. There, the trail went cold.

What they did during their time in Blackpool was unclear although I was sure their arrival and departure on the same flights was no coincidence. This was the evidence I needed that the two women were connected; that Family Guy's victim selection process had acquired an underlying motive that no one had previously suspected. If I could find out what this was, we would be significantly closer to catching him.

Further inquiries showed both women had been employed as executive assistants at a corporate hospitality firm called Gazelle Services. A call to the Department of Trade in Old England showed the company went into voluntary liquidation twelve years ago after its owner had died earlier in the same year.

I also asked about high-end tattoo ink businesses that manufactured the colours Dodgson had identified.

There were only three in the whole of Old Britain, one in Coventry, the other two in Blackpool.

Finally, this *was* a punch the air moment. I wasn't a punch-the-air person, though, and contented myself with an under-my-breath 'Bingo.'

And whether I liked it or not, the breakthrough was taking us back to PopRep®©.

30

BLACKPOOL, ENGLAND

The arrow plane come into PopRep®© airspace and it were ziff I ain't not never been gone. IngoLingo®© were all as I could gab, all as I could think. But we gotta come here so it were smin I gotta accept.

We was back in Old England to the find ink maker what selled speshlist colours called Billion Buck Vermilion, Canarybreath and Vert De Cyclops to a tat parlour before Kiera and Brunhilda arrived in Blackpool on 5th May 4036. If we nailed this, we be monstamoster closer to scovering why they was singled out by Family Guy. And if we cogged this we be monstamoster closer to cogging what made the bastard ticktock.

As we flied low over Blackpool I zeroed the old seaside town where I come as a kiddy with Mum and Dad. No need of climate control here to rip the rijnal. Weather were shite two thousand year back and were shite still.

Ebbaplace else also specked pretty much as it done last I were last here. The Tower, a half scale rip of the Eiffel, were a girdery steel spike what stabbed skywise over the slow-shelving beach and the wrinkly tin sheet of the Irish Sea. Into this poked three boardwalk piers, each calling to mind a freight train of vivid boxcars what somehow come cross the water and hit the buffers at the prom-prom-prom, knowed local as the Goldy Mile. Nowhere on earth like it, save praps Coney Isle in New York City. And like Coney, Blackpool were on its rijnal site, with lotsa rijnal buildings.

Casting back, I membered donkey rides on the sands, candy floss spinned hot and sticky pink. I membered gnasher-cracking sticks of "rock" candy. And plastic bowlers with "Kiss me quick!" on the hat band, and vingry whelks eated with cocktail sticks from paper cones. And stringed along the prom-prom-prom was bingo gaffs and slot dives, palm readers, fortune tattlers, pubs and more pubs and more yet where Dad drinked pints of Tetley bitter and mum Babychams and me a can or two of Bass shandy.

And, acourse, there was tat parlours. Probs more tat parlours than pubs.

We landed at Blackpool Airport and was met by a pangendry det sarge name of Georgie Humperdinck. They was a low and narrow spud with smooth skin and a charmy grin, decked out in a fashny maroon earl and sharp-tip boots. They taked us to our rooms at the Imperial Hotel, a redbrick palace from Blackpool's 19th Cent heyday. There we eated and freshed up, turning in early for a fast start the next day.

Sept for Bogart. I sended him on the Whizz Train to Coventry where one of the three top-end tat ink makers was based. I were near sure the firm we was after were in Blackpool – why would parlours in the tat cap of Old Britain go so far south for their ink when there was spliers right here on their doorstep? But I gotta be sure. And I were counting on Bogart's influsser smarts to get an answer from the longshotters.

*

First thing next day, Humperdinck taked us to the first of these top-end ink makers. This biz went by the name Thinking Inking and their big jumbly factry were a five min drive inland on Mansfield Road. The boss were bigmost helpy. He showed us to his office and give us instant access to his records. No joy though. Thinking Inking never selled the colour combo we was intrested to any tat parlour in Blackpool or any udda place in Old Britain in 4036 or any udda year. And while the tat parlour what inked Kiera and Brunhilda mighta got their colours from diffrent spliers, it maked biz sense to source all from one. So, leastwise for now, we was gonna focus on any what ordered the three shades at once.

As we was leaving I got a call from Bogart. He come up short in Coventry and were on his way back north by Whizz Train.

This leaved just the one ink maker.

We drived south to Ink Inc, a littler but swisher factry than that of Thinking Inking what were on an indstrial park off Yeadon Road. A monsta delivry truck in Top Tat

Ink Inc livery were waiting at a side gate while the scurity spud checked some docs what the driver give him.

Humperdinck pulled up at the glass-fronty gaff and we finded the uber boss, waiting by the ception desk. She were a slim jane with a pointy viz, garbed smart in a biz earl.

As we proached I could gog from her expression that she weren't not happy to speck us.

'You that Serial Killer Miller lass, ain't you not?' she tattled. 'I don't wanna get in with you and you franksteiny stuffs. We at Top Tat Ink Inc got a solid rep and I ain't not gonna let you bojo it.'

Once more, I thinked, the high profile what Simz and Jesusly and Confucius give me had come back and bited me in the cut.

'We ain't not gonna take up much of your time,' I gabbed. 'And your sistance will get treated real discreet.'

'No it won't,' the uber boss zeroed me gressive. 'Coz you ain't not getting no sistance.'

I turned to Humperdinck, Comanche and Puritan. Cept Old Bob weren't not there. Humperdinck shrugged pologetic and Comanche made a little backwise nod, ziff to tattle *Let's go – nada to be got here.*

I turned back to the boss jane. 'We can get a warrant.'

'Then get one.' She were real sure of herself. 'But I knows my rights. You ain't never gonna get no warrant.'

'I'm sure it won't come to that.' This were Puritan. He come outta no place and went close to the boss jane.

'I saw your delivery truck arrive with a consignment of mercury sulphide.'

Her spression went creasy. 'So what?'

'Transported with dioxytropin.'

'*And*?' The uber boss zeroed Old Bob like he were a daft un.

Monstadick error.

Coz what Old Bob were up to when he vanished soon come clear. 'Are you familiar with section IV(h) of the Haulage of Hazardy Chems Act of 3983?'

'We is licensed to carry both of them chems,' she tattled, 'if that is what you're getting to.'

'I'm sure you are.' Old Bob give her one of his gap-toothy grins. 'But not together. The Act stipulates clearly that these chemicals must be transported separately.' He got out his phone and showed her pics what he just taked of the delivry truck. 'I'm sure the Health and Safety people will be interested in these images. You see, the statute lays down severe penalties for non-compliance. As much as ten per cent of gross annual profits, with up to three years jail time. And, of course, there's the reputational damage you alluded to earlier. I can picture the media headlines: *Top Tat ink maker fined godzillions for flouting safety laws.*' He waved his phone. 'And I can send the pictures right now.'

Old Bob done a number on this haughty lass, no two ways.

'That were done without my knowing or consent.' She tattled ultra giddyup and somewhat shrill.

'That's not relevant,' Old Bob gabbed thorative, which acourse, he were. 'You're the CEO and principal shareholder of this business and that makes you legally responsible for everything it does or does not do.'

This the uber boss were frozed to the spot. Only part of her to move were her gobbler, what come agape.

The lawjaw give her the coop de gracias. 'You'd be out of business and in prison before you could say ClapTrap®©.'

I taked Bob's cue. 'Nuddaless, I is sure Mr Puritan here could turn a blind eye to this law-snappy stuff if you was to co-op with us. That right Mr Puritan?'

Old Bob nodded solemn. 'It is indeed, Det Top Boss Miller.'

The uber boss shutted her gobbler. Her fusebox were going whizzy-whizzy plus-plus-plus. Then she gabbed, 'You best come with me.'

31

The uber boss taked us to this swishy big office and give Bob permish to zamine all the archives on the screen.

Clickety-clack went Bob. Up come the sales ledger for 4036, the year Kiera and Brunhilda flied into Blackpool. We all zeroed squinty over Bob's shoulder as he scrolled down, slots scanning the lines of data: *Custmer Name; Order Date; Product Type: Quant; Order Code; Delivry Date; Payment Got.*

Down and down them dizzy-dancy lists we went till our slots got itchy blurry. 4036 nada; 4035, nada; 4034 sames. And so on. We was all starting to think them three colours was never selled as one.

Then Bob striked gold.

On 17th Feb 4024 two custmers buyed all three shades. Twelve zucking year fore they was used on Kiera and Brunhilda. That's some serio shelf-life.

That shuddabin anudda air-punchy moment but we was too capboggled by all them squiggly numbers to punch anything.

Even so, this were a monstadick breakthrough.

And praps not all.

Waybacker and waybacker went Old Bob.

Jiggly-wiggly come them lines of data. Sorer and sorer got our slots.

Down and down and –

Then we got anudda custmer.

And anudda and anudda.

This gived us five toto.

Nuddaless, Old Bob never give up. Not till the date when Top Tat Ink Inc first stocked them inks thirty-five year back did he shift his gnarly dedos from that keyboard.

If we never catched Family Guy, I thinked, none of it wuddabin the fault of our bulldoggy old lawjaw.

*

Spite this majormost chievement, it soon come clear that we was still a big way off where we had to get. Of the five tat parlous what buyed the three ink colours, one were in Glasgow, anudda in Derby and the rest here in Blackpool. Least for now the local ones gotta be the places to check – why would them two murdered lasses fly into Blackpool, Tat Cap of Old Britain, then get tatted two-hundred mile north in Glasgow or one hundred south in Derby?

I didn't wanna spook none of the local tat parlour popeyes by arriving mob-handed so I sended Puritan and Comanche back to the local copshop where we been gived an incident room. Next, me and Humperdinck went to gab with the tat parlour spuds. The sarge's broad Lancs accent would play well when we telled em we was lawdogs.

First, we drove back to the town centre, parking up at the Metropole Hotel on the prom-prom-prom. From there we legged to the apt named Queen Street, the resort's gay village. This time in the morning though it never specked neither gay nor villagey. But there were lottsa touristy spuds sitting with pints of yellow beer at tables outside pubs; and just as many going in and outta the cluster of tat parlours.

The one we was after were a ramshaky store – not what you wudda thinked were high end.

It were called Skin Deep and the dark grey and purple store front give a draclary vibe.

Inside were sames: low-lighted cavern of a gaff with lottsa mirrors and a black justable chair like them as what dentists used. Next to this standed a work-stool and a glass-top stand with tat guns, a big tub of Hustle Butter, squirty sanitizer and vac-sealed tat needles.

The owner, Stoker Fangly, were a goth jane with chain strewed garb what went jingly-jangly as she come from a back office and legged slow tward us. Her black-dyed rug were spikey, skin lardy and covered in spidry tats. She were mid-forties, dumpy and low – though still higher than my pangendry amigo Georgie Humperdinck.

'All right, Stoker,' gabbed he.

'All right, Georgie,' gabbed she. Her voice come throaty with heavy Lancs vowel sounds, sames as Humperdinck. 'What you want o me?'

'We thinks you mebbe can sist with some queries,' I tattled.

She gimme a knowy look. 'You a Manc, ain't you not?'

'In another life,' I gabbed. Gottasay I were pressed by how she picked up frags of my Manchester accent.

'We gets lottsa Mancs,' she tattled. 'And Scousers, Glasgies and Irishes. Even Yanks. We gets em all here.'

I taked out the blowed-up passport photos of Kiera Sinatra and Brunhilda as they was fourteen year back. Then I laid em on the glass top counter so she could speck em good.

'We need you to toss you mind back fourteen year,' Georgie gabbed. 'Can you member tatting these two lasses? Wuddabin same little tats on their upper arms. Probs Jan or Feb 4036.'

'Holy Cowell, Georgie,' gabbed Stoker, 'that a bigmosterest while back.'

'That it is, Stoker.'

I scanned Stoker's bleachy features as she zeroed the photos.

She blinked a frag flinchy.

Were this a sign she cogged the two lasses? Or were she just tryna focus?

She nay-shaked her fusebox. 'Nada come to mind.'

'Think real hard, Stoker,' tattled Georgie. 'This bigmosterest portantest.'

She zeroed the pics again, nearer, but still shaked her fusebox. 'Apols, Georgie, no can help.'

There were nada more to be done here so Humperdinck give her they card, told her to call if smin come to mind, and we left.

On the street, I turned to Georgie. 'Think she's tattling true?'

They shoved they dedos through their slicked back hair. 'Tough call, boss. She's a rum un, that's for sure. Gotta record for all sorta petty stuffs, nada serio though. What you thinks?'

I taked a few steps, flecting on that dithery frag when Stoker first zeroed them pics. 'I mebbe wrong,' I tattled. 'But I reckons she's holding smin back.'

'Want Stoker bringed in, boss? Give her some stewy time in a cell?'

We legged awhile tward the prom-prom-prom.

'Leave her be for now, Georgie,' I tattled. 'If we goes too heavy she might dig in deeper yet.'

'Where next then?'

'Eye of the Needle,' I tattled.

This were number two on the list of Blackpool tat shops what buyed in all three of them colours at the same time. It were on East Park Drive, a posh neck of town oppo Stanley Park. Georgie drived real frisky and we was outside the place in fifteen mins. It were more what I spected of a top-end gaff: big house, high chimneys and lush grass with a long gravelly driveway and proper nice views of the park.

The popeye what come to the door were a pudgy spud with smooth olive skin and white hair. On his fusebox he weared a round lamp, medic-like and a short white doc coat. Bit pompy for a tat lad, I thought, but if it bringed in the punters, who were I to judge?

Getting a hoity-toity popeye like this spud to co-op were easy-peasy. Any whiff of a nabber quiry into his practice wuddabin nuff to send his minted clients legging it. He taked us into his office, a lavish spread, all walnutty and frame pics of him and famey spuds what got tatted here. But even though he tattled nonstop about how he loved, *loved* the nabs and their work, and he maked all his files vailable, he got nada for us. His records showed not a sausage and he never cogged the pics of Kiera or Brunhilda.

I gogged at Georgie and he gogged at me and we knowed right then that this lad were way too frighted to lie.

So we drived deep into the sticks to the last on the list. This were deffo not you avridge tat shop – even the previo gaff specked humble by compo. It were an ancient country pile what been changed to a hotel-spa for the uber-rich. And them as was running this place was corprate types. The venue were part of the Lux-Finesse Group, which, we was telled by the signs, were a global biz.

We gabbed with the ception lad who picked up a phone and tattled with the ops chief.

We was keeped waiting thirty mins.

After half of these, I sensed a prob and maked a call.

At last, the ops chief strided into the lobby ziff he really were smoddy. Lad had a thin face with a wonky slash of a gobbler and long nose what he used to speck down at us.

'This jack gonna be difcult, boss,' tattled Georgie and I agreed.

This were a multi-nat gaff, we was telled, not cowed by lawdogs anyplace and the ops chief been telled by his ubers that it were the policy of the biz not to gab to us.

'You gotta get a court order,' he tattled haughty, 'uddawise I ain't not gabbing nada.'

Georgie leaned close and tattled soft so the ops chief never heared him. 'He's right, boss, even if we takes him in, he is entitled to keep his gobbler clamped.'

'No worries, Georgie,' I plied.

Then, to the ops chief, 'I thinks that court order is gonna come real soon.'

I gogged out the window just as the Arm and a Leg Roller drived into the car park.

Few nanofrags later, Old Bob legged rickety into the gaff, toting a sheet of paper. The lawjaw got what I called him about foot-to-the-floor ferrari. He come right up to this the ops chief and smacked the court order on his chest.

The ops lad strided away to read it. Spent a bigwhile specking the doc, then anudda bigwhile specking it again. Then he maked a phone call what I assumed were to his uber boss. *Then*, he come back, viz stormbroody boohoo.

'Now,' tattled I, 'you gonna play nice?'

He specked at me easter-islandy. 'I just tattled with the corprate lawjaws in Zurich and they told me I gotta give full, abso and toto co-op.'

The ops chief scorted us into a side room and scanned the pics of Kiera and Brunhilda what I laid out on a table.

He zeroed em close, closer yet. Thinked awhile, then nay-shaked his fusebox.

'I been at this gaff twenty three year and I never laid slots on neither of them lasses.'

Puritan moved in close, tattling soft, 'You know it would be contempt of court, punishable by fine, imprisonment or negative ClapTrap®©, GibGab®© and Howler®© exposure, to lie or withhold information from this investigation?'

'Yo, Mr Lawjaw,' tattled the ops chief, now big serio. 'We at Lux-Finesse respects and obeys the Laws of This Land What is Under The Flag.'

He taked out his phone and summoned all the tat salon staff what been here fourteen year back. They was all wearing smart corpratey uniform: black waistcoats and pants; white shirts and ties. Them as were on days off joined on vid links. The ops boss readed em the Riot Act about the pens for not co-opping with us lawdogs.

We showed em pics of Kiera and Brunhilda, plus the fake names they was using when they come to Blackpool. All zamined the pics intense, gabbed mong emselves, gabbed some more with their boss. But none of em could help. All nay-shaked their fuseboxes and sweared on Holy Cowell that they never zeroed neither of the two lasses. They cuddabin tattling lies but I thinked not, spesh after the ops chief threated em again with badmost punishings.

Georgie's phone buzzed. They taked the call then mouthed to me that the caller were Stoker.

I yo-nodded and taked the phone.

32

'This is Miller,' I tattled. 'What up, Stoker?'

No reply. Crickly-crackly lectric noise. At last she began gabbing. 'I been thinking about them pics of the lasses what you showed me.' Her vox were wavry-taut. 'And I thinks I members em. There was in a bunch of spuds what got identic tats and ... '

Stoker breaked off – I magined she were specking round nervy, checking nubdy were earwigging. She went on, hurried. 'I members them tats coz I got top-frog cash from this high and narrow frighty jane. Only condit were that I did the job-lot in two day.'

This were anudda monsta breakthrough. Having all them tats done identic and one after the next gotta mean them as had em was linked. Not just Kiera and Brunhilda, but uddas too.

'Smin else – ' Stoker's vox cut out sudden.

I heared street noise, kids skriking, radio music and DJ lickertangle. 'You okay, Stoker?'

'Yeah, all good,' she gabbed at last. 'But listen, not all them tats was in the same place.'

'What you mean?'

'Spuds could choose where I did the tat.'

'That's real good, Stoker,' I gabbed. 'What sorta tats was they?'

'Dunno. Small, but I forget the details.' Stoker's voice were real quivry now.

'Sure you good, Stoker? Smoddy threated you?'

'Nah,' she tattled blasé.

This were bullshit. Stoker got the frighteners aright.

'You got copies o them tats?' I quizzed. 'This is monsta portant.'

'Poss. I do all my design stuff on speshlist apps. But if I do still got em they at my udda place down in Revoe.'

'How soon can you get there?'

'Ten, fifteen mins.'

'Go there right now, Stoker, and we be waiting,' I tattled. 'Never stop for nubdy, never make any udda calls. You hears?'

She said she did and ended the call.

I turned to Georgie. 'You knows where Stoker's parlour in Revoe at?'

They yo-nodded and off we setted, bustagut giddyup, blues and twos flashy and waily.

We was there in five mins. The gaff seemed empty. I skriked Stoker's name through the mail slot. No response. Then I structed Humperdinck to break the door open and this he did, ultra frisky.

Inside were sames as the Queen Street parlour: heavymetal goth; mirrors ebbaplace; justable recliner; glass-top work table with tat guns, Hustle Butter and needle packs.

But no Stoker.

We searched the whole place but no sign. Nada disturbed, outta place or broked.

'Praps Stoker got stuck in traffic,' Humperdinck gabbed.

We both knowed uddawise.

Georgie called her phone. No response.

'We gotta get back to Queen Street right this nano,' I tattled. 'And get a drone up – if she *is* stuck in a jam I wanna know pronto.'

We drove breakneck thundybolt to Queen Street and leaved the motor right outside Stoker's gaff.

Humperdinck tried the door. Locked. They never needed telling to break in.

Stoker were laying in the recliner, arms dangling either side, not moving.

On the floor under her fusebox were a dark pool. We both knowed it weren't Hustle Butter.

We rushed over. Stoker's swallower been opened lug-to-lug. Wound were agape, airway and food pipe and all big vessels cut clean.

'Poor Stoker,' Georgie tattled. 'She were a ripe un aright bit never deserved nada like this.'

Georgie called in the killing, then we searched the rest of the parlour. I didn't spect to find nada and that were zactly what we finded. Killer wuddabin long gone. Next I sended a team of techs to the Revoe place where Stoker thought she stored the tat designs. This work were gonna take time, though I wuddabin sprized if they come back with anything helpy.

Soon after, Puritan and Wham!®© arrived with the CSI spuds.

'Where Comanche?' I quizzed frowny.

'She went to see an associate who lives locally and knows something about the tattoo business,' Bob splained. 'Said she was bored sitting on her backside at the police station.'

Made sense I guessed. I turned to Wham!®©. 'Enjoyed your trip to Coventry?'

'All good, boss,' he gabbed.

Smin sheepy in his manner maked me wonder if he were aright. 'You sure you good? You was gone longer than I spected.'

'I meeted this old amigo. We had some scran and gabbed so long I missed my train. Gotta wait two hour for the next un.'

'Not so good at lying are you, Tweetie Pie?'

All slots went to Comanche who come backwise into the gaff, dragging smoddy who were struggling and shouting.

'Look who I found spying on us.' She hauled Plato Tomsky into the room and shoved him hard tward me.

'This isn't what it seems.' The media olly holded his palms skywise and gimme a twisty grin. 'I can explain everything.'

33

The spud what got morer votes than Cally and New York City turned to Wham!®©.

But he were lickertangled and eye-shy. Only time I ebba gogged the lad so red-viz barrassed.

'You under arrest,' I told Tomsky. 'Georgie, take this popeye to the cop shop if you pleases.'

'Under arrest?' Tomsky vox were shrill. 'But what for?'

'How do the first degree murder o Stoker Fangly sound?'

'It sounds absurd!' Tomsky skriked. 'This is a dreadful misunderstanding. Tell them, Bogart!'

But Wham!®© keeped his gobbler clamped as Humperdinck cuffed the media billy and taked him to a nabber car on the street.

'You.' I poked Wham!®© in the chest. 'In my office the nanofrag we gets back.'

'And *you.*' I give Comanche a stormbroody speck. 'Wipe that grin off you viz.'

We drived to the Big Cop Shop in seprate cars and I went straight to the office what been set aside for me.

Wham!®© were standed antsy at the door and followed me in.

'What the zuck, Bogart?' I tattled fierce. 'I thinked I could trust you.'

Bogart gabbed he were real sorry and big boohoo. He sisted I could still trust him, that he meeted Tomsky, but it were pure chance. Tomsky were here in Old England fore we arrived, prepping for his new docmentry on Family Guy. There was nada spicious going down and this Bogart sweared to this on his mama's grave.

'And you swallowed that yarn about just happening to bump into you?'

He had no answer and never tried to gimme one.

'Even if you never telled him we was in Old England, you deffo telled him we was in Blackpool. Fact, I bet the two of you come up on the same Whizz Train.'

He tattled nada and I knowed what I just gabbed were true.

'Smoddy got inside skinny,' I gabbed. 'That's how Stoker got her swallower cut. That's how we lost a key witness. Did *you* deepthroat us, Bogart? Coz it specks that way from where I is standed.'

'No I never, boss.' His vox were pleady. 'You gotta believe me.'

'After what you done, gimme one reason why I should keep you on this team?'

'Coz I is a proper geezer, a bustagut spud with a tiktok honest and true.'

I shaked my fusebox and holded my temples in my dedos. There were a short quiet and I let it play, let him stew.

'Look, boss,' he tattled after a bitwhile, 'It's true I wanna use Plato to get profile and build my audience. But he's a bigmost media olly with a lotta sway in a lotta places. And nubdy know Family Guy like what he do. Strue and you knows it.'

It *were* true and I *did* know it. But I heard all this before from Bogart – and Tomsky hisself. And Wu Mei aready warned me about letting Tomsky get too close. Against this, I had to think on the probs he posed if he were left to meddle. One thing I knowed – I could never stick a murder rap on Tomsky. I were sure Bogart could give him an alibi till the moment the Whizz Train arrived in Blackpool. Which were way too soon for Tomsky to get anyplace near Stoker's parlour at the time she were killed. Sides, why would the sixth richest popeye on the planet get tangled in the killing of a tat artist?

What it come down to were the old Lyndon Johnson line about a bothersome spud in the tent pissing out being betterer than outside pissing in. Even so, Wham!®© were obvio under the spell of Tomsky and both would need gogging close.

So I turned to Bogart and gabbed, 'You can tell your buddy that no charges gonna be bringed and I will coop with his docmentry work *where poss*.'

Bogart's viz lighted up fireworky.

'*But*.' I give him a razory speck. 'This gotta be a two-way deal: he help us, we help him. He gets access only through you; and you comes to me first. I never want nada of this snoopy biz again. You gets me, Bogart?'

'I gets you, boss,' Bogart tattled.

Next day I were legging lazy along the prom-prom-prom, specking cross the blond sands where the ebb-tide scooped meandry channels what runned parallel to the coastline. Spiky breeze shivered their surfaces ziff the beach itself were wobbly. The two-tone sea were stained brown by sand grain on the gentle tilt of the beach. Only wayfar out, where the sea were deep, could you speck blue water.

Latest news on the murder of Stoker were not great. The frensik spuds never finded no tat designs at her Revoe gaff coz the hard-drives been wiped. This meant the Queen Street killer got a complice. I never knowed a serial killer what worked with smon else in this sorta way, which give the case anudda twist. Sure, serials done double acts. Like the Moors Murderers in Manchester, the Hillside Stranglers in Los Angeles and the Ken and Barbie Killers in Ontario. But them spuds never did nada like this. This were no pervy thrill kill. It smacked of dirty tricks by some creepy state outfit. Them as offed Stoker had a rational motive and their biz were getting the job done slick ferrari. No psychosexual shit, no freddykreuger torture, no horrorshow sign-off. And, acourse, no family.

Mebbe Family Guy had no role in Stoker's death. But there was no way his latest victims Kiera and Brunhilda was not connected.

So what did this tell me about the case itself? Were some high-up spiracy shit going down? Smin portanter than nabbing Family Guy?

Smin else: Family Guy becomed a plitiko deal. I been fetched here for plitiko reasons by the bosses of the three feds. They *made* this case plitiko. So should I be sprized if the killing of Stoker were part of some deep state spiracy?

On the udda grasper, serials was aways diffrent, aways sprizing, aways morphing. We knowed Family Guy were a clever lad with monstadick resources. Praps they was no plitiko doings. Praps Family Guy knowed we was onto him via the tats. Praps he were covering his tracks and hired smon to wipe them drives while he taked care o Stoker.

Either way, we was into some deep murky shit.

Anudda quesh: how did them as did for Stoker know what were going on inside my team? To get ahead of us in the way they done, they'd need smoddy on the inside. Or at least real close. How the zuck did they do this?

Again, Plato Tomsky come to mind. Wham!®© gived him an alibi, but what if Bogart was lying. Could I *really* trust the influsser?

My phone ringed and I zeroed the caller were Comanche

'It's the Grey Lady,' she tattled. 'The one who's been tailing us. I've got eyes-on.'

'Where is you?'

'Queen Street. Opposite the tat parlour.'

'Where is she?'

'Half a block away. If you can get here quick I think we can catch her.'

'Gimme two mins.'

34

stowed my phone and went to my lug-piece, then hustled cross the prom-prom-prom giddy-up ferrari. Slowed right down, though, as I come to Queen Street. It were thronged with tourists and that could work for or against us, pending on how this went.

I clocked Comanche at a newsstand. She knowed I were there but showed no sign as I walk on by.

'Seventy-five metres on your two o'clock,' Comanche gabbed in my lug-piece. 'Street table, Bonanza Café. Wide-brim straw hat, dark green jacket, blue jeans, trainers. Drinking a cup of something hot.'

I spotted the lass right then. If she got half the field savvy I spected, she wudda knowed I were there. After all, I were the boss of the invention she also been watching in Berlin unter dem Himalaya and probs lotsa udda places we never knowed of.

I moved tward her casual, like I were heading for Stoker gaff.

Closer, closer.

The jane zactly matched Comanche's previo description. As far as it went – which were not far. Which, in turn, were down to Grey Lady counter-sveylance smarts. All as I could tell were that she were late mid age, avrage build, avrage height. There were nada about this lass what weren't not avrage.

'What you wanna do, boss?' Comanche asked in my lug-piece.

'When gets the udda side of her,' I tattled, 'we move in pincerwise.'

Comanche never needed telling we gotta do this sly. Littlest mistake and Grey Lady wudda maked us instant.

She maked us anyway.

She sprinkled some mickles and mimes on the café table and giddy-upped cross the street. Me and Comanche went after her. As we was closing in she ducked into a fancy dress store. Partygoers was filling the aisles, hunting up costumes, trying em on, fooling around. Not by chance she picked this gaff. Smart work.

I keeped my slots on Grey Lady's straw sombrero and moved in, Comanche following and –

Come viz-to-viz with a pair of cowboys tryna twirl their six-shooters. I tried to shove past one of them but crashed into smin solid. Stepping back, I realized it were never two cowboys, but one gogging hisself in a long mirror. This were what I banged into.

I feeled like a fragwit.

The cowpoke gogged at me like I were eastbound but I pushed him aside, thundybolting down the next aisle –

Into the path of a circus clown. As I were tryna get by him, I shoulder-barged Draclar, then bumped into Wonder Woman, Winston Churchill, a nun in fishnets. Shoving em aside, I cracked on.

We was halfway cross the shop floor when I stopped and turned to Comanche. 'What if she aready changed into some costume – like Porno Mother Theresa there – and we gone right by?'

'It's a risk.' Comanche zeroed me grim. 'But if I were her, I'd head straight through the store and out the back, knowing we'd be standing here thinking exactly this. We can't check everyone in the store and we can't waste any more time.'

Comanche were right. Off we set. There were no back entrance but Comanche spotted a mergency exit side door. Flashing my shield, I asked a sales lass if she zeroed smon with a straw hat go out that way. The sales lass yo-nodded and on we went, through the side door, onto the street.

'Zuck and musk!' I cussed, specking the herds of shoppers and party spuds milling jostly in all directions.

There was four options: left, right, straight on, or double back. She cudda taked any.

Plus, how long had we been in the costume store? She cudda vanished even in ten secs. And we cuddabin off the scent much longer with the cowboy and clown and Churchill and all.

'Boss!' Comanche grabbed by arm. 'Left on Abingdon Street, hundred metres!'

I zeroed the straw sombrero proaching the corner of Talbot Street. But tween us was some kinda hen party with a *Sound of Music* theme. There was more janes dressed as nuns in fishnets, coupla lasses in Maria gear with silicone penises strapped to their fuseboxes; a Captain von Trapp in a Tyrolean jacket and a thong; and a lass wearing split-crotch lederhosen and toting a six-foot blow-up cock. We barged tangly through this horde. We closed the distance, all focus on the straw hat, the dark green jacket.

Grey Lady turned left onto Talbot.

We followed, running panty.

Gaining… gaining… gaining …

I dived at her, wrapping my gypsies round her waist. We tumbled wriggly to the pavement.

'Gotcha!' I skriked, pinning her by her shoulders.

'Boss, I don't think you have.' Comanche were kneeling next to me. 'This isn't the woman.'

I pulled back, zamining the lass under me. Comanche were right. This jane were much younger – praps thirties, praps a junkie, praps homeless, praps both. And she stinked bad.

'Who the zuck is you?' I gabbed.

She zeroed me feral. 'Who the zuck is *you*?'

I got my shield, pushed it in her viz.

'You a nabber, so what?' She tried to squirm free hut I holded her fast. 'Why you attacked me?'

I let her stand and backed off. The reek of baccy, booze and body filth were one zuck of a defence mech.

'Why were you wearing that hat,' Comanche gabbed, 'and that coat?'

'Zuck off, bitch.' Stinky Jane zeroed Comanche withry. 'I ain't not no snitch and I never tattles to no nabs.'

Comanche's punch sended her back to the sidewalk.

I give Comanche a hard speck. 'Did you gotta to bojo her so hard?'

Comanche rolled her slots. 'We want her to talk, don't we?'

'She can't tattle nada if she's out cold.' I taked Stinky Jane by the gipsy and tugged her up.

'You got three choices,' I telled her. 'I can let my friend bojo you some more; we can tattle at the Big Cop Shop; or you can answer the quesh right now.'

Stinky Jane nursed her bleedy viz, specking Comanche wary. 'This old lass come up to me outta no place. Telled me she gimme a fifty frog bill if I weared the hat and jacket and legged to Talbot Street.'

Anudda smart play, I thinked. Grey Lady spotted a downy-outy what obvio needed gelt and used the lass to monkey me and Comanche. Then she wudda switchbacked and left us chasing Stinky Jane.

I telled her we needed the bank note for spection, though I knowed Grey Lady were way too smart to leave DNA or dedo prints or anything help for us.

Stinky Jane opened her gobbler to argue but Comanche taked her by the choker and slammed her against the wall, frisking her with her free grasper. No luck with the front search so Comanche spinned her round and finded the fifty frog note in her cut crack. Cuddabin worser, I spozed. If she had more time it wuddabin up her vance-hole.

I telled her she could get the gelt from the Big Cop Shop when we was done zamining it. Meantime, she were free to go. She wandered off, rubbing her bruised cheek and grumbling of nabber vilence.

We legged to the prom-prom-prom and taked a rest on a wooden bench. Grey Lady beat us again and we flected on how she cudda got them field skills. But, like last time, we come to a dead end foot-down ferrari. All we knowed were them smarts gotta come from some murky state agency. Just as portant, I gabbed, were how, or if this were linked to the doing in of Stoker Fangly. Were Grey Lady part of some black ops team? This putted us back into tricksy plitiko shit and I aready done nuff capwork on that to gimme a sore fusebox.

After some while, I turned to Comanche. Like me, she were hot, sweaty and still jacked on drenaline.

'I could use a drink,' I gabbed. 'You?'

She gimme a yo-nod.

'I got cold beer and a bottle of single malt at the hotel. How's that sound?'

'Sounds real good,' she tattled. 'Just one thing first.'

I frowned puzzly. 'What?'

She come close, closer yet, ziff in slo-mo. Then she pressed her gobbler on mine. This time, no stractions, no dither. Her puckers glided silky moist on mine. If they were any friction in that snog I never wudda knowed. Then again, if they were a nuke blast right there, right then, I never wudda knowed that neither.

I waked next morning as Comanche padded naked to the bathroom and turned on the shower.

The night previo I got the best sex since, well, mebbe ebba. We drinked a few beers and a little whiskey. Then we went to it uber peppy. Comanche were hot and strong. But she were never clumsy, never hasty. She rided me like she rided her Vincent, caressing and coaxing, smimes frisky, smimes sprizing gentle.

When I heared the shower running, I taked a smoke from Comanche's pack and lighted it. Shudda never started again, but I were in a zuck-it mood.

Shudda never zucked Comanche neither but after that almost-kiss in the parking garage, smin were gonna happen us sooner or later.

I taked a long drag on the smoke and thinked on what this might mean. As a one-off, nada. But I knowed this were no one-off. Wu Mei were not gonna be happy and that gotta mean trouble. Right now, though, I sucked my smoke and dwelled in the fugitive joy of just me and Comanche in that hotel room.

That moment died sudden when my phone ringed. It were Wu Mei. At first I thinked she knowed what had gone on with me and Comanche. But I soon scovered diffrent.

'I'm in Rio de Jerusalem,' she tattled. 'The authorities have received credible intelligence on the whereabouts of Family Guy. I think we have the bastard.'

35

RIO DE JERUSALEM, BRAZIL

When the arrow plane was airborne Bob Puritan read a message on his phone. 'We'll get a full briefing from the Harpo when we land.'

'The Harpo?'

'*Häresie-Polizei* – Heresy Police.'

'Why the German name?'

Bob pocketed his phone. 'The Trumpian law enforcement system was founded two hundred years ago in a German-speaking community in the South Region of Brazil. The idea of a religious police caught on right across the federation and the Harpo's first director-general was Manfred Luther-Koenig, hence *Häresie-Polizei* and the contraction *Harpo*.'

I had to admit German speakers had a rare gift for turning longwinded titles into cool and often chilling acronyms – like the *Kripo* (pronounced Creepo), the abbreviation for the *Kriminal-Polizei*, CID in English.

Then there had been the *Stasi*, from the *Ministerium für Staatssicherheit* in Cold War East Germany. And the big daddy of them all, the Nazi *Geheime-Staatspolizei – Gestapo*. There were lots of others – including, of course, the word *Nazi* itself.

'You might think of the Harpo,' Puritan explained, 'as a synthesis of the Gestapo, the Soviet KGB, the Spanish Inquisition and, in particular, the ultra-misogynistic *Gašt-e Eršād* – religious police – of Iran.'

'Them Harpo spuds is cut-holes,' Bogart added. 'Musk em off, they zuck you up bad.'

I didn't care to think what it would be like working as a woman with the Holy Trumpian Empire's instrument of terror. Nor what the second oldest Marx brother might make of his stage name being used in this way.

'Tweetie Pie is right,' Comanche added. 'I've had dealings with just about every law enforcement and security agency on the planet and the Harpo are by far the worst.'

'But ain't you gabbing the Harpo is the best?' Bogart's tone was provocative. 'If they is the worst for you scummy crims, they gotta be good for us law abiders.'

'No I ain't not not not, you fucking pea-brain.' Comanche reacted as I knew she would. 'What I mean is they have unchecked power and sadistic licence.'

I made a cough and came to my feet. 'Comanche, a word please. In private.'

She followed me to the rear cabin and shut the door.

'I know, I know,' she said. 'But Bogart pisses me off – '

The rest of her words were silenced my mouth pressing on hers. We kissed long and hard and borderline aggressive. It was entirely unprofessional but I didn't care. If I wasn't really here, if I didn't exist, it didn't matter. And even if I was really here and did exist, it still didn't matter.'

When we finally broke the embrace, she gave me a forlorn look. 'I don't know where this is going.'

'Nor me,' I said. 'But it will be fun to find out.'

Her face stayed solemn. 'There's a lot about me you don't know.'

'That will be even more fun to find out.'

She craned forward and kissed me again. This time, though, the desire had been replaced by something else. Urgency perhaps; desperation even.

I thought of her sixteen-year-old daughter – the one she didn't know I knew about; the one whose safety depended on Comanche's many enemies not finding out about. I was certain this was the source of her despondency but there was nothing I could do. I'd been sworn to secrecy by Wu Mei, but more importantly, Comanche knowing that I knew would only heighten her anxieties.

---
*

When we returned to the forward cabin, Bob was fixing himself a coffee. 'There are some other things you should know about the Holy Trumpian Empire, boss,' he said. 'The ground rules of gender, if you like – although I'm sure you won't.'

I waited as he poured a small carton of milk into his coffee.

I knew from what he and others had told me that Trumpian women were oppressed by a theocratic patriarchy in a way that made the Shiite ayatollahs of my era seem like freewheeling liberals. Clearly, though, I needed to know more before we landed.

Stirring his coffee, Puritan came to sit in front of me. 'You'll have heard a lot of bad things about the treatment of women in Trumpia,' he said. 'You shouldn't believe them. The truth is much worse.'

I glanced at Comanche, sitting diagonally opposite, and she nodded her agreement.

'Women in the empire have similar rights to chattel slaves in antebellum American South. Which is to say, none. Trumpian females can be bought and sold, are forbidden from owning anything, and can be beaten – even killed – by their husbands without consequence. They are not allowed outdoors unless on a lead and wearing a "chastity orb". These resemble motorcycle helmets and are operated remotely by their husbands. Features include vision-restricting blinkers as well as audio blockers that can be turned on and off by husbands or "responsible males". The leashes and orbs are, according to the authorities, intended to protect women from themselves by curtailing their ability to seduce and fornicate with weak-willed men.'

'Like you see women doing all the time in the public spaces of Scientia and PopRep®©.' Comanche spoke with angry sarcasm.

'I'm not defending it.' Puritan sounded usually exasperated. 'I'm explaining it.'

He went on more evenly, 'There are, of course, moderates like me who want rid of the whole oppressive theocracy. But we are few and our voices are often stifled.'

'By them scroaty Harpo spuds,' Wham!®© added.

'Exactly.' Puritan's old hearing aid started its R2D2ese monologue and he adjusted the volume with an irate expression.

'But if women are so severely restricted,' I said, 'how will Comanche and I operate in Trumpia?'

'You will be cleansed.' Puritan was still fiddling with a tiny dial on his hearing device.

I made a suspicious frown and asked how that would work.

Finally, he finished his adjustments and looked up with a more obliging expression. 'It's a formality,' he said. 'You will simply be issued with digital trumpifixes that will give you complete freedom of movement, along with all the rights enjoyed by men.'

I gave him a puzzled look.

'The trumpifix is similar to a crucifix,' he said, 'but with the top cut off to resemble the letter T for Trump, worshipped as a second cousin of God and best friend of Jesus.'

I thought of the T symbol in Aldous Huxley's *Brave New World*. In that novel, the sign of the cross was replaced by the sign of the T, from the Model T Ford – the world's first mass produced car. I didn't think Henry Ford would be worshipped much in the Holy Trumpian Empire though.

'The ones you'll get,' Bob went on, 'will be fitted with a microchip that tells the Harpo and other state authorities that you are cleansed and must, therefore, we treated as if you were men.'

'So how come some women can have these so-called male privileges and others can't?'

'The overwhelming majority of women can't,' Puritan said. 'There are no hard and fast rules, but in general you need a husband with a few billion shekels to donate to the Holy Quadity – in other words, state coffers – and/or a husband of religious or political significance.'

This made sense, I guessed, in the way a dictionary without any words made sense, or removing the horses from Manet's *Horse Race in Longchamp* made sense.

'I once tried to blag my way into Trumpia,' Comanche said. 'but it didn't work so well. All Harpo men carry UFADs – "Unaccompanied Female Alert Detectors" and Harpo are everywhere. I was arrested before I got half a block.'

'What did they do to you?' I asked.

'I was publicly thrashed and deported back to Scientia.' Comanche sounded disturbingly blasé. 'But I'd learned my lesson the time I went back to Trumpia.'

'Clearly you hadn't,' I said. 'Otherwise you wouldn't have gone back.'

Comanche gave me a sidelong look. 'I was contracted to do a job in Constantinople, Texas so I had no choice. Also, I knew a tech whiz who owed me a favour. He cooked up a fake trumpifix microchip and I got the job done without getting stopped once. In fact – '

'The point is,' Puritan cut in, 'you won't need fakes and you won't need to worry about the Harpo. In fact, Wu Mei will be the ranking officer for this operation. The Harpo chiefs will absolutely hate it, but the order will come from Judgment Jesusly himself.'

This sounded very grand, though I got the impression that we we'd been set up to play one chess match while moves were being made in a different game we knew nothing about.

---
*

The arbeiterbots of Scientia may not have builded Jerusalem on England's green and pleasant land, but they *had* reconstructed the holy city on Brazil's Janeiro River in the place where Rio once stood.

As we came in to land at Holy Ghost International, Puritan explained the huge statue of Christ the Redeemer was all that remained of the old city of Rio de Janeiro. Through the window I saw that Christ the Redeemer was accompanied by an equally enormous effigy built of a burnt orange substance that I'd never seen before.

'That's Trump the Triumphant,' Bob said.

Then I saw the side-parted quiff and the too-long tie and thought, *of course it is.*

'But why no Rio?'

'The city was considered too hedonistic,' Puritan said. 'So the Founding Fathers of Trumpia had the remains of Post-Calamity Rio de Janeiro demolished to make way for Rio de Jerusalem.'

'No worries though boss,' Bogart chipped in, 'Us PopReppers rebuilded Rio de Rhône on the Med coast of Old France. We gotted a monstabigmost statue of Ole Jesu too, but not the Orange One. He just been de-Godded by Vox Popeye®© when our Rio were structed. Though he were *re*-Godded after.'

We were met off the plane by Wu Mei, who was standing at the head of a convoy of six SUVs. The body of each vehicle was riding low and I guessed they were armour-plated.

'You ready for the Harpo briefing?' she asked as we walked across the apron. 'It's important that you and your people can move quickly on this.'

I told her we were ready.

She gave me the names of the two senior Harpo officers we'd be meeting and directed us to the fourth SUV. I expected her to follow, but she went to the vehicle in front. Wu Mei was a cold fish any day of the week, but there was something oddly taciturn about her manner and I wondered if she'd found out about Comanche and me.

We were driven to *Beit Aghion*, the historic residence of Israeli prime ministers, at Smolenskin and Balfour streets. There wasn't much to see as we coasted along empty highways and silent streets.

'Today is Monday, the Second Sabbath,' Puritan explained. 'That means nobody is allowed outdoors unless they are attending Sacred Worship. The same goes for Sunday, the First Sabbath.'

'Except the Harpo,' Comanche said. 'The Harpo are as good as their motto: *Semper Ubique* – always everywhere.'

36

Nothing said brutal dictatorship like jackboots and jodhpurs. A squad of Harpo troopers, uniformed in the trademark garb, was standing at attention outside the entrance to *Beit Aghion*. This was a squat structure that looked more like a stack of Weetabix biscuits than the official residence of a mighty ruler.

Two officers emerged from the building and came towards us. The more senior man would be Harpo's commander-in-chief, Witchfinder General Derek Anti-Satan. He was a slight, short man, early fifties, with stoaty features and black eyes magnified by round-framed glasses. I thought he looked more like Stalin's henchman Lavrentiy Beria than Lavrentiy Beria. Multiple decks of medals formed a glittering breastplate across the front of his gilt-trimmed tunic. He was known as the Fist of God and judging from what we'd heard from Puritan on the drive over, the moniker wasn't unmerited.

The second man was Chief Special Inquisitor All-Saints Geddes who had been leading the inquiry in Rio de Jerusalem and would technically be my number two.

Unlike his boss, Geddes was tall and athletic-looking with affable expression. His cap was titled at a jaunty angle and his face smooth skinned with powder-blue eyes. I wasn't fooled by any of this apparent civility. According to Puritan, Geddes was the knuckleduster to Anti-Satan's fist.

Wu Mei made the introductions and indicated a group of reporters, photographers and camera crews being herded by Harpo troopers from the side of an outbuilding. I never saw a more biddable bunch of media people – including at the PR event at the Élysée Palace in Paris-sur-Euphrète. Even the Harpo troopers seemed more at ease than these guys. Not so much a hack-pack as a hack-flock.

They formed an orderly crescent around us. Wu Mei told them who each of us was and invited questions.

A young TV reporter pushed a microphone towards me. 'May I ask, ma'am, how confident are you of making a quick arrest?'

'We have some strong lines of inquiry,' I said, 'and we are here to chase them down.' I felt ambushed by this unexpected encounter and was determined not to give any hostages to fortune.

Anti-Satan made a discreet cough and stepped forward. 'First Father Jesusly has placed immense faith in Detective Superintendent Miller and her team – including our own well-known advocate Bob Puritan – and we are confident in her abilities. Every soul in the federation has been praying to the Donald for deliverance from this monster among us.'

A man in a sackcloth suit with wild boar hair and the sign of the T daubed in ashes on his forehead moved his microphone towards Anti-Satan. He spoke as if I wasn't there. 'If I may presume to inquire, Witchfinder General, sir, is a woman the most Godly – and indeed Trumply – choice for this important work?'

I sensed news antennae twitching. Other media men redirect their microphones and TV cameras.

Anti-Satan smiled at the questioner. 'I understand your concern, Pilgrim Guru Japeth. However, this commandment was given direct by the Lord Our God to the First Father. And the Lord Our God said, "First Father Jesusly, you shall appoint Miranda Miller to lead this Holy Quest".'

There was an excited babble from the hack-flock but the man called Guru Japeth stayed focused. 'Witchfinder General, sir, may I quote the Lord Our God as having spoken thus? And if so, are His words embargoed until any particular time?'

Anti-Satan's smile stayed put. 'The Lord Our God also told the First Father that his words were not subject to embargo and for immediate release to the media. So, yes, Pilgrim Guru Japeth, you may use that quote right away – as all you pilgrims here-present this day may use it.'

With the meat of their story delivered, the reporters and camera crews were dismissed and I was escorted with my team into *Beit Aghion*. The unadorned plainness of the interior was much the same as the exterior. *Functional* was the word that came to mind as we crossed an understated lobby and entered a corridor that made me think mid-market hotel chain.

'*Beit Aghion* is for show,' Bob whispered as we walked. 'It has been kept this way for reasons of historical accuracy but Jesusly doesn't live here. He has an out-of-town palace for his domestic requirements.'

The witchfinder general lead us through a modest reception area to a meeting room with chairs around a long table.

Here we were greeted by the First Father of the Holy Trumpian Empire, Judgment Jesusly. As I shook his hand I noted that he'd swapped the Italian silk suit he wore at our last meeting for a more folksy bootlace tie and country music style jacket with treble clef breast motifs in black piping.

'Welcome, y'all, to *Beit Aghion*.' His full-fat west Texas accent sounded even more pronounced here in Trumpia. He looked at Anti-Satan. 'Derek, I want you and your boys at Harpo to give Randy here every assistance she needs. That clear?'

Anti-Satan said yes, Pilgrim First Father, entirely clear.

He turned to Geddes. 'And All-Saints, Randy is the senior investigating office on this case – you know the lay of the land locally, but she knows this fiend we're after better than anyone.'

Geddes made an accommodating expression. 'Understood, Pilgrim First Father, sir.'

'And you will all, of course, report in the first instance to FIB Director-in-Chief Wu Mei.'

Wu Mei made a gracious nod.

'Now, as this is an operational meeting I'm, gonna leave you lawdogs to it.'

As he made his way to the door, I wondered why we'd been brought to his official residence if he wasn't taking part in the briefing.

Then I thought of the media opportunity and it made a worrying sort of sense. I'd been endorsed by the First

Father as well as by the Witchfinder General; I was leading this operation – ahead of a senior Harpo man; and my name and face would be all over the state media. This was why Jesusly wanted me in Trumpia so badly. Because he was, I suspected, very publicly hanging me out to dry.

As if the emphasize this, he paused on the threshold, and gave me a direct stare. 'Randy, I do hope you can make more progress here than you have so far. A lot's riding on catching this bastard. You hear me?'

'I do, sir,' I said.

When the First Father had shut the door behind him, Geddes handed Comanche and me our digitized trumpifixes, Harpo shields and shoulder-holstered pistols – I presumed Wu Mei had already received her accreditation.

When we were seated around the table, the special chief inquisitor began the briefing with an audio-visual presentation.

'This is our person of interest.' he pushed a laptop key and a man's face appeared on a screen at the end of the table. We were looking at a middle-aged individual with a bulbous brow and hairline so receded that all we could see was a faint ginger fuzz at the top of his head. His grey eyes were wide-spaced and small; his mouth was broad over a small jaw; the nose snubby with dense nasal hair bristling from cavernous nostrils. The overall impression was a face that had been stretched sideways by a distorted mirror. He was wearing a sloppily knotted mustard tie and mismatched plaid shirt. If ever there was a man who didn't give a shit about his appearance, this was him.

'Meet Charles-Henry McMartyr,' Geddes said, 'a lecturer in comparative cultural demography at Holy

Quadity University here in Rio de Jerusalem. This fellow came to our attention after an anonymous tip-off from a man claiming to be a member of McMartyr's faculty.'

Geddes scanned the room, as if to make sure we were all paying attention. 'According to the voice message left by the informant, McMartyr has always been obsessed by serial killers – allegedly from an academic standpoint – but his so-called research had recently plunged to fresh depths of deviancy.'

Geddes leaned over the laptop to change the slide and we saw an image of a family slaughtered by Family Guy; then another; and another; and more and more as Geddes tapped the laptop key.

'According to our informant,' Geddes said, 'McMartyr claims to be using these images as part of a research paper on the metrics of wickedness in the context of serial killers. His thesis is that Family Guy tops the index.'

I leaned forward on my elbows. 'And, what? You hypothesize that this premier league of serial killers could be a reflection of Family Guy's narcissism, compiled by Family Guy himself?'

'We thought it possible.' This was Anti-Satan. 'And certainly enough to investigate McMartyr further.'

Geddes went on, 'We listened to his phone conversations and read his messages. It seems he is actively trading in these depraved photographs.'

I examined the image still on the screen. 'Are the pictures genuine?'

The chief special inquisitor shrugged. 'We were hoping you could tell us that.'

'Very well,' I said, 'I'll look into it.'

'Next, we ran some routine checks,' Geddes said. 'And his passport was scanned by border control officers at all the crime scene locations around the times of Family Guy's "born again" murders.'

Interesting stuff, I thought.

But Geddes wasn't done. 'We then contacted colleagues through InterNab who carried out some door-to-door work. They found witnesses who saw McMartyr in each of the areas where Family Guy struck most recently – Fremont Street in Las Vegas, England and in Führerbunker Platz in Berlin unter dem Himalaya.'

I was about to protest about not having been told, but Wu Mei raised her hand. 'I knew about this, Miranda, but you and your team had a lot on your plate and this may well have come to nothing. In retrospect, I should have alerted you and for this, I apologize.'

I was royally pissed off but there was no point letting it show. And besides, I couldn't refuse an apology from the director-in-chief of the FIB. So I forced a smile and said I agreed she had done the right thing.

'What are your thoughts, Superintendent Miller?' Anti-Satan asked.

I wondered why they hadn't moved on McMartyr already and said so.

'We can't risk a false arrest,' Geddes said. 'Because if we collared McMartyr and Family Guy struck again, we'd look like a bunch of fools.'

'Also,' added Anti-Satan with a thin smile, 'McMartyr would have a huge compensation claim and there would be a fat pay-cheque for our friend Counsellor Puritan here.'

Bob said nothing though I could guess his thoughts.

The Harpo men had made sure it was my head on the block, not theirs. And with Puritan as part of the team making the arrest, he'd be conflicted out of any litigation.

I looked from Geddes to Anti-Satan. 'Next steps?'

Anti-Satan's reply was predictable. 'You're in charge, Superintendent.'

37

After the long, dead quiet of the sabbaths life had returned to abnormal on the streets of Rio de Jerusalem.

Puritan agreed to walk with me from our rooms at the Waldorf Astoria on Gershon Argon Street to our incident room at the Harpo offices on Shne'ur Kheshin Street while Comanche and Wham!®© went by car. I insisted on going on foot because I needed to get a feel for this place and that would have to start by walking its streets.

Even though I'd been told what to expect, the scenes on the mall section of Queen Shlomziyon Street were a shock. Every woman I saw was wearing a spherical maroon helmet – an "obedience orb" – and was linked to her husband by a synthetic cord leash. Many were clad in grey robes from their neck to their ankles. A few, though, strolled along the street in bikinis with half-cup tops and thong bottoms and high-heel shoes. Their skin was ochre and smooth and their hips moved with an accentuated sway. Yet they wore the same obedience orbs as the women in robes.

'Trophy wives,' Puritan explained, 'owned by rich men who like to show them off.'

As we talked, four nearly naked women appeared from a department store, attached by leads of different colours to a bald, chubby man in his late middle years.

I said they looked outrageous and Puritan agreed. 'The authorities justify this by reference to the scripture that tells of how the Donald had sex with the porn star Stormy Daniels before taking her as his wife and bringing her to the Lord.'

'But Trump never married Stormy Daniels, still less bringing her into the fold of the religious right. He paid her to have sex with him and that was the end of it.'

'You know that and so do I.' Bob gave me one of his weary, gap-toothed smiles. 'But these people don't and nor do they want to.'

A commotion ahead caught my attention. There was a series of yelps and shouts before a robe-clad woman came running down the street, a red light flashing on top of her obedience orb.

A Harpo street cop targeted her with a taser-like device.

The woman's orb made a loud buzzing noise, the red light turned green, and she crumpled to the ground. Her husband came forward carrying the unattached leash with a look of what's-a-guy-to-do? abashment.

The Harpo man gave him a stern look. Did the husband know how dangerous runaway wives could be? What if she'd escaped and corrupted some innocent male? On this occasion the husband would be let off with a warning. However, the event had been recorded and if this wife slipped her leash gain, there would be serious consequences – a heavy fine for the husband and the wife may even have to be put down.

'This is appalling,' I said.

Puritan looked at me with an expression half way between concern and pity. 'This is just the beginning, boss. I'm afraid there's worse to come.'

As we got closer to the intersection with Jaffa Street I spotted two women without orbs crossing the road. They wore sharp silk pant suits and moved with an assurance that I found bewildering. One asked a Harpo man for directions and he answered obligingly, tipping his cap as they approached him.

'Cleansed women,' Puritan said. 'Like you and Comanche.'

'Except Comanche and I aren't married to powerful dickheads.'

'What, like him?'

He nodded towards a tall man wearing a peculiar hat that looked like a bishop's mitre with the curved brim of a Stetson. He was coming towards us along the centre of the sidewalk, decked out in a purple satin frock-coat with gold lapel facings. A diamond-encrusted trumpifix hung on a gold chain from his neck. People hurried aside to make way and I sensed a feeling of panic and awe ripple along the street.

As he drew nearer, I made out bold features – jutting jaw, long nose and shiny brown eyes.

He touched his hat to Puritan as he walked by and Puritan made a short bow.

'Who is that?'

'Judge-Bishop San Miguel Jeffreys.' Bob gave me a dour look. 'Also known as Microwave Mike on account of his fondness for sending people to the Oven.'

'He was the judge who sentenced your elderly female client to death by microwave, wasn't he?'

Puritan nodded and watched Microwave Mike disappear among the shoppers. 'He's an oceangoing arsehole. But there are others as bad.'

A little further down the street we entered a business district. There were professional services firms and banks, stockbrokers and corporate head offices. But others too, that I'd never heard of.

I turned to Puritan. 'What's an indulgence broker?'

'Indulgences can be bought from the Office of Anti-Heresy in much the same way as in pre-Reformation Christian Europe. No matter what sin you've committed, you can acquire an official certificate of indulgence – for the right price. These brokers are the middle-men between the theocracy and rich sinners, or God's Givers as they are known.'

Through the front window of one indulgence broker I read the text of a large ad:

Save your eternal soul from the Flames of Hell *AND* save money! Huge discounts for multiple sinners - the more you sin, the more you save!

Across the street was a Post Mortem Realtor touting "Luxury graves to suit your pocket".

Puritan anticipated my question. 'With many religions of the past,' he said, 'the size of a soul's grave was fixed – a small, cramped space where you had to wait for Judgment

Day. But the Trumpian dogma states that the graves of souls awaiting judgment are infinitely expandable.'

'Let me guess,' I said, 'the bigger your bank account, the bigger your grave.'

'Some have three and four bedrooms, sea or mountain views, even swimming pools. But that's billionaire-oligarch territory.'

'But we're not talking about subterranean chambers, right?'

'Of course not. People are paying for afterlife real estate. Metaphysical or spiritual property if you like.'

I frowned. 'How crazy are these people?'

Puritan looked at me as if I should have known better and I took his point.

'They're only crazy,' he said, 'when observed from outside the sphere of their consciousness by people like you and me. But inside that sphere, everything makes perfect sense.'

'And what the fuck is this about?' I peered through the window of a post-mortem home improvement store and read the sales pitch on a banner-ad:

Taken your sinning a little too far?

Hell is hot – but you won't be with our
ultra-efficient air-conditioning systems
Interest-free finance – terms apply

Bob's gaze followed mine. 'The idea of spending eternity in the infernal pit without air-con is plenty to part wrongdoers from their cash. They see it as an insurance policy in case Judgment Day goes sideways.'

'This place is worse than Trump's America,' I said.

'That's a little harsh.' He made an ironic smile. 'Although you were there and I wasn't.'

38

Ten minutes later, we arrived at the Harpo Head Office and Heresy Correction Centre on Shne'ur Kheshin Street. This was a straggly complex of high walls topped with rusty razor-wire and gazed down upon by search-light towers. Entry and exit points were marked by candy-cane checkpoint poles, hydraulically raised traffic barriers and guards with assault rifles and body armour. I'd been expecting a grand statement of a building, like the SS-Gestapo building in Berlin-unter-dem-Himalaya, or perhaps the Lubyanka, once home to the KGB in Old Moscow. But this place looked more like a shanty town. It was located in the Russian Compound, close the magnificent Orthodox Cathedral of the Holy Quadity and the contrast could not have been sharper.

We walked to the main building where *DEATH TO HERETICS* had been emblazoned above the entrance. Inside, we presented our credentials at the front desk and were asked to wait in a reception area with cold metal seating and wall signs that forbade almost everything except breathing.

An enormous notice at the end of the room drew my attention and I went for a closer look. It was headed *The Thirteen Commandments (Exodus 20)* and laid out the twelve injunctions I recalled from high school religious education – with a strange addition:

13: Thou shalt <amend/delete as appropriate>

'This is an enlarged replica of a two-thousand-year-old parish newsletter found in the ruins of an Old World Anglican church,' Bob said.

'But it's obviously a typo.' I squinted and examined the poster more closely. 'The writer would have been using wordprocessor software set to auto-numbering with copy & paste. They must have accidentally hit the return key and somehow the error ended up in print.'

'That's the received wisdom among the cognoscenti.'

'So what happened? How could *13: Thou shalt <amend/ delete as appropriate>* possibly be interpreted as an extra commandment?'

I realized how naïve I was being before I ended the sentence.

'It's commonly known as the Harpo Commandment,' Bob said.

'You're going to tell me something horrible, aren't you?'

'This *is* the Holy Trumpian Empire.'

'Go on. Tell me the worst.'

We walked back to the seating area and sat as far as we could from the reception desk. 'The word "amend",' he explained, 'has been taken to mean physically altering a person, especially by amputation and mutilation. "Delete" translates into the Harpo lexicon as remove, eradicate, liquidate. And the phrase "as appropriate" is regarded as a divine right to maim or kill anyone deemed by the state to be suitable for the bone-saw, stoning pit or oven.'

'That's utterly absurd.'

Bob gave me a grim look. 'Try telling that to someone about to lose a leg or get stoned or microwaved to death.'

'Ah, Superintendent Miller, Counsellor Puritan!'

We turned to see Chief Special Inquisitor All-Saints Geddes striding towards us with a congenial smile.

'Welcome, welcome to your new home.'

He was here to take us to the second floor space we'd been allocated as an investigation room and asked us to follow him upstairs.

In the stairwell, a ululating shriek penetrated the cinderblock walls. I guessed it had come from some poor wretch being amended or deleted or both in the adjacent Heresy Detention Centre.

Geddes looked over his shoulder with an amused expression. 'Don't look so alarmed, Superintendent, those sounds are part of our psychological operations. No one is tortured here. However, detainees are often more willing to co-operate if they are in a conducive frame of mind.'

The wailing noises were guillotined when the stairwell door closed behind us and we went into the main administration block.

Geddes guided us into an area of glass-walled offices set up with desktop computers, a wall-mounted plasma screen, a crazy-board and other investigation room staples. There were no windows – I guessed to stop us seeing the people who weren't being tortured – and the fluorescent strip lighting leeched colour and lent the room a fuzzy staleness.

Geddes didn't stay long. Anything we needed, just call him. His office was only around the corner. Nothing would be too much trouble.

With Geddes gone, Puritan gave me a wry look. 'The word "torture" is forbidden in Harpo-ese. They prefer to say that they *shrive* detainees here at the Happy House, as it's colloquially known.'

Comanche and Wham!®© had arrived earlier and were waiting in the conference room for the team meeting I'd called.

Bogart piped up first, clearly excited. 'Boss, we just gotted the lab results on the Family Guy crime scene pics what them Harpo spuds found at McMartyr's gaff. Fakes, all of em – but real good uns what quired real spensive quipment.'

This was fast work. I was impressed.

And puzzled.

'They must have got started last night. But isn't all work in the Holy Trumpian Empire prohibited on the sabbaths?'

Bob made a humourless chuckle. 'When Derek Anti-Satan says jump, folks here go running for their vaulting poles.'

'I'm not surprised,' I muttered. 'Who wouldn't?'

I wasn't surprised, either, about the high quality fake photos. I could imagine a thriving black market for that sort of merchandise and Family Guy obsessives like McMartyr would be regular customers. Moreover, a narcissistic individual like Family Guy would get all sorts of pay-offs from crime scene porn produced in his name.

'I want to find out more about McMartyr,' I said to the group. 'Childhood, career, social life, friends and associates, rivals and enemies. Also, any low-level antecedents outside the Holy Trumpian Empire that may have gone under the radar. Juvenile offences too – particularly serial killer tooth-cutting activity such as cruelty to pets and other animals.'

'Anti-animal stuff wouldn't have been low-level in Scientia, boss,' Comanche said, 'even in the juvie court.'

This was a good point. 'Very well, concentrate on PopRep®©, but keep in mind that no system is infallible. If we draw a blank in the Land of the Wordless Dictionary, we'll need to refocus on Scientia.'

'But ain't we gonna collar this scroaty spud right away now, boss?' Wham!®© sounded disappointed.

'Anti-Satan and Geddes will be expecting swift action,' Puritan added. 'As will Jesusly.'

'Not until I'm ready.' I glanced around their faces to make sure they were taking my point. 'If McMartyr *is* Family Guy, he'll have many more resources than your average college tutor. I don't want him slipping through our fingers because we moved too quickly. We secure the ground. Then we consider our options. You all on board with this?'

There was a nodding of heads, then I turned to the assignment of work. I asked Puritan to talk to McMartyr's campus colleagues because I was sure he'd tell the wily lawyer much more than Geddes' Harpo goons. Comanche's job was to check out black market sales for Family Guy and other serial killer porn, while Wham!®©

would look into any misdemeanour raps McMartyr might have picked up in PopRep®©.

As they were filing from my office, Wham!®© turned back. 'Boss, I gotta confesh.'

I didn't need long to realize what it was about. 'It's Plato Tomsky, isn't it?'

He looked shamefaced. 'You gotta unstand that what happened ain't not my fault. I never knowed nada. Swear on all what's orange.'

I found myself believing him and asked what had happened.

'Plato rived in Rio de Jerusalem with his film crew first thing. But I never told him nada. Trump alone knows how he scovered we was here.'

'Don't worry, Bogart, you're not in trouble.' I gave him a reassuring smile. 'I'm sure Plato has a lot of sources. And he'd have found out where we are in any case after the press conference was broadcast this morning.'

'Smin else, boss.'

I frowned.

'Plato and his spuds is waiting out on the street. They wanna come in to do some filming.'

My frown deepened.

'Just a bit of footage of us at work,' he said. 'Nada portant or senstive.'

I saw the need in Bogart's eyes. He hated the PopRep®© establishment and was determined to make his own way in a tough world. Just as importantly, he needed a career to go back to when this was over. And Plato Tomsky's backing would be important to both. Moreover, I had agreed that Tomsky could be the investigation's documentary maker.

'Okay,' I said. 'He can come in for thirty minutes, no longer. And I don't want anything – you hear me Bogart? – *anything* filmed that could compromise our work.'

'You got it, boss!'

The man who was more important than a million municipal workers arrived soon afterwards with his production team. He thanked me profusely for allowing this, then loped around the office with giraffe strides, weighing up camera angles, checking light readings, directing his team. When he was done filming his establishing scenes, I agreed to a five-minute interview. We sat in my office and I talked in general terms about the threat posed by Family Guy; how we were working several leads here in Jay-de-Jay; and how we wouldn't stop until we caught him. Nothing I said was remotely newsworthy. It was the sort of guff that would make the headlines if I'd said the opposite.

He was about to ask a final question when Wu Mei Leclerc entered the office.

---
*

She kept her manner professional while Tomsky and his people gathered their equipment and left. She was even moderately polite when she said she wanted to talk to me in my office.

I got both barrels, though, when she closed the door. What the holy fuck did I think I was doing letting Tomsky in here? How did I think that would look to the likes of Jesusly and Anti-Satan? Not to mention Confucius and Simz? How many times did she need to warn me about Tomsky? What did I think she'd meant when she told me not to trust him and not to let him get too close to the investigation?

I gave her my in-the-tent-pissing-out spiel and assured he this wouldn't happen again.

'It shouldn't have happened at all.'

I wanted to ask her what, beyond personal dislike, she had against Tomsky. But now was not the time. She seemed to be done tearing strips off me and I wanted to let this lie.

Until, this was, she turned to the next subject of her anger.

'I know about you and Comanche,' she said.

There was no point denying it.

'Most senior investigating officers would be dismissed for less,' she said.

'But I'm not most SIOs.' I was tired of taking this battering. 'And this isn't most investigations. So fire me if you want.'

'Don't think I wouldn't, she said, 'if it was within my power.' Almost to herself, she added, 'I never wanted you in the first place.'

'Sorry I'm not Harry Bosch,' I muttered. 'Or Miss Fucking Marple.'

She glared at me across the desk, but seemed to decide against continuing her rant.

'You must be as careful with Liz Comanche as with Plato Tomsky. They are both dangerous people albeit in very different ways.'

'How so?'

She paused to consider this. 'Tomsky and I have history going way back. Believe me when I tell you he's egotistical, unprincipled and highly ambitious.'

Perhaps enough to be challenging for a seat at the top table? I wondered. Did she hate him because he reminded her too much of herself?

Wu Mei stayed quiet. I gave her a nudge. 'And Comanche?'

'You know, of course, about her teenage daughter – the one she'd do anything to keep hidden. Well, she has a criminal past she'd also do anything to keep hidden.'

'I know about her background in organized crime, I already – '

'This isn't anything to do with organized crime.' Wu Mei cut across me quickly then seemed to realize she'd said too much.

She took a few moments to collect herself, then fixed me with a stern gaze. 'I can't tell you more because her records were sealed by order of the Supreme Court of Scientia as part of her deal with the Justice Department. But you should be very, *very* careful with Liz Comanche.'

I thought about this. I understood why old scores and new rivalries might have caused friction with Tomsky. But why was she trying to drive a wedge between Comanche and me? Where did this fit into the labyrinth of secrecy and deception and truth as a relative construct that Wu Mei inhabited?

'It goes without saying that this conversation stays between you and I. You can't say a word to Comanche – for her sake as much as anyone's.'

I gave her a defiant look.

Then I understood what she was getting at. If I mentioned to Comanche what Wu Mei had just told me, Comanche would realize I'd known about her daughter all along. She'd see my covert knowledge of her deepest secret as a betrayal. And that would be the end of me and Comanche.

So I nodded my agreement and walked her to the main exit of the Happy House.

On my way back to the office I entered the stairwell where the screams of heretics being amended and deleted as appropriate pierced the cinderblock walls. I was halfway to our second floor office space when

the world wobbled.

I slipped backwards, expecting to fall down the stairs.

But they had vanished. The whole Happy House had vanished, the whole of Rio de Jerusalem, the whole everything. I stopped sliding. I was standing on an open page of a vast book. I felt the grain of the paper under my feet, smelled the camphor-like odour of printed ink. Around me was a sea of serifed letters, each one enormous and fuzzy-edged. But this close up, I couldn't read them.

I knew this book though.

It was Nico Nyro's final novel in the Miranda Miller quintet – *The Big Happy*.

I was in the middle of its pages. Trapped yet somehow free. I was an unended sentence, a half-told tale. I needed a resolution.

But it wasn't here, it wasn't now.

I recalled my similar experience in the Parisian bookstore. That ended with my discovery of the Nico Nyro books. Now, though, as the illusion dispelled, there was nothing. No revelation, no new insight.

All I could see were the grey cinderblock walls, steeped in the wails of the untortured.

39

I decided to walk back to the hotel because I needed time alone. The conversation with Wu Mei had given me a lot to think about.

As I moved west along Shne'ur Kheshin Street, I noticed large illuminated billboard ads above the sidewalk.

One read: "*Have you beaten your wife today? You might not know why, but she will. Take home one of our quality leather whips, straps or restraints TODAY*".

Another asked: "*One of your wives giving you ear-ache? Why not have her tongue removed? Just 300 shekels. Credit available, rates apply*". After this I stopped looking.

At the Jaffa Street junction I entered Yosef Rivlin Street, a narrow thoroughfare with little bistros and bars that might be described as quirky or seedy depending on your proclivity for optimism.

The questions dominating my thoughts could be neither asked nor ignored. What was this criminal record of Comanche's that a senior judge had sealed? If it wasn't linked to her organized crime activities, then what? I had a strong suspicion that, in one way or another, it concerned her daughter. But how?

There was the issue of Wu Mei's motives. I knew I couldn't trust her, but even devious people told the truth when it suited them. Clearly Wu Mei had a problem with me having anything to do with Tomsky and Comanche. They were two very different individuals who didn't even know each other. At least not that I knew about. And the fragmented nature of Wu Mei's revelations told me she was only telling me these things when she absolutely had to. This suggested there was some truth in what she'd told me. But there was a huge question mark over what she *hadn't* said.

'Hey, wait up!'

My chance to reflect disintegrated as Comanche came hustling towards me.

I'd left the office discreetly because I needed time alone. And I was good at doing things unobserved. So Comanche must have been keeping a close eye on me. Then she'd obviously tailed me.

But why?

True, we were lovers in a relationship of sorts so maybe she just wanted to talk. But there'd be plenty of time for that back at the hotel, over dinner, or a drink.

Had Wu Mei had one of her sly chats with Comanche? One that manipulated her in a similar way as Wu Mei was manipulating me? Was I being excessively paranoid? Was that possible in this place?

'You're going somewhere in a hurry,' she said, slightly out of breath.

I forced a smile. 'Only back to the hotel. I could use a coffee that doesn't taste like the dirty dishwater from that dreadful Harpo vending machine.'

She said she'd join me if that was okay and I said yeah, sure it was okay. What else could I say?

As we walked further along the alley I noticed increasing numbers of people with physical disabilities – a man without ears; a woman with no legs; another without arms; a pig-faced boy lacking a nose.

Then I realized they weren't disabled in the usual sense but surgically mutilated. The human subtraction all around me was shocking. Everyone I saw was, in one way or another, incomplete. Not by a congenital problem at birth, or in a road accident, or a war. They'd been *made* incomplete. And it had been done with a precision and deliberateness that was beyond anything in my experience. Sure, punitive mutilation wasn't uncommon in medieval times and earlier. But this wasn't medieval times. This wasn't about a hand being hacked off with a battle-axe, or an ear with a rusty knife blade. These people had undergone hospital operations – I hoped under anaesthetic – carried out by surgeons in a digital society. They were not only disfigured by their amputations, they were defined by them.

'This neighbourhood is known as Satan's Waiting Room,' Comanche said. 'It's where state mutilatees are forced to live. Their families and former communities won't have anything to do with them in case they too become tainted by sin.'

'What? So sin is treated as if it's a virus? As if you can catch it from somebody?'

She nodded. 'These people eke out an existence in areas like this where liberal types use their services – shoe repairs, clothing alterations, carpentry and so on. There are also doctors, lawyers and accountants here who work at a fraction of the going rate. Liberal benefactors also donate money, clothing and food.'

'Liberals?' I gave her a baffled look. 'Here?'

'It's a relative term,' she said. 'But not everyone in Trumpia is a Harpo snitch or a bigoted sadist. There are good people who hate the system and defy it when possible.'

'Like Bob Puritan?'

'Exactly.'

'But, let me guess, they are massively outnumbered and have no political power?'

'You got it.'

'So why does the system allow them to help these poor fucked up sinners?'

We entered a quadrangle where folk with missing body parts were queueing outside a soup kitchen. 'The high-ups like to keep mutilatees down but not quite out. They want other people to see what happens if they step out of line.'

I wasn't sorry to leave the alley and enter the broad thoroughfare of Menashe Ben Israel Street.

Until the crowds of men began to appear. They reminded me of British soccer fans walking to a match – most were covered in tattoos and many bare-chested with huge flabby bellies. They bantered raucously, swigging beer from cans and munching burgers and kebabs. One started chanting "You're gonna get your fucking head caved in" and others joined in.

Comanche grabbed my arm and tried to stop me. 'Come on boss, we need to leave. Right now.'

I stood firm. 'But where are they going?'

'You don't want to know.' She made an imploring expression. 'You don't want to go there.'

'Yes, I do.'

She placed her hands on her hips and stared at the ground, shaking her head. At last she said, 'They're going to a stoning game.'

'A game? In which somebody is stoned to death?'

'I told you wouldn't want to know. Or see.'

'But I do,' I said. 'I've got to.'

With Comanche trailing behind, I followed the raucous, beer-chugging men to a disused parking lot near the junction of and Menashe Ben Israel and Gershon Argon. A crater-like amphitheatre had been excavated in the dusty ground. Crowds of men like those we came with were standing around the rim and perching on the slopes. Bookies were moving between them, taking bets.

Without turning, I asked Comanche what was going on.

'The stoning match is between two teams.' She pointed at a large wooden scoreboard displaying the names of the competitors – "The Rolling Stoners" and "Rock and a Hard Place". 'The bookies have just shortened the odds, making the Stoners very narrow favourites. That's why there's a rush to place bets.'

My focus turned to the rough ground on the amphitheatre floor. On one side were the two teams, each comprising four men. One was wearing blue baseball-style uniforms, the other red. Between them stood a man in a black and white striped shirt who I took to be the referee. In front of him was a steel brazier containing rocks of a similar size – bigger than pool balls but smaller than tennis balls.

'Tell me what's going to happen.'

Comanche moved in front of me, her face close to mine, lined with concern. 'It's still not too late to leave. Once you've see one of these spectacles you'll never be able to unsee it.'

'I'm staying.' I took her wrist and squeezed it. 'Now tell me how this works.'

Comanche glanced over her shoulder at the players, who were now limbering up. 'The game is especially cruel,' she said, 'because the team hitting the victim most *without* a kill is the winner. The losers are the team that kills first. As you can imagine, this is deliberately designed to prolong the suffering.'

'But where's the condemned person?'

She pointed to a galvanized metal bucket at the far end of the crater floor.

The referee walk across and raised it with a theatrical flourish like a chef lifting a cloche food cover at a posh restaurant.

At his feet was a teenage girl, buried her up to her neck in dirt.

The crowd roared.

The girl blinked in the sunlight. She couldn't have been older than fourteen.

The crowd roared even louder.

Comanche leaned close so I could hear her above the cheering. 'The word is that this girl was sent to the stoning pit because she refused to have sex with her husband. I'd bet my boots he's old enough to be her grandfather and she'd never had sex before.'

The referee went to the brazier and picked up a stone, apparently at random, then handed it to the first pitcher, a hefty Rolling Stoner. He went to a square marked-out in white chalk, perhaps twenty metres from the girl. There, he started tossing the missile up and down, assessing its weight and trajectory.

Comanche was right: I'd never be able to un-experience this. But then I'd never want to. Because if that were possible, I'd have become a monster like these men.

I looked back at the girl. I saw no fear on her face, no defiance, no anger, just horrible adolescent self-consciousness. Her eyes darted from the pitcher to the referee, as if to say, 'I'm so very sorry to put you to all this trouble.'

This is the last day of the rest of your life, I thought. *And you're more concerned with not making too much of a fuss.*

That was what cut me deepest – her humanness until the very last.

The pitcher adopted a throwing stance and cocked his arm.

The crowd went quiet.

The referee blew his whistle.

The rock struck the teenaged girl between the eyes. Her head snapped back, then lolled forward, forehead in the dirt.

Howls of outrage came up from the crowd.

The referee rushed to the girl, shoving her head back. But I could tell from the glaze on her eyes and the deep wound on her forehead that she was dead.

My eyes followed those of the spectators to Comanche, standing at the base of the slope.

'She threw it!' somebody shouted. 'I saw her do it!'

Instinctively, I crossed the rough ground, placing myself between Comanche and the group of men forming around her. She and I may have been "cleansed" women, but that didn't seem to count for much right then. Comanche's mercy killing had cheated these men of their entertainment. They were mightily pissed.

I understood why Comanche threw the stone. Nothing could have saved the girl but at least the end had been so fast she knew nothing about it.

A bald, bush-bearded man stepped forward. He was topless except for the Rock and a Hard Place scarf around his neck. A pale belly hung like a suet pudding over his sweat pants.

'You had no right doing that shit!' He jabbed a finger at Comanche. 'This is no place for bitches, even cleansed bitches.'

Somewhat predictably, Comanche told him to fuck off. She and I could go where we liked, she said, and what was he going to do about it?

'Me?' Bushbeard's belly wobbled as he guffawed. 'You mean *we*.' He made a backward nod to the growing crowd behind him.

'Listen,' I said, trying to sound reasonable. 'We're Harpo officers.'

Bushbeard shook his head. 'Bitches in the Harpo? Who you tryna kid?'

I made another attempt. 'We don't want trouble.'

Another belly-quiver chortle. 'Trouble, bitch, is just what we *do* want.'

Bushbeard reached forward to grab me and –

The wooden stick whacked his wrist with a snap of bone. In the same movement, the stick slammed backwards, smashing his mouth. Bushbeard staggered, his beard gooey with blood and shattered his teeth.

Bob Puritan returned the stick to his side, advancing on the crowd with one hand held high, palm facing outward. 'Did Jesus not say, "let he who is without sin cast the first stone"?'

'But this was a woman,' someone protested. 'The scriptures never said nothing about a woman stoner.'

Old Bob moved further forward, his hand still raised. The crowd edged back as the lawyer continued to berate them. 'Did not the Lord Thy Trump renounce unto death all who would trespass against any cleansed soul?'

There was a disconcerting muttering among the men. Puritan had sown seeds of doubt and raised the prospect of retribution.

'As surely as Jesus drives a Lamborghini Urus, The Holy Donald came down from His Tower and spake thus unto the masses thereunder: "Let all that do vexatious or malicious wrongs unto they who are cleansed be schlonged bigly and cast into the pit of flames for eternity plus-plus-plus."'

'How do we know the Holy Donald really did say that stuff?' A weaselly man with sparse hair stepped forward. To the others, he said, 'He could be making that up!'

Old Bob kept his hand high. His voice never wavered. 'O, ye who doubt The Testament of the Lord, take out your iBibles and scroll to Alt-Right chapter 17,567, verses 210,919 to 210,922. See with your own eyes the truth of the Donald's words.'

There was a scramble for digital Bibles. Some clearly hadn't brought theirs and stood around, gazing at the ground in shamefaced avoidance.

'He's right,' somebody mumbled. 'Every word he said is spot on.'

The knot of men surrounding us began to loosen. Those at the back started to move away, then those at the front, including Bushbeard, still picking teeth from his beard.

The stoning pit was empty in two minutes, leaving us alone with the dead girl.

Without turning, Puritan said, 'I'll take care of that poor soul's body. You two go straight back to the hotel. Go now and go quickly.'

40

I cupped my hands in a mask over my nose and cheeks and breathed warm air to take the chill off my skin. It was cold and dark under a slim crescent moon and my watch told me it was 4.00am. We were waiting on Kasila Street in north east Jerusalem for the Harpo breach team to take up their positions.

Puritan and Comanche had told me not to dwell on the girl who died in the stoning pit. But it was tough to think about anything else. Her name was Ruth Francis and she'd just turned thirteen. Comanche had been right about the nature of the offence: refusing sex to her husband of sixty-three years. She'd protested that she had no sexual experience and tried to fend off the husband's advances because she was scared. As a child, she had every right to be. But the judge rejected this out of hand. I knew this because I read her file when I got to the Harpo's Happy House the next morning. By all accounts, Ruth Francis had come from a good family and was doing well at school until her education ended soon after her twelfth birthday, as it did for all girls – except, of course, for cleansed ones.

Then she was married off to a wealthy old man who paid her father a life-changing dowry. The suitor already had eighteen wives, but three were approaching sixteen, when he would divorce them. In any developed country in 21st Century, he'd have been a convicted paedophile.

Not here. Oh no, not here.

'You okay, boss?'

I felt Comanche's hand grip my arm and with it, a flurry of difficult emotions. But this was not the time for reflection, so I told her yes, I was fine and gave her a confident smile.

'Looks like we're nearly ready.' She indicated a squad of black-clad breach troopers moving into position and I refocused on the matter in hand.

Charles-Henry McMartyr lived alone in a ground floor apartment in a condominium two kilometres from his workplace on the main campus of Holy Quadity University. This was located where the Hebrew University had stood in Old Jerusalem and I'd spent the previous day there covertly observing his activities.

If anything, the headshot I'd seen in the briefing room was flattering. His broad face and balding head had the pallor and texture of old parchment, even though he was not yet forty-five. He had a habit was walking quickly along corridors and his greying red hair trailed behind like a wispy flame. A baggy tweed jacket with thick corduroy pants, four inches too long, and sandals over diamond pattern socks completed the shabby ensemble. In the brief conversations I overhead with colleagues and students, his tone was prickly and pedantic and he spoke fast, as if his time was too valuable to be spent on matters he didn't consider important. All in all, McMartyr was not a man who would be liked, or wanted to be.

But did any of this make him Family Guy?

As a mid-ranking academic with something of a reputation in his field, he was neither the under-promoted technician the FIB profile described, nor a high-flying creative type as Puritan hypothesized. Moreover, McMartyr was a statistician rather than a technical or artistic individual, which also made him an unlikely candidate for either the FIB's or Puritan's assessment.

Puritan's portrait was right about one thing though: Charles Henry McMartyr would be insufferable for anyone working under, alongside or above him.

This said, I'd known serial killers who defied the most diligent of profilers. And one thing McMartyr certainly shared with family Guy was self-absorbed cleverness.

I checked the time: 4.12 am. The breach team should have gone in at least ten minutes ago. I turned to Comanche. 'What are we waiting for?'

'The television people aren't ready.'

I rolled my eyes. Witchfinder General Derek Anti-Satan had insisted on TV coverage and when I went over his head and protested to Jesusly I was told the idea was his in the first place. We could have arrested McMartyr with a tap on his door at a decent hour; or even at work. But the breach team and the television crew were part of the politics behind this. Somewhat sarcastically, I suggested Plato Tomsky as the director of the production and got a dark look from Jesusly that told me he shared Wu Mei's opinion of Tomsky.

'Ready in ten, boss,' Comanche said.

I looked at my watch as the seconds ticked down.

On zero, two Harpo troopers swung a steel ram and the front door crunched open. I imagined McMartyr's terror as the breach troopers stormed into his apartment. I followed them inside with a TV cameraman right behind. This wasn't police work, it was theatre.

Not surprisingly, McMartyr was in bed as a trooper hauled him from it. With half a dozen flashlights in his face his features looked distorted, almost inhuman.

All-Saints Geddes entered the room, standing by the cameraman.

At Geddes' signal, the ceiling lights went on and, with the camera rolling, one Harpo trooper slammed his fist into McMartyr's belly. As he jack-knifed, another punched him hard in the face.

'What the fuck – '

I moved forwards to stop the beating but I was too late. McMartyr went down fast and lay on the carpet, not moving, blood oozing from his mouth.

I shoved the cameraman aside and knelt by the academic. He was unconscious but breathing. 'Get a medic in here right now!'

'Cut it there,' Geddes told the cameraman, 'the lead investigator giving this sick bastard first aid isn't the sort of scene we want to broadcast.'

I gave Geddes a withering look. 'Thanks to your stupid publicity stunt, we have a suspect we can't question. In fact, we can't even arrest him.'

'Worse still,' Puritan added, '*he* may have a case against *us*.'

Geddes made an acid smile. 'With you representing him, you decrepit freak.'

'You know the law,' Puritan said. 'Even in the Holy Trumpian Empire there's a presumption of innocence until proved otherwise. And if this absurd pantomime goes on air, you'll prejudice a fair trial and that could lead to the case being dismissed.'

The chief special inquisitor shrugged. 'He was resisting arrest.'

I made a sour chuckle. 'On his way between his bed and your men's knuckles?'

'I have twenty-odd Harpo troopers here who would testify to whatever I tell them to. And even *your* reputation, Counsellor Puritan, would be ruined if you supported this disgusting deviant.'

By this time the medics had arrived and McMartyr was checked over, then stretchered away to an ambulance.

'Hey, boss!' Wham!®© called from a dressing table near the window. He was peering into an open drawer and picked out a transparent plastic bag. In it was a large kitchen knife with a snapped-off tip. 'I finded smin what you gotta speck.'

I crossed the room and took a closer look.

What were the odds, I wondered, that this was the knife that broke when it struck Brunhilda Mozart's femur?

41

'**S**atan is everywhere,' Judgment Jesusly told a stadium audience of a hundred thousand and billions more on television. 'In the words of our revered prophet, Robert L'Éponge, "Debil come, debil go. Where he is, no one know." Deep words indeed, fellow pilgrims. So what did the revered L'Éponge mean by this?'

The First Father of the Holy Trumpian Empire strode from one side of the stage to the other, shimmering in a gold lamé suit with silver trim, along with a gold shirt, silver bootlace tie and golden cowboy boots with silver heels.

Swivelling on one of them, he pointed to the huge screen above the stage depicting Donald Trump in a court room with an improbably Aryan-looking Jesus beside him. The image had been drawn in the idealized heroic style of Soviet-era Russia: both men were fierce eyed, strong jawed, defiant.

'The Lord Thy Trump and his best friend Jesus always knew where Satan was. *That*, pilgrims, was for sure!'

Electronic organ chords sounded across the stadium. The audience cheered. Showtime was here.

'Sometimes the whereabouts of Satan is obvious – indeed we need look no further than the life of the Second Cousin Himself when He was persecuted by the elitist cabal of Satan-worshipping paedophiles who ran the 21st Century world. Did the Lord Our Trump bend or buckle under their wicked torment? Did he cave and collapse? Did he run or relent?'

Jesusly paused centre stage to allow cries of *No! No! No!* and *Never! Never! Never!* to rise from the crowd.

I was here because Charles Henry McMartyr was still lying unconscious in the hospital bed where Geddes' Harpo goons had put him. I couldn't fathom the unprofessional stupidity of beating him so savagely. The doctors told us McMartyr had suffered severe concussion and was in a coma. His skull was intact, though he may have brain damage. There was no telling when or if he would regain consciousness. Until that happened, he couldn't be questioned, still less charged. And Puritan assured me that even in the Holy Trumpian Empire he couldn't be convicted without being charged.

In the meantime, my team and I had been invited to attend this missionary event of Judgment Jesusly's. Wham!®© and Comanche refused to come and I didn't blame them. However, Wu Mei told me my attendance was essential for inter-federation relations. And Bob was too much of a gentleman to let me come alone. It was no recompense that we were given box seats.

'When you're on God's side,' Jesusly was saying, 'you're always on the right side. And Our Lord Trump was on God's side.'

There were shouts of *Hallelujah!* and *All praise to the*

Donald! Worshippers came to their feet, hands held high in devotional pose.

Jesusly regarded his audience, nodding solemnly as he moved to one side of the stage. Electric organ notes sounded again. Jesusly raised his arms in a V-shape and threw back his head.

The chords rose an octave.

'O, Second Cousin,' the First Father beseeched the roof, 'let God who made ye mighty, make ye mightier yet!'

The congregation responded with chants of *Make ye mightier yet!* All arms were lifted, all voices joined in. And all this happened under the gaze of Harpo troopers standing at the end of each row. What better incentive to participate if failing to raise your hands high enough cost you both? Or not chanting loud enough lost you your tongue?

On went the chanting.

And on.

And on some more.

And more on top of that.

It was like the end of one of Stalin's speeches when nobody dared to stop clapping for fear of being seen as less loyal than others. In the end, they had to be ordered to stop, and so it was here. A klaxon sounded, drowning out all other sound. The chanting ended, arms were lowered, worshippers sat back down.

Jesusly fell silent while the tumult diminished.

At last, he said. 'Yes, it's true that sometimes, pilgrims, we know exactly where the devil is and what he's doing. But there are other times when the whereabouts of Old Nick isn't so clear, when his activities aren't so easy to discern. For he is nothing, pilgrims, *nothing* if not subtle, if not devious, if not scheming.'

He talked at length, urging all to practice "Satan-spotting"; for fellow pilgrims here in this hall – and at home – to turn on the "radar of their souls"; to "patrol the ramparts of goodness". He never stopped talking. The pitch of his voice rose and fell, the rhythm sometimes urgent, sometimes measured.

I got a sense he was building up to something when the organ chords sound again. '*This* is how we defeat the Evil One,' announced the First Father.

'We say to him, "Devil, you can't have my house!"' He stamped a silver boot on the floor.

The organ volume escalated.

Jesusly stamped his foot again and moved across the stage, left to right. 'We say to him, "Devil, you can't have my children!"'

One more, the organist increased the volume. 'We say to him, "Devil, you can't have my soul!"'

When Jesusly reached the right side of the stage, he swivelled on his heel. Heading back where he'd come from.

'And *this*,' he proclaimed, 'is how we kick the Devil's butt.'

Another stamp. 'We say, "Donald, I hear your call!"'

The organist went to reverb. His two-tone chords bounced around the arena.

Again, the silver boot cashed down. 'We say, "Donald, I'm coming to you!"'

Bass pedals joined the ensemble.

The first Father's leg rose, bent at the knee. He held it there for three, four five seconds, then threw back his head and slammed down his foot harder than ever. 'We say,' he bawled, '"Donald, help me in my need!"'

The organist held down his keys and went to full volume, full reverb. Jesusly stayed still, staring at the tip of his boot.

When he stood straight, the organist signed off with a jiggly curlicue.

Uproar erupted. Arms went skyward. Hallelujahs crammed the space.

When the klaxon sounded a full thirty minutes later, the transcended worshippers returned to their seats.

Jesusly asked his pilgrims what they wanted next and they responded with calls of "Let us share!"

The First Father nodded and made an *aw, shucks, you got me* grin. Very well, he told them, they could share.

This triggered whoops and whistles.

'Who,' he said, 'can share with us an experience of defying the devil?'

It was impossible to tell which of thousands of arms went up first. Nonetheless, Jesusly pretended to and picked out a young man near the front.

He came to his feet and received a microphone from the nearest Harpo trooper. The man, whose name was Obadiah Rasputin, recounted how his toaster malfunctioned that morning. His toast burned, fumes filled the kitchen and the blazing toaster had to tossed into the dishwater. Such was the chaos and alarm that Obadiah Rasputin thought he might not be able to attend Worship. *This*, he said, was when he realized the malfunction had been caused by the devil in a calculated attempt to stop him hearing the Word of Trump.

The congregation loved this.

'It's easy to imagine,' Puritan whispered, 'why His Satanic Majesty would want to spend time sabotaging Obadiah Rasputin's toaster.'

Next up was an older man named Salvatore Stonehouse, who caught a bad cold and was thinking about taking a sick day from his job stocking supermarket shelves. Until, this was, the Orange One laid it upon him that the devil had given him the virus to prevent him working. So Salvatore Stonehouse went to work despite – indeed, because – of this dastardly ploy by the Evil One.

Puritan gave me a sad look, as if to say *This is what I'm up against.*

There was no shortage of others eager to share their tales of sticking it to Satan. I got the impression that the listeners weren't all that interested in other worshippers' stories. Like people hearing about someone else's dream, all they really wanted was to tell their own.

I zoned out. I could hear more and more of these folk disgorging different versions of the same story. Later, I was vaguely aware of Jesusly burbling away in his west Texas twang, talking trash, quoting crap, blabbering bollocks dressed up in language that sounded grandiose and revelatory and profound. *When God looks at us*, I heard him say, *He sees what he sees.* Later I caught, *Truly, God is God – is He not?*

A soft nudge from Bob made me tune back in. Jesusly was now talking about the fleet of luxury planes used by him and other high-ranking Trumpian leaders.

'If Jesus was alive today,' he said, 'he sure wouldn't' ride a donkey.'

Puritan put his mouth to my ear. 'There's been some criticism of the cost of operating this private fleet when most of the population is starving. Each Father of Trumpia, from the first to the thirteenth, owns his own Angel Squadron. Planes range in size from smaller executive aircraft to enormous solar-nuclear three-deckers with palatial suites, swimming pools and movie theatres. Jesusly even has a low-orbit clipper – the Rolls Royce of short-haul space travel.'

'What matters more?' Jesusly asked his flock. 'The cost of Trumpian Fathers using their own air and space craft? Or the saving of souls from eternal damnation? The faster we get to a place, the faster we can deliver salvation to those poor hell-bound wretches.'

The worshippers applauded with a tempest of enthusiasm.

'So I ask you, pilgrims, which would Jesus prefer if he were alive today? Space speed or donkey speed?'

There was an outpouring of 'Space speed!' *clap-clap-clap*; 'Space speed!' *clap-clap-clap*. After a good while this morphed into 'Down with donkeys!'

Jesusly surveyed his audience, nodding and smiling and pointing his finger at one worshipper, then another and so on as if he recognized them. The congregation luxuriated in this moment of rapture. If the First Father hadn't noticed them individually, he'd pointed out someone nearby, a family member, a friend, someone they knew.

With his audience purring, Jesusly made his pitch. 'Of course,' he said, 'you will be blessed for giving your money to charities for those in need. But imagine how much more you will be blessed for making cash donations to keep our Angel Squadrons flying. Because, pilgrims, in so doing, you are helping the Fathers of Trumpia to save souls otherwise damned to eternal torment in the flames of hell. Think on this and pray, and above all, ask yourselves what we must always ask ourselves: What would Trump do?'

The Harpo men handed out plastic buckets to be passed along the rows of seats. I saw fistfuls of bank notes being rammed into the buckets. Many were removing valuables – gold rings and medallions, watches with diamond-encrusted bands, all sorts of other precious possessions, and tossing them in the buckets. Others were frantically tapping their phones, no doubt transferring substantial cash sums to the Angel Squadrons fund.

I thought of Palm Sunday and GK Chesterton's poem *The Donkey*, and Jesus' choosing precisely that creature to demonstrate his humility. I recalled the widow's mite; the camel passing through the eye of a needle easier than a rich man entering heaven. I remembered the devil tempting Jesus on the heights of Quarantania with promises of vast worldly power and Jesus saying *Get thee behind me, Satan*. And I was reminded of Jesus' view of God and money: *Ye cannot serve God and mammon*.

More than anything though I was struck by the wrongness of the First Father words, *If Jesus was alive today*. I'd never been much of a believer but I knew the precept of Christian doctrine was that Jesus was resurrected after dying on the cross and remained alive, always and for ever. So if you were a Christian, Jesus *was* alive today.

But then these people weren't Christians, they were Trumpians. Perhaps this was as much and as little as I needed to understand about them.

Puritan leaned close and his voice came in a raspy whisper. 'This is why I despise Trumpia so much. Despite their wrong-mindedness, the rulers of PopRep®© and Scientia want to make the world a better place. The rulers of Trumpia just want to make money.'

When the buckets had finished their rounds, the organist struck up with the old hymn *Onward Christian Soldiers* but with different lyrics.

Onward Trumpian soldiers, marching as to war
With the T of Donald going on before …

The arrival of a Harpo officer with a message gave me enormous relief – and an excuse to leave: Charles Henry McMartyr has regained consciousness.

42

'I killed them all,' Charles Henry McMartyr said. 'I'm him. I'm Family Guy.'

I looked at him across the interrogation room table between us. His left eye was a small purple balloon, the gap between his eye-lids a dark seam. He was wearing a prison jump suit of yellow sack-cloth – orange being the Sacred Colour of the Second Cousin. The attire had been given to him after he was discharged from hospital and brought to Harpo Headquarters. Here, he'd been formally arrested and charged under Puritan's supervision – I was determined to have no more of Geddes' publicity antics.

Despite his traumatic experience, McMartyr was relishing this.

'In your apartment,' I said, 'we found a lot of books, recordings, porn movies all relating to Family Guy. Can you tell me why you collected all that stuff?'

'I like to see how others interpret my work, what they say about me, how I've influenced them.'

'So nothing to do with your academic studies of Family Guy?'

'My job at the university, my research, everything, was part of my cover.'

Before I could say anything more, he leaned forward, smiling. 'You know, Superintendent, how much I've been waiting for this encounter. I've so much enjoyed pitting my wits against yours since you arrived. We're both geniuses in our fields. Worthy opponents, wouldn't you say?'

He wriggled in his chair. He'd had a psychological erection since he was brought in here and I got the impression he was close to orgasm.

After processing McMartyr in the Harpo custody suite, Geddes insisted that he be left to stew in a cell for a few hours. He'd been cooking all right, but not in the way Geddes expected. Because instead of being consumed by fear, he'd realized that Trumpmas had come early. He'd used his cell-time to prepare for this interrogation, to hone his narrative, polish each detail. This would be his apogee, the start of his global celebrity.

I nudged a transparent evidence bag containing the snapped-off knife across the table. 'Can you tell us how this came to be in your possession?' I asked.

Without looking at the evidence bag, he said, 'I used that knife to do the Mozart woman.'

'How come the blade broke?'

'I stabbed her so hard, the tip sheared off.'

'Where did you stab her?'

'Everywhere.'

'I mean when the knife-tip snapped.'

'I don't remember.' He glanced at the mirrored wall where he sensed Derek Anti-Satan and All-Saints Geddes were observing. His pointy tongue licked his upper lip.

He was getting properly warmed up. 'I was in a psychotic frenzy.'

I'd had my suspicions but this was when I knew.

When I said nothing, he went on, 'You should have seen the rage I stoked up. I was stabbing, slashing, gashing. That place was one hell of a bloodbath.'

'Was it?'

'Of course it was.' Charles Henry McMartyr was in a state of rapture. 'I never stop cutting them. You know me, Superintendent.'

I gave him a weary look. 'Yes, Mr McMartyr, I do.'

'Then you'll know how brutal I am, how my lust for picquerism is unquenchable.'

'Picquerism?'

'Yes, it means a compulsion to stab and cut and – '

'I know what it means, Mr McMartyr.' I made a thin smile. 'It's just that I've never heard it used by a serial killer.'

Another silence. I had the impression he was recalibrating his story.

I leaned back in my chair, stretched my legs and looked at th ceiling. 'You must have known you'd never get away with this.'

He laughed. Licked his upper lip again. 'I've been getting away with it for nineteen years.'

'Have you?' I gave him a hard look.

He didn't respond.

I opened the file on the table and pretended to study it. Without looking up, I said, 'Why didn't you take Brunhilda Mozart's ?'

'I don't recall.'

I gave him more eye contact. 'But you took all the wedding bands of all the other women, right?'

'Right.'

I kept my eyes level with him. 'But it's not right, is it, Mr McMartyr?'

He frowned, glanced away. The penny hadn't dropped yet, but it was rolling towards the edge.

'Why not?'

'Because Family Guy didn't take wedding rings from any of his victims. And only Family Guy would know that because it was never in the public domain.'

'I'd forgotten that. Of course I didn't.' He placed his palm against his forehead in a *Doh!* gesture. 'Too much going on. All the chaos and confusion. And my concussion. Everything is a bit of a blur. I'd like a break now, please.'

'You aren't Family Guy, are you, Mr McMartyr?'

'What? Of course I am. Why wouldn't I be? I just confessed, didn't I?'

'I have no shortage of reasons why you aren't him. Do you really want more?'

There was a long, still quiet. I could almost hear the hum of the recording equipment behind the mirror. In McMartyr's head, I sensed the final fall of the penny.

I said, "Family Guy killed one hundred and seven people in those nineteen years. There's an awful lot of stuff that he'd know and you don't.'

I picked up the evidence bag containing the broken blade. 'You've never seen this knife before, have you?'

'I forget.'

'You better remember – and fast.'

He stared at the table.

'You're a smart man,' I said. 'You'll know Family Guy investigations have been inter-jurisdictional since the early days. And you'll also know that because of this, he won't face the death penalty. It's been abolished in Scientia for nearly two thousand years and taking capital punishment off the table was the price of their cooperation.'

'So what?' He was trying to pretend off-hand uninterest but it didn't work.

'Perverting the course of justice, however, is a microwaveable offence in Trumpia, which is where you'd be sentenced. Then there's wasting Harpo time, for which you'd likely lose a hand, and that porno stuff we found at your place, well, you can call it research if you like but it would still cost you your cock and balls. And all, of course, before you went to the oven.'

I let this sink in. It wasn't unknown for serial killer wannabees to press their bogus claims even in death penalty American states. But the needle was one thing; the oven, preceded by mutilation without anaesthetic was different level.

After a good while, I said, 'You ever seen someone cook from the inside? What happens is – '

'I want a deal.' All pretence had gone. Now, McMartyr was terrified and so he should have been.

'Admit it, Mr McMartyr,' I said. 'You're not Family Guy, are you? That knife was planted in your flat and you used your time in custody to work out your story. World fame, adulation in some quarters, plus a place in the history books in return for a comfortable life as a super-star inmate in a Scientian supermax? That must have seemed like a trade you couldn't refuse.'

I took out the Informant Immunity Contract I'd asked Puritan to prepare before I came in. 'Sign this right now,' I said, 'before it's too late.'

McMartyr understood what I meant.

'I admit I'm not Family Guy,' he said, grabbed my pen and scratched his signature on the document.

The ballpoint had barely left the paper when the door burst open and Geddes rushed in with Anti-Satan close behind.

I gave Anti-Satan a disgusted look. 'This man is one sick bastard but he is now officially cooperating with this inter-jurisdictional investigation. And in any case, he doesn't deserve Harpo justice. Nobody does.'

'That scrap of paper he just signed,' Anti-Satan said, 'whatever it is, I'll get it quashed.'

I shrugged. 'You could take that up with Counsellor Puritan. But you'd be wasting your time.'

The anger in Anti-Satan's eyes told me I'd just made a powerful enemy. Maybe it was unprofessional of me. We'd never have been able to work well together, but the smartest play for me would have been to keep him relatively neutral. Then again, having an odious creature like Derek Anti-Satan as my enemy made me feel a little more better about myself.

As for McMartyr's admission, I was left with many more questions than answers. He'd obviously been framed, possibly by a state actor, possibly by the real Family Guy.

But why?

It must have been clear to anyone with the resources to plant the knife that I'd see through the fit-up very quickly, whatever McMartyr told me. It was standard practice to ask serial killer wannabes about information that only the true killer would know. Even the most assiduous pretender could be weeded out in short order.

So the question I was left with was this: Why had someone taken so much time and trouble to plant the knife, as well as inducing McMartyr's colleague to rat him out?

This wasn't a matter of who would benefit, but *how*?

43

Late that night Family Guy killed again.

I'd have been as much of a monster as him if I welcomed news like this, though I had to admit I was glad of the distraction.

I was in bed, unable to sleep and thinking about Comanche. Everyone had secrets, but hers were the sort she'd kill to protect. There was simply too much I needed to ask and too many reasons why I couldn't. And this emotional paralysis had kept me awake at nights since Wu Mei gave me the talking to.

I grabbed my gear and met the others in the lobby. Bogart was impeccably groomed and I wondered how he managed to look like that in just a few minutes; Old Bob looked as shabby as always; and Comanche, like me, appeared to have had no or very little sleep.

With flashing lights and wailing sirens, it took a little over five minutes to reach the crime scene at a detached house on Benjamin Disraeli Street. The first thing I noted as we pulled up outside was that the neighbourhood was in a city centre location – detached houses and stylish apartment blocks. Not as densely populated as the Sinatras' apartment or the Mozarts', but still a high-risk spot compared to almost all of Family Guy's previous outings. I wondered if he might have started doing this to add more challenge to his activities. Maybe he thought this was all getting a little too easy for a man of his accomplishments.

The victims were Nebo Discipleson, a thirty-three-year-old accountant; his wife, Melania, twenty-nine, and their three children, Aquinas, eight; Ignatius, six; and Ivanka, four.

The ages of the adults was another huge departure – as significant as his sparing of the Mozart kids and the switch to higher risk targets. Before now, all husbands had been much older than their wives – on average, eighteen years. This was clearly integral to Family Guy's psychopathy. So why, suddenly, had he killed a couple separated by just four years?

The Disciplesons' home was a large detached villa and we entered a parquet floored hall with walls adorned with a polished wood sign of the T and a portrait of the Holy Quadity – Donald Trump sitting alongside a stern beardy man in white robes who I took to be God, a younger version, apparently Jesus, and most alarming of all, a blurry phantom comprising elements of the other three, presumably the Holy Ghost.

We put on full barrier whites and shoe covers provided by a plainclothes Harpo man.

'Where are the kids?' Comanche asked, fastening her suit.

'Upstairs,' the Harpo man said. 'The medics are with them.'

She gave me a look that was both hopeful and anxious. In that instant I saw the face of Comanche as a worried mother. 'After what happened with the Mozart twins,' she said, 'these kids may have a chance.'

I followed her upstairs, leaving Puritan and Wham!®© to take a look at the mother and father in the living room.

The two brothers were lying in twin beds with medical team members crouched over each child.

'How is it looking?' Comanche said to the medic attending to Aquinas, the eldest child.

The man didn't respond and Comanche had the sense not to press him.

She crossed to the bed of Ignatius, the six-year-old middle child and asked a similar question of the medic with his ear pressed on the boy's chest. Again, no reply; again, Comanche moved on.

She was about to check on the youngest child, Ivanka, when the first medic called out, 'This boy's alive!'

I crossed the room. 'Will he survive?

'Touch and go.' The medic was giving the lad a shot of naloxone. 'Depends on how quickly we can get him to the ICU.'

A stretcher with a drip-feed was brought in and Aquinas lifted onto it.

The medics were still adjusting the straps when a shout came from Ivanka's room. 'The girl! She's coming around!'

We crossed the landing into the little girl's bedroom. Her eyes were open – glazed and unfocused, but there was no doubt she was starting to regain consciousness. Another stretcher arrived and Ivanka carried to one of the ambulances outside.

The prognosis was less optimistic for Ignatius, the six-year-old middle child. The medic had found a faint pulse but wasn't confident the boy would survive the journey to the hospital. All the same, at least all three children had a chance.

Which was baffling. Clearly, Family Guy had developed a conscience, or at least a simulation of one. The Mozart kids plus the Disciplesons must mean this was not a miscalculation but a deliberate act of mercy. Serial killers evolved for sure, but I'd never experienced anything remotely like this.

I stowed these thoughts for later and realized Comanche was at my elbow.

'I want to go to the hospital with the kids,' she said. 'The girl is showing more awareness and maybe I could get something out of her soon. And I could keep you updated on the boys.'

This made a lot of sense and I agreed.

Downstairs, I joined Puritan and Wham!®© in the living room.

The scene was all too familiar.

Yet it wasn't.

At first glance this was trademark Family Guy. Melania Discipleson lay supine, legs open, left nipple sliced off, covered in knife wounds. Nebo had been bound, castrated and his genitals rammed into his wife's mouth. Also textbook Family Guy.

But there was more: Nebo's chest was severely mutilated.

As I moved closer I saw that his sternum had been cut open and his ribs prised apart.

'The heart is missing.' A chubby middle-aged man with a horseshoe moustache and round-frame glasses turned from the window and introduced himself as Thomas O'Testament, the state pathologist. He would carry out the post mortem along with Baudelaire Dodgson who was on his way on a military arrow plane from Paris-sur-Euphrète.

I went down on my haunches and observed the big space in Nebo's chest cavity. 'Is this what killed him?'

O'Testament shook his head. 'The heart was removed post mortem. Cause of death was asphyxiation, the mechanism, ligature-strangulation. As you'll know, Superintendent, that's entirely in keeping with Family Guy's antecedents.'

'We ain't not never specked no tiktok snatch before, boss.' Wham!®© crouched beside me. 'Why you think he done this?'

'Your guess is as good as mine.' I looked a little closer at the enormous wound. Although Family Guy had made a mess of Nebo's chest, the rib cage had parted cleanly. I gave O'Testament a quizzical glance.

'Surgical cutters,' he said.

'Or pruning shears, like Dodgson's?' I added.

'Indeed.' The pathologist wagged his head from side to side as if playing ping-pong with his thoughts.

Wham!®© peered over his shoulder. 'What you reckon, doc?'

O'Testament craned his neck to get a different perspective. 'What we have here is furious stabbing and hacking – even by Family Guy's standards – combined with neat and precise surgical work to excise the heart.

If I didn't know better, I'd say it had been done by two different people.'

'Or,' Puritan added, 'the same person with two different objectives.'

'What you mean, Bob?' Bogart asked.

Bob raised his palms in a you-tell-me expression. 'I'm not sure. But it appears he wanted Nebo's heart intact. Perhaps he's developed a thing for hearts. After all, it's the organ traditionally associated with romantic love. This may be a symbolic action. Not only has he castrated his male victim, he's physically stolen his heart.'

'It's further evidence that he's evolving,' I said. 'He's taken small personal items from female victims previously, but never from a male and never a body part. And we also have the question of why he's switched from much older husbands and much younger wives to a couple who were only four years apart.'

I went to Melania's body and looked for a stab cluster that could have obliterated a tattoo like Kiera Sinatra's and Brunhilda Mozart's. But there was nothing.

So what did this mean for my hypothesis that the latest batch of female victims were linked? Maybe only Kiera and Brunhilda were. But what were the chances of Family Guy selecting two women who just happened to have arrived in Blackpool together and left together for Old New York fourteen years ago? If these two victims were linked, I was convinced others would be too. There had to be something about Melania Discipleson that wasn't immediately apparent. I could only hope that this would be revealed at the autopsy.

44

Family Guy was the strangest serial killer I'd come across or heard of – and that was a lot of serial killers. Sitting in my office in Harpo Central the next afternoon, I sipped my coffee and considered the current situation.

The Discipleson children – like the Mozart twins – would live. It had been touch and go with the younger boy, but he was now responding well to treatment.

As welcome as this was, it again raised the question of why Family Guy had started sparing the children. With the Mozart children, we couldn't rule out them surviving because of a miscalculation. But we *could* rule it out after the same mercy had been shown to the Discipleson siblings. Now I had no doubt that this was an active choice.

Was this what serial killers did?

The Discipleson girl and elder boy had been able to talk to Comanche but couldn't tell her anything except that they went to sleep and woke up in ICU beds.

Meanwhile, the autopsy revealed no trace of a tattoo, or wounds inflicted to conceal one, anywhere on Melania's body. This was another puzzle. As was the difference between her age and Nebo's. Just four years compared to the previous average of eighteen.

Was this what serial killers did?

Then there was the clean, almost surgical excision of Nebo's heart – diametrically opposite to the stab and slash savagery of his chest wounds. After the autopsy O'Testament and Dodgson were as baffled as anyone. They agreed with Puritan's postulation that the dichotomy may have been down to the same person having two separate but related aims: to mutilate Nebo and obtain his heart.

But why?

Family Guy had never before inflicted such grievous injuries on a male victim.

And why the fuck did he want Nebo's heart?

Was this what serial killers did?

*

I wasn't left wondering for long. Puritan came into my office with the gap-toothy grin that told me something relatively good had happened.

'The blood work has come back from the lab,' he said. 'It shows Nebo Discipleson's blood contained traces of cyclosporine, an immunosuppressant for people who have had heart transplants.'

I frowned and indicated the visitor chair. This would explain a lot. But I couldn't imagine what. 'We didn't find *any* prescription meds in the house.'

Bob took a seat. 'I checked the whole family's medical records. Apparently no one living in that house had a heart transplant.'

I recalled looking through the bathroom cabinet and being struck by its tidiness when the rest of the house was a little scruffy. I mentioned this to Bob.

'You think these heart drugs were removed by Family Guy?' he said. 'And he made too good a job of tidying the bathroom cabinet afterwards?'

'It's possible.' I tapped my keyboard and brought up the lab report. 'But why had Nebo been taking these drugs if he never had a heart transplant?'

'Perhaps he did.'

I glanced up, bemused. 'If so, why isn't it in the medical records.'

'This is Trumpia.' Puritan gave me a sardonic look. 'Medical records – like any records – can be made to say whatever the Harpo wants them to say.'

'What are you thinking?'

He pinched the bridge of his nose as if it helped his concentration. 'Family Guy removed the whole heart – very, very carefully. But why this near-surgical excision? It must have taken a long time, painstaking attention to detail and significantly greater risk.'

'He's a resourceful man who seems to thrive on risk. But what are you getting at?'

'What if Nebo *did* have a heart transplant and the new organ was wholly or partially synthetic?'

I thought this through. 'It could be identified.'

'Exactly.' Bob's hearing aid started doing its R2D2 thing and he took a moment to adjust it. 'Any synthetic product used in this type of operation would have a serial number or at the very least, components that could be traced to the manufacturer. This would allow us to find out a number of things – where and when he had the transplant; why he needed it; who performed it; and possibly the name Nebo went by at the time.'

I stated the obvious. 'So Family Guy took the heart to stop us discovering something about Nebo Discipleson that he didn't want us to know? Such as an alternative identity?'

Was this what serial killers did?

'And that,' Puritan said, 'would mean Nebo – not Melania – was the reason Family Guy chose the Discipleson family.'

'We need to be one hundred per cent about this, Bob.' I spoke with a cautious inflection. 'Because a lot of things that haven't made any sense suddenly would.'

He gave me a weary look. 'And even more things that *do* make sense wouldn't.'

45

ate the next morning and the crowds had started to
thicken on the Greek Orthodox Patriarchate Street, a
narrow pedestrian thoroughfare in the former Christian
Quarter of Old City Jerusalem. Most of the shoppers were
men with women on leashes wearing obedience orbs and
long grey robes. Every so often, though, I saw cleansed
women and men with trophy wives in half-cup bikini tops
and thong bottoms.

As Trumpia's premier pilgrim destination, this was a
swirling torrent of religion and retail. The holy sites were
still there but all the old faiths had been swept away by
the tide of Trumpism. Judaism, Islam and Christianity –
with all its orthodoxies and denominations – had been
rebranded and repurposed by the Holy Quadity. The
only concession to ancient beliefs were discreet plaques
with text such as: *Formerly Church of the Holy Sepulchre
(circa 4th Century Christian chapel)*. And for every spiritual
edifice there were dozens of outlets selling spiritual
trinkets, fake designer gear, tobacco and fast food. I passed

a tattoo parlour claiming to have been founded in 1341 and a neon-fronted money changer whose predecessors had their tables overturned by Jesus at a nearby temple.

Comanche was showing me around the Old City streets and I had to admit the walk was a timely diversion. I'd been wrestling all last night and most of this morning with the implications of Family Guy having gone after Nebo Discipleson rather than his wife Melania. In order to think about it some more I had to not think about it at all and let my subconscious go to work. Which made a sight-seeing tour like this ideal.

We'd just entered a marginally broader section of alleyway called St Dimitri Square when Comanche spoke without turning her head. 'Grey Lady is back.'

I kept my eyes front too. 'Where?'

'Right behind, about fifty metres. Wearing a Boston Red Sox baseball cap, light blue coat and dark sweat pants.'

'How do you know it's her?'

'Something about the way she moves. She has a springy stride for such an elderly woman. Also, the set of her head – her neck is slightly tilted to the right.'

'How sure are you?'

'Not very. But I'd rather assume it's her and risk embarrassment than let her slip away yet again.'

'Okay,' I said, 'Technically we're Harpo agents so if things *do* get messy, we should be fine.'

We carried on walking. In a narrow, crowded alley like this, catching her was going to be tricky.

I saw a banana on the street near a fruit stall three metres ahead and said to Comanche, 'I'm going to try something. Play along.'

As we approached I placed my left foot right on the banana, pressing down hard. I felt it squelch, sliding one way as I slid the other, tumbling sideways onto the cobbles.

The fall made me look like a klutz but this was what I wanted. As I hit the ground I glanced sideways and saw the woman in the Red Sox cap, now about twenty metres away.

She was exactly as Comanche described – nondescription as an art form.

Then there was a moment of eye-contact and I knew she'd seen me seeing her.

I came up on one elbow, expecting her to turn and run back through the crowded the alley.

She did the opposite. Rushing forward, she barged into Comanche. They clutched one another in a chaotic swirl, as if they were dancing. Grey Lady swivelled, switched direction and slipped Comanche's grip. Then she was away, swaying and swivelling matador-like through the crowds, ditching the baseball cap as she went.

Comanche hauled me up and we ran after her. The ruse had put her forty metres ahead and it was difficult keeping sight of the back of her head – a short bob of mousy hair that was hard to pick out, even among the bobbing mass of obedience orbs.

The chase took us along Al Qdees Demetrius and the Greek Catholic Patriarchate Street. It was a gruelling pursuit but this worked in our favour – she'd be fifteen years my senior.

We'd closed to within twenty metres of her when she led us out of the alley and into the big public space outside the Tower of David.

I thought *Gotcha!*

Then I saw her talking to a Harpo officer, showing him a Harpo shield, pointing at me and Comanche. I realized she'd lifted Comanche's shield as the two of them grappled.

And I thought, *Oh, fuck!*

The Harpo officer was bearing down on us, big, aggressive, certain he was protecting one of his own.

Even as I took out my own shield, I knew this guy wasn't in any mood to listen. And even the slightest delay would see Grey Lady getting away from us yet again.

So I waited for the Harpo man to come close and jabbed him in the throat with my middle finger knuckles.

He went down fast, clutching his neck.

I ignored the gasps from people around and went after Grey Lady. Comanche knew what I was doing and stayed with me. We pursued our quarry along the façade of the New Hotel Imperial, then into the Latin Patriarchate Street. But this was wider, straighter and less crowded than the bustling maze of alleys we'd just left.

Gray Lady was running out of steam faster than Comanche and I were. There was nowhere to hide, no one to help, no more plays to make.

'Please stop!' I shouted between gasps. 'We just want to talk! We aren't going to hurt you!'

Maybe there was something in my tone; maybe she was just too exhausted to run any more, but she stopped, leaning forward with her hands on her knees, panting heavily.

When she'd recovered sufficiently to stand, she turned to face us. Her face was sheened in sweat, her lungs still sucking air. Up close, she was much the same as from across a street: unremarkable. Grey-blue eyes and round features that could no doubt be made to look attractive or dowdy, whatever was needed. I thought Comanche's estimate of mid-sixties was about right.

'What do you want from me?' she said.

'That depends.' I was still catching my own breath. 'On what *you* want from *us*. We know you've been tailing us in Berlin unter dem Himalaya and Blackpool and probably other locations we weren't aware of.'

'Am I under arrest?'

'We'd like a chat.'

'Do I have a choice?'

'What do you think?'

46

'Why don't you save us both a lot of time and trouble,' I said, 'and tell me who you are?'

Grey Lady stared back at me across the interview room table. Her expression was an odd blend of defiance and amusement. 'I'd have thought your Harpo friends would have my fingernails out by now.'

'I told you we wouldn't hurt you and I meant it. And they're not my friends.'

I made an exasperated sigh. We'd been at this for an hour and I'd made zero progress.

I tried again. 'Your fieldcraft tells me you're consummately skilled in intelligence work. You've clearly operated at a high level for PopRep®© or Scientia – maybe even for Trumpia. I'll find out sooner or later.'

'Good luck.' Her accent, like everything else about her, was difficult to place. She'd been carrying no identification – not even the top quality fake I'd been expecting – and said nothing that wasn't unhelpful or obstructive. I'd asked the authorities in all three federations to run fingerprint, DNA and facial recognition software on her and they all came up short. I suspected whoever she was – or had been – working for was covering up. Which told its own story about her value as an asset. Even if I did let Harpo torturers go to work, I was confident she'd resist indefinitely.

I leaned back and looked up at the ceiling. I couldn't persuade, threaten or coerce her.

So what could I do?

The answer came to me so quickly I wondered why I hadn't thought of it in the first place.

'Very well,' I said, 'we'll end this interview for the time being.'

I came to my feet with a smile intended to puzzle her, and left the room.

All-Saints Geddes was waiting at my office door. 'You get anywhere?'

'Not yet.'

'Give my boys a little time with her.'

'That'll never happen. Besides, I have a plan to trick her that involves deploying a secret weapon.'

He looked at me askance.

What I had planned for Grey Lady wasn't really a trick, nor especially secret and definitely not a weapon. But I wasn't going to tell Geddes this.

And who knew? It might work.

—
*

Bogart Wham!'s®© expensively manicured fingers shimmied between keys, bringing up one set of records, then another, almost as fast as I was requesting them.

He hadn't struck me as a keyboard jockey and I gave him a questioning look.

'What up, boss?'

'I'm surprised,' I said, 'and impressed. I never had you pegged as tech-savvy.'

He made a wry grin. 'How you thinks I come to be a celeb influsser? Gotta know you way round them PubComMedia plats uddaways you ain't not never gonna get no place.'

We were doing a search of men born in the same year as Nebo Discipleson who had had a heart transplant due to a congenital heart defect. The data showed one hundred and eighty men in this category had undergone this kind of operation. However, only forty-one were from South American states.

Of these, six died in the operating theatre and twelve after leaving hospital – which didn't reflect well on Trumpian medical care. This left twenty-three. Close, but we could get closer.

Bogart glanced up from the screen. 'Where you wanna go next, boss?'

If my hypothesis was correct, Family Guy had taken Nebo's heart not as a newly developed fetish but to cover up something important. My best guess was this was a feature of the missing heart that could expose a hidden aspect of Nebo's medical history.

Perhaps a cardiac abnormality, but more likely synthetic components.

'Narrow this group down,' I told Bogart, 'to those whose operation included non-organic material.'

Again Bogart's fingers skated over the keyboard. A new list appeared – thirteen names remained.

I thought about this some more. Family Guy took the entire heart and did so with intricate precision. A wholly synthetic heart would make the job of tracing the manufacturer significantly easier. This in turn would lead us to the records of the individual who received it. Maybe this was why Family Guy removed everything in the way he had. No heart, no way to find out where it came from.

'Now,' I said, 'exclude anyone who received their heart from a donor.'

Another short burst of keyboard clicking left seven males, now aged thirty-three, who had received completely synthetic organs.

I leaned over Bogart's shoulder. 'That's got to be near enough. Bring up the records of each one. We're looking for Nebo Discipleson as a boy, youth or young adult.'

Wham!®© did his stuff. Each record contained personal details and a photo of the transplant recipients. The main difficulty was the extensive age-range at the time of the operation, from pre-school to late-teens. The teenagers shouldn't be a problem – Nebo's appearance couldn't have changed all that much between the ages of eighteen and thirty. Matching little kids to a grown man, though, would be more challenging.

We went through the records in age order, starting with the oldest. The biometric scanner told us the first three were definitely not Nebo, the fourth a very remote possibility. This left us with three very young kids, aged seven, five and four. Nothing biometrics could do now, at least not with Trumpian software.

I focused on each face, not knowing what I was looking for except that it would be nothing obvious. I went from the oldest to the middle boy to the youngest. I looked at each again from youngest to oldest. Next, from middle to youngest to oldest, and finally in no order at all, over and over.

'Speck anything in them kiddy vizes, boss?' Wham!®© asked. 'I gotted nada.'

'Same,' I said. My eyes were sore, the images had started blurring into one another. Time for a rest.

Which was when I found myself staring into the face of Nebo Discipleson as a five-year-old. I couldn't pin down specifics – maybe the shape of the eyes, the set of the jaw, the expression of shy assurance. The more I looked, the more convinced I became.

I asked Bogart. He couldn't see it.

He looked again, again.

'Now I gog it,' he declared, 'I gog it bustagut giddy-up plusplusplus!'

Perhaps we were seeing what we wanted to see. But I thought not.

The boy in the picture wasn't called Nebo Discipleson, which was precisely what I expected. His name twenty-eight years ago was Creflo Bakker. He was born and raised in Sao Paulo state to Galilee and Mary-Margaret Bakker, who owned a small farm about fifty miles outside Sao Paulo city.

'What next, boss?' Bogart asked.

I perched a buttock on his desk, thinking out loud. 'My gut tells me Family Guy chose Nebo/Creflo for the same reason he chose Kiera Sinatra and Brunhilda Mozart. And if the women were linked by the tattoos they got in Blackpool, why not Creflo too?'

'Makes sense.' He pushed his chair back from the screen. 'That gotta be why Family Guy texas-chainsawed Nebo's chest. That way he wudda killed two birds with one rock: hided the scar tissue from the tiktok op *and* bojoed the tat outta zistence.'

'Agreed,' I said. 'We need to contact the facial recognition specialist in Scientia. They should be able to confirm that Nebo and Creflo are the same person. And, assuming so, whether Creflo arrived in Blackpool on the same flight as Kiera and Brunhilda. He would have been nineteen – the same age as Brunhilda and a year younger than Kiera. I'd say it's a racing certainty that he was on the same flight in and the same flight out.'

Wham!®© nodded. 'And with the same tat smare easy to zero on he body.'

It wasn't long before the facial recognition expert came back. Nebo and Creflo *were* the same individual and Nebo/Creflo *was* on that Blackpool flight with the two women fourteen years ago. Back then he was going by Exodus Tomlinson.

'So it deffo were them tats what gotted the Sinatras, the Mozarts and the Disciplesons killed.' Bogart looked angry. 'And poor Stoker Fangly got she swallower sliced to stop us scovering what them tats was bout. This ain't not no serial killer stuff, this is badmost plitiko shit, ain't it not?'

'Exactly. Somehow the people behind it recruited Family Guy to do their dirty work and dress it up as his own. We have to find out how and why a serial killer was repurposed as a black ops assassin.'

Wham!®© made a disgusted noise and slid his chair back to his desk. His fingers skimmed across the keyboard again as he called up a list of "new wave" Family Guy victims. 'If you leaves out the Sinatras, Mozarts and Disciplesons, they still anudda twelve vics, six of em childs. But they wasn't not sasnations, so why was they killed?'

I thought about this. Then I said, 'Camouflage. I'd say Family Guy's first three "rebirth" events were staged to make the second three look like part of the previous series. But the resources needed to pull this off had to be much greater than one man working alone – no matter how skilful and experienced he might be.'

'We gotta nab this cut-hole, boss, bustagut ferrari.'

'We do, Bogart. And we will. C'mon.'

I headed for the door and he followed. 'Where we go, boss?'

'You been to São Paulo?'

He shook his head no.

'Nor me. But that's about to change.'

47

We arrived at the village of Santa Rita da Ribeira in São Paulo State after a forty-five minute flight from Rio de Jerusalem to São Paulo City. From there we hired a car for the two-hour drive into the countryside. The land was lush and green with impressive mountain backdrops, but we saw a lot of rural poverty. Santa Rita was no exception. With a population of around two thousand, the community comprised a dozen streets lined by single storey wooden houses brightly painted in yellows, blues and reds. The main street was a row of run-down businesses – an auto repair shop, grocery store, pizzeria, café and four bars. It was the kind of place a young man like Creflo Bakker would have wanted to leave behind.

His parents, Galilee and Mary-Margaret owned a hardscrabble farm on the edge of the village. The farmhouse walls were faded green, peeling to reveal bare timber. An ancient tractor and rusted steel harrow had been left under a tarpaulin shelter. A few hens pecked the dusty ground and a pair of undernourished goats watched us leave the car and head for the farmhouse.

Creflo's father, Galilee Bakker, came onto the balcony holding a shotgun at hip height. He was a small man with narrow crumpled features in bib denim pants and no shirt. We were downwind and I smelled his armpits at ten metres.

Mary-Margaret appeared at his shoulder. She was a plump woman, taller and bigger-boned than her husband, with scraped back hair and a round face. I knew from the Harpo records that she and Galilee were fifty-seven.

We showed our Harpo shields and I asked Galilee to put away the shotgun. We'd come about their boy, Creflo, I said, and needed to talk.

Galilee squinted at our shields, lowered the gun and beckoned us indoors.

The living room was unsurprisingly spartan – a sofa, two armchairs and a low table on a thin carpet. In the hearth a fire had been lit and was boiling a pot of something that smelled of meat and onions. Whatever, it did a good job of masking Galilee's pit stink and for this I was grateful.

The Bakkers sat on the couch, Wham!®© and I took an armchair each.

I had no idea what kind of relationship they'd had with their son so I did this by the book. I told them Creflo and his wife had been found murdered at their home in Rio de Jerusalem. The three children had been in the house at the time but had survived without serious physical injury. I offered our condolences and explained that we were here to ask some questions as part of our pursuit of the killer.

As I spoke, their faces stayed expressionless. They were hearing what I said but it didn't seem to be registering.

'Poor Creflo,' Mary-Margaret said at last and a tear rolled down one cheek. Then her emotions took over and she wept, sucking in gasps of air between long sobs.

Wham!®© handed her a handkerchief and she took it with a trembling hand.

'He'll be with the Lord,' she said, mopping tears from her face. 'They all will.'

'More like the damned devil.' Galilee's face was unyielding, his voice gravelly. 'That boy was hell-bound from the moment he entered this world.'

'Hold your peace, Galilee! That's our son you're talking about!' Mary-Margaret gave her husband a spiky look. Normally, this would have earned her a beating, but Mary-Margaret was a cleansed woman from a wealthy family. According to her Harpo file, she'd married below her station. Way below, I thought. It seemed Galilee – then a groundskeeper – got her pregnant, forcing them to marry and quit São Paulo city for this backwater, where Creflo was born.

'No son of mine,' Galilee muttered, shaking his head. 'I disowned that boy twenty years ago. He was a goddamn sodomite.'

'That's a holy slander, Galilee.' Mary-Margaret stuck out her heavy bosom and cocked her neck in the way of an angry mother hen.

'No, it ain't, Mary-Margaret. Creflo's death and the death of his wife and them little ones was divine retribution. Vengeance is mine, sayeth the Lord.'

I glanced at Bogart and he mirrored my astonishment. Did these people usually carry on like this in front of strangers?

'Creflo did nothing wrong,' Mary-Margaret insisted.

'He never needed to *do* nothing wrong because he was thinking about it and that's as sinful – worse. I used to see the way he looked at them other boys.'

'You saw what you wanted to see, Galilee. Because he didn't take to sports and was shy with girls.'

I made a polite cough to remind them of our presence. 'When did you last see your son?'

My question was directed at both, but Mary-Margaret replied. 'Fifteen years ago. He would have been eighteen.'

She went to a sideboard and started rummaging in one drawer, then another.

'So you never met Creflo's wife Melania and your grandchildren?' I asked her over my shoulder.

'More's the pity,' she said, still searching for something.

Finally, she found it – a framed photograph.

'This was taken the day he left.'

She crossed the room and handed me the photo.

I looked at it.

I looked again.

The picture showed Creflo in his late teens, standing with a slightly gauche expression on the porch of the farmhouse. Next to him was Judgment Jesusly, tall and lean in a cowboy shirt decorated with treble clefs. Both were smiling as if something momentous had just happened.

'Judgment was the Thirteenth Father back then,' Mary-Margaret explained. 'A rising star in the firmament of Trumpian politics. A few months later he was promoted to Twelfth Father.'

'What brought him here?' I tried not to sound disrespectful of Santa Rita.

'He married my cousin and we knew one another from our undergraduate days at the University of São Paulo.' Mary-Margaret was gazing at the photo as if it evoked memories of brighter times. 'Creflo was a smart boy. Too smart to stay here. I wrote to Judgment, asking if there were any openings for Creflo on his staff.' Again, her eyes filled with tears. 'And he came. He *came. In person*. He met our boy and they got along famously.'

I guessed what was coming before she confirmed it: Jesusly offered Creflo an internship on his staff and that was the last she time she saw her son.

'I didn't resent him going. Or never coming back.' She glared at her husband. 'Creflo was too good for this dreadful little village, much too good.'

'Not the way I saw it,' Galilee said. 'Even in them days the First Father could see sin in folk and always tried to help them back onto God's path. He took the boy to cleanse him, but some souls are beyond the power of cleansing. Sure he married; sure he brought children into this world; but he forsook all help and became a secret sodomite.'

I'd heard enough of this endless dispute.

I took a photo of the framed picture and handed it back to Mary-Margaret. 'This was the last you saw or heard from Creflo?'

'It was.' She returned the picture to the sideboard and stopped half way back. 'Unless I can find …'

She left the room and I heard her footsteps on the stairs. A few minutes later a heavy object was moved across the floorboards, causing tiny spirals of dust to fall from the ceiling.

There were more sounds of Mary-Margaret's searching – bumping and scraping, tinkling of metal or glass, slamming of lids or drawers.

'She's rooting through that old chest of hers,' Galilee told us. 'Keeps all sorts of junk in there. Trump knows what she's looking for.'

At last Mary-Margaret's search came to an end. More footsteps on the stairs, then she was back in the living room, holding another photo, smaller than the other and unframed.

'He sent this in an email and I had it printed.'

She handed me the picture. It showed Creflo standing on a beach with sun on his face and wind in his hair. Behind him were some hut-like buildings on top of a promenade wall. He could have been anywhere.

I looked at Mary-Margaret. 'Do you still have the email?'

She shook her head. 'I don't even have the computer. It was old, even back then.'

'Can you remember what that email said?'

'Not much. He was happy, had found his perfect job. No regrets about leaving Santa Rita. Sent his love. That was it.'

I took a picture of the photo, though I doubted it would be of any use.

There was no more to be done here so I turned to Wham!®© with a time-to-leave expression. We came to our feet, gave them our condolences again, thanked them for their cooperation and left the farmhouse.

'Glad that franksteiny spud Galilee Bakker ain't not *my* pop,' was all he said as he started the car and we headed back to the airport.

This silence was welcome because I had some thinking to do.

My first thought was that Creflo may not be Galilee's son and this was the root of his disdain. But something of this nature would almost certainly have been on the couple's Harpo file. Next I considered the possibility that Jesusly was Creflo's father – which would certainly have been omitted from the file. As Mary-Margaret said, Jesusly's star was in the ascendant even fifteen years ago. A word in the ear of Derek Anti-Satan and the record could easily have been altered. Exile in San Rita would have been a high price. I could imagine Mary-Margaret being willing to pay it, but not Galilee. Perhaps this fuelled his rage.

Then again, if Jesusly was a party to assassination-by-serial-killer, why would he have allowed his own flesh and blood to be targeted? Or was this *exactly* why Creflo had been killed? If so, what did this say about the other two victims who had the same tattoo? Were Kiera and Brunhilda also Jesusly's children?

After a while I realized I was unearthing many more questions than answers.

For now, though, we had solid evidence linking the First Father of the Holy Trumpian Empire to one of Family Guy's victims and this in itself was a major move forward.

Bogart suggested turning on the radio and I said yeah, why not?

We tuned into to some righteous roots songs by Lord Huron and John Hiatt and James McMurtry. And with this soundtrack we drove through the abundant land of underfed people and bigotry and suspicion.

48

The secret weapon I'd told All-Saints Geddes about had done the trick: Grey Lady was ready to talk. My secret weapon – Bob Puritan – had pulled off what I couldn't. I'd been counting on his peculiar honest charm, his reputation as a champion of the underdog, and the advantage he had over the rest of us – he was of a similar age to Grey Lady.

Her name was Ariana – we didn't have a last name yet – and she was waiting for me in the interview room. Walking in that direction, I swallowed the last of my vending machine coffee and focused on the work ahead. Wham!®© and I had arrived back in Rio de Jerusalem late last night after a tedious drive back to São Paulo City and a bumpy flight thanks to severe turbulence. I'd told Bogart to take the morning off, but there was no lie-in for me.

Ariana was waiting at the table with Puritan, carefully positioned so he wouldn't be sitting next to either of us.

I sat opposite her and made a friendly smile. 'Bob tells me you've agreed to cooperate, Ariana.'

'Up to a point.' She didn't return the smile. 'Which will be determined by me. Also, for the purposes of this interview, Bob has agreed to represent me as legal counsel. And I want inter-jurisdiction immunity from prosecution, which Bob is handling.'

I gave Puritan a sharp look and he made a whatever-it-takes shrug.

He was right. As I expected, he'd already prepared the document and witnessed Ariana and me signing it.

Geddes wouldn't be happy – my day was looking up already.

'Very well, Ariana,' I said when the formality was complete, 'would you please tell us your full name and age.'

A quick glance at Puritan, then her eyes returned to mine. 'My name is Ariana Bad-Bunny. I'm sixty-four.'

'And what's your interest in this investigation?'

'I want to catch Family Guy and kill him with maximum pain before you can deliver him to a cushy Scientian supermax to live out the rest of his days.'

'Why?'

'It's what he deserves.'

'A lot of people in all the federations would agree. But why did you decide to this was something you should take care of yourself?'

She asked for a cigarette and I nodded to Puritan. He took out a pack and pushed it towards her with a disposable lighter.

When she'd lit her smoke, she said, 'The bastard killed my niece.'

This pulled me up, no two ways. 'He's killed a lot of women. Which one was your niece?'

She took a long pull on her cigarette. 'Kiera Sinatra.'

She let this sink in.

'I'm the sister of Rihanna Doonican, formerly Rihanna Smedge and Rihanna Bad-Bunny.'

She let this sink in too.

'You got it,' she said, seeing that I understood the implication. 'I'm also related to Gonzales Smedge.'

I took a cigarette from the pack and lit it. I shouldn't have but the nicotine hit would help me to focus. 'Related how?'

'My late sister Rihanna was the mother of Gonzales and Kiera, making me an aunt to both. They had different fathers – Nacho Smedge and Dean Doonican – hence different last names.'

'So Kiera was Gonzales' half-sister. Is that why she had a secret job at Smedge's night club?'

'In a way.' She tapped cigarette ash in a paper cup provided by Puritan. 'She had a great singing voice and loved to perform. But she was Gonzales' kid sister and they wanted to see each other. She'd married a good man, got a steady job, had two lovely kids. Gonzales respected that and understood why she wanted to keep her links to organized crime from her husband and children. This was why they kept her visits to Fifi's to themselves.'

This sounded plausible. I asked her to talk about her own relationship with Kiera.

'I loved her dearly and we were close, mainly because of my sister's lousy choice of men – both Nacho and Dean were from crime families. I suppose Rihanna liked living on the edge. Nacho was killed in a revenge attack and Dean is serving life-without-parole for multiple murders. Even when they were at home, those men were really somewhere else. I suppose I was the nearest thing to a father figure that Kiera had – mother figure too when Rihanna died of liver failure eleven years ago.'

'Your sister was a big drinker?'

'That often comes with living on the edge.'

I probed a little deeper. 'You like living on the edge, though, Ariana, and you don't strike me as a boozy type.'

'Heavy drinking and my job don't mix.'

'What *is* your job?'

She said nothing.

I gave her a nudge. 'C'mon, that level of field craft doesn't come from working a nine-to-five job. We asked around all the intelligence organizations and whoever you work – or worked – for thinks highly enough of you to cover your trail.'

She glanced at Puritan and there was an unspoken communication. Somewhat weirdly, he said, 'Under the terms of the agreement we just signed, my client isn't obliged to respond.'

I wanted to challenge him about conflict of interest but reminded myself of his whatever-it-takes approach and changed tack. 'Did your nephew Gonzales ask you to use these skills to find Family Guy?'

'He knew what I was doing and advanced funds when I needed them. But the idea was mine. Also, I want to say for the record that I've been operating entirely alone – I'm not working for anyone else.'

This may have been true. I couldn't imagine her working for Harpo. The FIB was also out of the question because in that case Wu Mei would certainly have known. And why would she want the chaos Ariana's involvement had already created?

She was most likely a retired officer from Above Average Intelligence, the PopRep®© intelligence agency that took its name from the Vox Popeye®© that proclaimed all PopReppers to have above average intelligence.

I considered making an approach to its chief. Their identity was secret and they were codenamed A++ because in the alphabet A came before C, head of the old MI6. The two plus symbols had been added to elevate the title even higher in PopRep®©'s absurd hierarchy. I had to wonder, though, why they stopped at two plus symbols. Why not three? Or ten? Or infinity?

Whatever, I was fairly sure A++ would know Ariana. They would have been contemporaries, perhaps friends. But if that were so, A++ would never betray an old comrade, so why bother asking? For now, I'd play along with her claim to be operating alone.

'Okay, Ariana,' I said, 'this is the way this will work: we share what we get with you and you with us. That sound fair?'

'It *sounds* fair.'

'Very well, tell me what you've got.'

She dropped her cigarette in the paper cup. It sizzled in the coffee at the bottom. 'Why don't *you* tell *me*?'

I turned to Puritan with an appealing expression.

He got the message and told Ariana that her immunity deal was contingent on her co-operating with me. Whatever I gave back would be a bonus. Also, he added, she could trust me.

Ariana thought about this for a short while. Then she said, 'Fourteen years ago Kiera was working for a PR agency as part of a team that handled Dreezy Simz's account. Back then, Simz was on the edge of bigtime success in PopRep®© politics. She'd recently become a junior Alister and was highly ambitious.'

The theme Bogart and I uncovered at San Rita began to take on even greater significance. I could guess what was coming next but wanted to let Ariana tell me in her own words.

'Simz singled Kiera out for special praise. She told her she was a gifted comms professional and asked her to join Simz's personal campaign team with greater opportunities and a big boost in pay.'

'Kiera was flattered, delighted. What twenty-year-old wouldn't have been? She took up the offer and within a few days had left Old Britain without telling anyone where she was going. She returned three months later a different person. Withdrawn, anxious, introverted and no longer working for Simz. It was obvious that something bad had happened, but she refused to tell me where she'd been or what had gone on.'

This was extremely interesting. I hadn't been able to find out what happened to Nebo/Creflo after he was recruited by Jesusly because he never saw his parents again. But it was likely that whatever happened to Kiera also happened to him – and Brunhilda.

'Time passed,' Ariana continued, 'and Kiera began to recover something of her old self. She didn't work in PR or comms again but found work as a school secretary. Didn't pay much, but enough to live on. Then she met Kanye and pretty soon was back to normal. Well, almost.'

She took another cigarette and lit it. I guessed this was tough, even for an old campaigner. 'Then, shortly before she and her family were murdered, she returned to square one. Worse than square one. Anxious, hyper-vigilant, restless, stressed. I asked what was wrong. Was someone threatening her? She told me she was under pressure at work. I knew this wasn't true, but short of calling her a liar, there wasn't much I could do.'

She pulled on the cigarette and blew the smoke into the grainy strip-lit air. 'One thing she did let slip was that she should never have been in touch with some people from Apex San José. At least I think that was what she said. I asked what she meant but she wouldn't say and pleaded with me to forget she'd mentioned it. Two weeks later, she was dead, along with Kanye and the kids.'

There was an extended hiatus.

'In my line of work,' she resumed, 'I know the effects of acute paranoia when I see it. There's a motto: if you're not paranoid, you're probably dead. I saw this. I could have helped but she was too scared to let me. Even so, I blame myself for not protecting her better.'

'You think she was being stalked by Family Guy?'

'Who knows? It's possible. But I got the impression that whatever the threat was, it was to do with her past. Maybe she'd had a brush with Family Guy in the past and he'd come back to get her. And I've been wondering if it's a coincidence that his so-called first wave of killings ended fourteen years ago – the same year that Kiera vanished with Dreezy Simz for those three months.'

This was something I hadn't thought of, although I couldn't imagine how the disappearance of Kiera, Nebo and probably Brunhilda could be linked to Family Guy's decision to end his first sub-series. All the same, I told her it was something we could look into.

I asked, 'What did you find out about this Apex San José?'

She made a longsuffering expression. 'There are a lot of places called San José – more than seventeen hundred worldwide.' She made a frustrated sigh. 'As for Apex, it's an extremely common name for all sorts of businesses and other organizations. I tried cross-referencing the two but came up with nothing.'

'At least it's something to go on.' I made some notes, then looked up with a smile. 'That's all, for now, Ariana. You're free to go.'

She frowned. 'I thought we had a deal. Aren't you sharing anything with me?'

'Not right now.' I glanced quickly at Puritan. 'Bob will stay in touch.'

I could tell by her savvy nod that she understood what I meant by this. There were aspects of the case I wanted to share but didn't want Geddes or Anti-Satan finding out. Instead, I'd tell her off-the-record through Puritan.

We were wrapping the interview up when my phone vibrated against my hip.

I took it out. It was Wham!®©.

'You gotta come, boss!' He sounded close to panic. 'It Plato – them Harpo bastards taked him!'

49

excused myself from the interview and left Puritan to make follow-up arrangements with Ariana Bad-Bunny. Then I went with Wham!®© to the incident room.

'You say Tomsky has been arrested by the Harpo?'

'Well…'

Comanche looked across from her work station. 'What Tweetie means is that he's been stood up by his new boyfriend.'

'Ain't not so!' Bogart turned on her, chin jutting. 'Plato wuddabin there for the meet less smin real serio gone down.'

Comanche chuckled. 'All that's gone down is someone who can give him a better suck-job than you.'

I gave her a give-it-a-rest look. She was right Wham!®© was over-reacting. But there were ways of dealing with him and mockery wasn't one.

'Boss, I knows this ain't not right,' he said. 'We was gonna plan some filming here in Rio de Jerusalem. We gotted chit-chats lined up with neybaz what lives near the Disciplesons' place. This were portant shit.'

This was starting to sound more concerning than I first thought. 'What did they say at his office?'

Wham!®© gave me a helpless look. 'Just that he gone outta town. The jane at the front desk telled me she never knowed where he went or when he were coming back.'

I called All-Saints Geddes. He said he knew nothing of Tomsky's disappearance and insisted it was nothing to do with the Harpo. I had no idea whether he was lying or not but at least for now I had to take what he said at face value. I asked the airport and the seaport to run checks and both came back within the hour to say they had no record of Tomsky having left the Holy Trumpian Empire.

'He may have travelled in-country,' Comanche said. 'Old Brazil's a big place.'

At last, I thought, she'd contributed something helpful.

'Also,' Puritan added, 'he could have crossed into Old Argentina or Old Uruguay or any of the other eight countries that Old Brazil has land borders with. No need for a passport so no one would know.'

This was true enough but it did nothing to mollify Bogart. He needed a distraction so I sent him back to Tomsky's downtown offices to see if he could turn up any leads on the media oligarch's whereabouts.

Comanche suggested contacting a heroin exporter she'd done business with. He knew what was happening on the streets and might have heard about Tomsky's vanishing act. She looked at me as if I should have been surprised that the drug trade existed in the Holy Trumpian Empire. But after my trip to Santa Rita da Ribeira with its fertile land and wretched people, I'd have been a lot more surprised if the trade *hadn't* existed here.

When she'd left I headed for my office and heard Puritan following me, moving heavily with his stick.

'Something I need to tell you, boss.'

I indicated the visitor chair and he made himself comfortable.

'What's on your mind, Bob?'

He twiddled a dial on his clapped-out hearing aid then looked up. 'It's about that portrait of Family Guy you asked me for. You remember the gist?'

I précised the main points. 'He's creative, intelligent, talented. He sees his "work" as art. He's the Caravaggio of serial killers. Charismatic and socially connected, but unpredictable, volatile and nightmarish to work with. Probably from a professional background, but more likely creative rather than tech, which differs from the original FIB profile. And a highly successful artist, not the gifted under-achiever with a technical background described in earlier profiles.

'Also, much older than originally thought. Not mid-twenties when he started, then mid forties when he made his comeback. More like mid-thirties first time out and mid-fifties now. So, a late developer in the serial killer world.'

I made a quizzical expression. 'How did I do?'

'Spot on.' He looked at me through his one eye, long, piercing and intense. 'Does all that remind you of anyone?'

I thought about this.

A name came to mind.

But that was ridiculous.

'We should also consider that serial killers like to insert themselves into investigations. You know the deal, it heightens their hit and allows them to relive their fantasy.'

The name came back to me.

No longer ridiculous. Suddenly obvious. The man described in Puritan's portrait – the man who had worked his way into the investigation – slotted perfectly with the man in my head. Like seeing the two elements of a gestalt image at the same time.

I spoke the name. It sounded even weirder aloud than in my head. 'Plato Tomsky?'

'Think about it, boss.'

I thought about it. The more I thought, the more sense it made.

'It's not just the personality fit,' Bob went on. 'Or his persistent offers to help our inquiries. What kind of resources would enable Family Guy to operate as effectively as he has?'

I didn't need to dwell on this for long. 'The ability to travel internationally; a network of global contacts – movers and shakers in all three federations willing to pull strings or look the other way; and, when these people couldn't or wouldn't help, the financial clout to buy information or other assistance with big bribes.'

I went to the vending machine and brought two cups of tepid murk. 'You could probably add blackmail. And all sorts of other inducements.'

Bob nodded, then winced as he sipped his coffee. 'On top of all that, I did a search of Tomsky's whereabouts when Family Guy struck – not just at the three most recent episodes, but all of them – including the first wave of homicides.'

I knew from my own experience that Tomsky had been in Vegas, England when the Sinatras were killed; in Berlin under dem Himalaya before the Mozarts were murdered;

and here in Rio de Jerusalem in plenty of time to visit the Disciplesons. And I had no doubt that the rest of Puritan's analysis would be flawless. Then, of course, he'd turned up in Blackpool around the time Stoker Fangly's throat was opened.

One thing still puzzled me. 'What about sparing the Mozart and Discipleson kids? How might that fit with Tomsky as Family Guy?'

He handed me an electronic tablet. When I swiped it open I saw a document headed:

Federation of Scientia
Freedom of Information Department
application reference AH-BP-1293-CXV

'I took the liberty of applying for this a few weeks ago when I began to feel curious about Tomsky's background. I may well have been going down a blind alley so I kept my mouth shut until today, when I received this response.'

I was looking at recently unclassified psychological, social services and police reports on Plato Tomsky as a seven-year-old. A fifty-year confidentiality period had been introduced following legislative reforms in Scientia. As a result, the documents became subject to new freedom-of-information laws. And nobody could have been better placed to know about and exploit this that Bob Puritan.

I scanned the densely typed documents. They concerned the removal of Plato and his twin sister Emmeline from the family home shortly before their ninth birthdays. The children were taken into care after witnessing their father, Ulysses Tomsky, having sex on numerous occasions with their twenty-one-year-old stepsister, Valeria. Ulysses, then fifty-three, had married Valeria's mother after his first wife – and the twins' mother – left him when they were aged eight. Ulysses' second wife was a fashion designer who spent much of her time abroad and it was during these periods that the intercourse took place. The evidence had come from Plato who used his phone to video the pair on the living room floor from the vantage point of the landing outside his room. He had sent the video to Emmeline and she showed it to a teacher.

Later reports took up the narrative when the twins were sixteen and in the care of their maternal grandparents. Neither had seen their father after being removed by social workers and both insisted they never wanted to. The reason for these reports was that Plato and Emmeline had been caught using heroin and Plato convicted for harming one neighbour's dog and another's cat. It seemed he had cut off the dog's ears and the cat's tail. In addition, the remains of several tortured wild animals were found in the neighbourhood and Plato admitted responsibility for these acts too. Both Puritan and I knew hurting animals was a common feature in serial killer development. Tomsky's offences had been committed in Scientia where animal cruelty penalties were unsurprisingly harsh. Plato was given a two year sentence at a juvenile correctional institution which, like many such places, did exactly the opposite of its moniker. The first thing he learned was how not to get caught; the second, how to hurt humans. After his release, police linked a number of violent sexual attacks on girlfriends, but all complaints were either withdrawn or nothing could be proved.

In the same year Plato was released, Emmeline was found dead in a junky squat. A coroner recorded that she died of a heroin overdose.

The next and final document was a police record concerning the disappearance of Plato's step-sister, Valeria, the year after Emmeline died. She had gone to work one morning but didn't arrive and was never seen again. Once more, the police had their suspicions but couldn't find any evidence connecting Plato to Valeria's disappearance. The report also noted that Ulysses Tomsky had died of cancer while his son was in the correctional institution. The cops didn't say so, but their thinking was clear: if Ulysses *had* been alive when Emmeline died, he wouldn't have lasted long.

'After this.' Puritan said, 'Plato kept his hands clean. He threw himself into his career, first as a photo-journalist, then a documentary-maker and eventually the media oligarch we know today.'

I drank some coffee. It had gone cold but somehow tasted better. 'Except he also became Family Guy. Your portrait paints a compelling picture of the serial killer. And Tomsky's personal history is an ideal launchpad for Family Guy's psychosis.'

'You think this is enough to make a case, boss?'

'More than enough. It explains everything: the torture and abasement of the older man and much younger woman; the use of anaesthetic on the children – and later, sparing them. And we have a very clear idea of where Family Guy's signature comes from: the posing of the older man as Tomsky's dad, the younger woman as his step-sister and the kids as himself and his sister, innocent victims of the adults' wrongdoing.'

I leaned forward with my elbows on the desk and my head in my hands.

'What's up, boss?' Puritan sounded concerned.

'Why did he vanish *this morning*?'

'You think someone tipped him off?'

'It's too much of a coincidence that he disappeared a few hours before your freedom of information documents arrived. He hasn't been arrested, snatched off the street or kidnapped. He's on the run.'

'I agree. But you should stop thinking what I think you're thinking. This has nothing to do with Bogart.'

I raise an eyebrow.

'Come on, boss, why would he?'

'Why *wouldn't* he?'

'Bogart is the most loyal person I've ever met.'

'Loyal to me? Or loyal to the career boost coming his way courtesy of Tomsky?'

'You do him a disservice.' Bob sounded disappointed.

Nonetheless, I couldn't entirely dismiss the suspicion that Wham!®© might have let something slip. And despite all this, I had to feel for him. It seemed his great benefactor had been manipulating him since the get-go in order to insinuate himself into the investigation.

I finished my coffee. 'So who do you think gave Tomsky the tip-off?'

Bob levered himself to his feet with his walking stick. 'Someone powerful enough to recruit the most famous serial killer in two thousand years and the imagination to use him as an assassin.'

50

Wham!®© returned from Tomsky's downtown office with no answers and even greater anxiety.

He needed another diversion so I asked him to help me to repeat Ariana Bad-Bunny's worldwide checks on places called San José with any sort of connection to an organization with Apex in its name.

I followed him to his work-station and stood by his chair as he went to work.

'Nada,' he said at last.

This was to be expected. Although we had to double-check Ariana's research, I was confident her work would have been thorough.

Next, I thought of the photo we'd brought back from Santa Rita – the one Creflo Bakker sent to his mother, showing a happy young man on a sunny beach. I asked Bogart to bring it up on his screen, then to enlarge it. We stared at the image, still extremely grainy despite the enhancement software.

We saw nothing we hadn't seen before but still carried on looking.

'We ain't not gonna get nada from this, boss,' he said at length. 'Sept sore slots.'

'Try enlarging that blurry area.'

'Which one?' He rubbed his eyes. 'Ebbathin is blurry.'

'Here.' I placed my index finger in the top left of the image, next to an area with a green and white tinge. 'What do you think that might be?'

He focused in and magnified it. 'Dunno. Smin maked of cloth. Maybe a parasol, awning, some sorta flag.'

I peered a little closer. I thought I could see a ripple in the material. 'Let's try a flag. Run a search on all national, state and regional flags with green and white colours.'

Bogart's fingers clickety-clacked on the keyboard and the screen filled with the flags I asked for. He scrolled down. There were too many to make much sense of – eight regional flags with green and white colours in the small country of Old Guatemala alone.

'Magnify again,' I said.

'We just gets morer and morer blurry stuffs.' He sounded weary, though at least his mind wasn't on the disappearance of his benefactor. 'But you the boss.'

And he was right about the image quality. Every magnification sacrificed resolution. All we could see now was a blizzard of pixels.

I stepped away from the screen. Then went closer and away again. I tried viewing the screen from a different angle. I didn't know what I was looking for – an idea or some kind of inspiration rather than anything tangible.

Then Wham!®© saw something.

He indicated a vague yellow-red scatter of pixels amid the mass of green and white.

'What are you thinking, Bogart?'

He ploughed his fingers through his hair. 'Poss smin behind the greeny white bit. Mebbe anudda flag.'

I thought about this. A lot of places flew federal, state and regional flags at the same location – a town hall, for example. 'What if that's a state or regional flag behind a national one?'

He keyed in these search parameters. A single option came up: the green and white colours of Old Nigeria and the yellow and red flag of Taraba State in the east of the country. But Taraba State was landlocked which meant no coastline.

'All right,' I said, close to giving this up, 'try the opposite: a national flag with yellow and red behind a regional one of green and white.'

This time the search produced the yellow and red national flag of Old Spain with two green and white regional flags – Andalusia and Extremadura. Like Taraba, Extremadura had no coastline. However, Andalusia did.

Bogart didn't need telling to run locations in Andalusia called San José with a connection to an organization named Apex.

The first came up – a small resort town on the Mediterranean coast.

But the second didn't.

'Leastways we got a place,' Wham!®© said with an optimistic grin that fooled neither of us.

'Let's give it a rest for now,' I said. 'Come on, I'll buy you lunch.'

His grin became genuine. 'Can I get bonus peeky flamingo wings?'

I said of course he could and took him to a nice restaurant on Jaffa Street. I wasn't especially hungry but I needed to recycle my thoughts, find a fresh perspective. And, as always, the best way to do this was to stop thinking completely and let my subconscious do some heavy lifting.

We chatted shit, which was a lot easier for Wham!®© than me. All the same, I was determined to press on with my non-thinking thinking process. So I forced myself to dive into the morass of trifles that formed a celeb influsser's world – fresh developments on Howler®© and BlahBlah®©; self-correcting eyebrow implants that eliminated the need to cut or shave; why *Who's Who* had changed its name to *Woo-Hoo* and who was new in the latest edition. And, having decided to embrace the conversation, I found myself becoming worryingly interested. I asked questions and was keen to know the answers. I formed views on issues that were beyond banal.

He was less than half way through his extra spicy flamingo wings when the idea popped up from deep in my mind.

'Sorry, Bogart,' I said, 'we're going to have to leave.'

He glared at me with a rare hint of defiance. 'What you got boss, morer portanter than bonus peeky flamingo wings?'

My idea had come from the words I used to describe my technique of non-thinking thinking. From some obscure niche, I dredged up a similarly constructed phrase: "non-subsidiary subsidiary". This was a practice used in a corporate fraud case I'd worked on in the early 2000s that involved moving debt from the parent company's balance sheet to overseas subsidiaries that weren't included in the parent's domestic accounts.

'Indulge me, Bogart,' I said. 'I've got to play a hunch. If it pays off, I'll buy you flamingo wings for the rest of the week. That sound fair?'

He seemed happy enough with this and we returned to the incident room in Harpo Head Office.

Back at his screen, I asked him to run a search for subsidiaries in San José, Andalusia named Apex with foreign parent companies.

Again, nothing.

After the surge of hope, this was dispiriting.

But I wasn't ready to give up yet. This two-flag thing was looking like a dead end. Until I was certain, though, I was going to persist.

We spent more time gazing at screensaver images of ocean scenes, mountain vistas, bucolic landscapes. I began to wish we'd finished our lunch. I was certain Bogart did.

At length he looked at me. I thought he was going to suggest calling this a day and I was ready to agree. I was wrong. 'All this corprate monkey biz,' he said, 'went down fourteen year in the wayback, right?'

I gave him a hopeful look.

'That a bigwhile, ain't it not? Lotta stuffs cudda gone down.'

I folded my arms across my chest. 'Such as?'

'Bizzes what was around then ain't not ness around right now. Ebba day they is bizes what goes busted. Or they flits to anudda place with cheap labour or tax breaks and whatnot.'

'That's great work, Bogart.' I placed my hand on his shoulder.

His expression was an uneasy alloy of delight and sheepishness.

'All right,' I said, 'let's look for businesses with Apex in their name – including subsidiaries of offshore parents – that were operating San José, in 4035 but later ceased trading or relocated.'

Bogart punched the keys so fast they sounded more like a constant tone than a succession of clicks.

He hit return, sat back and breathed out.

I wasn't breathing at all.

Until the logo of Apex Leadership Services appeared on the screen. The firm had been liquidated in 4036. It was an offshore subsidiary of Miami-based Resource Solutions, which folded later the same year.

'Bingo!' Bogart punched the air. 'I can taste them peeky flamingo wings aready.'

'You've earned them,' I said. 'Now, let's see if there's a list of shareholders.'

There was – including the majority shareholder and CEO of Apex Leadership and Resource Solutions. Her name was Ladybug Boo.

Not surprisingly, there was no address. But the Harpo database lived up to the organization's motto – "Always everywhere" – and brought up a home address for this Boo in Almeria, Old Spain. Made sense I guessed because Almeria was the capital of the province where Boo's training centre in San José was located.

As far as breaks went, this was as big as any since the investigation started.

Until we hit the first brick wall.

51

Finding Ladybug Boo was not as easy as I first imagined – even with the resources of the Harpo, Above Average Intelligence and the FIB.

A call to Above Average Intelligence's Madrid bureau told us she left Almeria six months ago after narrowly surviving an attempt on her life. A bomb had been planted under her car, which was detonated by a car thief who never knew how unlucky he'd been. She next turned up in San Francisco del Mediterráneo in Old Turkey where the FIB reported a further assassination attempt, this time a knife attack that missed her heart by five millimetres. After discharging herself from hospital against medical advice, she went silent. There were no records of her having left Scientia, or having returned to her house San Fran del Mediterráneo, or her place in Almeria.

None of the intelligence agencies had much on Boo – she was not known to any of them in relation to her past or present business activities. Nor were Above Average Intelligence or the FIB aware that she'd made enemies. Their only vaguely plausible theory for the attempts on her life was that she'd offended Zooist extremists the previous year when she acquired a meat processing company to service her core hospitality business.

As far as her personal history went, she was fifty-three and was born in Miami, which made her a PopRep®© citizen. There was a headshot photo showing a middle aged woman with strong features and dark hair. But I knew well enough that people's appearances changed – particularly when they'd survived two assassination attempts and didn't want to invite a third. Yet this curious dearth of information spoke for itself. Clearly, somebody powerful had taken a lot of trouble to conceal everything but the bare bones about this woman.

With no leads on Tomsky's disappearance, or any other developments with the Sinatra, Mozart or Discipleson cases, the investigation was losing momentum.

Once more, though, Wham!®© had a solution. Because Boo was a PopRepper®©, he suggested using his influsser network to find out more. He made some calls and came back quickly.

The word was that Ladybug Boo had been a gifted entrepreneur and rising star of the fast-growth start-up firmament. Resource Solutions had been an umbrella for subsidiaries in sectors ranging from life sciences to executive training. It was here that she seemed to have over-reached herself. In March 4036, Apex Leadership Services – which operated high-end training centres across the world – went bust amid mounting debt and plummeting revenue. This created a chain reaction and the entire organization collapsed six months later. Boo's reputation was destroyed and she vanished from the public eye.

'Something isn't right here,' I said. 'The executive training business isn't exactly high-risk, high-return. Who goes bust in that line of work?'

'Someone who someone else wants rid of.' This was Comanche. 'Boo must have pissed off some bigshot or found out something she wasn't meant to.'

She was right. 'According to Bogart's contacts, Boo's businesses were well-funded and managed,' I said. 'An enterprise like that wouldn't go under overnight unless it was made to. But how?'

Puritan shrugged. 'With sufficient political muscle there'd have been lots of way. For example, pressuring equity firms to withhold funding; or leaning on blue-chip clients to take their business elsewhere. And the fact that these exotically located training centres were worldwide suggests that whoever was responsible for the failure of Boo's business empire had global reach.'

I looked at Bogart. 'Did you pick up anything more on her background?'

He nodded. 'She come up Miami, Old USA. Never done well at school. Skipped lessons. Fighted with udda kids. Taked drugs. Got in bother with the nabbers. But this badstuffs come to an end when she were fifteen and set up a stand selling Old Cuban street scran what she cooked at home in Little Havana. Parently this nosh sold real well and in two year she maked nuff gelt to start she own bistro. Next come morer bistros, and morer still. Then she went into corprate catering and events. Lass were a millyaire at twenty-five and a billyaire fifteen year later. Final venture were exec training gaffs in zotic places like the one at San José. That were the flagship gaff.'

'Which was where something happened fourteen years ago that wrecked her life's work.' I looked around the group and gave them a short recap. 'We know from the beach photo that Creflo Bakker, who later became Nebo Discipleson, was in San José that same year. And from Ariana that Kiera said she regretted being in touch with some people from Apex, San José. In addition, we have strong evidence that Kiera was recruited by Simz and Creflo by Jesusly, again both in the same period. I think we can extend our hypothesis to include Brunhilda – who had the same tattoo as the other two – being enlisted by Confucius. That being so, it's reasonable to assume she was also present in San José. What we strongly suspect but can't prove is that Simz, Jesusly and Confucius were there. They'd have been up-and-coming politicians back then, probably being groomed for high office by attending events like leadership training. But we need evidence and I strongly suspect Ladybug Boo has it, which would explain why someone high up wants her dead.'

'Nubdy I gabbed to knowed where this Boo jane scarpered after San Fran del Med,' Bogart said. 'But if I were on the lam and them sassin popeyes was coming for me, home gotta be my numero uno place to lie low.'

'Bogart's right,' Puritan said. 'She came up in Little Havana. That's where her family and old friends will be. It's where there are people she can trust. Exactly where I'd go.'

'Me too.' I pushed back my chair and came to my feet. 'So let's get there as fast as we can.'

Our arrow plane was waiting at a private airstrip on the edge of the city. The others were already boarding as my SUV pulled up outside the hangar.

I stepped out of the vehicle and
the sun turned black.

Earth went dark.

And something weird happened to the laws of physics.

I was falling, but my descent was slow – I was soft and without substance.

The blackness paled to grey but dimensions had lost definition. The world had been flatpacked. The airstrip, the city, everything lost depth. Except the enormous typewriter I was standing on – a squat metal beast of a machine from the 20th Century. The kind with keys you had to thump and a carriage return lever you swiped with south paw hooks. If there was a more brutal writing instrument, I had yet to see it. I was standing on a key the size of a flagstone. It was the "f" key. Like my experience in the Paris bookstore, everything around me was familiar but not; everything made total sense and no sense. I was somehow part of it, yet remote.

From the belly of the machine I heard grumbles and moans, as if the typewriter was a sentient being. Diagonally ahead of me the "t" key began to sink, as if being hauled downward. I heard one of the great steel typebars creak from its housing and arc forward. The typeface struck a sheet of paper with a vicious thwack, rattling the steel frame. I staggered, fearing I was going to fall into the chasm between the keys. I regained my balance in time to see the nearby "h" key depress, sending its typeface smashing against the paper. Next it was the "e" key, after this, the space bar, then more keys and more and more still in a tattoo of almost simultaneous thunderclaps. The machine shuddered and clanged under the barrage of key strikes. After five I went on my knees for better stability. By the tenth I was prone on the key's Bakelite surface.

The keystrokes stopped.

A story was being written and I was in it.

But who was moving the keys?

Who was the author?

Was it *my* author?

One thing I did know was the order of keystrokes. They had spelled out a book title – *The Big Happy*.

'Boss! Are you okay?' Puritan's voice reached into wherever I'd been and hauled me out of it.

The lawyer was waiting at the foot of the aircraft steps.

I looked around, bewildered. But my surroundings were back to normal. And like the experience in the stairwell of the Harpo Happy House, there was no pile of books waiting for me; no epiphany; no new understanding.

Unless some sort of message or insight was bound up in the surreal events themselves.

If so, I had no idea what this might be.

'You seemed a little confused.' Bob approached me with a concerned expression.

'I'm fine,' I said. 'Let's get on with this.'

52

MIAMI, FLORIDA

Guess what. We was back in PopRep®©. Oh, the lovey-dovey of it. You mighta thinked I were getting customed to gabbing IngoLingo®© by this time. But it were the zact oppo. Morer I speaked, morer it drived me eastbound. Anyways, needs musted.

We flied arrow plane into Miami Internat where the local nabs was waiting. They gived us a gaff at the Miami Big Cop Shop on NW 2nd Avenue and we finded rooms at the Hyatt Regency.

Next we taked a cab cross town to Little Havana and legged the streets round the house on SW 6th Street where Ladybug Boo growed up. Gottasay, it weren't not the tough neybrud what I were specting. Frayed at the edges praps – graffiti on the walls of back street auto-repair shops and light indstry units. Some houses had chicken wire fences and dirt yards and wanted a lick of paint. But most was keeped spruce and spectable.

'Boss,' Bogart tattled. 'Looks like we got bother.'

The blade boys was standing on the street corner in their fashny garb and high-neck Doc Martens.

'Ignore em,' tattled I. 'They full of piss and wind.'

'*They* ain't gonna ignore *us*,' Comanche gabbed.

She were right. The bladies spread theyselves cross the sidewalk, blocking our way, grinning leery. Then out come their blades – zombie-gutters and switches, razors and bowies.

A long-beardy jack with a shaved fusebox come tward us.

'Give us you gelt and we won't cut you.' He chuckled. 'Well, not so bad that fifty stitches can't fix.'

He threw back his fusebox and hawked up phlegm with a scrapy-glotty noise. Then he spit a gob what falled on the ground, green and wobbly like smin living.

His pals crowded round the still-shivring phlegm, clearly envious.

'Look what Bez done!' gabbed one.

'That the bestermost green un what I ebba specked,' tattled anudda.

And there were me thinking this weren't not such a bad neybrud.

The lad named Bez come at me frisky, zombie gutter flashing this way and that.

I were ready but Comanche were readier. She catched his wrist full lunge and twisted it outways. Zombie clanged on the sidewalk. Bez howled wolfy. But Comanche weren't done. No, not by a long ways. Next, she winded his knife-arm through one-eighty. He jacked-knifed, yowling louder as his shoulder popped.

Yet again, I thought, Comanche gone way too far. She cudda hurt the lad without flicting such serious harm.

By now, Bez's pals was bailing bonus giddy-up.

'Ladybug Boo.' Comanche tattled hissy into the lug of Bez. 'Where did she hang out when she lived her? Who with? Where did her folks work?'

Bez's viz were knotted in pain. 'Dunno, lady, honest. I were nada but a babby in them days.'

Comanche wrenched his gipsy. Anudda armour-piercy screech.

'But you heard stuff as you were growing up, didn't you? Someone as famous as Ladybug coming out of a small neighbourhood like this, there must have been stories and you must have heard them.'

One more jerk. Musta sended Bez's pain level to the max and then some. He screeched falsetto like his balls got cut off and started whimprin sobby. 'All I heared were that Ladybug used to work shifts at the 7-Eleven on SW 12th Avenue. And her pappy shooted the old-timer shit in Domino Park. But I never knowed Ladybug. Never meeted the jane. Please lemme go, lady, *please-please-please.*'

Comanche released him and he hobbled off, still moaning, clutching his popped shoulder.

I give Comanche a stinky speck. 'Did you gotta bojo the lad so grievous?'

She made a stubborn spresh. 'He was asking for it and he deserved it. Maybe he'll think twice before pulling a zombie on someone.'

'And mebbe he'll won't think at all,' I tattled. 'Can't you not go anyplace and not put smoddy in the hospital or the morgue?'

'I was protecting you.'

'I never needed it.'

'And I got some useful intel, which is more than you, or anyone else has managed.'

'We all gotta calm down.' Wham!®© were never a fan of Comanche but even he cogged that this bickering were getting us nowhere. 'Comanche's right. She did get us a coupla leads. So let's chase em down.'

There were no disgreeing with this so we quitted the area and legged to SW 8th Street, a busy thoroughfare what some specked as the tiktok of Little Havana. Proaching lunchtime and the neybrud were filling with popeyes out for some scran.

Lot of em taked their grub to Domino Park and sitted eating fresco at the tables and chairs under shady canopies. Smov of the old-timers give these lunch spuds zentful glances, but most was too deep into their games to notice. These seniors was zactly the spuds what wudda membered Ladybug or her pappy.

I leaved my three amigos near the entrance and went alone. But nubdy at the first table were up for gabbing. The old boys was focused on nada but their dominoes as they maked their plays. Same with the second table, and the third.

So for the next, I taked out a fifty frog bill and tossed it on the table. 'That plus anudda fifty is for any of you good spuds what can help me,' I gabbed. 'I just after info about the Boo famly from the wayback.'

A player in a blue beret turned his rheumy slots real slow tward me.

'You with the nabs?'

'I am.' I showed my shield. There were no good lying – these lads wudda knowed aready. 'But I ain't not here to make no trouble. Just tryna contact Ladybug. She ain't wanted nor nada like that. I just wanna gab.'

I give em a bitwhile to digest this, then went on. 'I knows you popeyes played doms at this gaff with Ladybug's pappy, Lil Richard. I reckon Smov you is mebbe still in touch. Mebbe Lil Richard can help. We tryna help his lass, not hurt her.'

There were a slow quiet. It were ziff these popeyes got a joint cap and was mulling my quest as one.

At last the rheumy-slot one gimme a wary stare. 'If we can help – and that a monstabig "if" – we come to you. Where you at?'

I told him the Hyatt Regency.

He taked the fifty frogs and tattled, 'That for good faith. We gets the rest – *each* – if this come to smin.'

Then he turned back to the game.

---
*

I give up hopes a bigwhile back of Lil Richard Boo turning up at the hotel. The old lad with rheumy-slots and his amigos at Domino Park wudda necked a few bottles of rum real yo-ho-ho on the fifty frogs I give em.

Worster yet, we got nada from the 7-Eleven on SW 12th Avenue. Ebdy heared of Ladybug coz she were a famey biz jane, but nubdy knowed her personal and nubdy membered her from her days at the store. Not so sprizing as this wuddabin nearmost forty year in the wayback. I feeled capboggled, zasperated and kippered.

Meantime, Tomsky were still in the wind. The most wanted popeye on the planet and nubdy knowed nada about where he'd gone. I smoked too many cigs and drinked too many bourbons and were left feeling muddly and stale. So I left the hotel and went outside, thinking to take a stroll and clear my fusebox.

The evening were humid-hot as I legged down SE 4th Street tward the bridge on Brickell Avenue. But the air what blowed off the Miami River tasted briny fresh and this were zactly what I needed.

I were halfway to the bridge when I realized I got a tail. In the corner of my slot I specked a slim figure come out the shadows, legging quick in my drection. This spud were clad in dark pants and a hoodie with the hood pulled over their fusebox. In my sperience popeyes only went hood-up when it were cold, rainy or they was hiding smin. And it were deffo not the first or second.

I giddy-upped. Hoodie giddy-upped. I slowed right down. Hoodie done likewise. Nada subtle about this fieldcraft – Hoodie were no Arianna Bad-Bunny.

Over the bridge, I turned sharp right down a service road what went to Brickell Point. This one-ninety switchback abled me to be abso certain I were the mark. If I weren't, Hoodie wudda gone straight on; if were, they'd turn down the service road and come after me.

No sprize when Hoodie did just that.

Ahead were the Miami River, to my left a high retaining wall, to my right the W Hotel. The façade were fronted by seven twenty-foot high pewter and bronze pillars with easter-islandy vizes moulded into em. Passing the first, I stooped, ziff tightning my boot lace, and grabbed a small stone from the road surface.

As I come to the seventh pillar, I tossed the stone to my right.

The stone maked a loud bang as it hit one of the hotel windows – not so as to break the glass but plenty to draw Hoodie's attention.

I specked the hooded fusebox turn tward the hotel façade and, in the same secsplit, dodged behind the seventh pillar.

I waited, breathing quiet. Then I heared feet steps coming tward me bustagut ferrari.

Then Hoodie peared from the side of the pillar and stopped with their back to me. If I wanted to do em harm, they wuddabin easy meat.

But though I were ready for a scrap, I spected Hoodie weren't.

'You ain't not much of a tail,' I gabbed. 'I maked you from the get-go and cudda taked you out easy.'

He turned, shocked.

In the light what casted through the hotel windows, I gogged an old-timer – even older than Old Bob and Arianna. Early, mebbe mid-seventies. Which tattled a lot about his fitness.

'I just wanna gab,' tattled he.

'Then why all the cloak and dag hoopla?' tattled I.

He pushed back his hood and I gogged a thin viz with solid features and round slots – clear and alert unlike his rheumy buddy at Domino Park.

'Gotta be sure nubdy were specking us.'

'Why is that?'

They were a nano-frag of wavring, then he tattled, 'I is Lil Richard Boo, Ladybug's pappy. She wanna meet.'

53

M e and Lil Richard Boo got out the cab at the Ball and Chain Bar and Lounge on SW 8th Street.

The gaff were crammed with punters and pulsing with live salsa music from an open-air stage out back. No sprize that Lil Richard were well-knowed here and a path through the jammed space opened up as he legged round the bar to some horseshoe-shape booths at the rear.

He taked me to a booth and telled me to sit and wait. I ordered a bottle of Cacique Cuban beer and specked the layout. Wood panel walls was painted green and decked out with bills and pics of famey jazz spuds what played here. Out back, spuds was dancing salsa under a high timber-frame roof what give the place a mid-20th cent vibe

I waited. And waited. And kept on waiting. Fifteen mins. Thirty. No doubt Lil Richard were busy checking scurity rangements. Even so, this were getting tiresome.

I just got anudda beer when I sensed smon standing behind me.

'So, what you wants from me, Det Top Boss Miller?'

I turned tward the voice and gogged Ladybug Boo sliding into the booth.

For fifty-three she were in good nick and specked real snapped in a Tom Ford dress of purple taffeta and Louboutin pumps.

Setting down my beer bottle, I maked a friendy smile. 'I blieves we can help one anudda.'

'That so?'

She sounded dubious and I got why. Tables turned, Ida bin the same.

'Look,' I tattled, 'I cog you scaped two sasnation attemps. But you might not scape the third, or the fourth or the fifth. And we both knows the popeyes what is after you ain't not never gonna stop.'

She tattled nada.

I sipped more beer then pressed my point. 'No matter where you hides, Ladybug, you best hope is to help me figure out why them three poor popeyes with them specific tats suffered death by Family Guy.'

A bar lad bringed her a gaudy cocktail with a red paper brolly sticked in it. She ditched the brolly and necked the cocktail. Without looking up, she tattled, 'What you gotta offer? Witno scheme? Munity from proscution?'

I nay-shaked my fusebox. 'The spuds what is after you ain't not never gonna let them stuffs stop em. They is above the law. We gotta nail em, that's the only way.'

She lifted a slot-brow. '*We*?'

'Look, I knows the killing of the Sinatras, Mozarts and Disciplesons is someway linked to Confucius, Simz and Jesusly. But I gotta find out how. And I think you knows zactly how – am I wrong?'

At this, she gimme flinty speck and glanced round nervy. 'Keep you zucking vox down!'

She had a point. But I had to tattle loud to be heared over the bar noise. 'Some place private we can gab?'

She kept her gobbler shut and her slots on the table.

A shitfaced popeye stumbled against the table, knocking Ladybug's shoulder. She come to her feet bonus thundybolt, punched this lad in the viz and pulled a snub-nose. Then she realized this were just a clumsy drunk and putted the gun down. Two bouncers grabbed the drunk lad and frogged him to the exit.

When the kerfuffle died down, I tattled, 'You wanna go on living like this?'

At last she looked up. 'I gotta place we can gab.'

54

We arrived early next morning at Ladybug's flat above a grocery store oppo the Bay of Pigs Monument. A muscle-bulgy jack in sweatpants and black T come to the counter and showed us through to a stock room, then up some narrow stairs. She were waiting in a modest-size living room.

She'd agreed she gotta know who she were working with so I bringed my team.

When I done the intros we sitted round a low table laid out with a pot of coffee and stuffs.

'I got some vid files what's gonna blow your caps,' Ladybug gabbed. 'They is my evidence, but first you need the background.'

'Go ahead, Ladybug,' I tattled. 'Take all the time you need.'

She poured a cup of coffee and added cream. 'It beginned when I spanded my hospitality biz into leadership training in 4033. The San José site were the first and we used it as a template for the rest. Corprate clients was happy to pay top frog and I growed the biz bonus thundybolt.'

She specked into the coffee cup and went on tattling without looking up. 'I were specting bright future when Big-Lad Lee-Lewis turned up outta the blue. Back then, he were Uber-Top-Boss+++®© of PopRep®© so I were monsta capblown.

'Big-Lad told me he come with a deal and I cogged from the tone of his vox that he were never gonna take nada for an answer. So I banked the ten mil frogs he offered and got on with the rangements.'

Finally, she taked a sip of coffee. 'This ten mil frog deal give the govment of PopRep®© sclusive use of my gaff for fifteen rising-star plitikos, five from each fed. And – yeah, you guessed it – they cluded Confucius, Simz and Jesusly.'

This were anudda of them times when lotta stuffs what never maked sense bruptly did. But I keeped my gobbler closed for now and let Ladybug go on with her tale.

'The process were setted up as a knock-out contest and them as done worstest got booted. This happened every week till there was only the three left.'

I fixed myself a coffee. 'And in the years what followed Confucius, Simz and Jesusly was groomed for the top?'

Ladybug yo-nodded and drained her cup. 'I never knowed nada about what were teached. The instructors come direct from BigLad. Only role for me and my popeyes were scheduling seshes, comodation and food and drink. It were a three-month course what volved lotsa hard work. But the motto were them as worked hard got to play hard and nada were too good for them spuds – cluding what was called PlayPals.'

Ladybug paused, gogging round the room ziff to check we was keeping up. Happy that we was, she pressed on.

'Each rising-star – or Candidate – were gived a PlayPal. Kiera, Brunhilda and Nebo was gived to Simz, Confucius and Jesusly. Them and the udda PlayPals was sexed reglar during PlayTimes what happened ebba night when the learning sheshes was done.'

It were easy to speck where this were headed. Again, though, I keeped my peace and let Ladybug tell the tale.

'When the slection were done, the Chosens, as they was knowed, had the gaff to emselves. They was gived spesh briefings by Big-Lad Lee-Lewis and the udda fed bosses. By this time, Kiera, Brunhilda and Nebo was getting sexed swappy. Smimes they'd be all six going at it bustagut squirmy; smimes three PlayPals and one Chosen; udda times the three Chosens on one PlayPal. Then it were every zucking combo you cudda thinked of and uddas what you cudda never.'

'Was this sex consensual?' This come from Old Bob. 'From the PlayPals' perspective?'

Ladybug give him a what-do-you think? look.

'After two week of these spesh briefings the big bosses left, leaving the three Chosens to emselves. This were when ebbathin wierded up monsta. They throwed booze and drugs and sex parties ebba night, I spoze to mark the end of the contest. Them Chosens was getting into off-planet shit: sado-massochy and eastbound fetishy. They done bondage; whipping; strangling; all kinda object inserts and udda stuffs I wish to Trump I never got in my fusebox but knows I got till they puts me in the ground.'

Lotsa more pennies began dropping and carried on till I were neck-deep in em. If these pervy capers come out in the public domain it would be THE END for all three bosses. And spesh Jesusly. Multisexing were common in PopRep®© and Scientia where Freedom of Sex were shrined in law. But never in Trumpia. In Trumpia, ebba kinda sexing sept non-devo hetro were forbidded under pain of microwave.

Even for the First Daddy.

Spesh for the First Daddy.

'They did all that shit in front of you?' Comanche sounded capblown.

Ladybug give us a nay-shake. 'I zeroed through remote cameras. They was rigged discreet all over the gaff, each with a feed to monitors in the control room. The system were meant to upgrade our training ops. Spuds was told of the cameras but not where they was located – simlar to reality TV shows. But soon as Big-Lad Lee-Lewis gimme that contract what I couldn't refuse, I knowed some bad shit were gonna come down. So I left the cameras running and never telled nubdy.'

'You is one smart jane, Ladybug,' I gabbed.

Bob leaned forward. 'So the footage of these extreme sexual activities,' he tattled, 'is the basis of your evidence?'

'At first I keeped them vid files for revenge. See, when they done with my exec training gaff, they shutted me down. They wanted no trace of what gone on and me going bust suited them vance-holes bigmost. All my existing biz dried up; new biz never come; invoices was never paid; credit got withdrawed; cash ran out. The vid files was my best and only way to hit back and… '

Ladybug words ended sudden. She sucked air into her breathbags.

'Sorry,' she gabbed. 'Sorry.'

I knowed what she were going through. Reliving trauma like she done could do that to the pluckiest spud.

Bogart went to the kitchen and fetched her a glass of water. 'Take your time, Ladybug,' he gabbed. 'No rush. We got all day. You is with amigos now.'

She thanked him kind, drinked the water and taked up her yarn. 'Then I started specking just how cunning these three rulers was. In PopRep®©, they was whizzing up Vox Popeyes against Simz's rivals. Them as gabbed against her ended up banished or busted as Enemies of the Popeyes. In Trumpia, the Harpo was gived fresh powers and them as come under spicion went to the oven without trial. In Scientia, they was more subtle but just as frighty. Spuds what tattled out against Confucius and his Meso-Liberal Party started vanishing, then turning up in sewers and landfill with their swallowers slitted or radio-active shit in their veins.'

She finished the rest of her water. 'It were then that I started flecting on what were morer portanter: getting revenge or staying alive. I still keeped them vid files, but only as insurance. If they leaved me be, I'd never go public. Years rolled by – five, ten, nearly fifteen – and I rebuilded a life of sorts. Can't say as I were happy but I come to cog I were never gonna be super rich again and found a little peace in that.'

She breaked off, zeroing the ceiling, ziff moving back in time and tryna figure out how she cudda done stuffs diffrent.

'So what happened?' The nudge come from Puritan.

Ladybug maked a tired sigh. 'That peace come to an end when I were proached two year back by Kiera Sinatra.

335

She'd been in touch with Brunhilda and Nebo and they was gonna start a compo campaign for what were done to em at my gaff. Kiera told me they all suffered serio fusebox probs after their speriences as PlayPals. Also, their careers, like my biz, got snuffed. There was no high-fly jobs back home. They was cut adrift by Simz, Confucius and Jesusly. Kiera come to me coz she knowed they also zucked me over bad. She asked – begged – me to join em.'

One more time, her slots swivelled to the ceiling.

This time Bob had the sense not to press, to let Ladybug work through her tangled feelings.

Bogart fetched anudda glass of water. By the time he come back, she were ready to go on. 'I mustabbin eastbound, but I joined em. The idea of getting some kinda justice were too tempting. Like Kiera and her amigos, I come to be obsessed with the hobba stuffs them rulers done to me, the way they bojoed my life, stealed away the biz I builded. I telled them about the vid files and sended em copies.'

She run her dedos through her thick hair and sweared savage. Then she drinked more water and went on. 'But the three of em zucked up bad. Stead of biding time, waiting for the right oppo, they went full-bull with blackmail threats. Less they got full compo, they was gonna spoze the three monstadickest spuds on the planet as sex pervs. At first, they thinked they pulled it off. They was each gived twenty mill frogs to sign NDAs and gab nada in public, with promises of more gelt to come. But it never. What *did* come were Family Guy. And after he done he work, their bank accounts was emptied of them payments, like they never been maked.'

By now it were claro that Ladybug nerves was shredded. She leaned forward, fusebox in her graspers, rocking back and forth.

Comanche realized she needed morer than water and poured a big glass of Scotch.

'C'mon, Ladybug,' Comanche tattled gentle, 'drink this.'

Ladybug nay-shaked her fusebox but Comanche stayed there, patient. Ventual, Ladybug taked the Scotch and downed it fast. She asked for a smoke and Comanche give her one.

We all kept quiet, giving Ladybug the space she needed.

'Them three rulers got jawdrop power.' Her vox started low and small and quivry, like she were mumbling crazy shit. 'I mean, who the zuck cudda hatched a scheme what forced the most frighty serial killer of our age – of any age – outta retirement to do their biddings?'

She were right. The idea of focusing all that malice and wielding like a rapier gimme the freddykruegers – and I were never a target.

Yet.

'When did you work out what had been happening in relation to Family Guy?' This come from Bob.

Ladybug holded out her empty tumbler for Comanche to refill. After anudda belt of whisky, she answered. 'When Family Guy killed Kiera and her folk, I thought that was plain bad luck. But when sames was done to Brunhilda and her family, I knowed bestermost. I cogged ebbathin. I warned Nebo, but he never taked no notice. Reckoned he and his was gonna be fine. I messaged him, I called him. But he told me he were gonna be ready for whatever come at him. Poor daft lad.'

Last of the Scotch went down her swallower. 'All of them deaths was on me. I never shudda give em them vid files… ' Her vox petered. I got why. Reliving all them grim stuffs mustabbin bonus screamy.

'The rulers,' gabbed Bob, 'do they know about your role in this?'

She shrugged blasé, like she were too zucked to care no more. 'I spoze so. Who else wudda give the order to sassinate me? But whatever, they is gonna know footdown ferrari now that I tattled to you spuds.'

She were right again.

I tattled, 'We better zero them vid files.'

*

'I gotta warn you.' Ladybug gogged each of us hard. 'What's on these vids is way beyond X-rated.'

'We ain't expecting *Finding Nemo*,' tattled I.

'Okay then.' Ladybug come to her feet and we followed her cross the room to a wall-mounted TV screen rigged to a laptop. She flipped a switch and the show started.

In my time working with vice nabbers I specked some jawdrop porn but Ladybug were right – this were smin else. Smimes it were so deep-space it were almost yo-ho-ho. I specked Confucius with his Mount Rushmore viz prancing round in bondage gear; Simz as a teacher with a mortarboard hat and her mams out and bouncy; and Jesusly in nada but a jock-thong and leopard fur calf-boots. All this funny stuffs ended, though, when we zeroed what they done to Kiera, Brunhilda and Nebo. They was bound tight and beat savage, punched in their vizes and object zucked, lectrodes sticked up the lasses' fancies, cut-holes and on Nebo's balls. Later, they was waterboarded, hanged in chains, maked to gobble turds.

On it went, grimmer, grimmer, grimmer.

No sprize them three PlayPals was leaved psycho-zucked after all this. No sprize they went home different popeyes. No sprize Ladybug blieved she'd never get these sights outta her fusebox. Right then, I feeled the same.

Then they bringed in a donkey and I stopped gogging. One thing were for sure, though – if Jesus would never have rided a donkey in the modern age, Jesusly abso would and abso had.

Soon after this, Ladybug sensed we all zeroed nuff and stopped the vid.

At Old Bob's request, though, she frozed the screen and bigged up a shot of Brunhilda's tat.

It were a butterfly design done in the same colours what Stoker Fangly used – Billion Buck Vermilion, Canarybreath and Vert De Cyclops. True, I were no tat buff but I could discern the grasper of Stoker in the bold yet delicate design.

I turned to Ladybug. 'That tat same as what were on Kiera, Nebo and the udda PlayPals?'

She yo-nodded.

I thinked of Confucius and Simz and Jesusly. This were never case closed, not by a distance. But now I knowed we was closer than we ebba been to nabbing them crazy eastbound bastards.

55

Back at the Big Cop Shop, I called a team meet.

To Bob, I tattled, 'We gotta verify that them ink colours is what we thinks they is and come from Stoker's parlour. That smin you and your popeyes can handle?'

Puritan gabbed yo.

'Gottasay,' I went on, 'I got worries, no truer words.' What's to stop the three fed bosses claiming the vid files is deep fakes? Any way we can prove they ain't never not?'

'My firm has video analytical technology,' Puritan tattled, 'as well as voice recognition software. They can give us all the proof we need.'

'Sounds too easy,' I gabbed frowny. 'What gonna stop them power spuds shutting us down and nixing the vid files?'

Bob maked a wry spresh. 'Normally it *would* be too easy and that's exactly what would happen. But this is an election year. This is when their rivals are most vocal and get most media attention. If these files were released to the public by us and endorsed by one or more of these opponents, it wouldn't be so easy to deny.'

'Also, boss,' he added, 'you have your own credibility. You were brought here specifically to carry out this investigation and Confucius, Simz and Jesusly have gone to enormous lengths to publicise your credentials. Remember those photo opportunities with the bigshot politicos that you bridled against? Now they can work in our favour.'

'That kind of you, Bob,' I told him. 'Fact is though that all you spuds come with heavyweight cred of you own.'

I breaked off, not one bit keen to gab what were on my cap. Needed tattling though coz they might not be anudda chance. So I come out with it. 'I never been one for dishing out plaudits,' I gabbed, 'but we wudda never got this far if you three hadn't gimme such bustagut commitment. Whatever come next, you done me proud, no two ways.'

A fast glance round the room told me what I cudda guessed: Bogart smiley-blushy; Bob sheepy; Comanche voiding slot-contact.

Even so, I keeped gogging her and, after a bitwhile, she gimme a sly glance.

I maked a small smile and she did likeways. The exchange last nada but a nanofrag but I feeled a gut-poke and my tiktok go giddy-up. Mebbe I were wrong, but I reckoned she feeled likeways.

But what to do?

We'd tattled very little since she bojoed Bez the blade boy. Popping his shoulder when she never needed to showed – yet again – bad impulse control. Yet again I flected that though this were common among vilent fenders, crime bosses was different. They needed to keep their shit together uddawise their ops gonna go sideways bonus thundybolt. So what happened with Comanche? Why were she so near the edge? Gotta be to do with she daughter – the one I were sweared to secrecy about. Whatever, it were time to mend fences.

Right now though, I needed to gab with Bob.

I catched his slot and nodded tward my office. 'A word in your lug, Bob, if you pleases.'

When the door were shut and we was seated, I tattled, 'I gotta job for you – and your client Arianna. If, that is, you is both up for it.'

'What's the job?' His viz stayed deadpan.

'I needs ebba detail what you can find on interacts tween Kiera, Brunhilda and Nebo and the three fed bosses since that slection process in San Jose.'

'That might take some doing.'

'But you can do it, right, Bob?'

'I'll do everything possible.'

I picked up a dubio tone in his vox. 'Arianna a prob?'

He nay-shaked his fusebox but I spected uddawise.

'She *is* here in Miami, ain't she?'

He yo-nodded, which were what I already thinked.

'Well,' I gabbed, 'if she wanna keep her part of our deal, she gotta help us. We needs them field crafts and spy-smarts Tell me if I is wrong.'

'You're not wrong, boss,' Bob said, 'but I know what she'll say: what about going after Family Guy? After all, that's why she's here.'

I maked a shrug. 'Best way we can do that is by nailing them fed bosses. If we stablishes that they been using Family Guy as a hit-man, we can find Family Guy hisself.'

I went with Puritan to my office door. 'Sides,' I added, 'there ain't not nada else we can do. Tomsky is in the wind and no amount of sleuthing gonna snag him. We gotta leave manhunting to the feds and intel orgs. They gonna shout soon nuff when they collars him.'

As he went back into the incident room, I added, 'And member, Bob, nubdy gotta find out Tomsky is Family Guy. Not even Arianna. You cog?'

'Understood, boss.' He yo-nodded and legged limpy to his desk.

Comanche were still at hers and I went over. I been putting this off too long, so I gabbed, 'We should tattle. Wanna grab a drink later? Mebbe some scran?'

'I'm busy tonight.'

'Tomorrow then.'

She gimme a wary speck. 'You buying?'

'If that what it takes,' I gabbed weary, 'yo.'

'Okay,' she tattled, 'you got a date.'

*

I heared Arianna Bad-Bunny long fore I gogged her. She were musked off monstamost, no truer words.

The rumpus rupted in the corridor outside the incident room. Arianna first, obvio not happy; then Bob's soothy tones getting cutted off, then smudda guy what I sumed were a nabber tryna judicate.

Fastwhile later, Arianna come through the door full rhino, straight to my office.

'Why didn't you tell me Tomsky is Family Guy?' She zeroed me cold. 'I thought we had a deal.'

I lifted my graspers. 'Hold on there, Arianna. You wuddabin telled when you needed to know. But that ain't not yet. Right now, that intel is top secret and we gotta keep it that way.'

But Arianna were never gonna be mollied.

'I'll end that bastard.' Her whispry vox frighted me more than any ranty stuffs. 'One way or another, I'll get the justice Kiera deserves.'

I telled her that this were never gonna happen.

Mid this aggro, smin else striked me.

I taked her by the shoulders. 'Who telled you this stuffs?'

'What?' She specked me blank, lickertangled by this counter-attack. 'Nobody.'

'Smoddy musta telled you. Uddawise you never wudda knowed.'

I shoved her back against the wall. 'Who were it?'

'I don't know. Really I don't. A note was pushed under my door last night. I saw it this morning. But I have no idea how it got there.'

I glanced round the room at Comanche, Wham!®© and Puritan – the only popeyes on the planet what knowed about the Tomsky-Family Guy link. My slots skipped past Wham!®©, past Comanche, and locked on Puritan.

'You! Of all people!'

Puritan seemed capblown. 'I didn't write that note. Why would I?'

I scoffed bitter. 'Why *wouldn't* you?'

He opened his gobbler but nada come out. I got him bang to rights and he knowed it. I could see all as had happened, plain as the conk on you viz.

344

I give him a filthy speck. 'Ain't there nada you'd never not do to get in she knickknacks?'

Old Bob wrinkled his brow and shaked his fusebox. '*What*?'

'If you never wroted that note, Bob, who did? Gotta be you, Bogart or Comanche. Less it were me what done it in my sleep.'

'Cuddabin some spud outside the team, boss.' This come from Wham!®©.

I rounded on him sharp. 'Some spud what *you* telled, Bogart?'

'No I never! And that ain't not fair.' He gimme a withry look. 'You knows they is all kinda snoopy tech ebbaplace. I dunno how this come out, but it ain't not ness on Old Bob.'

'Save your breath, Bogart.' Puritan levered hisself up with his walking stick. 'She isn't listening.'

To me he tattled, 'I won't stay here and be insulted.'

And to Arianna, 'Are you coming?'

She give me a stingy look and followed Puritan from the room.

56

PARIS-SUR-EUPHRÈTE

Forty-eight hours later we received fresh instructions from Wu Mei and took the arrow plane to Paris-sur-Euphrète. I couldn't ditch IngoLingo®© fast enough, rejoicing as we left PopRep®© airspace and the language shackles fell away.

Despite my offer of protection, Ladybug had stayed in Miami, which was probably a wise decision. Little Havana was where she felt safe, where she could count on the protection of her own people. And in all honesty, nowhere would be safe for a woman who knew what she did. The only way we could help her now was to eliminate the threat at source.

Puritan was sitting at the back of the plane facing away from me. His only company was Wham!®© who occasionally went aft for a chat. I could tell from Bogart's attitude that he wasn't happy with what he considered to be my rush to judgment. True, this was a world of ultrasophisticated snooping technology and it was possible that someone outside our team had discovered that we'd connected Plato Tomsky to Family Guy. But the idea that Bob had told Ariana was too plausible to ignore. There was an affinity between the pair, a nascent relationship. And I could imagine how Bob's sense of justice would lead him to believe Ariana was entitled to know who murdered her niece.

Right now, though, I was too angry to do anything but let him stew. Ariana Bad-Bunny was out there, pursuing the same quarry as us, using her considerable skills, resources and contacts to find and kill Tomsky before we could get to him. As far as I was concerned this was down to Puritan's infatuation with the woman and his disregard for the test of the team.

I had, however, patched things up with Comanche who had traded her tenancy of the doghouse with Puritan. Comanche hadn't apologised but I never expected her to. We simply put the incident with the blade boy behind us and moved on. After an enjoyable dinner in downtown Miami we'd gone back to my room and she didn't leave until the next morning.

The plane descended with Ur of the Chaldees below the starboard wing and landed at Charles de Gaulle ahead of schedule.

Wu Mei was waiting on the tarmac as we left the aircraft and asked me to join her in an armoured SUV in the middle of a short convoy.

I sat opposite her. 'Any news on Tomsky?'

'Nothing.' A gloomy expression crossed her face. 'It's as if he left the planet.'

'He's had a lot of practice over a lot of years,' I said. 'Even so, you'd expect some leads given the assets deployed to find him.'

She didn't seem optimistic.

'I think he's had help,' I added.

She said nothing. I was sure she knew more than she was letting on. I wanted to say, *I think he's had* your *help*. I'd been mulling this hypothesis for some time and was now convinced that it held water. If Tomsky/Family Guy had been used as an assassin to silence Kiera, Brunhilda and Nebo, who better to act as his handler than Wu Mei? If *she* was giving him refuge it was hardly surprising that he couldn't be found by the global authorities.

'Why do you want us in Paris?' I asked.

'The federation leaders are attending a summit.' She gazed through the window as we cleared airport security. 'They want an update, while they're together.'

I frowned. 'There isn't one to give. You know that as well as I do.'

'They're politicians.' Still she didn't look at me. 'They don't really want information, they want reassurance. They want to go back to their people and tell them you're closing in on the monster who's been terrorising their communities.'

The one you're shielding, I thought.

I said, 'I'll come up with a suitable formula of words.'

'I was reading Milton last night,' Isambard Kingdom Confucius announced, as if he was in the smoking room of a Victorian gentleman's club. 'And I must say that I was enthralled by the magniloquent cascade of words, the unadorned grandeur of the language…'

Were you really? I thought. *Or are you just a pompous windbag?*

The Citizen Ascendant of Scientia was standing at the windows of the Salon Doré in the Élysée Palace – a perfect replica of the office once occupied by Napoleon III and Raymond Poincaré and Charles de Gaulle.

Listening without uninterest were Dreezy Simz and Judgment Jesusly. They were sitting on the cerulean silk sofas I recalled from my last visit here. And though I'd come to despise both Simz and Jesusly, I couldn't help but feel a modicum of pity, pinned down as they were by Confucius' bombast.

Mount Rushmore Man sensed my presence and turned to face me as the double doors closed behind me.

'Miranda, how very kind of you to come,' he said, as if I had any choice.

He invited me to take a seat on the sofa next to Simz, then sat facing me, beside Jesusly. We went through the pleasantries as tea was served. With this done, Simz went straight to business.

Elections were looming, she said. People everywhere were living in fear of Family Guy, but I seemed to be no nearer to catching him than when I took the case. This was fuelling criticism by increasingly vocal election rivals and increasingly frightened communities. A fast arrest could swing the election, she told me, but a failure to make one could swing it the other way.

I thought this was absurd – no electorate, even here, would judge its leaders on a specific law enforcement issue, no matter how much it dominated the headlines. Also, it was unfair to lay the weight of responsibility on me and my team. But then when had politicians ever been fair? In fact, I had a strong suspicion we were being set up as scapegoats. If we caught Family Guy and the three leaders were returned to power, they'd take the credit. If Family Guy wasn't collared and they lost, we'd take the blame. In fact, the more I thought about this, the more likely it seemed that I'd been brought here, and my team assembled, for exactly this purpose. Demeaning Wham!®©, Comanche and Puritan would suit a lot of agendas in a lot of powerful places.

Which raised another question: Did the leaders know Plato Tomsky was Family Guy? If so, did they know he'd been used to silence Kiera, Brunhilda and Nebo before they could go public with Ladybug's video? Almost certainly Wu Mei was the architect of Family Guy's "second coming". She had very probably helped Tomsky to flee before he could be arrested. But had she done this with the leaders' consent or had she gone rogue? I suspected the latter but nothing in this world would surprise me.

'Thing is, Randy,' Jesusly said in his easy west Texas accent, 'we wanna hit the campaign trail knowing this sicko is behind bars. Up to me and mine, he'd get a slow-roast in Old Crispy, but we made a deal and we'll stick to it. My point, though, is that you gotta give us something positive we can go home with, something to assure our people that you're hot on his bastard's tail, that you're gonna nail him soon.'

The idea of tossing a grenade into this conversation hadn't occurred to me until right then. There was no time

350

to think so I went ahead and pulled the pin. 'You could,' I said, 'tell your folks that I know Family Guy's identity.'

I studied their expressions – shock and bafflement, alloyed with a suspicion they'd misheard me.

The first thing this told me was that they didn't know Tomsky was Family Guy.

Which told me the second thing: Wu Mei Leclerc *was* working without their say-so.

Simz was the first to react. 'Who is he?' she asked. 'Who is this monster?'

'I can't give you a name,' I said, 'not without jeopardising the investigation. Which I'm sure is the last thing you would want.'

They glanced at each other, as if deciding whether to demand a name or accept what I'd said.

I pressed on regardless. 'However, you'll be the first to know the instant Family Guy is in custody. And in the meantime, news that he's been unmasked in itself represents significant progress that'll raise the confidence of your voters.'

'Darn right it will,' Jesusly said. 'But if you got a name, and with all the resources of the three federations, how come he ain't in jail already?'

'This is Family Guy.' I gave each of them a hard look. 'The most feared, adept and elusive serial killer in New World history. Even with a name, he isn't going to be easy to catch.'

'Does *he* know that *you* know?' This was Confucius.

'I fear so.'

'So he's in the wind?' Jesusly sounded aghast.

'He is.'

'And presumably all our law enforcement and intelligence people are scouring every corner of the earth?' Now the First Father was starting to sound angry.

I said nothing.

'Why weren't we told about this?' Jesusly looked to Confucius, then Simz, and finally back to me. 'Does Derek Anti-Satan know?'

Again, I let my silence speak.

'Gosh darn.' Jesusly banged his fist on the table. 'How in tarnation did this happen?'

I thought Anti-Satan was going to get hauled over the coals – perhaps literally – and relished a moment of schadenfreude.

It didn't last. I saw Jesusly swap glances with Simz and Confucius. And I learned in those two seconds more about the seat of New World power than in the weeks since I arrived.

The three of them weren't angry; they were anxious.

—
*
—

Comanche was waiting in my hotel room with a bottle of chilled Picpoul de Pinet, along with a baguette, some salted butter, camembert and pears.

She and I were back together, though Puritan and I still weren't speaking and Wham!®© had taken umbrage at the way I was treating the old timer. Wham!®© was good at many things but keeping his feelings to himself wasn't one. As a result, his attitude had become cool and distant.

We ate and drank before curling up on the sofa to watch a movie.

We were half way through our second bottle of wine when my phone vibrated and I took an idle glance at the message.

I looked again, closer.

And again, closer yet, then closer still until the device was an inch from my nose.

```
Dear Det Supt Miller, Miller of the Yard,
Serial Killer Miller - Miranda, if I may?
```

I was back at the murder scene at the Mozarts' home. Word for word, line for line, comma for comma, this was the opening salutation of the note Family Guy left for me.

I was still gazing at my phone when a second message appeared.

```
Do I have your attention?
```

I replied Yes.

Somewhere distant, perhaps on another planet, Comanche was asking me what this was about. I ignored her, unable to take my eyes off the phone, as if by looking anywhere else I might break the contact.

I blinked, relieved yet startled when the next message arrived.

```
Meet me under the Metro line station at
La Motte-Picquet. Fifteen minutes. Come
alone. I mean you no harm, but any sign
of your team and I will be gone. Do you
understand?
```

I replied. Yes, I understood. Yes, I would be there. Yes, I would be alone.

Five minutes later, I left the hotel on Boulevard de Grenelle. Five minutes after that, I was at the rendezvous.

The space under this elevated section of the Metro tracks was shadowy and damp. A train clattered overhead. I could have screamed full pitch and nobody would have heard.

But I was confident, without knowing why, that he didn't intend to hurt me.

So I lit a cigarette and waited.

Fobbing off Comanche had been hard. I told her the messages were from an important contact. The matter was urgent. I didn't have time to explain. I had to leave right then. I was not putting myself in harm's way. She could not come with me. She needed to trust me. Then I kissed her on the forehead and left.

I took another drag on my cigarette, looked at my watch. I'd been here three minutes.

Any moment now we'd be face to face.

I started thinking. The confidence that brought me here subsided.

I started overthinking. My confidence was shot. Now it seemed like negligence.

What if this was a ruse? What if he *did* plan to kill me?

I heard a movement from behind and swivelled, eyes skewering the dark.

I squinted, scanning the criss-crossed shadows of elevated railway girders.

Nothing.

I turned back.

Plato Tomsky's face was twelve inches from mine.

57

stared back at him, tripwired adrenaline stinging my body. My brain was going *fight-flight?-freeze?* Over and over, faster and faster. Then, faster still, *fight-fight-fight.*

I went into a combat stance, strike reactions on a hair-trigger.

In that same frantic instant, he made a disarming smiled.

Somehow I was confident once more that he posed no threat. At least not an immediate one.

'Hello, Miranda.'

'Hello, Plato.' I was vaguely aware how ridiculous this sounded. I came down from Defcon One. 'You've been leading everyone a merry dance.'

The smile was still in place. 'I try to entertain.'

'You wanted to talk.'

'Not here.' The smile vanished. He glanced around, double-checking I was alone. 'Come with me.'

He set off along the street, long loping legs carrying him fast.

'Where are we going?' I had to jog to keep up.

'Not far.'

A few minutes later we entered Place Cambronne, a busy seven-way intersection and an ideal place to disappear from. He headed across the broad cobbled square and took me into a bar called L'endroit Heureux. The place was crowded, hot and noisy, the air foggy with tobacco and marijuana fumes. He elbowed a path through the congested space and people closed up behind us as we passed. Another crafty move – we'd be almost impossible to tail. At the rear of the saloon he led me through a door. On the other side, a stone-floored corridor was flanked by stacks of wine crates and beer barrels. At the end he ushered me through another door and into a small parlour. Two chairs faced each other across a shabby wooden table with a ring-stained top. A bare light bulb hung from the ceiling. Its piss-yellow radiance fizzled and flickered.

'Please take a seat.' He found a bottle of Burgundy and two glasses then sat opposite, fiddling with the cork.

'Want a drink?'

I declined. Sharing a glass of wine with an infamous serial killer wasn't something I wanted in my memory bank.

This was the first time I'd got a proper look at his disguise. His blonde mane had been cropped short and dyed black and he'd grown a stubbly beard. None of this, though would have fooled any half-awake street cop, never mind advanced surveillance software. This strengthened my theory: he'd had help. I could see how this was unfolding. My hypothesis, I thought, was solid.

Which was when he shattered it.

'I just broke out of a secure psychiatric unit.' The cork

came out of the bottle. 'Wu Mei put me there with a false identity, bogus diagnosis and no records. Then she threw away the key. You've got to help me. If you don't, they'll lobotomize me and you'll never close your case.'

I struggled to process this information.

'You'd better explain,' I said. 'I know Wu Mei has been using you as an assassin, but – '

'No,' he said. 'She hasn't. Not as an assassin. As a consultant.'

I frowned. This didn't make sense. But why would he be lying?

That wine suddenly seemed more appealing. I told him I'd have some after all.

'You need to empty your head of everything you think you know.' He looked up from pouring my wine. 'You need to come at this without assumptions.'

'All right.' I took a glass of Burgundy and sipped it while he poured one for himself. 'Assume I have no assumptions. Assume my slate is clean.'

He took the chair facing me. 'Okay, here we go. You're right up to a point. I *am* Family Guy. But my career ended fourteen years ago. This so-called second wave you were brought here to investigate was carried out by someone else – an impeccably informed copycat.'

He swallowed a mouthful of wine and made a bitter chuckle. 'I was used as a consulting serial killer. Advising on my own work. Can you fucking believe that?'

I could. Mainly because I couldn't imagine how or why he – or anyone else – could have made this up. I said nothing though and waited for him to continue.

'This second coming ballyhoo was conceived by Wu

Mei after she became aware that Kiera, Brunhilda and Nebo were trying to blackmail those three shit-for-brains leaders. She wanted the blackmailers silenced, but in a way that wouldn't raise red flags among senior FIB colleagues who were already suspicious of Confucius and Wu Mei's relationship with him.'

I raised an eyebrow. 'And making them the victim of a born again serial killer wouldn't?'

He made a blasé shrug. 'There have been stranger coincidences. But the key aspect for Wu Mei was that nobody but a crazy person could imagine a link between her and Family Guy. And gathering the evidence to prove that link would be almost impossible.'

'*Almost.*'

'Well yeah.' He gave me a laconic smile. 'You were the surprise package. A spoof sleuth, conceived to fail. Yet you were onto me when all your predecessors never got close.'

He broke off to sip more wine and regarded me over the edge of his glass. 'Except one.'

'Wu Mei?'

'It grieves me to admit this, but she caught me fourteen years before you did.'

He'd told me to approach this assumption-free, but nobody could have made this leap. I was utterly baffled and didn't mind telling him so.

'My arrest never came to public notice, still less a court room.'

'You killed eighty-nine people – more than half of them children – and she offered you a *deal*?' I failed to keep the incredulity from my voice.

'To be fair, she was ordered to by my late mother. At

the time she was one of the Great Electors – a tiny elite made up of individuals with more than fifty million votes each. Between them, they could pretty much decide an election before a single ballot was cast.'

Despite what he said his mother had done for him, he sounded bitter when he talked about her. I risked a personal question. 'Was your mother part of the reason you chose your path?'

'Part of it,' he said, 'but only a small part. She was a self-seeking bitch but at least she accepted that the pain would never have happened if she hadn't abandoned us.'

'The pain of you and your sister Emmeline?'

He nodded. 'Dad was an abusive arsehole. I couldn't blame Mum for leaving him. But she could have taken us with her and she didn't.'

'Your dad remarried though.' I knew I'd entered dangerous territory here, but pushed on. 'Was that when the pain started?'

He contemplated the Burgundy in his glass but didn't drink any. 'Our step-mother was away most of the time. But my whore step-sister wasn't and that was just the way she and my pervert dad liked it. They fucked every night, all night. Every which way, every which place. The house was big, but we could always hear them. And whenever possible they made damn sure we could see them.'

He looked at me hot-eyed and I had a sense of peering into the pit where Plato the child began his metamorphosis into Plato the monster.

'If it hadn't been for those two disgusting deviants and their none-stop fucking, Emmeline would still be alive. I got revenge on Valeria. Before she died, I taught her what intense and extended hurt really felt like. But she was only one half of my tableau. The biggest regret of my life was not getting to my dad before cancer took him. Not teaching him a similar lesson. In the end I had to use my imagination and improvise. But I suppose from another perspective, this inspired the artist in me. After all, the need to innovate is the engine of all great achievements.'

He chugged his wine and smacked his reddened lips and I got the impression he imagined he'd been drinking the blood of his father or step-sister.

Time to move this on, I thought. 'As successful as you were, Plato, you still got caught. How did that happen?'

He rolled his eyes and shook his head. 'Like a lot of people of my calling, I became a little too fond of returning to the scenes of my creations. One is compelled to re-experience one's work and physical closeness to the event can have an addictive effect. Of course, I used various disguises and devices but Wu Mei was extremely diligent. She made some brilliantly intuitive connections, re-ran surveillance footage and that was that. I was brought down at the peak of my powers.'

'Tragic,' I said.

'Wasn't it?' He appeared not to have noticed my sarcasm and poured more wine.

Yet again, I marvelled at the dislocated psychosis of a sociopathic serial killer; the way he talked about his "calling" as if it was some kind of vocation; how he referred to gruesome torture and bloody slaughter and multiple infanticide as an aspect of his "work". The suffering, the terror, the destruction of human life weren't even collateral, weren't even by-products. They simply weren't anything.

I focused on the extraction of information. 'So Wu Mei collared you. What was your deal?'

'It wasn't easy, you know. Not for me or my mother.'

Again I was astonished by this walk-a-mile-in-my-shoes attitude. Poor Plato, poor mummy. What hardships they endured, what sacrifices they made.

'I had to agree to a violence inhibiting brain implant.' He tapped the side of his head. 'Once installed, it can't be removed. It was a long and painful procedure. Weeks in and out of hospital, but I got there eventually.'

By now, I was beyond sarcasm. 'So what? You were free to live the rest of your non-violent life?'

He gave me a reproachful look. 'You seem to think that serial killing is a lifestyle choice.'

'It's some kind of choice.'

'No.' He shook his head in a sequence of emphatic swivels. 'No, Miranda, it isn't. Not on my level. I wasn't some chop-house butcher, you know. I was practising art. Surely you've been dealing with people like me long enough to appreciate this?'

I've been dealing with people like you way too long, I thought.

But I went on with my next question. 'So Wu Mei used this information as a recruitment method when she decided to go after the three former PlayPals?'

His nostrils flared with the force of a snort. 'You may call it a "recruitment method". I call it what it was: despicable blackmail.'

'But why did she need you? Surely as the investigator who cracked the case, she had all the information she needed to resurrect your career through the agency of this copycat?'

Another vehement shake of his head.

I warned myself that I had to be more sensitive. Tomsky's oceanic narcissism demanded a measure of empathy no matter how disturbing I found it.

So I backtracked. 'I get it,' I said. 'She may have had the information, but you had the insight. She had the raw materials but the essence of the work had been yours.'

'Thank you, Miranda.' His pique diminished a little. 'Thank you for accepting my value to Wu Mei's entire operation.'

'You're welcome, Plato.' I kept my manner amenable. 'Now tell me, how did your new role as a consulting serial killer work?'

58

He poured himself more wine as he considered the question.

After a sip, he said, 'Wu Mei would send me a brief containing details of an upcoming piece – names, ages et cetera of family members, habits and routines, plans and photos of their home and the surrounding streets, that sort of thing.'

Clearly, I thought, the planning had been meticulous. But then I wouldn't have expected anything less from Wu Mei.

He continued, seemingly keen to demonstrate the effectiveness of his expert advice. 'I would then conduct an analysis and appreciation of the work and provide my input in a detailed report – what should be done and when; when it should be done and how, et cetera, et cetera. There were even times when a more direct contribution was needed, for example the note I wrote for you which obviously would have to stand up to calligraphical and syntactical examination.'

The validation of the note, I reflected, was exactly what convinced me that I *wasn't* dealing with a copycat.

Cute.

'I even suggested leaving the fountain pen as well as sprinkling the paper clips and a plastic ruler on the note paper. All details of a previous body of work, you see, that I knew your lab people would lap up.'

Even more cute.

I had to maintain his enthusiasm so I pressed on with my questions. 'Tell me about this copycat killer, Wu Mei's professional hitman.'

'Not much to tell. I never got to meet him. Wu Mei went to great lengths to compartmentalise the operation. But her guy was a world class operator. I was shown crime scene videos after each event and the work was almost identical to my own.'

'So what happened with the last two cases? Whose idea was it to spare the Mozart twins and the Discipleson kids?'

'I have no idea.' He looked me with an aghast expression. 'But it certainly wasn't mine. This was when Wu Mei's man got sloppy. Or soft. Or weak. But leaving work incomplete like that was a betrayal, a travesty, an insult to my work – my reputation.'

'I can imagine.' I made sure my voice was irony-free. 'If you had to guess, though,' I went on, 'what would you say caused this?'

'A colossal loss of nerve.' He kept his gaze on me. 'That's what should have told you that you weren't dealing with me after all. Why would I have ruined my own legacy in that way? Particularly when the Discipleson kids lived, you should have realized an assassin was at work. I would never-never-never have lost my shit like that.'

This *was* revealing. Maybe he was right. Maybe I should have drawn those inferences. Then again, we'd been trying to rule out a copycat serial killer not a hitman.

I went to my next question. 'So how did the arrangement unravel? What went so badly wrong that Wu Mei's goons snatched you and threw you into a lock-up psych unit?'

He pulled a despondent face. 'Same as last time. I may have my anti-violence implant but I still get the old urges. So I inserted myself into your investigation. I got ahead of you in Vegas, England and began to court your man Wham!®©, which I have to say wasn't difficult. It wasn't long before you agreed to give me inside access to the investigation. Wu Mei was unhappy about this from the start. My big bad, though, was when I was apprehended near Stoker Fangly's tattoo salon. That was when Wu Mei got really up-tight. She told me I was too close and posed a risk to the operation. She told me to leave you alone. Or …'

He raised his palms as if to fend off anticipated criticism. 'I know, I know. I should have paid attention. But the allure was simply too great. When I turned up in Rio de Jerusalem, she was even more pissed off. The last straw came when she caught me filming in your incident room. Soon after that she had me grabbed, flown back here and slung into that dismal institution.'

Thinking back, things that hadn't made sense now did. Such as Wu Mei's look of astonished disbelief when I first told her Tomsky had been socialising with Wham!®© And later, when I suggested Tomsky could help my inquiries.

What had she said? *You should be very careful with what you share with Tomsky.* Then she'd read me the Riot Act in Harpo headquarters after I let him film in the incident room.

Now I understood why she'd hit the roof.

'So,' I said, sensing that the conversation was ending. 'Where do we go from here? If you cooperate I can offer you protective custody.'

'We both know that isn't going to happen.'

'I had to ask.'

'Of course you did. But here's what's going to happen. I'll disappear again, but I'll be monitoring events closely. When I decide you're sufficiently close to bringing down Wu Mei and Confucius – and, by implication, their opposition numbers in Trumpia and PopRep®© – I'll be in touch.'

'About?'

'A deal. I'll give evidence for the prosecution in return for immunity and a form of protection of my own choosing.'

'I can't make that deal, not here and now.'

'No, but you're resourceful enough to get one arranged by the time I need it.'

He stood to leave.

'Will you be safe?'

He grinned. 'That's an odd question for a cop to ask a serial killer.'

'For sure. But you know what I mean.'

From the doorway, he said, 'Safe enough. Now, give me five minutes before you leave.'

Then he was gone.

59

'Don't ask,' I told Comanche when I got back to my room. 'It's a long story and not for now.'

She gave me a hard look and seemed to decide this wasn't a battle worth fighting.

'I need a shower,' I said. 'Then I need to go to bed.'

'How about a nightcap? You look like you could use one.'

I nodded and asked for a Scotch and soda.

She had it waiting when I came out of the bathroom and I enjoyed the fiery bite of the whisky as it slipped down my throat.

'I'm guessing you want me to go?' She picked up her bag and headed for the door.

I called after her. 'No, stay. I'd like you to stay. But I do need to sleep.'

She smiled. 'Fair enough.'

We went to bed soon after and I rested my head on her shoulder. 'It's been a hard night,' I said. 'I have stuff to process. We can talk tomorrow. That okay?'

She said sure, that was fine, and told me to get some rest.

I fell into a deep sleep fast.

Comanche was still asleep when I woke the next morning. I felt a little woozy, my throat was parched as I climbed out of bed. The events of the previous night returned in a torrent. I needed coffee, I thought, to jump-start my brain.

Before I could order some, my phone vibrated.

The caller was Wu Mei.

'Tomsky has been found,' she said. 'He's dead. His throat was cut.'

—
*
—

Tomsky's evidence died with him – a huge chunk of my case against Wu Mei and the three leaders had been wiped out.

Standing in the living room of his "safe house" on Rue Brancion, I surveyed the body of the man who had terrified the world. He was lounging in an armchair with his head cocked, as if in contemplation. His throat had been severed from left to right with a sharp edge. The right-handed killer had approached undetected and ended him without a struggle. The point of entry was a sash window of the second floor apartment. The chief CSI speculated that Tomsky's executioner had shinned up a drainpipe and it made sense. Scuff marks on the pipe were being examined but I was almost certain this would reveal nothing of value.

Some would say Tomsky had escaped lightly; others that he had a right to due process. Notwithstanding the loss of vital evidence, I thought this world, or any other, would be a better place without him.

Who was responsible? My money was on the man who had carried out Tomsky's second wave killings, very likely on Wu Mei's orders. No one could have benefitted more than the spy chief. The killer, or an accomplice would have been watching my hotel on the off chance Tomsky might show. When I left for the rendezvous I'd have taken Wu Mei's man straight to Tomsky. Next, he'd have followed the pair of us to L'endroit Heureux and waited for Tomsky to leave, then tailed him to this apartment a kilometre away. I was surprised at Tomsky's sloppy fieldcraft, especially because he was rightly paranoid. Then again, Wu Mei's assassin was a master of his trade – Tomsky himself had told me as much.

What concerned me most right now was how much Wu Mei knew about how much I knew after my talk with Tomsky. Given the time I'd spent with him, she was probably assuming he'd told me everything about his role as a consulting serial killer. Including that Wu Mei had caught and failed to bring him to justice him fourteen years ago. For the time being though, we were both behaving as if neither knew anything about what the other knew.

I watched the CSI people going about their work. I wasn't expecting a great deal of forensic evidence, if any, but everyone made mistakes and maybe we'd get lucky this time.

Comanche had come with me, Puritan and Wham!®© arrived together soon after. I'd barely spoken to Bob since our fall-out and my relationship with Bogart was also strained after the same rumpus.

But at least, it seemed, we were able to work together.

Which was when Wu Mei's message made my phone ding. I went out of the room to read it.

Puritan was talking with Comanche and Wham!®© when I returned.

'A word in private, please, Bob.'

He followed me onto the landing.

'Did you know Ariana Bad-Bunny arrived here yesterday using a fake identity?'

He didn't need to confirm this – the answer was written on his face. Fuck, it was up there in flashing neon letters.

'And you didn't think to tell me?' I heard my voice rising, the accusatory tone, the rising rage. I told myself to calm down, to be professional. But the fire in my head was already ablaze.

'Because,' he said, sounding like one of my ex-partners, 'I knew you'd react in precisely this way.'

I tossed back my head and rolled my eyes. Part of this fury stemmed from my own folly. Just moments ago I'd told myself no one could have benefitted from Tomsky's death more than Wu Mei – without even thinking of the one person in the three federations who actually would.

My focus returned to Puritan. 'Can you provide an alibi for Ariana between midnight and four this morning?'

'You know I can't, boss. Look, I know where you're going with this, but please take a few moments.' Now he was sounding like my father. 'Think it through. This isn't what it might appear.'

'Isn't it?' Now my temper was full *Towering Inferno*. 'A woman with the skills and resources to carry out any black op you care to mention, who less than a week ago vowed to kill Tomsky to avenge her niece, turns up in this city – with a fake ID – and Tomsky's throat is cut in less than 24 hours? And this happens because you, Bob, gave her classified intelligence about Tomsky being Family Guy. How do *you* think that appears?'

'Like a misunderstanding – '

I cut him short by shouting to the uniformed sergeant who was my liaison with the local police. I wanted a BOLO on Ariana Bad-Bunny. I wanted her arrested for the first degree murder of Plato Tomsky.

Then I turned back to Puritan. 'This is on you, Bob. If you told me as soon as she arrived I could have had her surveilled and we could have prevented this. We could have saved crucial testimony that could have proved our case – '

'Miranda, please – '

'Don't *Miranda* me.'

Bogart appeared on one side of me and Comanche on the other. I sensed their concern. I knew I needed to get a grip. But I couldn't stop venting. 'If it wasn't for your senile infatuation with this woman, our star witness would still be alive and your stupid girlfriend wouldn't be wanted on a murder charge.'

He said nothing and walked away.

I shouted after him. 'Happy now, Bob?'

He said something I didn't catch but didn't stop walking.

60

ack at the incident room in the old Sûreté building
I began the debrief meeting with what remained
of my team. I was still too angry with Puritan than
was good for me and needed the distraction. Besides, the
investigation had to move on.

I started by telling Comanche and Wham!®© what
Tomsky told me the previous evening.

There was a long quiet when I finished.

Bogart made a discreet cough and looked at Comanche.
I could guess what he was thinking: Plato's disclosure
meant Wu Mei had as much to gain from Tomsky's death
as Bad-Bunny. I expected Wham!®© to push back on this
but he stayed silent.

'I want to focus on this copycat assassin,' I said. 'He's
the key to closing this case – to bringing Wu Mei and
Confucius and the others to justice.'

'You think there is such a thing, boss?' Comanche
sounded dubious.

'Perhaps not. Perhaps everything we uncover will be
suppressed. But what else can we do? Do either of you
think we should walk away?'

Comanche stared down at the table. 'We couldn't,' she said. Her voice was bitter and I sensed a hint of fatalism. 'Even if we wanted to.'

'Bogart?'

He agreed with Comanche.

'Very well,' I said, 'until we get stopped, we carry on. So let's talk about Wu Mei's hitman. What sort of individual are we looking at here?'

'Smon what got monsta covert ops smarts,' Bogart said. 'Smon what got a real strong belly for getting his graspers real mucky. And the spud is either getting paid a shitload of frogs or Wu Mei got her talons in him deep.'

'I agree,' I said. 'Money, blackmail and revenge are the three recruitment tools for this sort of work. And although revenge is possible, I think it's least likely. Of the two remaining, I'd go for blackmail.'

'Why do you say that?' Comanche asked.

'No amount of money will buy long-term silence. There usually comes a point where more money is demanded, then more, and so on. The customary solution for that scenario is to take out the person making the demands. But getting to a guy with these skills and resources wouldn't be easy.'

She nodded. 'Makes sense.'

'What doesn't,' I went on, 'is that he began sparing the kids after the Sinatra homicides. Tomsky was appalled by this perceived incompleteness. He saw it as a betrayal and put it down to a massive loss of nerve on the killer's part. But that doesn't square with Bogart's correct supposition that this hitman is used to getting a whole lot of blood on his hands. What does this seemingly sudden change tell us?'

'That a quesh for Old Bob.' Bogart gave me a dark look.

'All right,' I said, 'what would Bob say if he were here?'

'An assassin isn't the same as a serial killer,' Comanche ventured. 'We're looking at two different creatures. Performing the same horrorshow over and over could have got inside this guy's head in a way that would have just bounced off a serial killer like Tomsky.'

'Go on,' I said, 'this is good.'

Comanche interlocked her fingers to form a platform and rested her chin on it. For a few moments she gazed across the room at nothing in particular and I sensed she was deep in thought. At last, she said, 'Professional hitmen, black ops operators, whatever this person is, must be able to distance themselves from what they do. They are, I guess, fulfilling their side of a contract. "It's nothing personal", as the saying goes. And it's probably true, up to a point. But I think our guy has gone beyond that point. I think he's into serious burn-out territory.'

'Top thinkings, Comanche,' Bogart said. It was a rare compliment so her insight must have resonated. 'But this burn-out gotta be snaily-slow. Musta eated into his fusebox ebba time he done one of them family jobs. When do you thinks this popeye gone into meltdown?'

'The signs were there at the Sinatra crime scene,' Comanche said. 'The tox reports showed the level of anaesthetic was barely above the lethal threshold. At a guess, I'd say he was trying to let them live as well but fucked it up. Almost as if it was the first step of a learning curve.'

More sharp analysis, I thought.

Comanche went on, 'I know he treated the kids in the first three "second wave" homicides with what he would have seen as kindness, even reverence. But he took extra care when he posed the Sinatra children. Best clothes, favourite toys, scented candles and those angel wings cut from the kitchen curtains.'

'I think you're right,' I said, impressed. 'This is really useful stuff.'

I didn't know how useful.

I would soon.

61

The human subconscious is a curious entity. It plays catch-up, but always in its own time – a gradual composting process of memory fragments and part-formed thoughts, unframed questions and undeveloped ideas. And it ambushes you when you least expect, sometimes as a deluge, sometimes as a trickle.

This time I got the trickle – at least to start with. I was sitting outside a café next to the Shakespeare & Company bookstore on Rue de la Bûcherie, sipping a double-shot espresso. I'd been brought here by my subconscious. Not to this specific place, but to *any*place where I could put conscious thinking into neutral and let my subconscious go to work. Thinking by not thinking, as I called it.

Across the street, a group of anti-ist protestors were protesting the declining number of protests in the previous twelve months. *Is demo decline down to deep state deceit?* some placards asked. *What won't they tell us?* queried others. One demonstrator had glued her tongue to the road surface, another his foreskin to an iron drinking fountain. Some cops were being barracked for

376

trying to unglue them. There were cries of police brutality, allegations that the Meso-Liberal government was secretly yet institutionally anti-anti-ist.

Of more interest, some pigeons were squabbling over crumbs of food on the pavement. One finally triumphed and flew off, morsel in beak. The others continued their quest.

Three metres to the left, a lone pigeon was approaching a tasty-looking french fry. I wondered why the others weren't interested. Then I saw a ginger cat, concealed in some bushes on a low wall. It was positioned behind the lone pigeon that seemed focused only on the titbit.

The cat tensed.

The lone pigeon went nearer, nearer.

The other birds continued their squabbles, oblivious to the life-and-death drama in front of them.

The lone pigeon was less than a metre from the cat. The pigeon picked up the fry.

Any moment …

The cat pounced –

– Missed.

The pigeon was flapping skyward with the fry before the cat landed.

I emptied a sachet of sugar into my expresso and stirred it.

That pigeon had known something it wasn't meant to know.

But what?

And how?

The other pigeons hadn't warned it. They didn't take flight until the lone pigeon was aloft.

The cat hadn't made a sound.

Pigeons had an exceptional sense of smell. But the air was unusually still.

So how?

Instinct? A sixth sense? Pure coincidence? Dumb luck?

This was when I noticed my subconscious had sent a message to my frontal lobe. It had been mirroring the cat-and-pigeon puzzle, asking the same question: how was something known when it shouldn't have been? *Couldn't* have been?

But the subject under question wasn't a pigeon.

And unlike the pigeon riddle, this one had an answer.

I drank more espresso and knew I'd need something much stronger very soon.

The answer began to crystallise. Misty outlines solidified. The more I saw, the less I wanted to see.

But I couldn't turn away.

Not now.

Not ever.

I recalled Comanche's comment about the special care the assassin had taken when he posed the children at the Sinatra family crime scene. *Best clothes, favourite toys, scented candles*, she'd said, *and those angel wings cut from the kitchen curtains.*

But Comanche shouldn't have known where those angel wings were from.

She'd never visited the crime scene because – like Wham!®© and Puritan – she wasn't on my team at the time. I hadn't met her, or them.

And I'd kept the source of the angel-wing fabric off the record specifically to screen out wannabees like Charles

Henry McMartyr. I was the only person on my team who knew this.

Except Comanche.

Had she spoken to Tom Roscoe at Vegas, England police? Or Ronnie Ortega, the senior crime scene investigator? Very unlikely, I thought. And even if she *had* obtained this information in this way, I had to ask *why*?

Unlike the pigeon conundrum, the answer to this one was horribly obvious.

Comanche was Family Guy 2.0.

Comanche was the assassin.

62

Ariana Bad-Bunny was looking at me with a deadpan expression from the other side of a bolted-down prison table.

I was not going to make the same mistake with Comanche I made with Puritan. Not least because if I was right about her, I was going to be wrong about him. So, there would be no more rushing to judgment, no more hasty presumptions.

I gave Ariana a straight look. 'I may have been wrong about Bob.'

'May have been?' She lifted an eyebrow.

'I need your help,' I said, 'to clear his name.'

'The name you besmirched?'

'That one, yes.'

'There's very little that man wouldn't have done for you. And you betrayed him.'

'I'm trying to make that right. But I need your help.'

'But I'm banged up for the murder of Family Guy, alias Plato Tomsky. So not in much of a position to help. Even if I wanted to.'

'I may have been wrong about you too.'

'Seems you may have been wrong quite a bit.'

I wasn't going to insult her by saying something trite. So I kept quiet and allowed her this moment.

After some while she gave me the strangest look – I sensed pity, insight, harshness, kindness bound up as one. I felt exposed, transparent. Then she said, 'What do you want me to do?'

*

The Moulin Rouge, like its patrons and performers, was better seen at night. Unlit by neon and exposed to the afternoon sun, the red oxide windmill seemed shabby and run-down – more like a Blackpool Pleasure Beach reject than the embodiment of *La Belle Époque*.

I watched Comanche leave the Metro station at Place Blanche and cross Boulevard de Clichy towards the windmill. She walked quickly and with purpose, though not so as to stand out. There would be an occasional look over her shoulder, as if she were a tourist checking her bearings. But none of these glances appeared to ring alarm bells.

In any case, she was never going to see me because I wasn't there.

I was observing her from FIB headquarters through a nano-camera in heavy-frame glasses worn by Ariana Bad-Bunny, now back in Grey Lady mode. Of course there was a chance she'd make Ariana – she'd done it before in Berlin unter dem Himalaya and again in Blackpool. But Comanche thought Ariana was locked up in La Santé prison, so she was the last person she would expect to see on the street. At least this was what I'd been banking on when I asked for Ariana's help.

Sitting in front of a screen in my office, I was smoking too many cigarettes and fighting hard to keep my emotions compartmentalised. Below a battened down hatch in my mind, I could hear them shouting and banging to be heard. But I was determined to let this play out, to reach conclusions when I'd seen the evidence.

Because, right now, the most obvious conclusion was unthinkable. It would have to be faced, I knew this. But only when I was sure. And in the meantime, I had to think like a senior investigating officer, not like a betrayed lover.

When Comanche left the office she said she was meeting an old Parisian crime family boss who may have some information that could help the investigation. She hadn't been more specific, but this was entirely normal. I'd always let my team chase their own leads and come to me only if they found something useful.

On the screen I watched Comanche move from the Moulin Rouge and turn left into Rue Lepic. Ariana followed at a discreet distance. Like Comanche, she was wearing tourist gear and blended easily with the visitors thronging the cobbled street. Comanche was soon in the mazy Montmartre alleys once inhabited by the celebrated artists of the *Belle Époque* – Renoir, Valadon, Degas, Monet, and many more. Guides with vivid umbrellas led groups of tourists from Picasso's former home to a café-bar Toulouse-Lautrec frequented and on to a favoured haunt of van Gogh's.

Comanche stopped often. She obliged a couple who asked her to take a photo; she browsed gallery windows;

she grabbed a coffee at the Starbucks on Rue Norvins. All of which enabled her to reconnoitre the street behind as well as the way ahead.

This in itself wasn't surprising. She was well-known to local law enforcement and if she was meeting the head of a crime family, it would be natural to avoid leading them to them.

Ariana followed, apparently undetected as Comanche carried her coffee across the street and into Place du Tertre, where artists were dabbing their canvases under the spellbound gaze of visitors. One took a picture of a work-in-progress and the artist went off at the deep end. He pointed to a nearby "No Photos" sign and demanded the tourist delete the picture. The tourist refused. There was a scuffle. Like any good operator, Comanche used the diversion to improvise. Dropping her coffee in a bin, she elbowed through the crowd at the edge of the fray and vanished from view.

Ariana went after her. I took an anxious drag on my cigarette. Ariana was swallowed by the tussle of tourists and artists. The camera images became shaky and blurry. I feared the worst.

Finally, she made it to the other side. She scanned the square. But Comanche couldn't be seen. There were a few seconds of panning back and forth. In the voice piece I could hear Ariana's heavy breathing. I wanted to say something, but I knew this wouldn't help. At last, the swivelling stopped and the camera was back on track. Comanche was exiting Place du Tertre and walking towards the Basilica of the Sacred Heart. I'd never known a stronger tourist magnet than the pale grey structure with its sweeping views of

Paris. Always crowded, and with multiple entrances and exits, it was ideal for a clandestine meeting.

I felt another twinge of concern as Comanche weaved through the crowds, but Ariana wasn't going to lose her again. She'd moved much closer and although this brought some risk, it was a sound decision. After taking the evasive measures I'd just witnessed, she'd be confident of having shaken any tail.

She moved to the viewing area to the left of the basilica and leaned against an iron railing. Ahead of her the cityscape stretched to the horizon. The day was clear, the sun high. Spread out below was the view that brought people here – the Eiffel Tower, the golden dome of Invalides, the pewter thread of the Seine.

Ariana took up a position twenty metres away and got out her binoculars, scanning the city below like other visitors.

This was going to be it, I thought. This would be the rendezvous. I lit another cigarette with the tip of the previous one.

'You getting all this?' Ariana asked.

I told her I was.

'Won't be long now,' she said.

She was right. From the direction of the funicular rail station, a slender man in grey T-shirt and jeans walked across the viewing area, a howitzer-lens SLR camera slung around his neck.

There was something familiar about the way this man moved. The springy gait, the athletic carriage.

'Recognize that guy?' I said into the microphone.

Ariana didn't. She asked if I did.

'I do,' I said, 'but I can't remember who he is or where he's from.'

He went to stand beside Comanche and began focusing his telephoto. Neither looked at the other.

The exchange was brief – they were together less than thirty seconds. Maybe a verbal message had been passed, or one of them had passed something to the other. Either way, it had to be important, otherwise why take the risk of meeting in the first place?

The man lowered his camera started to move away, moving back towards the funicular.

I'd definitely seen that walk before.

But where? My memory had picked a great time to let me down.

I looked away, screwed my eyes shut, massaged my temples. I looked back again. More temple rubbing. Back yet again.

A chunk of memory dropped into place at the back of my mind.

I did a double take.

A triple.

This was when I recognized him. He was out of uniform and this was what had confused me.

I was looking at Chief Special Inquisitor All-Saints Geddes.

63

What to do? I needed time and space and a new brain. But I didn't have the first two and was stuck with an old version of the last. I'd have to deal with Comanche soon enough. And I needed to mend my fences with Puritan. Then I'd have to talk to him and Wham!®© about next steps. This was the least they deserved. Besides, I was relying on them now more than ever.

Before any of this, though, I had to understand this fresh craziness. I'd been betrayed as a professional and as a lover. I felt like a fool. I felt angry. I felt fragile. But human emotion wasn't going to help me or anyone else. The only way out was to keep my feelings in check and do some proper detective work.

The first question was what All-Saints Geddes had to do with events in Scientia? He was Derek Anti-Satan's right hand, so it was fair to assume he was in Paris-sur-Euphrète at his boss' behest. And if Anti-Satan was part of this, Judgment Jesusly would be too. Nor was it much of a stretch to hypothesise that the Trumpian bosses were in league with their Scientian counterparts, Wu Mei Leclerc and Isambard Kingdom Confucius. And since these people came in threes, PopRep®© would also have a role. Dreezy Simz for sure, but who else? Who was Simz's equivalent of Anti-Satan and Wu Mei? This continued to bother me but I left it for now and moved to the next question: why were they involved in this conspiracy?

All three leaders were facing elections this year. Their chances of victory had been threatened by the former PlayPals' blackmail attempt. So they'd brought in their security chiefs to manage these issues. Their discovery that Ladybug Boo was also involved, and that Plato Tomsky had switched from a vital asset to dangerous liability stirred an already murky pot.

I could use some fresh air so I left the building and walked. I had no idea where to, but the simple act of moving through the sunny spring evening helped to clear my head. I moved briskly along the Quai des Orfèvres, then north along the tree-lined Boulevard du Palais.

The question I'd been putting off was how Comanche fitted into this?

She'd tripped herself up over the kitchen curtains used as angel wings at the Sinatra crime scene. And after seeing her rendezvous with Geddes, I didn't doubt she knew about those curtains because she had cut them out and placed them next to the children she'd just murdered.

I remembered Wu Mei's strange warnings about Comanche as well as Tomsky. Now I knew what was behind it. They were two halves of the same whole, Tomsky the architect, Comanche the executioner. And the closer I got to either or both, the greater the risk that something might go wrong. In addition, Wu Mei had told me about Comanche's daughter, who must represent her hold over Comanche. *What wouldn't a mother do to protect her child?* That was what I asked myself at the time. Now I had the answer.

As I crossed the Seine at the Pont au Change, the sun vanished behind a cloud and a cool wind shivered the river's surface. I shivered too, but for a different reason. I had a gut feeling that I was being shadowed. I looked over my shoulder. But apart from a group of joggers going the opposite way, I was alone on the bridge. Watching Comanche being tailed by Ariana must have sharpened my paranoia. My head was too full of spy stuff. I needed to get a grip.

I carried on walking.

I was close to the right bank when another question came to mind: Wu Mei had also warned me about Comanche's judicially sealed past. Whatever it was, I didn't doubt this would be another crucial part of her leverage. But, like the mystery of PopRep's®© version of Wu Mei and Anti-Satan, this would have to stay on the back-burner.

I walked on, turning right towards the Hotel de Ville. My blood was circulating faster now, and with it, my reasoning ability.

Thinking back, it seemed Comanche had ripped up Tomsky's grand design when she started sparing the children. I recalled her remarkably perceptive analysis of the assassin's mindset. Those insights – the despair, the regret, the burn-out – had come from the heart. I'd witnessed her anxiety at the Disciplesons' place when she rushed upstairs to check on the kids. Then she went with them to the hospital – not so much an act of compassion as desperation.

There was so much else I hadn't seen but was starting to. Comanche had been privy to my opinion that a note from Family Guy would enable me to rule out a copycat. Which was exactly what was left at the Mozart crime scene. Clearly, Wu Mei had Tomsky pen the note and Comanche put it in place.

I thought, too, about Comanche's return to Paris after apparently visiting her daughter. She'd been wearing a yellow bandana. At the time I thought this was a motorcycle gang thing. Then I recalled the lesion on Brunhilda Mozart's forehead and Baudelaire Dodgson's speculation that it may have been caused by her managing to head-butt Family Guy. The pathologist was probably correct. Odds on, I thought that Comanche had been using that bandana to conceal a cut or bruise where Brunhilda's forehead made contact. Another thing Dodgson had mentioned: the snapped off knife tip suggested a loss of control. And how many times had I seen this from Comanche recently? No wonder Dodgson thought this absence of restraint was unlike the highly disciplined serial killer whose victims he'd autopsied for nearly twenty years.

I turned left at Rue Saint-Paul and moved away from the river. By now, the sky had completely clouded over and dusk wasn't far away. I'd walked further than I'd realized. Maybe I'd take the Metro back. Or get a taxi. This was an odd time of day – too late for sight-seeing, too early for dining out – and the street was unusually empty.

The apprehension I'd felt on the bridge came back. I paused, pretended to study a bistro menu.

Was I being tailed?

I glanced in the direction I'd come from. The quietness of the hour made it easy to scan the street scene for tell-tale signs. But I saw nothing untoward. And now I was beginning to irritate myself. The problem, I decided, was that my brain needed a reset. Not surprising given what I'd witnessed at Montmartre ninety minutes earlier.

I put down the menu.

Focus, I told myself. *Focus on the case.*

I walked on. My thoughts re-ordered themselves. Just a few paces later, my hypothesis hit the buffers.

The problem was this: Comanche had left Paris-sur-Euphrète – and was apparently seeing her daughter – when Family Guy killed the Mozarts in Berlin Unter dem Himalaya. But she was back in Paris a little over an hour after the latest estimated time of death. So she definitely couldn't have killed them.

Except she definitely had.

I did some mental arithmetic. The journey would have taken at least five hours on a commercial route. Even on a military solar-atomic arrow plane, she couldn't have done it in less than three.

So how had she pulled this off?

I walked on.

My memory went to work.

I walked further.

I thought about our flight from Vegas, England to Paris-sur-Euphrète – when I'd watched Dreezy Simz deliver her Michael Gove speech in Trafalgar Square. I remembered that her low-orbit clipper had left Old England an hour after our arrow plane and *still* arrived in Paris-sur-Euphrète ahead of us. In fact, so far ahead that she'd had time for a make-over before I was presented to her and Jesusly by Confucius at their media conference. Our arrow plane flight had lasted just over three hours. So, factoring in our sixty-minute start and the time Simz spent with her beautician before we arrived, this low-orbit clipper would have made the same journey in less than an hour. I wasn't sure how fast those things went, but these timescales implied a median velocity of around five times the speed of sound. And shifting at that rate, Comanche could plausibly have travelled from Berlin Unter Dem Himalaya to Paris-sur-Euphrète in under an hour.

Of course she'd have needed the connivance of Confucius to use his clipper. But given what I already knew about the involvement of the three federation rulers, this wouldn't have been difficult for Wu Mei to sort out.

So Comanche remained in the frame.

I walked on.

Other aspects of the case began to re-configure. The more I looked at events in this different light, the more transparent various developments became.

Like the framing of Charles Henry McMartyr, which I could now see as another move in Wu Mei's multi-dimensional chess game. She'd no doubt worked with Derek Anti-Satan to fit up McMartyr in order to bring me and my team to Rio de Jerusalem. Once we were there, Comanche would have been in place to carry out the assassination of Nebo Discipleson and his family.

I turned left into Rue Saint-Antoine and went straight on at Rue du Rivoli. Dusk was falling. The street lights came on. I wanted to get back to the office where my car was parked, then to my hotel.

I quickened my pace.

Something else came to mind. The night Tomsky's throat was cut, I'd fallen asleep fast and woken up feeling woozy. In light of what I now knew, I'd bet my boots Comanche slipped something into the whisky-soda she fixed for me while I was showering. Then, with me unwittingly providing an alibi, she'd have left the hotel and followed Wu Mei's directions to Tomsky's safe house. With him and his evidence eliminated, she was back in bed before I awoke.

Wu Mei's planning was impressive, I had to admit. Before Tomsky was taken out, she'd have had Comanche slip that note revealing he was Family Guy under Ariana's door. Ariana's reaction would have been predictable, as would me blaming Puritan. All of which drove a wedge between me and Puritan and made Ariana the perfect patsy when Tomsky's body was found.

I'd reached Boulevard de Sebastopol when the sense of menace returned. Once more, I paused, scanned the street behind and saw nothing of concern.

But the animal part of my brain stayed on red alert.

I was five minutes from the office. I was tempted to run. I should have.

One way or the other, though, I was determined to end this.

So I slipped into Place de la Tour de Sainte-Jacques, a public garden around the remains of a Gothic church tower, with gloomy paths weaving in and out of plane-leaf trees.

Ducked behind a tree, I waited. I checked my watch. Two minutes passed, five, seven.

Nobody had followed me into the square. And by now, nobody was going to. I'd been wasting my time.

I sucked in a deep breath and exhaled a loud sigh.

'Silly girl, Randy,' I told myself.

'Not necessarily.' The voice came from behind me. 'It's just that I'm too good for you.'

I knew that voice.

I looked over my shoulder.

All-Saints Geddes emerged from the vegetation behind me, a blade gleaming dull in the grainy street light.

64

'Thought you were smart, did you?' he said, 'having Bad-Bunny tail Comanche?'

I kept quiet. My eyes stayed on the knife.

He was wearing the same grey T-shirt, sneakers and jeans I'd seen at Montmartre two hours earlier. I'd *felt* him right behind me. But how had I not *seen* him? My head must have been more fuddled than I thought.

'Comanche should have made Bad-Bunny from the outset.' He sounded bored, as if having to explain his superiority was a chore he really could have done without. 'But she had no idea she'd picked up a shadow. And she brought Bad-Bunny right to me. How fucking amateurish? Never send women to do men's work.'

'Is that what you're here to do?' I asked. 'Men's work?'

He laughed.

My eyes stayed on the blade so I couldn't see his face but I imagined him smiling. He was six inches taller than me and two hundred pounds to my one hundred and twenty. And I didn't doubt his close combat skills were at least equal to mine. He'd be thinking this was a done deal. Which was my only advantage.

So I took it. He never saw the heel of my hand until it slammed against his cheekbone. He staggered back. But he still held the knife. I kicked at his crotch but he half-parried my foot with his left palm. My ball-crusher missed by a few centimetres, striking his inner thigh instead.

I pulled back, assessing my next move.

He wiped a trickle of blood from his cheek. 'Wanna play dirty? I'll show you dirty, you fucking whore.'

I heard the rising fury in his voice. Now I had another advantage – you're not thinking straight when you're riled. I hit out again, this time with a toe-poke. It struck his shin and made him yelp. His anger ratcheted up another few notches.

Now he came at me hard, the knife flashing this way and that, stabbing, slashing, twirling. The blade whisked past my face once, twice three times. Then he went for my gut, thrusting low, forcing me back on the uneven ground. He tossed the knife from his right hand to his left and attacked again. His frenzy no longer seemed like much of an advantage. I retreated further into the earthy gloom, further, further yet. I felt my heel stub a tree root and I tumbled backwards, my shoulders thumping the ground, driving the air from my lungs.

I heard him laughing again. Then he was straddling me, knees on either side of my chest, one hand on my throat, the other raising the blade. I scrabbled with both hands for some kind of weapon. Any kind. But there was nothing but compacted dirt.

'While you're bleeding out,' he said, 'I'm gonna hurt you.'

I wriggled beneath him but he had me pinned. I smelled his sweat, spicy street food on his breath. My fingers reached a patch of softer, powdery soil. I scooped a fistful.

The blade came down. I flung the dirt.

Two things happened.

He dropped the knife, clutching his eyes.

And a blood-sheathed iron spike erupted from his chest.

He wobbled, hands moving from eyes to chest, gore coming from his mouth and nostrils. Then he keeled sideways, hitting the ground to my left. I levered myself up on an elbow and saw him wriggling and kicking. Not for long. He was losing too much blood to stay conscious and went still fast. This was when I realized a pointed upright from the nearby railing had been driven between his shoulder-blades and come out through his sternum.

Comanche appeared from the shadows.

'You okay?' Her question sounded distant and unreal, like it was part of another conversation in a different, uncrazy place.

'Yeah,' I said between gasps. 'Look, we need to talk – '

'Now's not the time.'

'Just listen – '

'Gotta go.'

'There's nowhere you can run.' I was panting hard and my words came in breathy intervals. 'You were compromised the moment Ariana saw your rendezvous on Montmartre. And after what you just did to him' – I indicated Geddes' body – 'they'll all be after you.'

'They've always all been after me.' She made a small smile. 'And maybe this time they'll get me. But first I have business to handle.'

'Your daughter?'

'Wu Mei told you.'

It was a statement not a question, but I replied anyway. 'She swore me to secrecy. Look, I get it, I understand the pressure she must have put you under.'

'No, you don't. One day soon, you might. But right now, you really don't.'

'Let me help.'

'You can't.'

'Where will you go?'

'A place you know well. I've never visited but I know some people there.'

'I don't understand.'

'You'll figure it out. But don't hang around. There isn't much time.'

She placed one foot on Geddes' back before yanking the railing shaft free. 'The parks department with want this back.'

She leaned it against the tree trunk, tipped me a wink, and walked away.

I was in no state to stop her and didn't try.

65

ob Puritan was not an easy person to apologise to and apologising was not my forte. His gaze was stone-jug. Even his good eye didn't blink. I talked a lot without getting to the point. I came close a couple of times but veered away at the last moment.

I was about to make another approach when he cut across me. 'I accept your apology, boss.'

'But I haven't apologised yet.'

'Your intention will suffice. Ariana told me what you did. And we really don't have time to waste, do we?'

'No,' I said, 'I suppose we don't.'

'Very well,' he said. 'To business. What next?'

'What would *you* suggest?'

'We need to get to Comanche,' he said. 'Before they do. She's desperate, on the run, and has a lot of reasons to expose this conspiracy. And, of course, she's facing charges of multiple homicide.'

I'd already briefed him, Wham!®© and Ariana on events in Place de la Tour Saint-Jacques the previous evening. Wu Mei had not yet reacted to news of Geddes' death.

The chief special inquisitor's visit to Scientia had almost certainly been off-the-books so there'd be diplomatic complications. Also, Wu Mei and I were still engaged in a game of who knew what about whom and she wouldn't want to move until she was sure of her ground. That said, the murder of Derek Anti-Satan's protégé wasn't going to go away.

'Agreed,' I said. 'But before we start looking for Comanche I want to know more about the hold Wu Mei has over her. Obviously, Comanche's daughter has been a big part of this. But it's not everything.'

He gave me a curious glance and I told him about the file relating to Comanche's past that had been sealed by the Supreme Court of Scientia as part of her deal with Wu Mei.

He shook his head. 'Documents sealed by the Supreme Court can't be accessed by any conventional legal route.'

'But you know a non-conventional route, don't you, Bob?'

He made a dubious expression. 'Possibly. A clerk to one of the Supreme Court justices owes me a favour. She may – and I stress *may* – be able to help. But at best this would be a one-off glance at the file – no copies, no notes, no anything that could leave my friend exposed.'

'This is important,' I said.

'It had better be. May I ask why?'

'According to Wu Mei, this file has nothing to do with Comanche's career in organized crime. And there's nothing Comanche wouldn't do to keep it hidden – including resurrecting Family Guy's horrors. That makes it an incredibly powerful bargaining chip. I think it would tell us a great deal about Wu Mei's power as well as Comanche's vulnerability.'

'Okay, boss.' He came to his feet. 'I'll see what I can do. But I advise you very strongly not to get your hopes up.'

*

As an act of premeditated negligence, this was remarkable. The office of Puritan's friend, Vera Wolfe, was located next to the chambers of her boss, Justice Louis Napoleon Schiller and close to the Supreme Court Central Archive. At the agreed time, I walked into the Quai de l'Horloge entrance and checked in at the reception desk. My appointment was with Vera, though I knew she wouldn't be there because she'd engineered a meeting with Justice Schiller and Puritan in a conference room. This was in relation to one of Puritan's longstanding appeals and was due to last a good while.

I was handed a visitor pass on a nylon lanyard and directed to Vera's third floor office. The door had been left unlocked and I went inside, then through an interior door, also unlocked, to the judge's chambers.

The décor was in the grand design of the ancient building, though the history of the place was not at the front of my mind. I crossed the room to a desk by the window and saw what I'd come for – a paper copy of Comanche's sealed file. Vera's plan was to tell the elderly and absent-minded Schiller that she left it there because he'd requested it. This, apparently, happened a lot and Vera was confident her boss would accept her assertion without demur.

I sat at the desk, looked down at the file, ran my fingers over its coarse manila cover with *Sealed* stamped in fuzzy-edged red letters.

And hesitated.

I was about to trespass in a sanctuary of hidden hurt.

But I had to know what was inside – for Comanche's sake as well as mine.

So I opened the file and read its contents.

It wasn't what I was expecting, even though I didn't know what I was expecting. Wu Mei had told me this was nothing to do with Comanche's organized crime activities, which I'd already discounted. Even so, the nature of the material came as a shock.

It seemed Comanche had been sexually and physically abused as a child by her father. According to the file, her mother knew exactly what was happening but looked the other way. Worse still, Comanche knew her mother was doing this. As the years went by, the paternal abuse and maternal betrayal became intolerable. On her fifteenth birthday, Comanche took an axe to her father and left it in his spine.

I stopped reading and thought of All-Saints Geddes lying face down, his backbone split by the railing spike. And I realized the manner of the Harpo man's death was no coincidence.

I returned to the file. It told how Comanche then went after her mother with a kitchen knife, killing her on the spot in a violent frenzy.

Little wonder, I thought, that Comanche wanted this kept sealed. I never doubted that Comanche loved her daughter. The lengths to which she'd gone to keep her safe testified to that. But what would any child think of their mother if they discovered she'd brutally murdered her own parents?

I closed the file and left the judge's chambers, then Vera's adjoining office and then the court building. Outside, the air was cold for the time of year though I welcomed the sting of the breeze on my face. It helped me to make sense of things, reframe events of recent weeks.

I'd been right, I thought, about her poor impulse control with the wannabe bee outside the Mozarts' apartment; and again during the arrest of Charles Henry McMartyr; and yet again with Bez the blade boy in Little Havana. She'd hospitalized all three when much less drastic action would have sufficed.

And I kept returning to the conversation at *Cabane de Christophe* when we stopped for lunch during that crazy motorbike ride.

When I asked about her parents she'd said, *They were both arseholes and I never shed a tear when they died. Oh, wait. Yes I did – of joy.* Now, this remark acquired a dreadful resonance.

So too did her comments about my actualization and whether I existed. *You look real enough to me*, she'd said, *and all this shit around us is all too real. I wish it wasn't. If there was any chance of it not being, believe me, I'd take it.* A few moments later, she'd added, *If you aren't real, you're the luckiest person I ever met.* At the time I thought these were throw-away comments. But, walking towards the Pont Neuf, I realized she'd meant every damned word. She'd been murdering children to protect her own. She'd been living a double life in every meaningful relationship, including the one she had with me. She was trying to save what she loved by committing acts she hated. Now I saw the source of that fathomless despair. It was that of someone who had nowhere to turn and no way out.

I'm not your enemy, I'd said.

You will be, she replied, *sooner or later*.

66

MANCHESTER, ENGLAND

You guessed it, we was back in the Land of the No-Word Dictiony. Never wudda came here less it were abso ness. And once more, needs musted. One thing good: I were back on home turf –Manchester, my home town. Madchester, Rainy City, Cottonopolis, as it were smimes knowed. And all pretty much sames as when I was last in town: heavyweight Queen Vic buildings of pale stone and red brick, juxted with post-mod skyticklers of gleamy cut and shiny steel. Yet never far from this was seams of dark; prosts turning a trick; meth dens under railway arches; blade boy hangouts; yeggmen gaffs.

Comanche were here. I never knowed this for sure but I feeled it strong. Mebbe it were eastbound working on gutfeel. But gutfeel were all I got. And if this were a bad call it were coz I were clean outta good uns.

I racked my cap tryna magine where Comanche mighta gone. I gabbed with Old Bob and Bogart and I asked Ariana to quiz old intel spuds at Above Average Intelligence. But all come back with nada. Then I membered what Comanche tattled about the place she were gonna run to as she yanked that railing spike from Geddes' spine. *A place you know well. I've never visited but I know some people there.* Next, I got to thinking that she knowed I growed in Manchester. And *she* knowed *I* knowed she never been here coz we gabbed about coming one day, even if we really knowed it were never gonna happen. On top of this, she knowed I knowed she had contacts here, again coz she tattled about em in that same convo.

We taked rooms at the Midland Hotel, Manchester's finest, and I put the bill on Wu Mei's tab. No point tryna hide coz she could find us easy if she had a mind. I were sure, though, that she were happy for us to find Comanche and do the dirty work.

A showdown was coming, though, no truer words.

When we was settled in, I sticked in a call to the local nabbers and were sprized when they was bonus helpy.

'Yo,' gabbed a Det Top Boss name of Chet Checker. 'You name it, Randy. Nada is too much bother. Swing by my office and we'll set you up with whatever you needs. Meantimes, we keep our slots peeled for this Comanche lass.'

Praps they were a sub-tone of *Come into my parlour.* Praps I were reading too much into this shit and Checker were nada but a co-oppy Manc.

Anyways, he come back foot-down ferrari. 'We got a hit, Randy.' His vox were cited. 'You gonna wanna see this.'

The Big Cop Shop were north east of the city centre and the drive taked us through Strangeways, the working class neybrud where I come up. To be fair, they builded lotsa tidy new homes since my day, though the same tower blocks rised up headstony under dull breastplates of cloud what come in low and moved slow.

Chet Checker were waiting in reception – a short spud with dark hair what growed so low that his brow specked like a flesh-tone headband. He shaked ebdy's hand and telled me yet again how rocks-off he were to be working with me. Gottsay I finded it a tad too much, but hey, better than the oppo.

He taked us straight to the ops room where they got banks of street cams rigged high up for all to speck. One of em were froze-framed and Checker pushed the Forward tab when we was gathered round.

We specked a dark-clad spud in a wool hat legging slow long a city street. This, I knowed to be Chapel Street on the Salford bank of the River Irwell. When this spud come to the Premier Inn hotel, they went inside. As they moved tward the entrance, though, they taked off the hat and gogged skywise – direct into the street cam.

This were Comanche, never a doubt.

Which shaked me in a way I never spected. Acourse, we was here to collar her. But a small bit of me wanted us to fail. Coz if *did* collar her …

I turned to Checker. 'How long ago did this happen?'

'Thirty mins. She ain't not come out since. We got the place covered. Ultra-low-key. Nubdy would know we was there.'

'Smart work, Chet,' I told him. 'You warranted up?'

He nodded. 'Ready to move on your say-so.'

'Then let's go to it,' I tattled.

We went to it aright, pelting bonus giddy-up in unmarked cars down Oldham Road and cross the Irwell into Salford.

The breach team was ready-steady. I give em the yo-nod and in they went, fast, ficient, fierce.

And come with nada.

'Trump in Stormy, she done a runner.' Checker scratched his thick-thatch fusebox, obvio capblown. 'How the zuck?'

'She got monsta-level black ops skills,' I splained. 'Don't beat yourself up, Chet lad.'

In a way I were not sprized Comanche taked off. Mebbe the zuck-up with the street-cam made her realize she gotta split. Mebbe the street-cam deal were never a zuck up at all. Mebbe it were to let me know she were in town. Like, *Here I am. Catch me if you can – but I bet you can't.*

The breach team boss come over and told us the gaff been double-searched top to toe and all were clear. 'Just one thing,' she gabbed. 'The hotel manager reckons he earwigged this Comanche when she were making a call. I think that popeye will tattle.'

The manager were a slim spud still young enough to have zitty cheeks, name of Groucho Speedwell.

And tattle he did.

Comanche maked a call from the hotel lobby, he telled us. He were in the back office, but the door were ajar and Groucho heared the whole convo. Comanche were calling some popeye about scoring smin not easy to come by and they agreed to meet at Mr Thomas's Chop House on Cross Street. This were all Groucho knowed so we thanked him profuse and drived through downtown Manchester to Mr Thomas's. This were a genuine Queen Vic gaff if ebba there were one, bonus narrow but crazy deep and gleamy with buffed brass and polished wood, rijnal flooring and arched wall tiles in green and cream.

I went in solo so as not to spook the locals and showed the bar lass a photo of Comanche.

'Never specked her,' she tattled without looking.

I shoved the photo nearer her viz. 'You sure?'

'She's sure.' I turned and zeroed a big moustachioed jack with neck tats and baccy breath.

'Praps *you* gogged this jane?' I holded up the photo for Mustachio to zero.

'This ain't not no snitch joint.' He come closer. 'So why don't you zuck off while you still can.'

'I can leave any time I likes.' I standed my ground. 'But I ain't not going no-place without answers.'

Mustachio were not gonna be telled. He bringed up his index-dedo and jabbed it at me gressive.

I blocked the index with the heel of my palm and clasped it in a fist. Then I cocked my wrist, levering the index backwise and down.

A yowl come from the gobbler of Mustachio. He sinked to his knees as I plied more pressure.

'Now,' I tattled. 'You gonna tell me what Comanche were doing in here?'

'Zuck you!'

I pushed harder on his index. He maked anudda yelp.

'Bar lass!' I called. 'You better call an amblance. Tell em to fetch splints for a broke dedo.'

I shoved some more. He whimpered feeble.

Again to the bar lass, I called, 'Oh, yeah, and tell em they gonna need lotsa morphine.'

'*Okay-okay-okay*,' wailed Mustachio.

I eased off a little. 'Why did Comanche come to this gaff?'

'She come to see this geezer.'

'What geezer?' Back went the dedo. 'Be specific.'

'She were after this popeye what can fix fake ID stuffs.'

'Name?'

'Elton. Elton Jones.'

'Where he hang?'

'Ordsall. Huddart Close. Oppo Salford Lad's Club.'

'That weren't so hard, weren't it not?' I let go of his dedo.

He sticked it tween his knees, ziff to stop me snatching it back.

I left Mr Thomas's and give Chet the name and dress of this Elton Jones.

'We knows old Elton from way back,' Chet gabbed. 'Won't be tough to find.'

He weren't wrong. Elton were cleaning out his budgie cage when we arrived at his place in Ordsall. He were an old school forger, well into his sixties, with a long list of previouses and a strong desire to stay outta his old cell in Strangeways. So he singed like a Canary Wharf. He were working on a counterfeit passport for Comanche. He never wanted the work but she leaned on him heavy. And he were gonna hand it over in return for ten thousand frogs the night after tomoz in Castlefields. He even zeroed Chet's phone map and showed us where.

Out on the street, Chet gimme a thumbs-up. 'We gonna nab her, Randy. Bang to rights.'

Logic telled me he were right. Yet I knowed too well that logic got a nasty habit of zucking you in the vance.

67

This late at night, Castlefields were Steampunk City and serio freddykrueger +++. The place got built when the lad Poe were still spinning gothicy yarns and specked more a haunt of Jack the Rip than Family Guy. It were a mass of iron tendon and stone muscle and brick bone. Its canals and railways was once the great arteries of trade what maked Manchester the world's first indstrial city. Over my fusebox, the steel lattices of the train viaduct was black against a fat yellow moon. Below, the canal basin glimmered dim, mist lifting raggedy off the water and groping cross the wharfs. Their cobbled surfaces was gleamy-slick from the rain. It slacked off a bitwhile back but the air still feeled like damp cobwebs on my viz.

I come here solo, spite the protests of Puritan and Wham!®©. Even the ultra-keen-to-please Chet Checker voxed his worries.

But I owed it to Comanche.

Sides, if she meaned me harm she never wudda kebabbed All-Saints Geddes with that railing spike.

I lighted a smoke and waited.

Ten mins passed.

Anudda ten.

I peered into the shadows, tryna make out form and shape. But ebba time I thinked I zeroed smin, it come to nada.

Longer I waited, colder I got.

I sticked anudda smoke in my gobbler and were gonna light it when –

'Sorry about the wait.'

I turned sharp.

She come from behind a steel viaduct column and leaned against its rust-flaky flank. She were not ten feet from me.

I tossed the smoke. 'Lemme guess. You had to be sure I were solo.'

'I knew you'd come through.' She maked a faint smile.

'I knowed you'd come too.' I give her one back.

'Got my passport?'

'What you think? But here's smin instead.' I taked a quarter bottle of Captain Kidd rum from my pocket and throwed it to her.

She catched it and gogged the bottle dubio. 'You know I like Captain Morgan. Only tossers drink Captain Kidd.'

'Well then,' I tattled, 'what's the prob?'

She gimme one of her cheeky winks, unscrewed the top and taked a swig.

'So, here we are.' She wiped her puckers on her sleeve. 'You worked it all out, then?'

'I did. The first puzzler were why you was so sloppy at the Premier Inn, though I spected from the get-go that you wanted me to find you. But why did you never used your crime gang amigos in Manchester?'

She gimme a you-kidding-me? look.

I thinked about this and then it hit me.

'You was using them all along. Young Groucho, Big Mustachio, Old Elton. They was all your people. They was the trail of breadcrumbs what you left to lead me right here, right now.'

'You should have been a detective.'

'Praps. But what still don't compute is why you done all this stuffs?'

She taked anudda swig of rum. 'I needed to buy some time. I got a job for you.'

This were some jawdrop shit. '*You* got a job for *me*?'

'The most important I'll ever ask anyone to do. Ever.'

She weren't being flippant, that much were for sure.

'I'm fucked,' she said. 'There's no good ending for me. We both know that.'

'But if we can just tattle – '

'For Chrissakes, Randy, just listen.'

I holded up my palms, ziff to say, *Okay I get it*.

Her vox went soft. 'There's nobody in this world I care about as much as you. Except the person I need you to take care of for me.'

'Your daughter. You spent the last forty-eight hours getting her free of Wu Mei. That were the time what you was playing for, weren't it not?'

'Like I said, you should have been a detective.'

'Where's the lass now?'

'Safe. For the time being. That's where you come in. I need you to make sure she stays that way.'

I maked a gimme-a-break spresh. 'I were never a mother figure. You knows that.'

'I'm not asking you to be. Victoria is a smart and capable sixteen-year-old. She doesn't need someone to hold her hand. But she's still a sixteen-year-old. And she *does* need someone to protect her, someone she can trust, someone to keep her on track.'

'And if I gabs no?' Even as them words come out, I knowed there were no real poss of me gabbing no.

'I'll provide all the resources you need.'

I telled her I could use a belt of rum. She slinged me the bottle and I taked a big swallow, feeling the neat spirit burn my swallower and belly.

Then she gabbed, '*But.*'

'Oh good,' I tattled sarcy, 'there ain't not nada like a "but".'

'This is serious shit, Randy.' Comanche glared piercy. 'Victoria can never know about the things I did to keep her safe. And she can never know I killed my own parents.'

'Coz you wants her to think well of you?'

'Because I want her to think well of herself.'

I cogged what she meant. What chance would any kid have growing up in the shadow of a mother like Comanche? Victoria might aready think there were smin wrong with her genetics. Add to that a family history of contract serial killing, patricide and matricide and, well, nuff tattled ...

'She knows about my career in crime, that she was born in jail. No escaping that. But I don't want her to become me. You're the only person who can stop that happening.'

'I thinks you is overrating me.'

'No, I'm not.'

There were a drawed out quiet. I gogged down at the damp cobbles and shaked my fusebox. But there was no way I were gonna scape this last duty she wanted – *needed* – from me.

'Assuming I is down with this,' I tattled, 'what next?'

'I don't want assumptions, Randy. I want your word.'

'Okay,' I tattled, all out of choices. 'You has my word.'

I waited a bitwhile, then gabbed again, 'So, what next?'

'There is no next. There was never a next.' She zeroed me straight. 'I won't be taken. You're gonna have to end me.'

She come to this blunt and cold and frighty ferrari.

'Don't be brickthick. We can work smin out… ' I knowed I was gabbing eastbound but still I gabbed. It were like, as long as I were gabbing, nada bad were gonna happen … as long as I were gabbing, Comanche wouldn't come to no harm… as long as I were gabbing, she… could not die …

Even when she pulled her gun, I never stopped gabbing.

Even as I pulled mine.

Even when the shot ringed out. Then anudda and anudda, anudda yet.

I did stop, though, when I specked the blossoms of gore on Comanche's chest. One, two, three, four …

But I never fired my gun.

My slots followed Comanche's gaze and I zeroed Wham!®© standing behind me, his Glock 19 fumey, four brass casings at his feet.

A sputtery cough come from Comanche. Still zeroing Wham!®©, she gabbed, 'Finally, Tweetie, you did good.'

Gore come oozing thick from her gobbler. Even so, she maked a smile. 'The boss could never have done it. You saved us a lot of pain.'

Bogart tattled nada.

Comanche tottered. Her gun falled clattery to the cobbles.

I tried to get to her. But my shoes was heavier than deep sea diver boots.

She went to her knees, tipped me one last wink, then keeled sideways and lay still, slots unshiny, life gone.

68

ST PETERSBURG, RUSSIA

Was someone inside my head? Or was I inside theirs? The question I'd asked myself so many times since I arrived here was bothering me again. Now, though, it was more persistent, more pressing. For a while I'd been able to compartmentalise the incidents at the bookstore and the airstrip. Now, though, with Tomsky and Comanche dead, the Family Guy investigation was over. And the puzzle of my existence, of who had written – or was writing – *The Big Happy* was back. I was certain it was inextricably linked to the reckoning that was about to happen as the vertical thrust plane landed in Palace Square, St Petersburg in Old Russia. Wu Mei had sent me a message shortly after Comanche's death. It was to the point, though curiously polite. She was sorry about Comanche and sent her commiserations. The global bosses were in the Winter Palace and she wanted me to be there as soon as convenient.

She hadn't said whether I should come alone, but I took this to mean Wham!®© and Puritan could come along or not. They wanted to, but I didn't. If anyone's head was going on the block, it had to be mine alone. Of course, there were protests but I stood firm. Bogart's head was a mess after he shot Comanche and I understood why. They'd never agreed on much and fought a lot, but a kind of kinship had developed – almost like sibling rivalry. Puritan's relationships were similar, though without the sibling stuff. He and Bogart were close and he'd never fallen out with either Wham!®© or Comanche. I was the only one he'd come into conflict with.

As for where I stood with Comanche, I didn't really know. Everywhere one moment, nowhere the next. Every feeling I'd had for her as my friend and lover came with an opposite; every sympathy for her predicament, an antipathy; every positive thought, a guilty one.

What wouldn't a mother do to protect her child? I'd once asked myself. The answer in her case was nothing. But could *anything* begin to justify the murder of eight other children and twenty mothers and fathers? What would *I* have done? Not that.

But then I never had a kid and Comanche was a sociopath, pushed in that direction by her own abuse by the parents she'd also killed. True, she'd ended the suffering of the young woman in the stoning pit; and she saved my life when she speared Geddes with that railing spike. But what she'd done at Wu Mei's behest was unforgivable. In the end, I was certain Comanche knew this. In the end, even someone with her psychopathy couldn't live with the pervasive horror.

As for her daughter, I'd received a call from one of her motorcycle gang comrades telling me Victoria was safe. When the time was right, a meeting would be arranged.

This was another issue altogether. I'd get to grips with it – I had no choice. But not right now.

The vertical thrust plane settled on the miniature steppe of Palace Square and I went forward as the door opened and the steps were deployed. A Scientian Army major was waiting to escort me and we began the long walk to the green, white and gold confection of the Winter Palace. As statement architecture went, I'd never seen anything grander or more imposing. I wasn't sure whether I was meant to feel intimidated or flattered but I felt neither – not by the building itself. What happened inside, well, that was something else.

As we neared the main entrance, my phone dinged. The message was from Wham!®© and its contents were significantly more diverting than the baroque pageant that awaited me inside the palace.

I was shown through halls of marble and granite and jasper, chandeliered by structures of gleaming crystal and flanked by tall columns with ornate entablatures. There was more overkill here than a Family Guy crime scene. What was it for, the excessive splendour? As art, I got it. As a meeting venue for a handful of people, it made no sense. But then, what did? Fortunately, the three leaders and two security chiefs were waiting in a relatively modest salon laid out as a reception room.

The first thing that struck me was the absence of the third intelligence boss – A++ of Above Average Intelligence. Surely now would be a good time to make an appearance, top secret identity or not.

'My dear Miranda,' Confucius said in his best Royal Shakespeare voice, 'how wonderful to see you.'

I was keen to get this business done so getting rid of the monkeys and focusing on the organ grinders topped my agenda.

So I said to Confucius, 'You should leave the room while we decide whether or not you're going to be arrested.'

'What?' Confucius' expression was stranded between bafflement and outrage. 'How dare you!'

I lifted an eyebrow. 'You need to start considering a return to your real job. I gather they're looking for a Widow Twankey for *Aladdin* at the New Bristol Hippodrome.'

'I don't know what you mean.'

'Yes you do, Gielgud. That's your name, isn't it? Gielgud Fanshaw? You were a jobbing actor whose best paid work was the occasional daytime TV commercial. You got lucky, though, when you landed the biggest role on the world stage: Isambard Kingdom Confucius, up-and-coming leadership prospect in Scientia. Tell me if I'm wrong.'

I knew I was right – or rather Bogart was – when neither Wu Mei nor Anti-Satan intervened.

I turned to Simz. 'And if I were you, I'd get ready for a return to the Liverpool tribute act circuit – I hear it's not been the same since Scouse Kylie quit fourteen years ago.'

She seemed bewildered.

'Well, Scouse Kylie, aren't you going to *Say Something*?'

It was a cheap play on words, but I *did* enjoy it.

'As for you,' – I glanced at Jesusly – 'they'll be glad to see you back in your travelling preacher tent in Abilene, "Buckle of the Bible Belt."'

I watched my words sink in, then addressed all three. 'Small wonder you couldn't behave yourselves at San José. You weren't competing in a leadership selection process, you were auditioning. And when you landed those roles of a lifetime, you went apeshit with your PlayPals – Kiera, Brunhilda and Nebo.'

A charged silence filled the salon.

At last, Wu Mei gave the three of them a brief nod and they left the room.

I called after them, 'Kiera, Brunhilda and Nebo.'

When the doors closed behind them I looked from Wu Mei to Anti-Satan. 'I have some questions.'

'We have some answers.' Anti-Satan's Lavrentiy Beria eyes gleamed with disturbing confidence. 'Safe to say, though, that you're not going to like them.'

I mustered an air of defiance. 'You don't know what my questions are.'

'I think we can guess. You'll have worked out by now that we are the power in this world. But what you're most curious about is the third person – the head of Above Average Intelligence.'

'Okay,' I said. 'Tell me.'

I didn't like the way this was developing.

'You're also curious about your author, your creator. Does this individual exist? If so, who are they?'

I liked this even less.

'I'm the one you're looking for, Miranda. I'm A++.' The voice came from behind me. I recognized it instantly. But it wasn't the voice of a spy chief.

This was every kind of crazy.

And every kind of sane.

'We need to talk,' said A++.

69

'You?' I said. 'This isn't possible.'

'It is, though, isn't it?' The woman I'd known as Ariana Bad-Bunny was standing at an open door to another room. 'It's more than possible, it's inevitable. Think about it.'

I thought about it. She was right. Through the lens of this fresh perspective, fuzzy details took on sharp definition. Such as how Ariana had clearly operated as a high-level intelligence officer but nobody at Above Average Intelligence, or the Harpo or the FIB had any information about her; such as her strange knowingness when I questioned her at the Harpo Head Office; such as that look of skewering look of insight and pity when I asked her to help clear Puritan's name.

'Come in.' She stood aside as I walked into the room she'd come from – similar to the one I'd left, but smaller and arranged as an office. Wu Mei and Anti-Satan stayed outside and the woman I'd known as Ariana closed the door. 'Take a seat. Tea?'

I sat on one of two grey silk armchairs either side of a low table. I said yes please, tea would be nice. My understanding of this world had just been exploded so we were having a nice cup of tea – a panacea more British than the band playing on as the *Titanic* went down. I hoped the parallel ended there, but had a nasty feeling it didn't.

'Milk or cream?'

'Just milk.'

I had too many questions, none of them conceivable just two minutes ago. The ones I'd come here to ask would have to wait. I struggled to order my thoughts. Implications, effects, repercussions. They all came together in the particle collider of my brain.

'Sugar? It's one lump you take, if I remember correctly.'

That would be lovely I told her and waited while she played mother.

'Well,' she said, bringing over a silver tray of tea-drinking paraphernalia, 'isn't this nice?'

There it was again, that word.

'Very nice.' I took a sip of tea and had to admit it was exactly that.

'I know you'll have many, many questions.' She poured some milk into her cup. 'And understandably so. First, though, let me explain something of my own position in all of this, which might resolve some of your concerns.'

I swallowed another mouthful of tea and sat back in the chair.

'First, I suppose, I should confirm that I am, indeed, head of Above Average Intelligence. The identity of the agency's chief has traditionally been a secret and, while I would have been happy for my name to be made public, I must also acknowledge convention.'

She took a sip of tea but her eyes never left mine. 'My real name is Nico Nyro.'

This was familiar. I should have recognized it instantly but the context was all wrong.

She gazed over the rim of her teacup, waiting for me to make the connection.

At last I said, 'You're my author.'

She returned her teacup to its saucer. 'Yes – or leastways I'm the writer who conceived the character of Miranda Miller. I make this distinction because your actualization process created the properly functioning individual that you are now, complete with free will, self-determination and independent thought. In short, I formulated the idea of you, but that's where the link ends. You have made yourself into a totally different person to the one I wrote about. And you have no idea how proud that makes me.'

I gave her a flummoxed look. 'Why do you say that?'

She seemed a little abashed. 'When any author conceives a protagonist, they tend to take on a life of their own. They develop in ways you hadn't imagined. This is the magic of prose fiction. When you hear your work read aloud, for example in an audiobook, that character acquires even more depth and texture. If you're lucky enough to have your work turned into a movie, I would imagine this takes the fictive evolution process one step further. But if you get as lucky as I did and your character is made real – as you were – that's on a wholly higher plain. My experience of your actualization has been similar to having a child. Except of course, you came as a fully grown adult. Observing you going your own way, making your own decisions was transcendingly joyous.'

Not so much for me, I thought. But another realization elbowed its way to the front of my mind. '*You* placed those Miranda Miller novels in the basement of that bookstore, didn't you?'

She drank more tea and gave me a subtle you-got-me look.

Something else occurred to me, something that had been bothering me for a while. 'Then you'll know I read the first four of the quintet. What happened to the last one, *The Big Happy*?'

'I didn't write that one.'

'You mean you didn't get round to it?'

'Not at all. I left that title for you. You wrote it. You're writing it right now. It's your story.'

I recalled my peculiar experiences at the bookstore and the airstrip. The sense that I was in the book and at the same time apart from it. And, of course, I recalled the title – *The Big Happy*. Perhaps somewhere deep in my mind I was aware that *I* was creating the narrative, that in a sense, I was my own author.

But I'd had enough of this metaphysical maze. Besides, I had more questions – concrete ones. 'Why choose me? Wu Mei said you could have actualized any fictional sleuth. Jack Reacher, Clarice Starling, Lisbeth Salander, you could have had any of them. I also believe I was set up to fail – so why not choose a proper spoof like Clouseau or Frank Drebin?'

'*I* wanted you. Maybe it was the ultimate vanity publication, but I was determined to give you a shot. Wu Mei and Anti-Satan were never happy because the scheme was theirs and they wanted a more traditional character.

But I dug my heels in. Eventually I sold Miranda Miller to them on the basis that you were a satirical investigator – closer to Clouseau than Starling – and would therefore be much more likely to fail.'

I sensed that Nyro was enjoying this, as any author might enjoy a media interview about their latest work. Clearly this conversation wasn't going any further than this building, but if anything I got the impression that the confidentiality heightened her satisfaction. She may well have been the first author to meet her protagonist face to face. So I grasped the opportunity, pushed on with my questions. 'You didn't really want me to fail at all, though, did you?'

'No I did not. You have nothing of Clouseau and everything of Starling.'

I poured milk into my tea from the silver pot on the table. 'Can you tell me why?'

She mirrored my actions. When we'd sorted ourselves out, she continued. 'I always opposed this plan of Wu Mei's. But the three of us had to work together and I was outvoted by her and Anti-Satan.'

'Work together? Isn't that something you three do all the time?'

She shook her head and made a light chuckle. 'Good lord, no. We're not some cabal of spy bosses. We lead rival organizations. But there have been times when we've shared the same problem and it made sense to pool resources. This was one of them.'

'The common problem being the blackmail attempt against the three leaders?'

'Exactly, though as you've gathered, they aren't proper politicians. They lead immensely privileged lives and in return take advice from senior specialists and act as mouthpieces for various interest groups within their federations.'

'So these upcoming elections are for real?'

'Absolutely. If this blackmail material gets out – and it will now that you've uncovered the truth – they'll be voted out of office. It's part of our roles to protect them from scandals like this. But we can only go so far, and in Wu Mei's case this has gone way too far.'

I got what she meant. Wu Mei's plan to revive the career of Family Guy was infinitely worse than the scandal it was meant to conceal. Small wonder Nyro had never been on board with it.

'What will happen to the leaders? And to Wu Mei and Anti-Satan?'

'Confucius and Simz could be allowed to pull out of the elections and retire on modest allowances. Jesusly's masters are less forgiving. He faces the real prospect of a date with Old Crispy – his phrase, not mine.'

I drank more tea. I couldn't say I felt much sympathy.

'As for Wu Mei, she's finished. If she was in any other federation, she too would be looking at the death sentence. In Scientia, she'll probably spend the rest of her days in a Siberian supermax. Conspiracy to commit mass murder, torture and violent rape must be made an example of.'

'And Anti-Satan?

She made a grim smile. 'As far as the Harpo goes, the notion of going too far doesn't exist. In any event, Anti-Satan kept his hands clean by delegating all the off-book work to Geddes. And he has evidence that the operation was mainly Wu Mei's doing. He'll silence criticism from liberal elements by claiming she went rogue.'

'And you?'

'I'm not under threat.' She finished her tea and placed the cup and saucer on the tray. 'I argued vehemently against the Family Guy plan. I warned Wu Mei and Anti-Satan not to do it and put this on the record. When they dismissed my objections and went ahead anyway, I devised a way to get inside your investigation and help bring the whole damn thing to an end.'

'Hence Ariana Bad-Bunny?'

'Hence Ariana Bad-Bunny.'

'And presumably that's why you, as your alias, told me about Kiera having been in touch with people from Apex, San José.'

'You needed a nudge. You and your people did the real detective work yourselves though.'

I thought she was being coy – that tip-off had changed the course of the investigation at a critical moment. But I kept quiet.

'Was Ariana's backstory also a product of your imagination?'

She shook her head. 'I wish I could say she was. The real Ariana was an Above Average Intelligence officer who died three years ago in the field. Nor did I need to invent very much at all. She was indeed an aunt to Kiera and related to Gonzales Smedge. Assuming her identity was the most tailor-made cover I've ever used.'

Resourceful all the same, I thought. But Nyro clearly didn't like compliments so I didn't give her one.

Instead, I turned to one of the main issues I'd come here to resolve. 'What about my team? Who picked them?'

'You know already that Wu Mei recruited Comanche as

the Family Guy copycat as well as her eyes and ears inside the investigation. Anti-Satan selected Puritan because he's been the Harpo's nemesis for many years. If the operation crashed and burned, Anti-Satan would not only be rid of him, but would also have a ready-made patsy.'

'And Wham!®©?'

'My choice. I was confident he wasn't going to fail, or allow you to fail. As you quickly discerned, there's a smart operator behind that man-boy façade. You could say he was my insurance policy.'

'Bogart and Bob have been incredibly loyal.' I swilled what was left of my tea around the bottom of the cup. 'Tell me, though, was either of them aware of your role in all this?'

'If either had been, do you think today would be the first you knew about it?'

'Silly question.'

'As you said, they are loyal people.'

'What will happen to them?'

'I'm sure they'll flourish – especially after taking credit for catching the original Family Guy *and* stopping the copycat killings. Bob will no doubt return to his legal practice and Bogart can look ahead to becoming a senior Alister. Who knows, he may even become a proper politician capable of effecting true reform.'

'Including a written dictionary?' I made a wry smile.

She reflected it. 'Why not?'

'What about me? Will I be de-actualized now my work is done?'

She gave me a hard look. 'Do you want to be?'

70

Did I want to return to the pages of her novel? Which was better – or less bad – a kind of living in the tripolar hokum of The Big Happy? Or a one way ticket to unknowingness?

But then I had to consider my obligations. I'd promised Comanche that I'd look after her daughter. I'd yet to meet the girl, but I was certain every time I did she'd remind me of her mother.

'I'm not sure,' I said. 'But the choice isn't mine.'

She gave me a probing look. I told her about my pledge and she nodded understandingly.

After a few moments' thought, she said, 'It's a big responsibility and you alone can decide how to deal with it. As far as I'm concerned, though, you're free to do what you want, go where you choose.'

'But?' I drained me teacup, 'Isn't there always a but?'

'Not so much a but as a maybe.'

'Okay, what's the maybe?'

'I could use you in PopRep®©. Maybe you could work alongside me as my deputy. I'm retiring in three years. You could replace me as head of Above Average Intelligence. And, of course, you could stay close to your friend Wham!®©. He's destined for political success and your paths would certainly cross.'

'That's a generous offer.'

'It's actually quite selfish on my part.'

'But I'd have to decline. Working with my own creator would be a little weird. No offence.'

'None taken. Very well, Wu Mei's position at the FIB will become vacant very soon. I wouldn't be at all keen on having you as a rival, but I'm sure the Scientians would be happy to have you.'

'Thanks. But again, I wouldn't be interested.'

'Even if it helped you to keep Victoria Comanche safe?'

'Even if it did.'

She took a tablet from the table and started scrolling through pages of information, stopping every few seconds to suggest one top job after the next. After I declined the fourth, she realized it wasn't the jobs themselves that I wasn't interested in.

She put the tablet on her lap and gave me a direct look. 'You don't want to work anywhere in the federations, do you?'

I didn't need to reply.

'I'm afraid there's very little else. There are a handful of non-aligned countries but they are impoverished geo-political hangovers from the Old World. North Korea, Libya, Afghanistan, Cuba – '

'Is there anything in Cuba?'

She looked at me as if I was mad, but shrugged and consulted her tablet.

'Here's something.' She looked up from her scrolling. 'The National Revolutionary Police Force is looking for a chief of detectives. The pay is rubbish, but you'd be based in Havana.'

I knew she was doing her best to find some sort of role for me, but even though I loved Havana, the prospect of more politicking did not appeal.

I said I was sorry, but wondered if there was any non-political police work.

She gave me a weird look. 'In Cuba?'

'Alright, relatively non-political.'

There was more scrolling, and more.

She'd been at it a good while when she stopped and looked up with a weary expression. 'All I can find is a vacancy for a lieutenant of detectives. The pay is below the statutory minimum wage in PopRep®©; living standards are dreadful; and the job is in Cienfuegos, a three-hour drive from Havana.'

'Worth looking into,' I said.

She still wasn't going to give up. 'It's the sort of work you were doing twenty years ago.'

'That's why I'm interested,' I said.

Epilogue

CIENFUEGOS, CUBA
FIVE YEARS LATER

Caribbean evenings were special where Arimao playa met the river that shared its name. The sun was under the horizon, casting a peach afterglow on ribs of cirrus, high in the delphinium sky. Flamingos stalked and sifted the estuary shoals for a late supper. Across the bay, the slim crescent of a sail fattened as the skipper put his helm over and steered for the shore.

I was watching from the porch of my home, a colonial villa of ancient timber, worn smooth by sand and brine. I should have had it painted, but I liked it how it was. I was fifteen kilometres from Cienfuegos city, but the drive was worth it for views like this; the transparent sea; the fine yellow sand; the breeze-borne scent of mariposa jasmine.

I'd visited Cuba in the 2010s – at least in the imagination of Nico Nyro – and remembered the elegant decay, the lived-in antiquity of its towns and cities. Which was why I wanted to live here. Unlike most of the states and regions of the federations, Cuba was largely untouched by Scientian arbeiterbots. Of course, there'd been restoration work, but the Cubans had done most of it themselves. Besides, the urban centres had been in such a mess since the 1959 Revolution that the apocalypse had arguably improved them. Even now, Castro-era deprivation and weirdness was widespread. A public lavatory attendant dispensed three squares of toilet paper per bowel motion. An orthopaedic surgeon I'd met claimed he earned more from a side-line cleaning swimming pools than at the hospital. I could believe it. My own salary as a police lieutenant was borderline breadline. I made ends meet though.

I sipped my tumbler of Cuba libre and glanced at the old Bakelite telephone, hoping it stayed silent. I was rarely called at night, but you could never be sure. Major Fernandez, my boss was a relaxed but effective officer who treated his people well. The city had a population of nearly 200,000 so it was big enough to keep me busy but too small for the hardcore political subterfuge that infected capital and big cities.

I saw the arrow plane come in from the east and land, remarkably on schedule, at Aeroporto Internacional Jaime González. My friends Wham!®© and Puritan would be here shortly, and with them my ward, Victoria Comanche.

I went inside and checked my security arrangements on a bank of closed-circuit screens and surveillance technology controls. There were hidden cameras, infrared devices, encrypted communication systems, and more. I even had a pair of combots that Nyro insisted on, though I rarely activated them. In the five years I'd been here I'd never felt threatened – which was something for someone as hyper-vigilant as me. When Victoria was here though, I went to amber alert. Even the combots were on standby. As the daughter of a professional enemy-maker, she'd always be a target. Not that she couldn't take care of herself. I'd made sure of that from the outset.

She was her mother's daughter in many ways, not in others. Not being a sociopath helped. And Comanche had done a good job raising her as normally as possible in decidedly abnormal circumstances. When we first met she was as diffident as I was. Over the years though, we'd become tight. She'd grown into a confident young adult while I'd grown into the oldest lieutenant in Cuban police history. Of course promotion was always an option, but I was happy doing what I did, making a difference in small but significant ways.

Victoria had completed a law degree and wanted to follow in the footsteps of Puritan, whom she regarded as her grandfather. She'd turned down a job offer from him though, and I got why. Maybe one day she'd join him, but first she was determined to make her own mark.

She and I rarely talked about her mother. We both harboured ambivalent feelings, though mine ran deeper. I knew Comanche had been Family Guy's copycat as well as the killer of her own parents. I'd continue doing my damndest to protect her from these secrets because whatever wickedness Comanche had committed, I didn't want her daughter carrying the burden.

As for Bob, he'd turned seventy last year but would never retire. Again, I understood why. I was the same – if I did change jobs it would be from the oldest police lieutenant in Cuba to the oldest private investigator. My retirement plan was to die at work and I suspected Bob's would be the same. He and Nyro had stayed friends since Family Guy 2.0 although I didn't know and never asked if things had gone any further.

Bogart was now a top Alister and, as Nyro predicted, was moving fast up the political hierarchy. Soon after we closed the Family Guy 2.0 case, he'd been appointed chief executive of BlahBlah®©, then GibGab®©, then both. Next he'd been elected Uber Top Boss of PopRep®© Old Britain and last year of PopRep®© Europe. Also, to his credit (and my frustration when he visited), he continued to speak IngoLingo®© outside the federation. This was a "first" for a PopRep®© leader and I had to admire him for staying true to his roots. He'd shown statesmanlike magnanimity, too, by pardoning Simz halfway through an eight-year jail term for events at Apex, San José, a gesture the Scientians repeated with Confucius. Jesusly had received no such leniency, though he had swerved a slow roast in Old Crispy and even kept his genitalia, an extraordinary achievement for a sex offender in Trumpia. Having said this, he did face the rest of his life cleaning human remains off oven walls as a reminder of what would happen to him if he transgressed again. Given a choice, I'd rather be dead.

Wu Mei Leclerc's life sentence in a Himalayan Supermax ended three years ago when she was savagely shivved by a female associate of Gonzales Smedge, Kiera Sinatra's half-brother. The wounds weren't fatal but the septicaemia that followed was.

My main regret was Derek Anti-Satan. The witchfinder general was still unfinished business and probably always would be. Evil was a word of many definitions, but he was all of them.

I went back to the porch. Night had fallen, an indigo blindfold pierced by a salvo of stars. Rollers boomed on the shore. The air was freighted with tangs of brine and begonia and ghost orchid.

Along the coast road, headlights were approaching when

somebody dropped the planet.

It only fell by an inch or two but when it stopped, the stars jolted.

A sheet of night folded around me. Objects lost depth. Everything around me was flat and grainy and grey – I was standing on a printed page. It began to turn. I was sliding off. I reached the margin, tumbled into a chasm. But instead of falling, I was swept up, as if gravity had been reversed. Higher I went, until I found myself standing on a pile of books as tall as a skyscraper. From there, I looked down and saw in *The Big Happy* the membrane between creator and created, the bare artifice of my story.

The illusion ended.

Everything returned to normal.

The planet went back to its proper place. Gravity was restored.

Perhaps I should have been worried but I wasn't. We were all characters on a page, actors on a set, tellers of tales. One day *The End* would come as *The Ends* always do. Until then, I'd live this life in this world. Like every other, old or new, brave or gutless, it was flawed and feckless and forsaken. Like any world with people in it, it always would be.

Appendix

A Scientian Visitor's Guide to IngoLingo®©

HISTORY AND DEVELOPMENT

The origins of IngoLingo®© can be traced to the introduction of the info phone in the mid 39th Century, along with the advent of script messaging, or scripting, and software applications such as AppForIt. These innovations required brevity, driving extensive linguistic contraction while promoting countercultural slang.*

Notwithstanding assertions by PopRep®© authorities, IngoLingo®© is not a language, or even a dialect. It is a form of urban cant that owes more to poor literacy than to any serious academic endeavour. It is, in fact, a product of old scripting habits; bad spelling; grammatical ignorance, and the anti-intellectualism widely regarded as a function of populist government.

It is true that IngoLingo®© contains elements of Old Word vernacular, in particular 1950s hipster expressions (fusebox – head), Cockney rhyming slang (bucket list – fist), fragments of Jamaican creole (smoddy – somebody), and the pioneers of Old World social media platforms (zuckerberg, vance) as well as other tech sector figures (musk, bezos).

Moreover, when convenient traditional English words are not at hand, IngoLingo®© appropriates shamelessly from other European languages (Influsser from German; serio from Spanish).

Most educated and professional PopReppers®© speak traditional English in private, while almost all use traditional English when visiting Scientia. However, in PopRep®© all public utterances must be in IngoLingo®© and the Scientian visitor should not expect otherwise in any formal or semi-formal situation.˙

NOTE ON GRAMMAR AND USAGE

The adverbial suffix *ly/ily* is almost extinct in the Popular Republic®©. This means adjectives are usually used instead of conventional adverb forms. So expect to hear constructions such as, 'the dog barked vicious rather than 'the dog barked viciously' and 'she worked diligent' rather than 'she worked diligently'.

Past tenses such as "came" and "did" are not used, so people say, 'he come at me with a knife' and 'he done it so fast I never zeroed.'

Most irregular verbs have been *"reglized"*. For example,

you will hear *thinked* for thought; *shrinked* for shrunk; *taked* for took; *knowed* for knew, etc.

Vowels are often omitted to shorten words, while some words are contracted to reduce syllables. For example, *scovered* – discovered; *splained* – explained; *dictiony* – dictionary; *nubdy* – nobody; *ebdy* – everybody; *smin* – something; *smare* – somewhere; *smuddaplace* – some other place; *smoddy* – somebody; *ebbaplace* – every place; *udda* – other; *uddawise* otherwise; *proach* – approach; *pology* – apology.

However, it is worth keeping in mind that figures of speech – especially alliteration and onomatopoeia, along with words or phrases that rhyme, or simply "sound good" – supersede all other rules and conventions.

Mono and disyllabic words are preferred. Trisyllabic forms are common, while quadrisyllabic words are considered "ignorant" and are avoided if possible. Words with more than four syllables must have special authorization. These "big words" will attract negative attention if used by visitors. You are strongly advised to avoid them when talking in public places.

GENERAL GLOSSARY

Abso:	absolute, absolutely
Acourse:	of course (contraction)
Allstuffs:	everything – 'allstuffs was identic'
Anudda:	another
Aright:	all right, alright

Backwise:	backwards
Bigbad:	very bad
Bigmost:	extremely, to the greatest extent; also even moster bigmost
Bigwhile:	a long time
Bitwhile:	a short time
Billyaire or billy:	a billionaire
Bojo:	(verb) to destroy, wreck, ruin – from the nickname of Boris Johnson, British prime minister 2019-22
Bojo:	(noun) a mess, a fiasco, a trainwreck
Boohoo:	sad, sorrowful, unhappy
Breathbags:	lungs
Brickthick:	stupid, daft, dumb
Bucket:	fist – bucket list, rhyming slang
Bustagut:	extremely – 'This jack were bustagut brassy'
Cap:	brain – capital gain, rhyming slang
Capblown:	mindblown
Capboggly:	mind boggling
Capzucked:	mindfucked, mindblown
Gore:	blood
Convo:	conversation

Holy Cowell:	Holy cow, mild expletive – after 21st Century TV personality Simon Cowell
Cuddabin:	could have been – see wuddabin and shuddabin
Curio:	curious
Cut:	arse/ass, backside – cut glass, rhyming slang
Cut-hole:	anus
Cut:	glass
Dedos:	fingers – appropriated from Spanish
Dictiony:	dictionary
Donald, The:	Donald J Trump – also see Donald J; 'Trump in His Tower'; 'Trump in Stormy'; 'The Orange One'
Dummied:	fooled, deceived or tricked (also see monkeyed)
Earl:	suit – Earl of Bute, rhyming slang
Eastbound:	crazy, messed up – from Cockney slang "eastbound on the District Line", an Underground line running from central London to the eastern borough of Barking, ie to be barking mad

Ebdy:	everybody (contraction)
Fastwhile:	very soon
Ferrari:	fast, quickly – see giddyup and thundybolt
Frag:	fragment, little bit
Fragged, fraggy:	broken up, mutilated – 'fragged savage'
Frankstein / franksteiny:	scary, horrific, awful, messed-up bad
Freddykrueger:	adjective – 'the scene were freddykrueger frighty' – from Freddy Krueger, central character in the 20th Century *A Nightmare on Elm Steet* slasher movie
Freddykruegers:	(noun, pl) the heebie-jeebies; 'the scene were freddykrueger frighty'
Frighty:	scary, terrifying
Fusebox:	head – mid 20th Century hipster slang
Gab, gabbing:	to talk, say or call (see tattle); 'I can gab proper when I wanna.'
Giddyup:	Fast – see thundybolt, ferrari

Gipsy:	arm – gipsy charm, rhyming slang
Gobbler:	mouth
Gobspew:	meaningless verbiage intended to impress
Gog:	to gaze or look inquiringly – 'I gogged him curio'; 'she gave me an odd gog'
Gogs and Sungogs:	glasses and sunglasses
Grasper:	hand
Identic:	identical
Importanter:	more important
Importanterest:	more important than Importanter
Inspo:	inspiration
Intresty:	interesting
Jack:	man, guy, fellow (male equivalent of jane)
Jane:	woman, lady (female equivalent of jack)
Jawdrop:	extremely, impressive – 'The lad were jawdrop sexy' 'The scene were jawdrop frighty'
Lawdog:	police or law enforcement officer (see nabber)

Lawjaw:	lawyer
Licker:	tongue
Lickertangle:	a tongue tangle, nonsensical talk or muddled speech
Mad Daddy:	a cool or impressive man – mid 20th century hipster slang
Mad Mama:	female form of above
Mightabin:	might have been
Monsta (sometimes monstadick):	large, plentiful or extremely
Moster:	more than; to a greater extent – 'This insult raged me even moster bigmost.'
Mindzuck:	mind blown – 'I were mindzucked'
Monkeyed:	fooled, deceived or tricked (see dummied)
Musk:	urine, piss – 'He musked me off bigmost' from Old World billionaire Elon Musk – also see Bezos, Vance, Zuckerberg
Nabbers/nabs:	police officers
Nada:	nothing – appropriated from Spanish
Nanofrag:	split second
Nay-shake:	shake the head to indicating no

Ness:	necessary
Nubdy:	nobody
Obvio:	obvious, obviously – appropriated from Spanish
Off-planet:	extraordinary, totally shocking – 'The scene was toto off-planet, gottasay'
Olly	Oligarch
Orange One (the):	after Donald J Trump, 45th President of the United States
Palling:	appalling
Peeky:	spicy or strong smelling
Plitiko:	political
Popeye:	the population, the people, also an individual
Popeyes:	people, individuals, folk (see spuds)
Previo:	previous or previously – 'She was the gill I seen previo'
Praps:	perhaps
Proach:	approach
Prob:	probably
Profesh:	professional
Puckers:	lips

Puckerplaster:	lipstick
Rip:	copy, replica
Rithtik:	arithmetic
Schlocks:	teeth
Screamers:	condition of intense fear – 'They put the screamers on me'
Serio:	serious, seriously – appropriated from Spanish
Shuddabin:	should have been (see wuddabin and cuddabin)
Signiff:	significant
Slots:	eyes
Smare:	somewhere – Old World Jamaican creole (contraction)
Smin:	something – as above
Smoddy:	somebody – as above
Smon:	someone – as above
Smov:	some of – as above
Snapped:	cool, splendid, perfect
Speck:	to see, observe or notice (see zero and gog)
Splain:	explain
Spresh:	expression
Sprize, sprized:	surprise
Spicious:	suspicious

Spiracy:	conspiracy
Stormbroody:	dour, aggressive, foreboding
Stuffs:	stuff, things
Sungogs:	sunglasses
Tattle:	talk, say, call (see gab)
Thundybolt:	fast, rapid (see ferrari and giddy-up)
Tickler:	joke, witticism
Tiktok:	heart
Tractive:	attractive
Trump in Stormy!:	Lord in heaven! – reference to Donald Trump and Stormy Daniels
Vance:	arse, ass 'he got a kick up the vance,' 'stick it up your vance – after, JD Vance, US vice president in Donald Trump's second term (also see Bezos, Musk and Zuckerberg)
Viz:	face
Vox:	voice
Vox Popeye®©:	voice of the people – Latin *vox populi*

Yeggman, yegg:	bruiser, gangster – mid 20thcentury hipster slang
Yo-nod:	to nod in a way that means yes
Yo-gabbed:	to say yes
Zact:	exact/exactly
Zero:	to look (see speck) – 'I zeroed him coming'
Zuck:	fuck, from Old World tech billionaire Mark Zuckerberg – 'Zuck off', (also see Bezos, Vance, Musk)

This book is printed on paper from sustainable sources managed under the Forest Stewardship Council (FSC) scheme.

It has been printed in the UK to reduce transportation miles and their impact upon the environment.

For every new title that Troubador publishes, we plant a tree to offset CO_2, partnering with the More Trees scheme.

For more about how Troubador offsets its environmental impact, see www.troubador.co.uk/sustainability-and-community